MARLEE JANE
WARD

ORPHANCORP

First published by Seizure in 2015, 2017, 2019

ISBN 9780646720647

To anyone who has ever felt like they were too much.
You aren't, you are just enough.

WELCOME TO
ORPHANCORP

I twist my hand at a weird angle to get to the itch on my wrist below the shackle. I mean, they call them 'the Consequences of movement violations', but shackles is what they are. When I forget to refer to them as such I get 'the Consequences of speech violations', which is pretty much just a gag. No one cares what I call that because everything sounds the same with a mouthful of rubber, doesn't it?

The bus is ancient and jammed with kids, skinny bums squeezed onto the bench seats. The bus is far noisier than the kids, the whole thing filled with a riot of squeaks and rattles and the odd bang from somewhere inside the engine, while us kids keep our mouths shut and our eyes wide, staring straight ahead. Sweat makes a thin layer between my thighs and the cracked vinyl and my bum aches, pressed into the unpadded bench seat. I bounce hard on my arse bones with every pothole jolt.

No one makes eye contact with me. I'm not the only one shackled . . . sorry, *facing Consequences*, but I am the only one gagged. Sometimes my mouth just starts going and even though in my head I'm all like, *shut up, oh just shut up*, I can't help myself.

We slow and the bus drags itself up to the curb, backfires and dies with a rumble-thud. Everyone kinda cranes their eyes slightly to the left. The Uncle up front glares, on a hawk-eye lookout for any minor infraction of the head-turning variety. They put the thickest, stupidest ones on transport duties, usually as a punishment. They like to make us pay for that. I've been enjoying this one's company for fifteen hours of this broiling hell-trip back to Sydney and when he motions for us to stand and file off, I make sure to catch his arm with one of the strings of drool that have spilled out the sides of my gagged mouth.

'It's been a pleasure,' I say, but it comes out all garbled.

'No talking,' he barks, looking like he wishes he could gag me a second time.

We line up on the footpath beside the bus. The sun is going down and everyone's always tired and grumpy as hell after a transfer, but they've got to stick to procedure, don't they? We all wind out our wrists and ankles as they scan our armband codes and make sure no one's pissed off or died during the trip. It happens.

I take a moment to look over the facility, though I'm not sure why I bother. Every Verity House is the same — a big grey box straddling an entire city block. It's like they knock them together off-site and heli them in or something. Maybe they do, I don't know. Broome or Blacktown, Albury, Cairns or that one they say is on that island down in Tassie, it doesn't matter. The dining hall is always to the right of the dorms; the watch quarters have those thick, double-brick walls that mean they're easy to sneak past if the door's closed; the bathrooms are sweet little Kidcam blind spots where I can read a non-reg book on my tab, have a cry or a quick-and-dirty interlude up against the wall without facing any of the related Consequences. In their hurry to manufacture heartless functionality, they've made me a home.

I breathe in, scanning the familiar rise and fall of the walls. I take every tiny victory I can, because eventually they add up.

Small victories are all you get in an Orphancorp.

SEVEN DAYS

'Miri . . . Mirya . . . Miriiyanan Mahoney?'

I hold up my shackled hands and wave them a bit. The Auntie, a red-headed woman wider than she is tall, comes over to remove the Consequences piece by piece. I wriggle my wrists and hinge my mouth open and closed to work out the ache in my jaw.

'That's a mouthful of a name, isn't it?'

'It means star. Shooting star,' I tell her, like she'll care, and I wipe the twin spills of spit off my chin with the hem of my shirt.

'So, you're some kinda big shot, are ya? A shooting bloody star?' the Auntie asks, shaking her head and paging through her tab.

'Nah. People just call me Mirii.'

'So, Mirii, what didja say to get the gag? You got a dirty mouth or what?'

I do. In my head I swear *a lot* but the Consequence of profanity is a write up. We work around it. Everything fun is a fugging infraction around here.

I don't want to tell her what I said because she'll probably slam a mark against my name and I *just* got here but I don't have much choice because the big oaf who gagged me in the first place is walking past and he puts a boot into the back of my knee that drops me to the ground.

'Likes to run her mouth, this one,' he says.

'I just pointed out the sweat-marks on Uncle Barry's arse to the bus while he was installing my hands into those Consequences there,' I say, crawling up to my knees and gesturing to the shackles in her hands. 'I mean, I shouldn't have mentioned it; it's pretty noticeable on its own. He's got a big bum.'

They both look down at me and he sinks the boot in once more for good measure before he wobbles off, red faced and sweaty-arsed.

'You're due for Age Release in a week, yeah? You might need to get a hold of your mouth before then.'

'Yeah.' She's got a point, but shiz, if I could control my mouth even the littlest bit, I reckon I mighta done it already.

'So, why'd they bother with the transfer?' she asks.

'I don't know. Why do you guys do anything?'

The Auntie laughs at that. 'You've got a pretty colourful file, little star. We're desperate for Nannies, but the notes say you can't be trusted with kids. You don't like kids?'

'Nope.'

'Nah, me neither. You should come work for us when you age out.' She cackles at that, like she made a super clever joke or something but it's not even funny, right? It's true. Aunties and Uncles must hate kids.

Kids. Shiz. Way to make my blood run cold. They cry and cough and tug my pants, seeking comfort I've got no idea how to give them. It's not their fault, those poor dumb jerks. I did the same when I was their age.

The Auntie scrolls further. 'We're gunna put you into electrical manufacture. You seem to bugger that up less than anything else. Think of it as a parting gift from Verity House.'

'Yeah, thanks,' I say, acting evasive and stuff, but I'm way glad. Tinkering with machines is my thing. Circuit boards and wiring comfort me: they make sense when nothing else does.

'Report at 8 a.m. to the E-wing for work detail. You do school?'

'Yep.'

'Figured. You've got a smart mouth. Classes start at six. Be on time or they won't let you in.'

She moves on to the shy cluster of toddlers next in line. The snotnose little bastards are all sobbing and piddling themselves because half of them have probably just been rounded up off the streets. Even if they were born into an Orphancorp, they're still too little to know what's going on. They let them cry. They let them cry up until they're about six, then after that, crying's an infraction.

The Auntie huffs and puffs until she's crouched down over her huge gut, giant bosom all mashing up into her chin, and she holds up the tab so that the little tykes can see. They stare, saucer-eyed, and a colourful cartoon starts playing.

'Hey kids! Welcome to Verity House!'

—

We shuffle up the steps and through the big red doors. The hallway's the usual concrete slapped over with pastel paint, gone all grimy. What's with that weird pinky-peach chalky colour? Everything's slicked with it – they've gotta buy it by the tonne. Right by the door are the offices for administration and there are heaps of Aunties and Uncles lazing around, joking and laughing, getting fatter by the second, probably thinking up a bunch of nasty schemes to torture us with later. The floor is cream linoleum, scuffed and grey up the edges and I drag my feet over it, leaving little rubber marks. Off to the right is the dining hall and it's already buzzing with the dinner shift of hungry kids who glance up at us and then look away, back into their plates of whatever crap it is they're serving us tonight.

The nursery is the first door on the left and it's jammed full of crying blobs from ages brand new to just big enough to know better. An Auntie leads our squadron of toddlers off into the room and through the door I see one of the Nannies shake a curly-headed blond wobbler off from clutching at her leg.

'Go away! Just bugger off!' she screams down to him.

The little dude falls splat on his big nappied bum and starts to wail and the Nanny looks up at me as I pass, her eyes scooped out deep with desperation. She's knocked up herself, pretty far along too, dressed in one of those hideous pink preggo-tunics they make the expectants wear and in no time at all she'll be adding her own spawn to the throng.

Fugg me, what a sad little tableau.

I worked extra duties for ten months to get the implant in my arm and it was worth the grind and then some. I can't imagine adding a kid to this mess. I'd never forgive myself.

There's two more dorms, for the four-to-sevens and the nine-to-twelves and they keep divvying up my little transport group until there's just me and two other kids shuffling to the teen bar-racks, clutching canvas backpacks to our chests, our extra pairs of boots dangling from the laces looped through the straps.

I get a relatively unstained mattress on an empty bunk below the big barred window in the Sixteen/Seventeen district of the teen dorm and I unload my stuff: one mint-green shirt, one pink. Two pants: lavender, and a kind of peach that matches the walls. One sky blue jacket. They dress us in pastels because they think it makes us calmer or something. I really don't know where they're getting this info from 'cause it doesn't seem to do much but make us look fugging stupid and stain up quick as anything. I've also got seven pairs of grey underpants and seven pairs of grey socks because we only get laundry privileges once a week, if we keep out of trouble. All this goes in the empty plastic crate under the bed, this one is blue and says AntipoDairy, Inc on the side. My second pair of boots go to the foot of the bed.

I feel along the edges of my mattress to find the hidey-hole — nothing is sacred to any of these little bastards except the mattress-safe. I jam the only thing I care about inside: a very battered, technologically obsolete and much-modified tablet: my prized possession. I've been working on that biatch for years and I have it just the way I like it. It holds everything I love: my books, saved copies of all my best assignments from the Free School, pictures of arbitrary things in places that I cared a bit about and lost and that I sometimes like to torture myself with. Look, I'm pretty well aware that it's probs a bit sick to love an inanimate object, but honestly, I'm just glad I can love anything at all. My tab, man. It's like a portal to the rest of the world, a window where I can get a glimpse of what could be if I can just make it out of here.

'Hey big star! Dining Hall, now, unless you want to go to bed hungry.' It's the Auntie from before, waddling past the door.

I follow her back down the hall and get in line for my food. The kid at Position One on the Foodservice line looks up at me with one eye. The other looks way over to the left, but lopsided or not, his eyes look kind.

'Just transferred?' he asks and I nod.

He slaps a little extra of the brownish glop on my tray. 'Welcome to Orphancorp.'

I grin. 'Thanks bru.'

'Newbz,' he says, nudging the next kid in the service row and she picks me out a nice roll that isn't too stale or too mouldy and she passes it on with a whisper to the next one who finds me a decent-looking apple. I nod them all thanks and sit down at a half-empty table, digging into what turns out to be a not-too-awful roo stew.

Everyone's all chattery but all of a sudden things go quiet. I look to the door 'cause a hush like this means something pretty dramatic is afoot. But nothing seems to be up, nothing's different except this one girl has come in through the door. She's got real white skin, almost-white hair and she's small, wiry and kinda beat up. She looks around with a sour expression and no one says anything.

'That's Ferguson. Freya Ferguson,' says a kid at my table, even though I didn't ask. She's a ratty little thing in a pale pink beanie, and she jabs her fork towards the bruised-up chick, who's now scowling at the kids on food service as they make her up a plate. 'She escaped a few weeks ago, she's only just got back from Time Out.'

'Oh. Do you guys do comis?'

Time Out is rough and when someone gets back everyone goes up to them and gives their, like, commiserations, usually just a nod or a fist bump or if you're okay friends maybe a clap on the shoulder or a chest bump. Depends on the kid.

'Yeah, we do. But I don't got no comis for Freya. I hope they beat her up real good.' Ratty curls a lip at her and goes back to chewing the tough lump of roo she's got between her teeth.

I look up at Freya, sat by herself at a table in the corner. Now and then a kid will walk past and give her a nod, but no line of supporters like usual when someone comes back all bruisy and morose from a long stint in Time Out. When I've gnawed my way through the entire bowl of chewy stew, I take my apple and walk past Freya. I give her a nod and put the apple on her table, 'cause I know all too well the dual emotional smackdown of a long pull in TO coupled with being an unpopular fugg, and jeez, everyone could use a present sometimes. She looks up at me and her eyes are the lightest green, like seriously sparkling emerald as shiz and she smiles, revealing a missing canine tooth.

—

The rules for bedtime go like this: everyone needs to be in bed for count, we call it 'tucking in'. An Auntie or Uncle ticks our names off a checklist on their tab. The Auntie on watch tonight is the big ginger chick from earlier. Her name's Auntie Beverly but all the kids call her Aunt Bev and she pretends she hates it but you can tell she fugging loves it because she flushes an even redder red whenever we say it.

Once lights are out and the door's locked, we can do whatever we like as long as we don't leave. I mean, we can, someone's always got a shifty set of keys that they scrape up in the metalshed, but that's just for special occasions, birthdays and stuff, though in a place like this it's always someone's birthday.

'Where you transfer from?' asks a rake of a girl with a mop of curly black hair and bloodshot black eyes. The 'one size' PJ's they give us swamp her and she's tied knots in the shoulders of the threadbare cotton to keep it from falling right off.

'Orange,' I say and bring my pillow to the cluster they've all huddled theirs into.

'Oh, I been out at Orange,' says a bru about my age with sun-bleached hair, tanned skin, a sixer and guns that he flaunts, shirt-less. A gardener for sure, and hot. He's got a righteous grin with a chipped front tooth.

'Was Uncle Jerry there when you were in?' I ask.

'For sure. He still trading shots of Phegia for blowjobs?'

'Oh yeah,' I say. 'He'll be under report any day now, half the babes in the teen dorms are junkified to the max.'

'Fugging dickbag,' he says.

I flash him a coy little sidesmile as someone else asks me some-thing and he sits back against the wall, folding his hands up behind his head, coysmiling right back.

I'm totally throwing this one down later on.

One of the kids who came on the bus with me sits on my seat with his pillow between us.

'Saw that dog Uncle gag you on the ride in,' he says, and throws me a fist bump. I bump him back and shake my head.

'Gotta get a hold of my mouth, I'm up for Age Release in a week and I have a strike against me already.'

'What happens if you get two more strikes?' asks a little twelver two pillows over.

'For strikes they can put me into detention for up to a month after I turn eighteen. So just late release. But if I commit one of the five deadly sins . . .'

'Right to a Prisoncorp,' says Blondie and I nod. Everyone kinda looks down for a bit. Verity House and all the other Orphancorps (Sunshine Gardens, KidsCo, and the most ruthless and diaboli-cal of all, Punkin Patch) buy unaccompanied minors from the state and can't keep 'em past eighteen. That is, unless they mess up, then it's right to a Prisoncorp. Once you're in there, it's pretty much the end of it.

'So, you got any skills?' asks a South Asian kid about my age with long, silky black hair. I can't tell if they're male or female, but it doesn't matter because sweet babes need no gender.

I pull up my sleeves and the hem of my nightshirt.

'I tattoo. No machine, just stick and poke.'

All the kids ooh and ahh over the blue-black designs that twist and dance all over my skin. 'You have to be over fifteen though, and if they see the tats and want you to spill, you don't know me, yeah?'

'Of course,' says Blondie and I'm hoping he wants some kind of complicated lower ab piece 'cause I'd be really into that.

'What about you guys?' I ask.

'I make a pretty good corn wine,' Blondie says.

'Toilet?' I ask.

'No way. Got batches going up in the roofs here and there. I can also get you some weed if that's your thing.'

Of course. Gardeners can always get you weed.

The S.A. cutie flicks their long 'do back over one shoulder.

'I'm Ara. I work in the metalshop and I can make all kinds of stuff. Keys and tools or whatever you need. No weapons though, I'm a lover, not a fighter.' Their name and voice are just as androgynous as the rest of them. I shake a delicate, long-fingered hand.

'I'm a doc,' says a stone-face girl with fierce grey eyes and acne-spotted cheeks. 'No-snitch stitches, tooth-yanking, terminations, that sort of stuff.'

There's the usual assortment of black market traders and pill-shillers, and one nondescript boy with wild, black-circled eyes who tells me he will cop the blame for an infraction and even do a stint in Time Out for the right kinda trade. Fugging weirdo.

We've moved onto a rundown on the general attitudes, tempera-ments and suspected menstrual cycles of the Uncles and Aunties when Aunt Bev throws open the door.

'You little shits need to keep it down, the bubs are trying to sleep.' Behind her I can hear a toddler wailing.

'Do ya think the crying might have something to do with the harsh realities of the conditions we live under, and not our pretty tame and quiet convo, Aunt Bev?' I ask her and all the kids snicker. She doesn't have her tab on her so I don't get a mark down but she gives me a withering look and we get into bed before she storms in and starts making a scene.

Kids are settling in, deep-breathing, sleep-farting and starting to snore when I see a shadow break the moonlight and spill over my bed.

'So, I was thinking of having you do a tat for me, but I'm not sure where,' whispers Blondie. I lift up my sheet and he slides in beside me.

'Wanna take a look at some of mine?' I ask and he pulls my nightshirt up over my head. 'It might give you some ideas.'

'I like this one,' he says, lifting my arms above my head and nipping at a little design on my bicep before burying his nose in my armpit hair. I twist my head to one side and stare at the thin ink lines. It's an image of a flower I found in the playground once. Blondie smells like earth and sweat and sunshine. He works his way down between my legs and pulls at my underpants with his teeth.

'So, I'm Mirii,' I say, and he comes back up and kisses my mouth.

'I'm Ben.'

'I'm going to call you Blondie,' I say, and he laughs. I roll him over and run my tongue all the way down his side. 'I think this is a good place for a tattoo.' I nibble at his hip and I can tell that he agrees.

—

After Blondie leaves I curl up under the sweat-soggy sheet. The thrum in my body almost drowns out the quiet night-sobbing in the littlies dorm next door, but then there's a great clatter-crash that jolts me up out of bed. It sets off the babies down the hall, which is just fugging great.

'Catch her, Mahoney!'

At my name, I jump up and before I know what I'm aiming for, I raise my hands and grab, getting handfuls of greasy hair. The lights come on and I see my hands are sunk into long, white-blonde strands attached to an oval-shaped face with green eyes flashing hate and glee and a mouth missing the right canine tooth.

'Please,' Freya says.

'Sorry babe, gotta do what the man says,' I say, and wrangle her into a good headlock until the Uncles catch up, puffing. Even though she's down and I've got a tight hold, they still taze her. She stiffens and tips over and the kiddie-prod catches me too as we topple towards the ground, zapping me right on the shoulder. All the parts of me go rigid and my teeth sink tight into the very tip of my tongue as the bolts peal around my body. When the pain subsides, I can feel I've pissed myself. The urine and the blood from my tooth-gouged tongue mix in a puddle on the floor as I shuddershuddershudder. Rage and voltage zing through me. I'm seeing stars.

'On your feet, Ferguson.' Freya untangles her limbs from mine and stands unsteadily. They prod her, make her stand again. This game goes on until it's not fun for them any more, then one of the Uncles twists her arm up behind her back and they march off. She looks down at me and mouths something that looks like 'truck you' but probably isn't, but then she smiles her marred smile for a moment before she disappears. For some reason, lying in a puddle of my own assortment of liquids, I smile too.

—

I don't know if it's the prodding that shakes me up so hard, but while I lie in the dark and try to breathe my way through the fizzy jump of all my muscles and nerves, I start to think about my mum and dad.

The lady who I reckon was my mum had really nice brown skin and dark eyes and wavy brown hair that went all the way down her back. I think I can remember the tickle of her hair on my face as she looked down on me. The dad, he had orange hair and a red nose and kind green eyes. I mean, I'm not sure if they even are my mum and dad because of the whole thing about how I must have been just a little dumbshiz kid when I came into the corp and all I have are these random memory flashes, but I reckon they are. I look like an even mash of the two of them: his green eyes and her brown skin and hair that's a weird mix of the two, brown and wavy, run through with threads of copper.

But too, I know they must be special because of something in the way they looked at me, yeah? Like I was theirs and they'd made me and they loved me just heaps and stuff.

I'm glad I've got that to hang onto. Most of the kids here don't. It helps to know that somewhere, sometime, a couple of folks loved me, even if it was only for a little while.

SIX DAYS

'What's that?' the little kid asks, pointing to the tattoo peeking out of my sleeve.

'Nothing. Bugger off,' I say, brushing him away like a fly and just like a fly, he buzzes back in.

'Is it a tattoo? Can I see?' he asks.

I huff and blow my hair out of my eyes, focusing in on the headset I'm wiring up. It's fiddly work and this kid's got me distracted. My hands are covered in little white circle-scars from drips of liquid hot solder and I'm not looking to add another right now.

'It's nothing. Now, piss off, kid.' I roll my sleeve down so he stops asking.

I hate kids. I think I even hated kids back when I was one and I try my very best to avoid them, which is no easy feat when you live in fugging Orphancorp.

The little dropkick is a runner for my section and I don't want to get him talking to me so whenever I need something I get up and get it myself, which of course makes the Auntie in charge of my section suspicious.

'Mahoney, next time I see you get up out of that seat, I'm going to put my boot so far up your bum you'll be able to see the tread on your tongue.'

'That's a good one, Auntie,' I tell her. 'I'm gunna use that.'

'My pleasure, Mahoney. I do it all for you.' She pulls out a tab and lifts one finger to the screen. 'Now, do I have to write you up, or are you going to sit down?'

I park my arse. 'I'm down.'

She gestures to the kid. 'Get this little kicker to get your wires or pliers or whatever.'

He grins. He's about eleven, a real goofy-looking kid with big ears, and a wide, tanned and freckled face.

'What's your name, fuggface?'

'Cam.'

'Right, Cam, I need a pair of needlenose pliers,' I start and the little brownnoser takes right off but I grab him by the sleeve of his grubby lemon-yellow shirt and pull him back. He's so skinny and insubstantial that I almost reef him right off the ground as he swings back towards me.

'But, I don't want any shizzy, busted up pair. No rust. No solder gumming up everything. And the grips need to be intact, no tears. If you're gonna run for me, you don't bring me any poor quality tools, got it?'

He nods, big dumb smile on his doofus face. He runs off to the supply shed and the joke's on him 'cause I've got the last pair of good pliers right there on my workstation, but at least this way he'll be digging through the tools 'til lunch break and that gives me a bunch of time to find another timewaster job to keep him out of my hair 'til knockoff time.

—

The toilets are in a line in the bathroom, no cubicles or doors because, fuggit, that would give us some dignity or something. For once the entire bathroom is empty until the door opens and someone comes in. It's that Freya chick from yesterday. I lower my eyes, because it's the thing to do in the bathrooms and besides, I'm halfway through the most epic piss and don't feel like making eye contact with some biatch-stranger I barely know while I void the three-hour-bladder I've had brewing all morning.

I'm watching a roach skitter out from behind the loo and run between my boots when I hear the thud of footsteps and I look up. Freya's skipping towards me and in her hand flashes something sharp and deadly-looking. Sick hot fear slices through me 'cause there's this emptiness in her gleamy green eyes and I jump up, staining my pants with a dark splatter of pee.

'*You hurt me last night,*' she hisses, jamming her hard, thin body against me, arm circling my neck like the headlock I had her in last night. Her hipbones drive into the base of my spine and her tiny breasts mash under my shoulder blades. She pulls me back down onto the toilet and wraps her legs tight around my waist, squeezing 'til my ribs scream.

'Dontcha age out in a few days? Dontcha think you should be more careful?' Freya asks. I feel the sharp edge of whatever she's holding dig into my cheek.

'I'm really sorry, Freya,' I say, breathing hard against her crushing thighs and the wiry arm across my neck. 'But you would have done the same as me.'

'Bugger off I would have,' she says.

'Bullshiz. When the man tells you to jump, you ask them if they'd like sugar on top.'

'Fuck the man,' Freya says, like a petulant little kid.

'Yeah maybe, but babe, I don't know you. I'm not risking my release for no one, let alone some fugging stranger.'

'What kind of attitude is that?'

'The kind of attitude that means I'll get out of here and have a chance at a real life.'

'You won't.' She collapses a little bit against me. The sharp point pulls away and the sting eases. Then she takes a big breath and goes rigid again and the knife digs in and this time I feel hot blood spill down my face and drip onto the floor. My face is on fire as she drags the spike against my cheek and my nerves scream as the flesh splits apart but I stay silent.

This is the second time I've spilled my own blood and piss onto the floor since I got here and both times have had a lot to do with this Freya chick. I wonder how much more I'm going to spill in the next week because of her.

—

The grey-eyed girl, Nerida, breathes sour breath into my face. She's one of those girls who looks right into you and so I look anywhere but into her black-flecked irises. I settle on a nasty looking, pus-filled volcano-zit by her nose. My fingers claw up as she catches the edge of the wound with the fine, curved needle and sinks it in.

'Fuggit! Don't you have any local or anything? What kind of doc are you?'

She lets go of the needle. I can see it, out of the corner of my eye, hanging out of my cheek.

'Do you want me to do this or not? The infirmary is right around the corner, and I'm pretty sure they won't use a local, and they'll probably slam you in the pokey as well, if you don't tell them who did it.'

'Okay, okay. It just stings, that's all. Got any corn wine? Potato punch?'

'No. Now please shut up and stay fugging still.' Nerida leans back in and I feel the needle pull through the skin and I gasp as it bites into the other side. Little zigs and zags of pain shoot through all the nerves on my face and I pant as she draws the split skin together and ties the thread off with a practiced flourish. Then the needle dives in again and I draw a sharp breath and grip hard onto the sink.

We're in the dorm bathroom and there's a little just-teen outside on watch so none of the Aunties come waddling in to bust us down to Time Out. It's lunch hour, so the dorms are deserted, but you can't be too careful.

'So Freya's mad that you turned her in the other night?'

'Yeah, I guess,' I say, wincing and trying not to move my mouth too much. 'I don't know, it seems like overkill, yeah? What was I supposed to do, say "nah"?'

'Freya doesn't think like that,' Nerida says, and ties off again, diving back into my screaming skin without even a pause to catch my breath.

'Does she have a thing with Blondie Ben the gardener? I may have had a bit of cuddle time with him last night.'

'Ben's good like that,' she says, and is that a hint of wist I detect? 'Nah, that would be too easy. She doesn't care about stuff like that. She's new. She was living wild out in the Western Suburbs until a year or so ago. I don't know how they caught her, but she's not like us. She doesn't get how it works. She's not, like, broken yet.'

Nerida digs in again and I clench my teeth. 'Last one, Mirii.'

'Thank fugg.'

'She's been here about three months and she's spent half that time in Time Out. She's even done a stint in the Naughty Chair. We thought that one might finally break her, but it's like it's just made her even more mad.' She pulls the last stitch together gently and I groan as she knots it. 'There, all done.'

I lie back against the tiles, the whole right side of my face thumping.

'I don't want a tattoo for the trade, but I know Ara Jadhav wants one and they've got what I want, so talk to them later.' She goes over to the sink and washes her hands. 'The kid we've got on watch for us? You owe her your fruit from dinner tonight. Don't forget, because she won't.'

'What do *you* want?' I ask her, but she just slams her little med bag closed.

'None of ya business.'

'Right-o then.' I'm in no mood to probe. She walks off without looking back and I take a few seconds to breathe through the pain, then I slam it back to the buzz shop because lunch break's almost over.

—

'Mahoney, what's that on your face?' The Uncle on watch in the buzz shop peers at my cheek, his forehead all crunched up above his big red honker nose. I can smell the booze coming off him in waves.

'Nothing, Uncle Jeff.'

'They look like stitches.'

'You're an observant old bastard, aren't you?'

'You're a mouthy little bitch, aren't you?' he says and he comes towards me. With that kind of tone I know better than to sass him back, and I shrink into myself as much as I can. See, I was thinking daffy-drunk-Uncle, when he's really aggressive-boozed-up-dude-in-power. My mistake.

'Sorry Uncle Jeff.' I put on my best beaten-dog look. If I had a tail it would be between my legs. Angry old jerks like him dig that submissive vibe. 'I got these back at Orange. Had an accident on the playground.'

'You run your mouth like that again and you'll be having another accident pretty soon.'

I nod and skitter back to my workstation before I piss him off any further. I add him to the shiz-list I've got in my head under the subheading of 'angry drunk arseholes'.

Cam comes up and puts a shiny-looking pair of pliers on the table. He looks up at me with a big, dumb grin on his dork face, like he can't believe what an impressive fugg he is for pulling this gleamy, almost-new tool from some magical tool-stash in the ether, but then the smile crumbles away.

'Wow, Mirii. What happened?'

'Nothing.' I say, trying to strip a piece of wire, the most basic of tasks that I'd even trust this jerk to do, and snapping it instead. My hands still tremble and Cam sees it and takes the stuff from me, stripping the plastic sheaths from the wires with surprisingly tricky fingers. He hands them back to me and I take a few deep breaths to steady myself.

'So, what's with the tattoos?' he asks, tapping my arm a few times for emphasis.

'I don't know. What's with your face?' I finish the delicate loop and twist of the wires and I don't even have to reach for the cover, because Cam is right there, handing it to me already.

'How come you have so many?'

"Cause I can. 'Cause they can't make me wash 'em off.'

The kid nods. He gets it. I smile, even though it stings like a bitch, and hand him the finished headset. He wraps it in a plastic cover, drops it in the box and starts gathering up parts for the next one.

I pull my sleeve higher and trace the inked pattern on my arm, six diamonds linked by a thin black line, remembering the midnight grey night I poked it; the heat of the needle, the sting of the ink.

'What is it?'

'This one? It's a constellation. That's a pattern of stars. It's in the shape of a boat. It's called Carina.' The talking hurts my face, but it helps to relax me a little bit. Helps me push Freya's mean green eyes away.

'Like the stars in the sky? Why'd you put them on you?'

'Why you ask so many questions?'

He shrugs.

'Okay, you ever been in a corp out in the desert?' I ask. 'Like out Bourke way? At night the stars are everywhere, not like here in the city where you can't see them at all. I looked them up on the net and it turns out the stars are how people used to find their way around before sats or even maps. They'd make the patterns in the sky to guide their way home. I liked the idea of being able to find my way around.'

'But how?'

'I guess they'd just look up and search for the patterns, yeah? Then follow them. Like, the first people who lived here, way back thousands of years ago.'

'The abbos?'

'Don't say that, that's a derogatory word.'

'What's dirogory?'

'Derogatory. It's like a mean word, a hate word. Don't say it. They're called Aboriginals. Or like, Indigenous.'

'Shiz, sorry,' he says, and his cheeks flush a mean shade of red that spreads out all the way to his batwing ears. 'I don't hate Aboriginals or nothing.'

'It's cool, just don't say that word no more. Anyway, they'd make up stories about the shapes in the stars and tell the stories to each other so everyone knew how to find home.'

'Are you an indigenous? Your skin is pretty brown.'

'I think so. My name, Miriiyanan, means shooting star in an Aboriginal language. Gamilaraay. I looked it up.'

'You know a bunch of stuff, huh?'

I nod.

'Do you go to school?' he asks.

'Yeah. Do you?' I raise my eyebrow and glare at him because too few kids do and it's a real shame.

'Nah. Too tired in the mornings.' He looks sheepish and he takes the box even though it's only three-quarters full and heads off down between the rows of workstations, weaving through the spotlit buzzshop islands 'til I lose him in the flow.

—

'I know who did that to your face,' says a husky girlvoice. The speaker slots herself in next to me. 'Vu, Adeline,' she says, and offers a fist. 'Call me Vu though, everyone does.'

'Mahoney. Miriiyanan. Mirii,' I say and bump her. She pulls her fist back and spreads her fingers out, like they're exploding in slo-mo. It's an inner-city thing. Vu has long dark hair on two-thirds of her head, with the rest scraped to the scalp. She wears a pair of too-big, ultra thick glasses and a dirty pale-orange shirt with darker orange sweat-stains in the pits and the buttons close to bursting across her chest.

'Was it Freya? It was her, right?' Vu asks. There's a twisted knot of scar tissue on her right cheek too.

'Was *that* Freya?' I ask, nodding towards the puckered skin.

'Sure was, when we were both at the Engadine house. She thought I dobbed on her to the guards.'

'Did you?'

'Totally didn't, not that time anyway. I did every chance I could afterward, though. I figure I earned it.'

'What's it to you, anyway?'

'Well, if it was Freya —'

'It might have been,' I say.

'Then we have something in common.' She dips a meat nugget into the squirt of brown-flavoured sauce on her tray, then shoves the whole thing in her mouth. I nibble at mine. A bunch of kids who seem to know and love Vu come and sit with us.

'Is everyone here cool?' I whisper to Vu.

'Yeah,' she says, spitting little bits of mystery meat and breading on my arm. I wipe it off as she gestures to a prissy-looking chick sitting near the door. 'You have to watch out for Kelly Karmine, she's getting it on with Uncle Dereck.' She nods towards a young, beefy and neckless Uncle standing on duty by the door. He keeps sneaking looks over at Karmine and it's pretty obvious and gross.

'Kelly's got a loose mouth, among other things. Everyone else from the teen dorm is okay, unless they're in the Naughty Chair, but who can keep their mouth shut there, really?'

'Cool.' I raise my voice to be heard by the rest of the table. 'So, who do I see about keys? I got a mish I need to do tonight.'

A tall, thin guy waves a hand. He's got a little 'fro going and tribal scars on his cheeks. 'I'm your man. Ade.'

I reach over and we bump. 'You need a toll?'

'Nah, sister. Danger is my reward.'

'Ah, a man after my own heart.'

Ara slots in across from me, shaking out their long hair so they don't sit on it.

'Hey, Ara?'

They raise a finely-shaped eyebrow at me.

'Nerida said you have something she wants. I gotta pay her for these stitches,' I say, waving at the tight, sore part of my face. 'She said you might want what I've got going.'

Ara rolls their eyes. 'Bloody Nerida. She's right, but. Can you do names?' Their voice is weird and low and kinda skips a bit when they say 'names'.

'Of course.'

'Good,' Ara says. 'I'm down to trade.'

—

'Don't you have, like, a week left until you go?' Vu asks. She presses up against me by the door and she smells like sweet sweat and like mandarins, which we got with our dinner tonight. Apparently she was owed fruit for something because she had a bunch of them and she peeled and ate them one by one as the kids told stories before tuck in. She didn't share with anyone else, but she gave a few of the little crescents to me. That meant something, but I'm not sure what.

'Five days tomorrow.'

'Then why are you going on a mish? Do you want to get caught or something?'

'Of course I don't, don't be stupid.' I say and I guess it's true, but I wonder . . .

'Most kids with as much time as you left keep their heads down and do the time. They don't go out on missions and they don't pick fights with unpredictable bitches *and* they don't back-talk to the A and U's.'

'I like living on the edge,' I say and grin at her, but it's all for show and I reckon she knows it. Inside I'm really wondering the same thing.

Like, I thought when I was almost there I'd chill out, but if anything, I've got worse. Kids always talk about Age Transfer with such gravity, like it's some golden time and they've got this big, gaping freedom coming up, and it's like that but it's also not. Freedom feels scary, feels too big and every time I think about what I might do I stop being able to think about anything.

'Mirii. Mirii! Mahoney, are you in there?' Vu asks, knocking on my head.

'Shiz, yes. Yes.'

'I don't think you're up for a mish, babe. You just voided out like, whoa. You been smoking up with Farmer Ben?'

'I wish,' I say. 'I gotta go out, Vu. I need gloves and alcohol wipes, gotta make some trade. I owe for these stitches. If you're worried, then stay here.'

'Nah, I wanna come. I haven't been on a mish in ages. I need some excitement. Do you get mad toey and hungry afterwards?'

'Who doesn't?' I say, then hush her. Auntie Carol's on night-watch and the girl at the workstation next to mine said that she always gets into the med supply cupboard and dopes out on Calmucet or Tarmiene. Perfect mish conditions. Through the grill on the door I can see her take a seat behind the watch station and within thirty seconds she's already on the nod.

'Time?' Vu breathes into my ear and it tickles: my ear and elsewhere. I brush her back a little, but she shoves herself up against me again.

'Nearly.'

Auntie Carol's head drops again, comes up. Drops, up again. Drops, drops, drops . . . She lets out a big, honking snore.

'Let's kick this baby,' I breathe and I open the door extra-slow and careful-like. Vu follows tight-close behind me and we whisper across the scuffed, moonlit linoleum in bare feet. I've got the key ring clamped tight in my hand so it doesn't jingle but I reckon I could stomp double time across the floor, shaking the keys like a tambourine, popping out cartwheels and singing the national anthem at the top of my lungs and Carol would keep napping through the whole thing. She's pretty gone.

Vu and I skitter into the watch station. She keeps an eye out while I slam a flash bead into the Systower. It's this mean little patch that I scored off a kid back out at the Lightning Ridge house when I was a little thirteen-year-old scumbag. He was this hack-genius and the patch runs a stealth prog that kinda pauses all the cameras but keeps the timers running so it looks like nothing's happening. I mean, half the kidcams don't even work, but better safe than sorry, yeah? Cost me a month's fruit and I ended up with bleeding gums but it's paid for itself about ten times over and it's never let me down. That or none of the cameras work. Either way.

That prog has spread through the Orphancorps like herpes through a teen dorm, and there's a bunch of copies floating around now. Standard issue for a mish, but I get off on using my old orig copy. Like retro hipster chic, yeah? I had it before it was cool.

'We're good to go?' Vu says and when I nod she pops her head back in the dorm and a few other kids run out and scatter down the hall on their own missions.

Me and Vu skip towards the Sick Bay. I do pop out a cartwheel now, 'cause I'm extra jolted to be out in the wee hours and it feels cool to have Vu padding down the hallway beside me, her hair and nightshirt rippling.

Sick Bay door opens with a massive crunch of the lock that has me wincing, but no rogue night-time Auntie or Uncle comes to check out the noise so we pop the door open and slink into the infirmary. I go right for the supply cupboard, snatching up a whole box of alcohol wipes because there's ten of them in there, then I empty the box of small surgical gloves halfway and muddle the rest around to disguise the missing bulk. Vu goes to the pharm supply cupboard and I throw her the keys. She pops the lock, takes a few Tarmienes from a bottle on the top shelf, but not too many because Auntie Carol's already piggied up a bunch of them tonight and she doesn't want it to be too obvs. Then she pockets a preloaded syringe of Calmucet and I'm like, not as cool with that.

'You into heavy shit, hey? Your arms look okay, I didn't think you jabbed. You a groiner? In between the toes?'

'It's not for me, it's for trade. I owe big.'

'Looks like. What did you do?'

'Got knocked up last month. Needed some of Nerida's special tea.'

'Oh, sorry. You okay?'

'I was once it was gone, right?' She lets out a big laugh, like, 'Ha!' and then claps a hand over her mouth.

'What does Nerida want the Calmucet for?'

'She's the jabber.'

'Wow. I didn't know.'

'It's not like she sings it from the tabletops at dinnertime.'

'Guess not.'

Vu pops the stuff into her bra and smooths her nightie over the lumps. 'So, you wanna go down to the admin offices and jimmy some of the Aunties' and Uncles' lockers? They've always got lollies and shit. We could be high-rolling traders for the rest of the week.'

'Sure, why not?'

I close the Sick Bay door behind me and pull it twice to make sure it's locked. Then Vu grabs me round the waist and we dance down towards the admin office by the front door, our night shirts flying up, bright in the moonlight. She dips me right by the door and I slide the key in while I'm upside down. She pulls me up, spins me and I push the door open with my foot.

There's a light on inside.

—

The light is a bright strip under the door to the Warden's office. Vu and I pause mid-breath, still cheek-to-cheek from our impromptu dance-number.

'Vile,' she breathes. She's still gripping one of my hands and she drops my waist and pulls me away. The door creaks as it closes. We race back up the hall.

'You're right,' I whisper as we pass the infirmary. 'Totally gross. What a waste.'

'Not gross,' she says. 'Vile. Warden Vile. Warden Kyle, I don't know what he's doing here, but if he sees us we're up the scheisse creek.'

'Paddle?'

'Yeah, nah,' she says, extra-grim.

And it's then that I hear the footsteps bouncing off the walls. Hard soled shoes. Squeaky.

Warden shoes.

My heart speeds up and my guts turn to water, start to churn like someone's pressed my flush button. Vu and I swing it past the nursery dorms and I make a quick eye contact with a night Nanny who happens to be peering out of the window. I press a finger to my mouth but I'm going too fast to see if she nods or not.

I'm pretty sure a bunch of kids are raiding the kitchen or up in one of the workshops on a light-finger mish but there's no time to warn them. We power past Auntie Carol who's drooling all over herself with her chin resting on her chest and her feet up on the countertop.

Vu opens the door real swift and quiet and I fly in behind her, skidding around to lock the door up tight. Ade's sitting up and I sling the keys to him across the bunkbed forest of snoring teeners. He catches them fast in one hand as I dive for my bed. In the hallway there's a shout and a yelp and a clatter as this Warden dude lays one out on Auntie Carol, busted asleep at the wheel. I wriggle further down under the covers and try to slow my heartbeat from a mad voidstep thump to something more ambient. The lock grinds, deafening and slow and then the door opens.

'Up. All of you up! Now. Stand next to your bunks.'

The lights go on and everyone's already up, blinking in the hum of fluorescence.

The Warden is a squat, portly fugger with slick black hair, a sharp, dark suit and a button-up shirt that's the cleanest, whitest thing I've ever seen. His tie chokes him tight under his loose, shaven neck.

'Five missing from their beds, Carol. Who are they?'

'I'm, um, I'm . . .' Carol slurs. She's probably in as much shit as we are, if not more.

'Get out, Carol. Call the watch down from the tower, then wait in my office.'

Carol shuffles off, tripping on a crack in the linoleum, mumbling and crying to herself.

Warden Vile paces through the rows of mattresses, tapping something in the palm of his hand. He does it on purpose, to slam up the tension. He's quiet and we're quiet and the air's all zappy like just before a storm. He passes by me, so close that if I lifted my hand just a little, it would brush across the fine stuff his suit's made of. What are suits made of? It looks itchy. I wonder if he can feel my heart trip-hopping under my ribs, smell the fear-sweat trickling out from under my arms.

He looks right at me. I've got at least twenty centimetres height-wise on him and it feels weird and wrong to be looking down at this man because his presence feels so mighty. I feel like I should lay flat on the floor to show him that I know my place. Show him that I know he could end me at any second if I so much as breathed wrong.

Then I stop breathing. Everything goes slow and liquid. I can feel my face desaturate. My legs cramp and my fingers turn to stone.

That thing he's tap-tap-tapping in his palm? It's my flash bead. My patch. I left it in the Systower and if he finds out it's mine, I'm crumpets.

FIVE DAYS

Vile points to a blinking, half-asleep kid with wild bedhead.

'You. Who is missing from their beds?'

The kid doesn't hesitate for a second. None of us would, not when it's this obvious. If he asked Freya right now, even she'd spill like a knocked-over cup.

'Belham. Hough. Chen. Smith, Clover Smith. And . . . I think that's Jadhav's?' he says, twisting up a brow, trying to remember.

Ara puts their hand up. 'I'm Jadhav. That mattress is Cook's.'

'Right,' the cyclone-haired kid says. 'Yeah, Praz Cook sleeps there. Sorry Ara.'

'Good,' Vile says. He still taps the flash bead in his palm. His hands are white and pink, soft like flower petals. The nails gleam like shiny plastic. He keeps up his pacing round the mattresses and every eye in the room darts from place to place, following his course.

'And who knows what this is?' He holds up the flash bead. From here it's just a tiny black dot between his thumb and forefinger, but we all raise our hands. He points to the closest girl.

'It's a flash bead.'

'Yes. And who does it belong to?'

No hands. The silence is long. The buzz of the light fills up all the spaces in between us. I see a slight dip of a white-blonde head by the window. Freya. I look at her. She looks at me. She raises an eyebrow and her eyes gleam with knowledge. They're asking me, *should I?* I try and make my face say, *don't you fugging dare, you twisted bitch*, but that's a lot for one expression to say and I don't know if my message is that loud *or* clear.

The door slams inwards and every kid in the room jumps half a foot. I jolt in the heart and in the guts and it feels like my blood starts running backwards. A bunch of the Aunties and Uncles from the night watches and up in the tower trot in, proud as pie, with all the mish kids by the collars. They look defeated as shiz.

'Take those children right down to the Consequence wing.'

Everyone winces, though I don't know why we expected different. It's not like they woulda tucked 'em back into bed. They march out and Vile gives us a cold once-over with those deep black eyes before he sweeps out. The door locks and the lights go out with a crump. I blink against the dark, blind in the absence of the sick white light and climb back under the covers. When I can see again I look over at Vu who looks over at me, her face heavy like a storm cloud. She crawls over and I lift the blankets for her. Cuddling up against me, I feel her body start to shake.

'If it wasn't . . . If we didn't . . .'

'I know. I know, Vu. This is our fault too and if they zing us to the man, we'll cop. If they don't . . . I don't know. We'll find some way to make it up to them.'

I let her tears soak into my nightie and when she's done crying, Vu pulls me hard to her and her tongue is in my mouth and she rakes her fingernails across my back. I know what she wants. I can feel the ripple of scar tissue in lines across her thighs. I catch glimpses of the long-healed, and less-healed slashes on her arms in the silver moonlight. I sink my hands into her hair, twist it up between my fingers and yank it back hard. She lets her head go and I follow her back with my teeth at her neck. She breathes sharp and presses herself tight against my hipbone.

Sometimes here the hurt and the good feelings get all mixed up. Sometimes they become the same thing. And sometimes you gotta feel your way out of the pain in your brain. There are lots of ways to do it.

This is one.

—

After, when Vu is curled into my side, exhausted and deep asleep and I'm laying there, eyes closed and mind racing, I feel . . . something. A presence. I open my eyes and Freya's standing there, inverted in my vision — legs-body-head-pale-hair — above the mattress. Her grey nightdress and hair glow in the dark but the bruises on her face make it into a void. She doesn't say anything, but then again, she doesn't need to.

—

It takes me three tries to plug in my tab in the purple morning light and I nod my way through two lessons on the free-school site until I give up and lay my head down on the desk for a bit before work starts.

It's still and quiet with only the low thump of a few fingers on tab screens, but I can't sleep because I can't stop the circles in my mind. I see the faces of the kids who got caught out of bed, a flash of the door to the Consequence wing, Freya's missing tooth, Warden Kyle's cold grey eyes. The classroom has bright lemon-yellow walls and an ancient whiteboard scrawled with the ghosts of old marker. There's a much-scrubbed but still not-gone epitaph of the word 'balls' in giant letters from the top to the bottom and I stare hard at it to escape the visions in my mind, trying to solidify the ghost-words. One of the lights in the left corner flickers and strobes across the gleaming whiteboard.

The dodgy light is a sign. When I get into the buzzshop Uncle Jeff sends me and Cam, who's unofficially appointed himself my personal runner, plus another buzzy and his runner over to the dorms to replace the wiring on some of the overhead lights. It's feeding time in the nursery and we peer into the zoo, get a glimpse of the mad, scrambling battle-royale of tots for their bots, get a whiff of the stink of milk-spew.

'The Four-to-Seven dorm first, yeah?' the other Buzzer, Gregor, asks me and I nod like mad.

'For sure.'

They've cleared off an area under the fixture, roped it off with some yellow and black checker-tape and opened up a rickety ladder. Gregor and I Fist-Peace-Faceplant to see who goes up first (fist beats peace, peace revives a faceplant, faceplant flops all over a fist) and I win. Cam and the other runner, Sticksy, hold the ladder while Gregor climbs up to suss out the sitch and I get busy laying out all the tools we might need.

While I'm digging through the rusty toolbox, I eavesdrop on a tight group of scummy tykes nearby. The boss of this gathering is a girl of about six with a runny nose and a long tangle of ashy-blonde hair. She sits in the middle of an arc of rapt kids, telling a story in a loud, nasal voice to be heard over the shrieks and giggles of a hundred other little jerks.

'. . . they eat the light, and drink the noise the lights make. That buzz sound. They eat it all up.'

She's talking about the grey ones. That's what we used to call them, but it changes. It always changes.

'I never seen no grey ghosts,' says a boy about her age. She throws him a look of pure malice, the way only a six-year-old can.

'That's because you're gunna die soon,' she tells him, pure and matter-of-fact. 'You can't see them if you gunna die soon. Then you'll be one of 'em.'

The little boy goes a pale green colour. He turns to a wide-eyed dribbler with a shocking bowl-cut next to him, punches him in the stomach, and storms off through the room.

Tangles takes the crying kid into her arms and rocks him 'til he shuts up. She sucks a noseful of snot back into her nostrils and continues.

'Grey ghosts come from all the kids who die here. They can't hurt you, but. They just can't ever die proper because they don't got no family to let them into heaven. You gotta know people in there to get in.'

The mouth-breathers sit there and nod.

'In the day time they live in the lights, eating and drinking lots. Then at night they come out and play in the hallways and in the stairwell down to the con-sa-kents wing, but they don't play fun games. They have to play hidey-findey all night and not ever find each other. Just look and look forever.'

'Can they see each other?' asks a tiny little golden-skinned boy with tight ringlets spilling over his brow and a rippled burn scar on his neck.

'Nope. There's lots of 'em but they feel like they're all alone.'

'Oh,' the kids chorus.

That's new, I haven't heard that one before. I reckon Tangles made it up on the spot. These stories get passed around like rumours and gossip, changing that little bit with every telling, but the base is always the same.

Tangles drops her voice to a loud whisper. 'That big girl and the boy up on the ladder, they're tryna help. She's got special tools to try and get the ghosts out of the lights and send them to heaven.'

The kids sneakily peer over at me and I look up and wink. Some of the real little ones gasp.

Fugg me, kids are stupid.

—

I'm up the ladder in the nursery, getting twisted in loose wire when I glance down and see Vu looking up at me. She's got a bub on her hip, winding its hand in her thick black hair.

'Hey Mirii,' she says. Her eyes are puffy and dark-circled and there's a row of little marks on her neck. Those are mine and seeing them runs electricity through me, but not real current because the power's been switched off in here. Like, the meta-phorical kind, yeah?

'Hey Vu, I didn't know you worked the nursery.'

'Yeah, I've been on this detail for four months, since my last transfer,' she says, bouncing the tiny blob. It waves its grubby little hands around, grins and lets out a laugh that even I think is cute. Then it opens its mouth and a big glug of white vomit comes out and goes down the front of Vu's lavender top.

'The spew smell never comes out. Did my hair reek of it last night?' She grins up at me.

'I didn't notice,' I say, coysmiling right back.

She hands the kid off to another Nanny and uses the thread-bare towel over her shoulder to mop up the mess on her shirt. There are heaps of older kids in here working Nanny detail. Apparently, if bubs don't get a bunch of attention and stuff when their gooey brains are growing, they end up useless and kinda crazy. Orphancorps need workers, not angry kids that prefer rocking back and forth over working in the factories, so they put a bunch of the older kids on Nanny detail. I wonder how long it took them to figure that out? Some of the kids are hopeless on daycare duty, but some of them are good at giving out the love and stuff. Not me, though. I did it once for a few months and it sucked the life right out of me. Kids are such little balls of need, aren't they?

'So, I heard from Bates this morning, he was on mop-up down in Consequences,' Vu says, popping a pacifier back in the mouth of some kid who spat it out. 'He said it was a pretty deep cleanup scene but that everyone's in Time Out now. A couple of them went through the corner and the chair in the wee hours, but it don't look like they're gonna spill. I think if they had we'd be toast already.'

'Makes sense, yeah. Still have those Calmucets from last night?'

She nods yes.

'Maybe we can trade 'em and get the kitchens to send some decent food down?'

Vu nods and folds her arms around herself. 'It's the least we can do. I wish we could do more.'

'Me too.'

From over in the corner there's a clatter and a scream. A blob-ber's toppled over or something and bashed a whole row of them down like dominoes. My jaw tightens as the room erupts in screams.

'I don't know if I could do this job,' I say, stepping carefully down the ladder as Cam and Sticksy hold it tight.

'I actually don't mind it. You stop hearing the noise after a while. I like working with the real little ones the most of all.'

We watch as Cam and Sticks try and settle the unrest by starting a game of Zoom. Soon the bubs are all giggling and clapping their hands like they're having the time of their blobby little lives.

'Real little bubs are easy, ya know?' Vu says. 'There's only, like four things they want. Food, to be changed, to sleep or a cuddle. That's about it. I like that.'

'If only all people were so easy.'

'Right?' she says.

—

'I want you to do a tattoo on me,' Cam says, watching as I wire up another headset, then another and another.

It's hell-hot in the buzzshop and everyone pauses now and then to mop up sweat, roll out their ankles and stretch out kinks in tight necks and shoulders. At this point in the day everyone's hit a good rhythm and we pick, prod, solder, sleeve and pack like we're manufactured for it, like we're windup. Cam hands me tools before I even know I need them. I guess he's okay, but that doesn't mean I'd break my rules for him.

'You're not old enough for a tattoo,' I tell him.

'Am too!'

I shake my head. 'Even if you were old enough, you couldn't afford it. It's a lot of work, I gotta charge bank for it.'

'Could too. I got mad trade,' Cam says, his skinny chest puffing out a little.

'Yeah right, you do. You got some gangster scam running in the pre-teen dorm?'

Cam goes red.

'Well, tell me more about the stars then,' he says.

That I can do.

I tell him about Crux, the Southern Cross. Carina, visible all year round. Of Eridanus and Gemini in the summer, Lyra and Scorpius in the winter.

'And you know that big smeary, glowy thing in the sky that you can only see proper way out in the remotes? That's the Milky Way, that's the galaxy our planet's in,' I say, getting myself in deeper with everything I tell him, because then I've got to explain it all. 'It's shaped like a big spiral, like water spinning down the drain, yeah? And the way we see it is, kinda looking across it and out into the rest of space, so it looks like a band across the sky.'

I draw a big slash through the air with my soldering iron and he ducks a little, looking totally lost, but that's okay, he's nodding because he's getting the vibe of the story and I think he just likes hearing me tell it. For some weird reason I like telling it to him, too.

'And it's weird but back in the day, the Indigenous people saw the Milky Way as this big, like, Emu in the sky.'

'Emu like in the stew? That rubbery crap?' Cam asks.

'Yep. You ever been at the corps with the emu farms?'

He shakes his head.

'There's one out at Gilgandra. They're these huge birds . . .'

'Birds?' Cam's totally incredulous.

'Yeah, they're these giant birds but they don't fly. They've got long necks and long legs and they're the grumpiest fugging birds you ever saw, Cam. Like, worse than an Uncle on transpo duty.'

I can see Cam trying to picture a big angry bird like the way I've described it and I know it's jamming his brain circuits up and that he's for sure got it all wrong. I make a mental note to show him a picture on my tab one day.

'Anyway, they looked up at the Emu in the sky and depending on where it was and what shape it was in, cause it always changes, they could tell what time of the year it was and what they should be doing with their hunting and stuff. Like stealing emu eggs or whatever.'

'Why does it move?'

'Oh, because of, like the rotation of the earth and the orbit around the sun . . .'

I've lost him again. I bring him back with peeks of the thin blue-black dotted lines that link the little star shapes under my sleeves and my shirt and I try to describe where to look for Crux and the Emu in the big night sky.

'How'd you learn all this stuff?'

'Looked it up. When you sign up for the Free School you get a tab. Like, you gotta pay it off with extra duties and stuff, but it's yours and you can use it to look up anything you want. Well, anything that's not blocked by the corp, but you can find ways to get around it.'

'Yeah, a buncha kids in my dorms do school.'

'Well, if you signed up you could get a tablet and learn stuff too. Look up whatever you want. You could even get some extra training for when you age out.'

He twiddles the blue-handled pliers in his hands for a bit, pulling at the handles.

'It's too long. I won't age out for years.'

I snatch the tool from him before he ruins the rubber grips —
they're the only good pair left.

'So what, you'll just fugg round 'til it's time to leave and then
end up in a Prisoncorp when you can't get no work outside?'

'Probably.'

I clip him round the ear.

'Mahoney! Contact warning one!' bellows an Uncle walking
up the row to our left. I throw my hands up and the Uncle makes
a note. It's worth it.

'I used to think I'd never age out, but now I've got five days
left. It goes so slow, Cam, until you look back and realise it went
really fucking fast.' I jab the point of the pliers at him with every
word and he ducks, shamed.

'Mahoney, language infraction!' the Uncle bellows. I twist my
face up as he puts the strike against my name, but it's worth it.

'It's okay, kiddo,' I say. 'I don't hate you or nothing. I just don't
want to see anyone stuck here forever.'

'Even Freya?'

'Not even Freya. Well . . . probably not.'

—

I scan the cafeteria 'til I find that unmistakable blonde head.
Freya's on the other side, sitting alone. She's mashing her potatoes
into a sad plateau on her plate, and even from all the way over here
I can see the fierce look on her face.

'I've never known someone to get so mad at potatoes,' Vu says,
stepping over the long plastic seat to slot in at the table beside me,
her tray teetering in one hand.

'So, I don't want to hurt her or get in any trouble,' I say as Vu and I bump fists. 'I just want them to chuck her into the Time Out cells or maybe give her a fat old dose of kiddie Calmucet to space her out and keep her quiet 'til I leave.'

'She wouldn't tell on us,' Vu said around a mouthful of over-boiled broccoli.

'Wouldn't she? How do you know?'

'Well, she's got the whole loyalty thing going.' Vu ponders for a bit. 'She's all "kids before skids", "damn the man", stuff like that.'

Cam slides in next to me with a tray and I unlock my tab screen and push it in front of him.

'That's an emu,' I whisper, pointing the picture I've pulled up.

'What the fug?' he says, and grabs it from me, studying the image intently. 'Are we having emu tonight?'

'Nah, I'm not sure what this is. Horse?' I take a big mouthful of the weird, grey meat and chew it thoroughly. 'Camel?' I chew a bit more and then throw my fork down. 'I have no idea. Whatever it is, it's terrible.'

'Welcome to Orphancorp,' Vu says. 'What did you expect? Cuts of the finest cow?'

'I'm a simple girl,' I say. 'I just like to be able to identify my food before I eat it.'

'Oooh, fancy.' Vu grins, her cheeks rounded with food and little green bits in all her teeth. What a babe.

I turn to Cam on my right and drop my voice.

'So Cam, what do you know about Freya? Do you think she's the type who'd spill? Like for revenge? If she, say, really hated some sweet and totally innocent babe who she thinks did her wrong?'

Cam thinks about it.

'I dunno. Maybe. Look what she did to your face.'

'Right? And let's say she's got some info on a certain piece of tech left in a certain Systower during what may or may not have been a mish last night . . .'

'That was you guys?' Cam hisses and I clap my hand over his mouth. He mumbles against my hand, more quietly this time, so I peel my palm away.

'You think she'd spill to Vile?'

'I don't know.' I feel the skin pull and pucker around the stitches on my cheek. 'That's why I'm asking you.'

'Shiz, Mirii. I couldn't say.'

'Maybe we could organise a cuddle party. Maybe some snugs might chill her out,' I say to Vu.

She shakes her head. 'She's never come to one.'

'Never? Wow.' I think on it for a bit. 'Maybe we should have one anyway. You know, just for the older kids.'

'You're gonna throw a cuddle party?' Cam asks.

'Yeah, maybe.'

'Can I come?' he asks.

'Ah . . . Um, I'm not sure you're going to be able to get out tonight. You know, after all the shiz last night,' Vu says.

'Maybe you could set one up for the pre-teen dorm,' I tell him.

He nods, like he's carefully considering something he hadn't thought of until now, then he grabs his tray and bolts off to a table full of pre-teen dormers and they all start whispering, excited-like.

I look at Vu and raise an eyebrow and she laughs, then I catch a glimpse of Freya behind us, spearing the last limp stalk of broccoli into her mouth.

Just before I turn away, she looks up and at me. My jaw clenches and my teeth press against each other, setting off the nerves in my rotten molars. I can just make out the black void in her smile where that missing tooth should go.

—

Ade gives us the all-clear, so I start. He's got an assignment for the Free School to finish and doesn't mind keeping lookout for us, though I promised him my next fruit from lunch anyway 'cause I don't like favours and Ade nods his thanks.

I'm cross-legged on the counter in the bathroom with Ara sat opposite, facing me.

'This is gonna hurt.'

'I know. I can handle it,' Ara says and with the look they give me, I can tell they're not lying. In those black-liquid eyes is a whole history of pain and I guess that this will be just another hurt on top of all the other hurts, but at least this pain will be real. With this kind of pain, the pain that you choose, at least you get to know when it ends. At least it *has* an end.

I glove up, unwrap a liner needle from a little sterile pack. When I first started out I jimmied up tools from whatever I could find around, but then, a while back, I gathered up the cash and got a sketchy Auntie to accept an e-parcel of some legit tools and ink. I feel, like, totally professional now, and virtually anti-septic.

I've drawn the name across the soft inside part of Ara's arm, just below the elbow ditch, in red pen. The letters sit inside a banner, with scrolled ends.

We begin and neither of us says a thing.

There's no sound but the drip of a tap into one of the metal sinks and the even whisper of our breath. I fall back into the steady rhythm of the needle like I never left, rocking into it, the shifting of the spike precise in my hands. The name takes shape gradually. My wrists start to ache.

When I get to halfway I pause and shake out my hand.

'Are you going to ask?' Ara says, their voice echoey in the empty bathroom.

'I figured you'd tell me if you wanted me to know,' I answer. I stretch my arms and roll my shoulders out. 'Ready to start again?'

Ara nods. 'I didn't think it would take this long.'

'How long did you think it would take?'

'I dunno. Not this long.' They prop their arm back on my leg and I get right to it, wiping the excess ink from the skin and dipping my needle into the little inkwell I've made out of aluminium foil.

'It's a lot of work,' I say. 'It used to take me longer.'

'How long have you been doing it? How did you learn?'

'Since I was about thirteen. A few kids in the house I was in did scummy pin-and-pencil tatts, and I thought they were so cool. I started looking stuff up and one day I saw a picture of this lady with blue lips and this pattern on her chin on the Wiki. I thought it was beautiful. Her tattoo is called a Moko and it's sacred to her people, the Maoris over in Kiwiland. It tells the story of their lives and their people and stuff. How rad is that? Anyway, yeah, I decided to learn and I practised on anyone who'd let me, which was pretty much everyone. There's a whole lotta kids out there with some shizzy-lookin' tattoos, thanks to me.'

'The tattoos tell the story of their lives?' Ara asks. I don't know if they heard anything else I said. They bite their lip as I move the needle to a new spot and start pressing it in, and in, and in.

'Yeah, in a roundabout kinda way. I mean, I don't do Moko 'cause I'm not a Maori but I feel like my tattoos kinda tell a bunch of stories about my life too.'

'Yeah. I get it. So you don't forget the important bits. Like a mark to make sure you remember.' Ara is nodding and looking sad and thoughtful.

'Yeah, I guess so.'

'The name. It's my sister. Our parents got caught up in the Queensland strife and we don't know what happened to them. She's a few years younger than me and when we came here I told her that I'd protect her, keep her safe. But they transferred her not long after we got processed in. I used hackies and bribed the admin to keep a track of where she was, but I lost her. She's not in the system any more.'

'Do you think she . . .' I don't even want to say it.

'No, she's not even listed as deceased, she's just gone. Like she wasn't ever in the system.'

I start on the last little piece, my wrist throbbing.

'I'm really sorry about your sister,' I say, making the last few jabs. I take a squirt of some antiseptic solution I stole from the first aid kit in my last dorm, and wipe away the excess ink.

The lines are dark and sharp against the soft skin of Ara's fore-arm, angry red fading to pink around the stark letters.

Raaya.

—

I lie in the dark, waiting for the time to come, the right time when you can feel the shift in the dorm from mostly awake to mostly asleep. I don't know how I can feel it, but it's plain to anyone. It's as if the room pulses with consciousness until it doesn't, 'til the thrum of caged kid-minds quiets to a low hum. When I feel it, I sit up. I can see a few other eyes scattered around, shining with excitement. I stand and gather my blankets and my pillow before I run down the little gap between the bunks, bare feet making a quiet thud, thud, thud on the linoleum.

Vu takes my arm when she gets close and we whisper between the beds. There's a bunch of us, a few of the oldest teens, snaking our way through the grey passages between each island of sleeping kids.

In the bathroom we all spread our covers out, throw our pillows around. Ara uses one of the blankets to block underneath the door. Everyone stands there for a second, sparks zapping between us all and eyes all gleamy then we all cuddle up on the floor, heads on bellies, feet in laps, arms draped across shoulders. Vu puts her head across my legs and I play with her hair, letting the soft strands slip over my palm, rubbing my fingertips over the buzzed parts. Blondie slides in next to me and puts his head on my shoulder, reaches up to take my free hand and I thread my fingers through his. He moves his hand over mine, calloused palm dancing across my palm. Ara comes over and puts Vu's feet in their lap and Vu starts to giggle softly as Ara's delicate fingers tickle her toes.

A little plastic bottle of potato punch appears from somewhere and we pass it around, taking sips. Blondie sparks a joint and some of us toke sips of that too.

My head's all swirly and it's like a weight lifts off the room, piece by piece, as everyone goes calm.

This is kinda sacred. It's our time.

In an Orphancorp, there's not a lot of physical contact, and the touches we do get usually hurt. Without each other, maybe we'd go through life thinking that hands are just slaps and fists, not for grasping or stroking.

The first cuddle party I remember, I must have been about four. A boy walked past me late in the night, caught a glimpse of my open eyes.

'Come on,' he said. 'It's time to hug now.'

I followed him, and a bunch of other kids were there, tangle-haired and sleep-sweaty in their giant nightshirts. We pushed a bunch of pillows together and everyone flopped onto them, pressing up against each other. We lay like that a long time. There were quiet sobs now and again. Some of the kids fell asleep. I clung tight to a little girl about my age and her red hair got all in my mouth. Then, the little limbs began to move and everyone just kinda came awake again and we unthreaded ourselves from each other, pulled the pillows apart, and went back to our beds.

I lay there, alone, but the warmth from the others still on my skin and a different kind of warmth inside me, something I hadn't felt before, or for a long time. Like I was part of something. Like I was loved, even just for thirty minutes in the middle of the night.

I'm feeling pretty loved right now, a dozy web of limbs woven around me and Vu is at my neck, nuzzling into it and Blondie is on the other side, nibbling on my earlobe and there's always this tipping point, this critical mass moment when all the chemicals in the room shift and turn electric. Sometimes it doesn't happen, and we all just snug and sleep like at cuddle party when we were kids, but more often than not, we reach that point and then? It's on. Sometimes it's just-touchies or everything-but-pants. Sometimes, like now, it's anything-goes.

Vu's mouth is on mine and Ara is at her belly, lifting up her nightie and burying their face in her side which makes her sigh under my lips. Blondie's hands are on my waist as he kisses up my neck. Then, somehow, Vu is devouring Blondie and I'm lying close by Ara, our tongues twining gently and I feel their hands all over me and I go to lift their nightshirt but Ara bats my hands away.

'No,' Ara says. 'I'm not . . . I can't . . .'

'It's okay,' I whisper. I drop the fabric and wrap my arms

around their neck instead. I let the delicate hands explore me as I run my fingers down through skeins of soft dark hair. Vu crawls back over and I peel off her nightie as Blondie slips in beside Ara and I watch them kiss as Vu undresses me too.

The room is alive with harsh breaths and sighs, everyone's in convoluted little groups that split off and merge with others. Someone's got a stash of black market condoms and everyone's digging in and giggling and the air is full of the sounds of quiet sighs, laughter and foil packets ripping open.

I close my eyes and let the zinging in the air carry me off. There's bodies moving around me, sweet lips on my belly, sweet lips pressed on my mouth. In the dark behind my eyelids, I am all embodied, like out of my head and not just because I'm drunk and stoned but because I'm not stuck in the swirl of my thoughts, I'm all arms and legs and torso and neck and fingers and the pulsing little core between my legs and then I hear a whisper.

'Open your eyes, Mirii.'

It's Vu. The dark splits and lets in the moonlight, glinting off limbs and eyes-closed, mouth-open faces and she's there. I look right into her and she into me and then everything turns to sparks. When I can breathe again, we kiss.

I feel so connected to everyone, and we all lie in a big, sweaty pile for as long as we can, trying to keep the threads between us whole. I feel like something inside me is full, and the easy swirl of thoughts that come from a mind free of fear. I didn't realise how scared I was until I stopped feeling scared for a minute. Scared to leave, scared something might happen and I might have to stay, scared of the void in Freya's smile and the empty-bed cold in Warden Kyle's eyes.

'You done?'

Everyone lifts their heads at once. Freya's standing in the

doorway, framed by the door and the dark room behind it.

I hold out my arms. 'Come cuddle with us, Freya. Let's be friends.'

'You're all disgusting.' She walks past us to the toilet and sits. Her pee spatters against the porcelain and into the water, loud like a waterfall. The explosive sound of the flush shreds the webs between us all and suddenly it's not a magic warm pile of loving bodies, it's a sweat-drying, cold-creeping bunch of stupid kids on the floor of a dark bathroom in the middle of the night.

'Way to harsh our refractory period, Freya,' I say.

'Do you think you're smart or something, with your big words?' she says.

'Well, yeah,' I tell her. Everyone's getting up and getting dressed and grumbling and this is not how cuddle party should end.

'Why you gotta come in and bugger up our good time?' Blondie says, sliding his pants up and hunting around for a shirt until he remembers he wasn't wearing one and then just stands there, arms crossed over his sweaty abs, glowering.

'You don't mess with cuddle party, Freya. This is, like, the only time we have that isn't totally shitty,' says Ara, smoothing hair down around their stormy face.

'What? I just took a whizz. You're acting like I'm the foot basher on duty in the Naughty Chair, for fuck's sake.'

'You wouldn't understand,' Vu says, gathering up her pillow and her blanket. 'It's special.'

'It's gross. I bet you all have the megaclap or something, flopping around together like that.' She goes out through the door and everyone looks at each other and the spell's been most definitely broken, so we just head, one by one, back to bed.

FOUR DAYS

Vu trails behind as I drag my feet to my mattress. I only know she's there when she reaches out for me.

'Mirii,' she says, not whispering, just speaking really low. Whispers hiss and echo across the big room, but soft voices get lost between the walls and rows and sleep sounds.

She and I sit, perching on the edge of my bunk, the vinyl cover groaning with our weight and a few of the lumps around us shifting and mumbling in their sleep at the sound.

'Way to ruin cuddle party,' she says, awkward, as if we didn't just have this convo back in the bathroom. It's weird and sad to see her like this, but I feel the same way. It's just weird and sad all around.

I've got lots of things to say about it, but all I can manage is, 'Yeah.'

'Yeah . . .' she says and we stare at the floor for a minute, almost touching. It's funny to think that not thirty minutes ago, parts of me were in parts of her, parts of her were in parts of me. It's sad how that connection can get all busted up so easy.

'I like you, Mirii,' she spits out, suddenly. 'Like, like-like.'

'I like, like-like you too, Vu.'

'But I don't want to. Not 'cause you're shiz or anything, but you're gonna leave soon.'

'Yeah,' I say. 'Me too.'

See, this is why I don't like-like anyone. Or that other one, the one we don't ever say. Because, eventually, everyone gets taken away.

'Yeah,' she sighs and we hold hands for a bit.

The silence hurts, sorta twists inside my chest.

'You could come find me,' I say. 'How long 'til you age out?'

'Seven months,' she says. 'If I don't muck it up.'

'We should try. You ever seen the old Town Hall building, right in the middle of Sydney?'

'No,' she says. I haven't seen it either, but I've seen pictures and I know people have organised to meet up there because it's so easy to find.

'It's one of the only old buildings left there. It's real small, and it's kinda like this tiny stone place in the middle of all these huge scrapers, yeah? You can look it up. We could meet there. There's a set of steps out front. Let's say, in seven months and one week, we meet on the steps at 6 p.m.?'

She brightens a bit. I do too.

'Yeah? You reckon?'

'Heaps reckon. If we still got the like-like, then we can do whatever we want, you know? If not, we can still be friends, hang out on the outside. See what that's like.'

'That's rad,' she says and she leans into me. We sit there, like that, for a bit. Then I lift her chin up and we're kissing again and she climbs up on me and I grip her waist, her hips, her bum, through her nightshirt and we do that for a bit, too.

—

'So, did you have your little pre-teen snugger session last night?' I ask Cam, elbowing him as I reach over for a mag-tip mini-driver.

He flushes so pink that I swear the tips of his ears are like, fire extinguisher red.

'I'll take that as a yes,' I say, elbowing him a few more times for fun.

'Did you guys not want me to come to your cuddle party because . . .'

'Because it's different from yours?'

'Yeah.'

'Well, yeah, but I wasn't gonna say that. Are things starting to get a bit weird at the pre-teen cuddle party?'

He doesn't say anything, just goes even redder, though I thought that wasn't possible. He's almost purple.

I'm struggling to get this tab back together, I don't wanna be too forceful, but being so gentle is getting me nowhere. We're done with our consignment of headphones and everyone else is wiring lamps together now, but me and a few others are on special duty, fixing up a load of junked tabs for all the kids in the freeschool program. I'm gleeful as anything because I've got mad skills with this sort of thing, and Cam's super keen to learn from the best.

He's not keen to look right at me right now, though. I peer up at him with teasy-eyes.

'So Cam, did you get some touchy-feely last night? Feel up any new boobs? Noobs?'

'Shut up!' he says, but he knows I'm just ripping on him. You always gotta rip on the ones you like the best.

'You gotta be gentle with those noobies, Cam. They're *sore* when they're just coming out like that . . .'

He pushes on my shoulder, still red and all sheepish and I can tell by the way he's looking at me, or not looking at me, that he probably did. Good for him.

'It happens like that once you get to your age,' I say. 'One cuddle party we were all just snugging each other and doing comfort stuff, and the next it was as if something in the air changed. Like the way we smelled just drove us crazy and we all went to a new place. It's fun though.'

Cam nods, all thoughtful and I feel kinda good that I'm here to say this to him. I had to figure all this junk out on my own. 'Just relax and go with it. Try and be safe, there's always condoms around if you know where to look for 'em. Don't do anything you don't want to do and don't make anyone feel like they have to do anything. If someone says something's cool and another thing's not, you gotta respect that, 'cause everyone is different, you know?'

'Did you and Vu . . .? At your cuddle party?'

It's my turn to go a little red.

'Yeah, yeah we did some stuff,' I say and it's not like me to be coy or anything, but here I am, being coy.

'You like her. I can tell. She likes you too,' Cam says.

'I don't know. I'm . . . not good with this kind of thing. And I'm leaving so soon, so what's the point?'

We both go quiet for a bit and let the clip and crump of the buzzshop take over for a while, my fingers fiddling with the inner-works of a battered Orion tab.

'Are you scared?' Cam asks out of nowhere.

For a second, all the things I'm scared of start tumbling through my head like a tonne-load of socks and undies in the giant tumble-dryer down in the laundry.

'Shizless,' I say. Then, 'of what?'

'Of leaving.'

'Oh, yeah. Totally,' I tell him, holding out a hand and flicking my fingers twice before he passes me a tiny screw from the square I'd drawn on a sheet of old paper. It's a diagram of the tab I've just pulled apart, with labels and squares for all the parts. *So you don't lose nothing*, he'd said. *That's genius.*

'You got a job out there?' Cam asks, placing the next screw in my hand before I need to wave at him.

'Nah, no job.'

'What about a place to live?' he asks as I fit the screw to the head of the mag-driver and twist it home.

'No. Not yet.'

'Wow. How come? When Byron Kirk left, he had work *and* a bed at a boarding place.'

'Well, isn't Byron Kirk a shining fugging example of life post-Orphancorp?'

'Shiz, Mirii, I'm just asking.'

I feel all jammed up on the inside, scared and my brain can't cope with it, so I'm just voiding it with anger. It's not even Cam's fault, he's just here, just pointing out things that are true. I hand him the tab and he cleans the screen with a rag dipped in Mrs Sparkle Screen Cleaner, then slips it into a softcover in a box at our feet. He brings up a fresh tab and I get to opening her up.

'I don't know why I haven't sorted anything out yet. I just . . . can't. It's like every time I try I can't make it past opening the browser on my tab. It just don't feel real yet.'

'Oh. That makes sense, I guess,' Cam says.

I don't have to explain anything else because the buzzer starts to drone for lunch. I'd take a half-cooked brumby stew over this line of questioning any day.

—

The hall is crowded with kids coming in from the workshops but I still spot Vu coming out of the dorms, her long hair gathered into a half-falling-out twisty bun on one side, the fine buzz of the shaved part showing her pale scalp through.

'Hey Vu,' Cam calls and she turns. Her eyes are almost swollen shut and there's tears all on her face and it takes me a second to realise what's going on. When I spot her backpack, stuffed full and gripped tight to her chest, extra boots swinging from one of the arms, clarity kinda rushes in.

She's being transferred.

Cam hasn't seen it yet, probably because he's too short to see over the line of kids shuffling in for lunch, so he's confused when I start running after her. There's three other kids with her, all bag-clutching and looking scared. There's got to be some mistake. The Aunties and Uncles always serve the transfer notice three full days beforehand, so how did she not know? Why would she tell me she like-liked me if she knew she was gonna leave?

'Vu!' I say and she turns, almost tripping on the bru in front of her and she drops her backpack. I grab it from the floor for her.

'What's happening?' I ask, pressing the thick canvas bag into her chest.

'I'm being transferred!'

'Where? How? Did you get notice?' I say, as she pulls me along in the line with her. Aunt Bev is at the head, leading them down the hall, but she hasn't seen me yet.

'No! I don't know what's happening. They pulled me outta the nursery half an hour ago and told me to pack my things.'

'There has to be a mistake,' I say and I jog up ahead. Aunt Bev scowls at me.

'Outta the way, Maroney.'

'It's Mahoney, Aunt Bev. So, where you taking this lot off to?' I try to sound light and breezy like I'm just curious but I'm puffing hard and my face is all creased and she can totally tell that I don't just have a general line of inquiry going on here.

'None of ya business. Now, mind yourself and get to lunch before I give you a mark.' She heads off through the door of the admin area and it's out of bounds so I just stop on instinct but Bev keeps going and the transfer kids all follow her. Vu pauses on the threshold and she's crying hard and I feel a few hot tears spill down my face when she wraps her arms around me. I grip her tight.

'You two!' Bev shouts from the door. 'Contact warning one!'

We ignore her.

'Don't forget me,' she says.

'I won't. You remember me too.' I squeeze her tighter.

'Contact warning two! Vu, get your arse through that door. I will not tell you twice,' Bev thunders at us.

'I'll find you. I'll get a hackie to track you for me.'

She nods, pressing snot and tears into my neck. I pull back and lift her face, kiss her lips, tasting the salt she's made all over the place.

'Contact warning three!' Bev says, and suddenly there's rough hands pulling us apart. They turn her around and she's through the door, getting smaller and further away.

'Mahoney! Admin area is out of bounds!' bellows some faceless Uncle behind me and I ignore him and race across the threshold.

'Vu! Seven months and one week! Town Hall steps. Come find me!' I call and they're pulling her so she can't look back but I know she's heard. I stop and my shoulders kind of sag because she's out the door now. She's gone. I should have known. I shouldn't have let the like-like creep in.

Then the impact comes.

I've seen folks tackled by a bunch of Uncles all at once, but managed to avoid it so far. It's not like I don't get up to naughty things, it's just that I don't often get caught. But it's pretty easy to get caught when you're standing in the middle of the admin wing, a good five metres across the yellow-dash line on the floor that indicates out-of-bounds. I'm in their den now, a different world of buzzing systowers and keyboard clicks, of bad kid-jokes and the rustle of junk-bar wrappers. I'm out of place and standing there like a giant whitehead on the tip of a nose, just waiting to get squeezed.

And squeezed I get.

The impact is what I imagine it might be like to get hit by a bus. One minute, my boots are flat-footed on the lino, the next, they're in the air and so am I, three thick, sweaty Uncles sweeping me up with their trajectory and we all hit the floor. My body breaks their fall and the sound of it feels like the pain. All the breath presses out of my chest and I can't suck in another. They climb off me and one flips me over and twists my arm back behind me, jams a knee into my spine that might hurt if I wasn't already in pain.

Then he lets me go.

I know why.

'I'm down,' I say, even though it doesn't matter. 'I'm down already.'

When the kiddie-prod hits and the first jolt zings through, I think I can hear them laughing. Then I can't hear much at all.

—

I'm not out for long, because I come back when they're dragging me into the hallway and I can't imagine they would have left me cluttering up the floor in admin for too long.

'That's a strike, Mahoney. We're feeling generous today. You're lucky you aren't hangin' upside-down in the Consequence wing right now.' The Auntie drops my legs and steps over me, back into admin.

'Mirii! Mirii, you okay?' Cam is there. Ara and Blondie too, and a whole lot of kids all come 'round me and I'm blinking hard and gasping like an asthmatic before a puff.

'Did . . . Did I . . . Did I . . .'

'What, Mirii, what are ya trying to say?' Cam asks, taking my hand while Ara squeezes the other.

'Did I whizz myself this time?'

The kids all around giggle and the tension starts to slip away.

'No, not this time,' Blondie says. He brushes everyone away, the little kids scattering back into the cafeteria and he gets his hands underneath me and scoops me up. He carries me back into the dorm and sends Cam down to get me some food and water from the lunchline. He puts me down, real gentle, onto my bed. Ara and a few other kids from cuddle party last night hover around and there's a crowd around the door that hums and jostles, looking in to make sure I'm okay.

'What happened?' Ara says.

'It's Vu, she got transferred,' I tell them, my teeth still chattering.

'Transfers don't happen on Sundays,' says Ara, hand jammed to their mouth, nerve-biting the long nails tipping each delicate finger.

'It's Sunday?' I ask.

I always forget it's Sunday. The days all bleed together because it's all just get up, work, sleep. But on Sundays, we get three hours out in the playground in the afternoon. Playtime.

'Oi, you little jerks. Go outside and play,' booms a thin-haired blonde Auntie, scattering the crowd at the door. 'Get some bloody sunshine,' she says, popping her head in through the doorway and glowering at us. 'Now!'

Everyone helps me up and Blondie and Ara hold my arms while I jerk and shuffle out along the hall, my heart still racing and the blood pumping in my ears, making a hollow noise that sounds like, *Vu, Vu, Vu.* We go past the workshops, past the stairs to the Consequence wing and out the door to the playground. I'm not sure that I'd consider it playful exactly: a blank asphalt square, weeds coming up through the cracks, fence-lined and barb-wire topped. But the air is fresh out here and the sun feels warm on my face.

They set me up at a splintered wooden table and Cam comes flying out the door and hurtling across the yard. He passes me a mandarin secreted in his armpit.

'Present,' he says. 'From the kids on Foodservice. They told me to give you this too.'

He touches me, gentle like a pillow or a kiss, on my arm. Comis. 'Cause a tasing hurts, so here's a thing that doesn't. I still feel my muscles vibrate under his hand, but it helps.

'I guess it's from me too,' he says. 'I'm sorry about Vu.'

I can't even force a smile because of all the hurt bubbling up just under my skin. I don't want to cry. I'm not going to cry, I can't, not here where everyone can see, but my eyes feel all gleamy with tears and everything blurs. I can feel my throat forcing up the sobs. *Not here, not here.*

'Thanks little bru,' I say, hardly able to get it out. I want to hug him, but Cam is already going all red so I punch him in the guts instead and he groans and shakes his head, going, 'nah, nah.' He tears off to join a bunch of kids playing some kind of weird balance game that I bet only they know the rules to.

One by one, or in little groups, kids come up to me, their faces flush with the air and the excitement, or the twin games of full-contact netball and bullrush going on in each corner of the yard. Some nod, some offer a solemn fist for bumping, most just place a hand on my arm or my shoulder.

Tangles, the storyteller from the kiddie dorm yesterday, she must remember me because she runs up and leaps onto my back, holding me tight for a good thirty seconds before an Auntie from her dorm watch screams at her from across the yard.

'Tompkins! Contact warning!'

Tangles drags herself up off me.

'Sorry you got tased, ghost-lady,' she says, and skips away. Little weirdo.

I'm touched for the comis, because these kiddos barely know me and they're making my heart hurt like whoa crazy, even more than before. It's the kinda hurt that aches from all sides.

—

Outside the bathroom I can hear kids banging and bitching as they go about their mandatory Sunday afternoon chores but here in my tile and porcelain enclave there's just me and the quiet hum of a busted toilet filling and leaking, filling and leaking.

My hand is still shaking but I'm making the shape anyway. The little trembles in the line will make me remember. I press and press, the points of the needle driving a hot pain through me, my neck aching from the angle, my wrist twisted and fingers pressure-white from how tight I'm gripping. I want to get the ink deep in there. I want to make the line as black and true as the night.

And it's not just for Vu and how I like-like her or whatever, this one's for everything. The way they can just take someone away one day and not even tell anyone why. The way they can keep those poor busted mish kids down in Consequences and do what they do to them, and no one knows and if they did, I doubt anyone would care. How they've had me working since I was six years old, how they teach us to read and write but make us pay to learn anything else, the way they lock us in together at night and let kids do what they're gonna do to make more babies for them.

How it's a cycle. How we're set up to fail.

When I'm done I keep my shirt hiked up and stare at the tattoo in the mirror, the black shape like a beacon branded into the soft brown skin above my belly, below my breasts.

V. For Vu, of course. For Vile. For voltage and vomit. For Verity House. For vengeance?

Yeah, maybe for vengeance, too.

—

'Who is this dipshiz?' I whisper, trying not to let him hear me.

'Berry. Costa Berry,' says Ara.

We're all jammed up by the door. Blondie's the tallest, so he's peeking through the window, taking quick little sips of the view and updating us on the stats.

'Well, what's he good for?' I say, my voice real low, but he still looks over at me.

'He's a hackie,' Ara tells me.

'He's like, twelve?' I hiss and he looks over at me.

His curly brown hair is just a bit too long and it spills down over his oil-slick forehead. He's a whole head and a half shorter than I am, with shifty eyes and every few seconds he clears his throat, this thin, weedy 'ahem' that drives me crazy. Every time he does it, I dare him to do it just one more time.

Wouldn't you know it, there he goes again.

'I'm, ahem, I'm almost fourteen,' he says, hitching up his pyjama pants. They're so long they bunch and puddle around his feet, and this just adds to the little-doofus vibe I get from him.

'He's really good,' Ara says, and I guess I trust them.

Just then Blondie waves for us all to get back. A torchlight shines in through the window and I can see the glass steam up where the Uncle presses his nose as he peers through. They're supposed to come in and shine the light around, but they never do. Who could be bothered? I mean, the door's locked, right?

The yellow beam slices right between us, me and Blondie on one side of the doorway, Ara and the little pinhead on the other. What was his name? Barry? Betty? Berry, that's it. We all crouch there, totally still and the light disappears finally. Footsteps echo away and Berry clears his throat again.

'You better get your airways under control before we go out there,' I tell him, but Blondie's up at the window again and he flaps his hand for us to be quiet.

'Uncle Rick's off to the dunnies. He usually takes at least ten minutes. Time to slam this shit,' he says and slips the key into the lock, quiet and careful as anything. The door cracks just a hair and we peek out.

The hall is empty but for the buzz of the lights dotted up and down the hall. I think of the grey ghosts for a second, their lonely games of hidey-findey in the halls and all my hairs stand on end.

Behind me, Blondie wraps his head in a spare shirt. He's wearing two, one on his face, one on his back, which is twice as many shirts as I've ever seen him in.

He slips out the door first and works his way up the hall, inching along the wall. When he gets to the corner, he monkeys up the wall like it's nothing, springing off doorknobs and finding purchase in the cracks in the wall. To be fair, some of those cracks are pretty wide so it's only like, impressive rather than magic or anything. Blondie hangs lightly off the bracket for the cam, shoulder jammed into the corner and bare toes crammed into a decent gap. He slings a pillowcase over the cam, long end dangling for easy grabbing on our way out. After the last mish-bust, we're not taking chances with the cameras - they might actually be working now.

The moment it's covered, we all flood out the door, closing it gently behind us. Ara's long hair trails as they tiptoe to the end of the hall, by the back door and the stairs to the Consequence wing, on lookout. Blondie jumps down, landing lightly on his feet and stays beneath the bracket for a quick jump-rip of the camera cover if we've gotta make a hasty exit. I push Berry out in front of me and we go right to the systower behind the watch desk. He slams a flash bead in the back and picks up one of the watch tabs.

'See, passwords for the main OS with all our records changes every day at midnight and, ahem, I've made this patch that temporarily changes the time to midnight and then changes it to MY password, so . . .' Berry says softly, his fingers dull-thudding over the keyscreen on the tab.

'Shhhh,' I say. 'I don't need to know how it works, just get me on there.'

We wait an agonising sixty seconds for the fake-clock to click over and before I even know it, he's on the OS, navving through to the state ward records.

'Vu . . . Vu . . . Hey, was she that Vietnamese girl with the shaved bit in her hair and, ahem, ah, the thick glasses?'

'Yes, that's her,' I tell him. 'Please be quiet.'

'Ahem, sorry. I liked her.'

'We all like her, that's why we want to find her.'

'Um . . . She's not in here,' Berry says, peering up at me, his face bottom-lit by the glowing tab screen. 'She's not even in here at all. Are you sure that's how you spell her name?'

I grab the tab off him and hiss, 'Of course I'm sure, it's two fugging letters!'

I scroll through. Vreen, Kevin. Vu, Aiden. She should be right in between them. I page through every Vu on the screen. No Adeline. No record, no transfer, not even an awful, red-tinged deceased page.

Just nothing.

Ara races down the hall, their footsteps quick and quiet.

'I heard a flush!' they whisper, and Berry leans over the desk, pulls his flash bead patch out of the systower and races back into the dorm room before I even realise what's happening.

'Hurry,' Blondie says and I wave him off.

'Just go, I need one more second.'

He leaps up to grab the shirt over the camera, blonde hair flying. I turn away from the camera and I scroll through 'V' again, eyes skittering over the text.

Uncle Rick doesn't come whistling around the corner, like I expect him to at any second. I hear another flush and I grimace at the thought of what he's doing in there. It's a false alarm, he's not on his way at all.

So it's not his hand that clamps over my shoulder, cold and hard and tight-pinching the nerves there. It's not his voice that startles me into dropping the tethered watchdesk tab on the floor,

the screen cracking into a thousand little fissures, each one cap-
turing the moonlight and the darkness of the hall in turn. It's not
his words that come, stinging my ear like acid, chilling my spine
like an icy shower in the Consequence wing, which is where I'm
off to, by the way. No doubt about it.

'Out of bed? Mahoney, is it?'

It's Vile. It's Warden Kyle.

And of course I can't help it. Me and my mouth. Like maybe
he's gonna go easy on me if I just cower and grovel, but I figure if
I'm already up the scheisse creek, how's a paddle gonna help me
anyway?

'Yeah,' I say, turning to give him a grin and I bend down and
peck him on the cheek. 'I thought I'd come and give ya a good-
night kiss, Vile.'

THREE DAYS

It doesn't feel real until after Vile's had the Uncles and Aunties on nightshift run a sweep of the halls, wakes all the kids up in the teen dorm, questions them in front of me, questions me in front of them. After he smashes the already shattered watch tablet to pieces, makes all the kids in the room jump. After he tears my mattress to bits, but doesn't find anything, even though I swear I put my tab back in my hidey-hole. After he drags me out of the room by the hair and I get a good long look at Ara and Blondie with their angryscared eyes, at Freya, who's got this weird combination of glee and pity on her mug. After Vile marches me down the hall.

—

After I realise what's coming to me, but before I get it.

—

I'm not getting out of here. I'm not going to try and make a life for myself. I'm going right to Consequences, to face 'em, then into Time Out for as long as they like. The broken tablet is 'destruction of property' and I try to remember what the Consequences of that are, try do the maths in my head to see if that's enough to send me over to a Prisoncorp, but the maths are arbitrary anyway, and besides, Vile's got me so tight around the arm that I can feel his fingers slip into the spaces between my muscles and tendons and I can't keep a track of much else.

The hallway is endless and far too short at the very same time. There's a growing group around me, led by Uncle Rick who's looking vicious because this happened on his watch and he'll cop a strike or a salary dock. By the flash in his eyes I can see that he's going to make me pay for it, in bruises and in blood.

The watch must be down to a skeleton crew because half the nightshifters come down to herd me towards the stairs. They laugh and joke and their eyes sparkle and some of their faces are flush red with excitement, which makes my guts twist and all the feeling drain out of my fingers and feet.

I don't bother saying anything. It's not gonna help and anyway, my mouth's gone so dry that I don't think I could squeak out a word.

The door to the stairwell looms up in my vision and I close my eyes as Vile kicks it open and pushes me through. The crash of the door against the wall bounces off the cinderblock walls and all around my head.

Down we go.

—

'Children need to know the Consequences of their actions.'

Vile tells me this over and over.

I'm not sure if it's blood or sweat or water that's dripping down my face. All those things? I'm sure my stitches have busted open and it is hot down here, plus my hair's still wet from the tub of water that's now red-tinged and forgotten by the door. The room feels airless. And electric, but not in the good way. It zaps with the kind of charge that grows in the space between the ones with the power and the ones without.

'Who helped you?' someone says. 'Who else?' they ask and they pull the balled up rag out of my mouth to let me splutter the same answer, which is not the answer they want.

'Just me,' I say. 'Just me.'

Back in it goes.

The chair isn't really a chair, it's more a swivelling kind of plat-form. I think the base of it was once a chair, but the top is a plank of wood. My knees ache against it. My hands are behind my back, but tethered to a spot on the ceiling, pulled up. I've been here for hours, maybe days. Maybe I've always been here. Every muscle in me screams, screams. Every part of me is ripe here, unable to be hidden. The soles of my feet take precedence now. An Auntie, her face flushed and dripping sweat, holds my face up to hers.

'Look at me,' she says.

I look to her left, to the pokey. A pair of frightened eyes peers from the cutout and I lock onto them.

'Look at me,' she says again, pulling my hair, my head, back. I remember pulling Vu's head back like this, but that was with lust, for pleasure. This is different. It's funny how the intention changes the action. I try to focus and lock my stare with the eyes in the pokey, try to make out who it is. The person behind those eyes aches for me, and for themselves. I ache for the pokey. The press of all the pointed bits driven through the steel locker walls seems gentle in comparison, peaceful. I could be alone.

'Don't look at him,' the Auntie says. She lets go of my head and picks up the hose, turns the tap until water jets out. She takes it to the pokey, shoves it though the cutout and closes the slider, trapping it there. There are gurgles and screams. Water glugs out through holes in the bottom and down the drain in the middle of the room.

'Look at me,' she says, and I have to pick my own head up this time. The chair wobbles and I almost tip off the side. My shoulders beg me not to tip. They don't want to twist that way in their sockets, but they will, if they have to. They'll jump right out. I've seen it. It doesn't look real when it happens but I bet it feels real and I don't want to find out.

I look at her and she pulls the rag out of my mouth.

'Who else?'

'Just me,' I say. This is not the answer she needs.

'Children need to learn the Consequences of their actions,' Vile says from off in the corner, far enough away to stay clean, close enough to see. Everyone laughs. I laugh. It's funny, or it's not, or I just don't know what else to do.

When the impacts come again, I try to keep myself upright. The pains just all slip into one, like a crescendo of noise or tone or a buzzing in my ear, but in all the parts of me instead. I look around, through the shifting bodies of the Aunties and Uncles, their twisted faces. It's bright in here. Brighter than anywhere else, and never dark. The cinderblock is white, or white-ish. The tiled floor is white, or white-ish. There's a red ring around the drain below. There's a bank of lights above, uncaring white light. Two steel lockers to my left, dotted with screw and nail-heads, sharp ends pointing inwards. Down the hall to the right, the

Time Out cells. The concrete walls ring with breaths, hard like gunshots, dull thuds of things striking flesh, the pulse of the hose, the gurgling drain, the buzz of the fluorescence.

I wonder if the grey ones are watching me from up there while they feast on that buzz.

—

They say you leave little bits of yourself behind in the Time Out cells. It's another kind of ghost story the kids tell each other in blanket-gatherings late at night. They say that every day you spend here grates another piece off you that seeps into the walls.

I believe it. Time Out feels haunted, but not like the hallways upstairs at night with their grey ghosts. These thick walls are full of fragments, little bits of everyone that's lost themselves in here. The time here diminishes a kid, takes away pieces they can't ever get back.

I wonder what parts I'll leave here? Hopefully it's something I won't need.

'I'll leave you the big mole with the hair coming out of it on my bum, yeah?'

My voice bounces around the concrete walls. It sounds thick and fuzzy coming out of my torn-up lips. I run my tongue around my mouth and I'm relieved to find all my teeth still there, though a couple of them have split through the fragile skin of my lips.

I try to stand, but can't. There's nothing in here to pull myself up on. There's almost nothing in here at all. Just a bucket for my waste. And me. I'm in here too. That's a bit of a waste as well. Or maybe I'm waste. I'm not sure.

Everything else is concrete. It's cold. I shrug off my nightshirt and bunch it up underneath me, but then my naked back presses against the wall and the chill creeps inside me, my bones going cold. It's so hot upstairs, the heat rising all day, so how is it so cold down here? Is it because we're underground? Is it because of the ghost-bits in the walls?

The cell's about the size of a toilet cubicle, but with no toilet, and a high ceiling. The paint on the cracking walls is white, or was. Grime and piss and dirt and blood stain everything, gather in the creases, between the concrete blocks, in the corners. It's tall enough to stand in, and sit, and lie down if you curl up, but not to stretch out.

Give it enough time and it will be my whole world. I've been here before. Not here, but here enough. Time Out cells are all the same. Time gets lost here, along with other things. When the cutout slides open and the food comes through I try to make a note of it, try to remember to count them, but I know I won't be able to. The bread is stale and the water warm. I shuffle so I'm close to the door, peering through the crack, hair-wide, and watch the shadow of shoes passing.

I roll onto my back and I cry.

I wonder where I'll go now. To a Prisoncorp? Wherever they sent Vu? Will I die in here? I've seen it happen. When I was buying out my second tab after the first stopped working, they put me on cleanup in Time Out on the weekends. I saw two blue bodies secreted up the stairs. Will that be me? Do I have blood rushing into my guts right now that will send me out slowly, writhing on the floor? Is that how I'll get out of here?

I never let myself really think about getting out. Like for-real out, into the world.

At first you don't because it's so long away. And then you don't because it's just so close.

Like, most kids will be diligent and get a dorm set up in the city, send in apps for jobs even though landing a job is like spotting a maggot in a pot of rice. Sure, it can happen but it's a slog.

I never did that. I don't know why. Maybe some bit of me knew it would end like this. I thought I had this well of hope or whatever inside me, but maybe I didn't.

Or maybe I do, and that's the bit I'll leave behind here.

TWO DAYS

The lights don't go off. They don't ever go off. They hum and zzz all day, all night, so you can't tell the difference and time gets all muddled.

Because there's nothing to look at, my mind fills in the blanks, the blank walls. First it's little twisting shapes in the corners of my eyes that I try to catch but always miss. After a while, forests of patterns grow in each cinderblock screen. I'm having whole conversations in my head, doing things differently with different outcomes, trying for different Consequences. They all lead me in here, to this room and I am convinced it is inevitable.

It was always going to end like this.

When Vu appears in the corner, whole and full-bodied, even I know that it's going too far, that I took one-too-many knocks to the head region. Vu is gone, she's been taken somewhere secret and scrubbed off the sys, or worse, she's filling out a shallow grave somewhere, but she's not here.

Still, I wonder for a second if ghost-Vu would be warm if I tried to hold her.

—

The food comes through the cutout. It could be anything; breakfast, lunch or dinner. It's not just bread and water this time, there's a little bowl of grey-meat and a mandarin. Someone upstairs paid a hefty price for this treat for me and the smell of the meat makes hot saliva squirt out from under my tongue and fill up my mouth. I shovel it in right there at the little shelf under the cutout, a pair of dark, dark eyes set in brown skin peering through the slit and watching me with sorrow and pity.

The mandarin. It reminds me of Vu, that first night that she shared the fruit with me. When I break open the skin the little cell fills up with the sweet citrus smell.

Underneath it is a little slip of paper.

Psynode, it says.

Brainfuckers, Inc.

Vu? it says. Then, *Vile knows.*

I crumple the paper. I eat it. I can feel the ink seeping off the paper and into my blood. I'll remember what it says forever.

ONE DAY

When Aunt Bev comes through the door I get a shock because it's like I forgot what the door was there for.

'Get up, Mahoney,' she says, and when I try and fall back onto the concrete floor, she holds a hand out for me.

I stare at it for a bit. It's as strange as if she was holding out a flower towards me, or a loaded rifle.

'Get up, Mahoney, now. There's not a lot of time.' Aunt Bev reaches down and takes my hand in hers, pulling me to my feet, my feet that sing and ache and cramp as I step out of the door of my Time Out cell.

'How long have I been here?' I ask her, my voice defeated and stew-thick and garbled around my swollen lips. 'Which Prisoncorp are you gonna take me to?'

'Bloody hell, Mirii, dramatic much? You've been in here a day and a half.'

Oh.

'And you aren't going to any Prisoncorp,' she says. 'You've got Age Transfer. I'm taking you upstairs to admin for processing.'

I can hear the words she says, but I don't know why she's saying them or how or what they mean. Is this real?

'But . . . Vile, I mean, Kyle, said . . .'

She stops in the middle of the Consequences hallway. I can see the room with the chair and the pokies just off to the left. It's clean now, the floor dry like nothing happened. But when I look at the cutout I see the flash of a pair of eyes and I feel like I can't breathe so I look away.

'The Warden says a lot of things. I follow the system,' Bev says and she holds up her tab. The words on the bright white screen swim in my vision. 'OS says you Age Transfer today, so I'm getting you ready for release, Mahoney. Now, let's get a move on.'

'But . . .' I start but she turns back towards me and her face tells me to plug my mouthhole. I do.

'OS says you're due for release, Mahoney,' she says. Her usually flush round face is pale and pinched. 'Now, that could change at any second so, unless you wanna try your luck in a Prisoncorp with the big girls, I suggest you get a wriggle on.'

Aunt Bev turns and hurries up the stairs, lighter on her feet than I'd imagined. I still gape for a second but then I limp after her. I get it but I don't, so I follow her anyway. How is this happening? Is Warden Vile here? Who changed the Sys? I look at Aunt Bev's giant bum fast-swinging side-to-side with each step, but it's got no answers for me, so I follow, mute, on feet that feel like blocks of wood.

The halls are jammed with kids weaving back and forth. Is it breakfast? Lunch? No, dinner. Processing out always happens after a full day of work, 'cause why not get another day of free labour from us? It's like a last little jab in the side before they turf us out on our arses. I'm trying to keep up with Aunt Bev but all the parts of me hurt and there's this kindling anger in my gut.

Everyone's staring at me with slack-jaws and I realise I'm looking totally knocked around. I stare back at them and think about how little it would take for them to all look like I do, just one step outta line. I hang my head because there's so much pain and rage and shame in me that it must be all across my face, and I can't bear the thought of them seeing that. Emotion is weakness. Weakness is like a big flashing, alarm-wailing beacon here. Even though I'm on my way out, I can't just switch that off.

At the dorm door, Bev points inside.

'Pack your shit, Big Star,' she says as I haul myself past her and into the dorm. 'I'll meet you down in the lobby for signout. Don't dawdle.'

I nod. She doesn't need to tell me twice.

Blondie and Ara come into the dorm after I get changed, just as I'm throwing my bloodstained nightshirt in the bin.

'Mirii!' Ara says, and rushes to me, pulling me to them and holding me lightly, hands catching in my matted hair and lips pressing to my swollen lips so softly that it's almost like they aren't there at all. Blondie wraps his arms around me from behind and I gasp at the feather-press of his arms around my shoulders. I can feel his lips plant kisses on the crown of my head.

'What did they do?' Ara asks.

'Oh, you know, torture and humiliation. The usual.'

'Bastards,' Blondie says, and he's got tears coming from his eyes and he'd be mopping them up with his shirt if he was wearing one, but of course he isn't. They're probably running in droplets through the ridges of his abs and the thought makes me smile. It stings.

'How did you hack the OS?' I ask, tying my boots to the arm of my backpack.

'It wasn't us,' says Blondie. 'We tried, but they beefed up

security, put double A and U's on all the posts on nightshift.'

I'm reaching gingerly into the remains of my mattress, feeling inside the twisted hidey-hole and I'm way confused, because if it wasn't them, then who? But something else has got my brain and it's not in any state to be running two strings in simult, yeah?

'Have you seen my tab?' I ask, talking right over Blondie.

'Nah, I thought you'd hidden it in the roof panels with your tattoo stuff,' Ara tells me. 'That's why Vile didn't find it.'

'No, it was here. It was right here.'

There's a little sound from over to my left. Like a laugh or a snort.

I fugging knew it.

'So, Mirii. I'm just reading about that baby magpie chick you found down at the corp in Umina when you were twelve . . . It was really funny how you spent so long raising it and hiding it and feeding it, and then that Uncle found it and cr-'

'Freya,' I hiss.

She's sitting propped up against the wall, legs crossed and my tablet in her lap. She's in her nightshirt already, white cotton in amongst her white sheets, pale skin poking out, pale hair spread over the pillow.

'I logged onto your Free School account,' she tells me, casual as anything. 'Your average was really high, but I did some of your assignments and, yeah, your grades went down a whole lot . . .'

The rage grabs my guts again. There's this pressure inside my head, like my anger is expanding outwards, through my muscles and flash-boiling my blood. I feel the old wound on my cheek, the pulled stitches, start to pulse and ooze with hot blood.

—

I didn't know a body so ruined could move so fast. I don't think Freya knew it either.

—

My hands are around her neck, her eyes bugging and a yelp of shock strangles through her throat, before she even registers that I'm coming for her.

See, I don't just have her by the throat, I've got every fucking Uncle and Auntie and sick-fuck older kid, all the Overseers and the district managers, up to the second-in-charge of Verity House with the plastic face that I met one time at the George Street corp, who shook my hand with a grip like a fresh-coughed hunk of phlegm.

I'm choking out Uncle Jerry from the house out at Orange with his stable of jabber-babes crying for their next hit and Uncle Rick too, who grinned, red faced in the harsh fluorescent of Consequences the other night, as he drove the club against my feet again and again.

I've got Auntie Helen from the Aberdeen corp, a steel-haired, god-bothering old biatch who danced the holier-than-thou jig with one foot while crushing your face underneath the other, and I'm just squeezing, squeezing the life out of her.

I'm pressing my thumbs into the windpipe of Uncle Martin, who gave me a hot little grin as he stamped on the frail body of my little Magpie chick, and I heard its breaking bones and couldn't do anything but be thankful it died quick.

And I've got Vile. I've got Warden Vile round the neck and he's struggling and trying to bat my hands away but I don't let up, won't let up until the black in his eyes spills out and swallows all of him, 'til the black runs out of the pit in my guts to join it.

He gurgles.

She gurgles.

And it's not Vile, or anyone else. It's just Freya, some hard little blonde chicky from the wild Western 'burbs, rounded up but not broke in yet. I look down into her crimson face, those eyes bulging, capillaries popping and the blood spreading out over the whites. In them I see how all *she* knows to do is hurt and rage and thrash out her pain on everyone around her because she can't take it out on anyone bigger. I split-second think about how all *I* can do to cope is turn everything into a big fugging joke but it's *not* a joke and wonder if it's not the same thing, but done different.

Maybe it's *all* the same thing but done different.

Freya punches on, feels the flesh split under her fingers and it helps her to forget. I get it on, and the flesh parts under my fingers and it helps me to forget. Like we're saying it in different ways, but the words are coming from the same place.

And maybe we're too hurt and too scared or too *something* to know that it's not really that she hates me or that I hate her or that we hate each other.

It's that we hate *this*.

So I stop.

I let her neck go and fall back onto the floor and it's like the room comes back. Everyone's frozen, watching. I realise that Blondie and Ara have been trying to pull me off her and so when I fall back, I land on them in this bony, groaning pile of pastel-uniformed limbs.

Freya scrambles to the end of the bed, crouching there with her hair wild and her eyes wilder. She looks at me with fear and awe, then hatred and finally defiance, the emotions changing in her eyes as the colour in her face changes from purple to red to pink then white again.

I hope she never loses that defiance.

I hope she manages to escape soon, 'cause there's no way she's not already signed up for a Prisoncorp the moment she turns eighteen. I hope that the next time she tries to steal away in the night, there's no Uncles on her tail, no close-by newbz to crash-tackle her as she goes past.

'Fuck you, Mirii,' she croaks.

'I'm sorry, Freya.' I am. I'm really sorry, for everything she's had done to her and everything I've been through and all the bullshiz every little bastard in this place has copped and will ever cop.

'Fuck you, Mirii!' she screams.

I reach for the tab and she sees me do it, and reaches out at the same time. She's closer and she snatches it up.

In one swift motion, she raises it up and smashes it against the wall.

It comes apart into chunks, chunks of all the things I've learned and all the stuff I'd cared about and the few contact details I'd managed to keep from kids over the years and some fuzzy pics I'd taken when we'd hacked the camera that one time. The little stories and poems and the bits I wrote out when it hurt too much to keep them inside. Chunks of plastic and steel and solder that she kicks towards me.

But I don't flinch. I don't fall for it. I don't have the urge to dive on her and rip her creamy throat open wide-red with my teeth. Well, maybe a little. But I don't do it.

I just take my pack, boots swinging from the arm, and I turn away.

She hurls a piece of my busted tab, hitting me in the back of the head. My neck rocks forward with it but I don't turn.

'Fight me, Mirii!' she wails.

I want to. I really do. But I don't, too. And all the bullshiz things I could say to her rise up in my throat and they wanna run right out of my mouth but I don't let them.

I keep it to myself because it won't help anything.

—

There are still strings of Freya's hair between my fingers. My hands shake as I brush them against each other, pulling them out. The golden strands float down. They're so fine that I lose them before they hit the floor.

Ara and Blondie fall in line with me as I limp out through the dorm, my feet aching inside my stiff boots and the press of the cotton socks against them almost too painful. Ara takes my bag and guides my arm while Blondie clears a path through the mute throngs of kids gathered around our corner of the dorm.

'Nothing to see here, ya little jerks,' he says, like an Uncle, his voice booming, and the younger ones scatter, giggling nervously while the older ones pull together into groups and whisper as we go past. I can hear Freya swearing and screaming, but the sound of it fades and I try to walk as fast as I can, get far away from her.

Poor Freya. She's like a swirling drain, trying to drag us in and down with her as she empties out. As we go through the door an Uncle comes in, stopping just a second to look at my face with shock and awe, then he pushes past us.

'Ferguson, if you don't shut your hole I'm gunna shut it for you . . .'

The sound of them fades out as we leave the dorm.

It's like I've been holding my breath and maybe now I can release it. It's like I've been holding my breath my whole life and now, maybe now, if I make it outside, I'll be able to take another breath for the first time.

'Mirii!' Cam is just a bobbing head in the after-dinner crowd, but I can't mistake his voice. He comes up close and throws his arms around me. The force of his skinny little body is almost too much to bear, but I bear it anyway and I smile into his hair.

'Your face, Mirii. What did they do?'

I pull back and look at him with mock-shock.

'Shiz! Is something wrong with it?'

He grins and all the freckles on his nose crease.

'Look, I signed up for the Free School. They assigned me a tablet. I've never had one before.' He holds up an old tab, a single crack creasing the corner. It catches the fluorescent light and it blinds me for a second with pure white. 'I've got to scrub dunnies in the pre-teen dorm for the next year for it, but check out how rad it is.'

I do. It's pretty rad.

'Isis seven. Good model. If the screen gets fuggity, recalibrate it to minus three, that helps.'

His eyes glow and I bet he spent all last night checking out Orion or the best ink recipe for a good, solid line in a fresh tattoo. Good on him.

'I've already had one of the hackies from my dorm show me how to use it. Sticksy. He's really good, like scary good.' Cam drops his voice. 'We wrote that patch that changed your record. They were gonna send you up to a Prisoncorp this afternoon, out to Eramus City.'

My eyes bug out so far that they almost pop right outta my head.

'What? Eramus City? Are you kidding? How did you do it?' I

hiss. My heart thumps as I think of how different this day might have been.

'Well, it was Sticksy mostly. I just supervised. He's a fuggin' demon on the tab. I'm thinking of taking over his extra duties so he can teach me.'

'Do it. But be careful. And when you learn how to hack around the firewall, look me up. My email is my name; one "r", two "i"s.'

Cam's lower lip trembles a bit so I take him real soft in my arms and let him spill his eyes and his guts out in tears that soak into my chest.

'Happy Birthday, Mirii,' he says, long string of snot clinging to my shirt and his nose in a gross little bridge.

That's right. I'm eighteen today.

'Thanks kiddo.'

'Contact warning, you two!' grunts an Auntie as she goes by and we spring apart. Cam wipes his face with a sleeve, tears and snot staining the fabric. Then he takes off down the hallway, skinny limbs pumping. He doesn't look back.

I walk down to admin and I toe the line between in-bounds and out-of-bounds, remembering the last time I was here and my body shudders. Aunt Bev beckons to me, gaze steely.

I turn back, just one last time. I've just remembered.

'Hey, who sent me the note?'

Ara and Blondie look at me like I'm talking nonsense.

'What note?' Ara says.

'When I was in Time Out. You sent the food, and under the mandarin was a note.'

'We sent some meat,' says Blondie. 'But no fruit. We couldn't swing both, not on this limited income,' he says, looking sheepish. 'And no note.'

'Shit.' I turn to Ara. 'It was about Vu. The note said something about *Psynode*. Do you know what it is? They called it *Brainfuckers, Inc.* Said Vu could be there. Said Vile knows.'

'I've never heard of it. Do ya think . . .'

'Raaya? Vu? Maybe. I'm gonna look into it.'

'Me too,' they say and this veil of ferocity slips over their face. Ara's hands start to twitch and they stroke the still-raised, ink-shedding tattoo below their elbow, without realising they're doing it.

'Talk to Cam. I'll look too and we can share info.'

Ara nods, long hair swaying. They pull me into a gentle hug.

'We're gonna find them,' Ara says, then turns and marches off down the hall, head up high and stride vicious. Kids scatter out of their way as they storm back to the dorms.

I look back towards Aunt Bev, shuffling papers furiously and eyeing me. She mouths something that could be 'bury the fudge cup', but is more likely something else.

'I gotta bail. I think my exit is not exactly above the board, if you know what I mean.'

Blondie touches my face.

'Seeya Mirii,' he says, his tanned face kinda sad and kinda happy in that way faces get when things are good and bad at the same time. I don't think Blondie's real good with ambivalence. I think it's throwing him.

'Seeya Blondie,' I say. 'I won't forget that first night. Your mad tongue skillz really helped me feel more at home.'

I touch his stomach one last time, feel the valleys and ridges of his muscles.

'Good luck, Mirii. I hope you find her. You know, Vu.' He turns and goes back down the hall, pausing to jump up and tap the doorframe as he passes through it, the muscles in his back tensing and releasing.

'Good luck,' I whisper, not just to Blondie, but to everyone. Cam and Ara and Ade and Berry and all the other teeners just waiting it out. The pre-teens racing around the halls, working off the evening buzz before bedtime lock-in, the littlies in the kiddie dorms telling stories, making myths. The bobble-headed blobs in the nursery, probably missing Vu's happy face, no idea that they're in it for the long haul. I hope they make it, even though they probably won't.

I toe the line between in-bounds and out-of-bounds, then I slam across it. No point delaying the inevitable.

—

Aunt Bev has everything done, what with all that time I kept her waiting, so all I need to do is sign a form. I scrawl my name across the tab, my finger dragging on the screen and making the letters spread out, far out of their bounds.

She doesn't hit submit. I reckon she'll wait until I'm out the door. I wonder if Bev will lose her job. I wonder if they have a Time Out for Aunties and Uncles who fugg up. Do they get thrown into cells? Will they hang her by the arms, beat her ribs and kidneys and feet? I don't know. I start to ask her but realise I don't want to know.

'Thanks, Bev,' I say, as she helps me stand up. And I mean it. I try and put it into the words, try to fill them up with all the things I want to say to her but can't.

'Shut up, Mahoney, and get a move on,' she says, but she goes a bit red around the ears. I get the urge to throw my arms around her, but I can't. The whole admin area is full of Aunties and Uncles, all quiet and glaring at us, chewing on sandwiches slowly, or paging through tabs. They know this isn't right but I don't know if anyone knows what to do. Sure, the OS is set in stone, but Warden Vile's face is pretty stony and his fists are too, and maybe they speak a louder truth than what any OS could say.

'Bev, do ya know what you're doing here?' says this beefy old Uncle, coming to stand right over me, looming and making me feel real small underneath him.

'Just following the OS, Jeff. You know how it is.'

'I get it Bev, but I'm not sure the OS is up-to-date, yeah? I got a feelin' that when Kyle comes in tomorrow, he's gonna have some pretty stringent OS corrections.'

'Might be, Jeff, but I'm doing my job. OS says she's gotta go, she's got to go.' Bev looks at him real pointedly. 'I'll cop the flack if there's some sys error I don't know about.'

Uncle Jeff grabs me by the arm.

'You could get Bev into real trouble for screwing with the OS,' he says, squeezing my bicep so hard that the nerves in my arm go fuzzy.

'I know,' I say. 'I haven't.' I'm not lying and I try to twist my face to show it, but I don't know if it comes through or not.

He looks down at me, his face a rough-hewn, stubbled mess, blackheads sprinkled over his nose. His eyes are bloodshot and the smell of potato punch oozes out of his pores. He's so big, his gut pressing into my elbow. He could squish me under his thumb and he looks like he wants to, so I try not to move or breathe or exist too hard under his gaze.

'It's on me, Jeff,' Bev says. 'Don't sweat it, yeah?'

His hands twitch. The vein in his neck throbs once, twice. Things go quiet, kinda white around the edges. Does he know he's one bellow, one gripped shoulder, one 'no' away from spinning my life off one way or the other? A bead of sweat grows heavy on his forehead, spills down his cheek, disappears under his shirt collar. I can almost *hear* it trickling over his slick skin, hear the fibres of his shirt sucking it up. My heart thuds, slow and uneven, skipping a beat that probably stops every clock in the house, jams the works in every systower, blocks all the dunnies, wakes up every blobby bub in the nursery and sets them to scream.

'I guess it's on you, Bev,' Jeff says, passing a sleeve over his sweaty head, turning, and waddling away. He looks back, once, jowls set, mouth twisted.

I don't let him look back again and catch me there.

—

'You made it,' Bev says, taking a deep breath of the warm summer air as she pulls me by the elbow out the door and down the first two stairs. I don't reply, just thud down the steps and onto the street, take a lungful of free air. Free air smells like burning rubber and biofuel exhaust. I look back at Bev, her red hair escaping from her ponytail, red cheeks glowing under the front porch spotlights.

'Got a job lined up?' she asks.

'Nah.'

'How about a place to go?'

'Haven't found one yet,' I tell her, and she shakes her head.

I feel really small out here, uncontained, but free too. It's a scary feeling. I look up into the sky. The moon's coming up, waxing, and there's this soft light cast over everything. No clouds. I pick out Crux, low on the horizon, Acrux burning bright at its foot. The tattooed image on my chest pulls a little like it's trying to get up there and join up with its twin. The ground feels different under my feet and the sky seems like it might never end, like I might just lift off and fall up into it.

I'm holding an envelope in my right hand. In it is a hundred whole credits, the reward for my lifetime of labour.

'*Thank you, from Verity House!*' it says, in bright red and yellow letters.

The night is falling fast and every spark in the sky gets brighter. I think about the city, and Vu, and Raaya, and whatever Psynode is. I think of credits and jobs, dorms and tabs.

I take out the money, stuff it in my pocket and crumple up the envelope, letting it fall away as I take the first steps.

PSYNODE

DAY ONE

'You electronic piece of shit,' I hiss as my tablet chimes with a dire low battery warning, a second after I hit send.

The charging pad is plugged into the one point in the room not in use, but it's all the way over on the far side of the room and the only place I get decent wireless signal is this corner.

I've already spent a few long, cold hours by the open window because of course the window has to be open to receive the signal. My hands are numb and my breath steams. Everyone complains about the open window in the dead of winter so I've gotta promise them my rice ration for tomorrow to get them to shut up and let me get on with it. Going hungry for a day is worth it to stop Mrs Gupta from kicking me every time she walks by or the Pierce twins threatening to slit my throat in my sleep.

So, do I risk my battery running flat but keeping the signal while I upload, or lose the sig, run and slap the tab on the pad for a minute or two? Either way, I'm gonna bugger my upload and have to start over. I've got four minutes 'til the midnight deadline and I'm pretty sure I'm not gonna make it. I watch the upload bar extending as the red-rimmed critical battery icon mocks me from the lower right-hand corner.

'Faster, you prick, faster,' I plead softly, but obviously not softly enough because Xue Xiang rolls over on her floor mat and throws a shoe at my head. I'd throw the shoe back but Xiang is pregnant and I guess it's probably wrong. Maybe if I aim specifically for her head and not her grotesquely swollen belly? Nah. I'll just spit in her water jug later on.

The upload progress bar creeps through the nineties and I beat the heel of my palm against the aluminium window frame silently. The battery life on this tablet is a joke. When I got the thing third-hand, from Elton at the Blue Market, he told me the charge lasted twenty-four hours (though I've heard that new, the model is good for at least a fourteen-day charge.) But the bloody thing is at least three years old, obsolete, practically useless, and the battery life is a few hours at most.

The upload bar passes ninety-five percent, my butt clenches, teeth too, and I grip the sides of the tablet. If I could power the bloody thing with my rage, the charge would last a lifetime.

Why does everything bugger up when it's the most important?

At ninety-eight the critical battery tone chirps again and the symbol changes from the 'low battery' to the 'no battery' icon.

'Oh, you crump of a thing,' I hiss, and I imagine smashing the tablet on the window frame, the pieces flying off in all directions. I imagine it sparking. I wish it would set fire to the entire god-damned place.

If only I'd charged it a little longer. If only someone hadn't stolen my extension cord (and when I find out who it was, I'm gonna strangle them with it.) If only one of these bitches would let me use a power point closer to the window. I'm sure they refuse out of spite. If only I was like everyone else round here, never trying anything and never having to fail. Why do I even bother? All this work, all this time spent wrangling, totally wasted.

Or not. The upload status bar winks out, then is replaced with 'Upload complete'.

I stare at the words for a second, then the screen goes black.

'Ha! I did it! Eat shit, all of you!' I bellow and my glee is then met by a barrage of shoes, pillows and one well aimed saucepan that corks me right on the crown of my head. I'll probs have an egg there for a week but it can't wipe the smile off my face.

I did it.

—

'Mrs Poluski's Single Women's Dormitory' sounds fancy, but what they should call it is 'Mrs Poluski's Grotty Firetrap for Nasty Bitches'. Mrs P crams in as many of us as she can. By day the dorm bustles with activity, windows fogged from the breath of sixty-five women and the steam from the fleet of rice-cookers that feed us all, each one jacked into an overflowing powerboard.

By night the floor is carpeted with seam-to-seam tatami mats, each one occupied by one very lucky lady. The less lucky sleep sitting upright on the benches that line the perimeter, strapped in to prevent slumpage onto the floor and the inevitable brawls that erupt when a floor sleeper is hit by a comatose bencher. The latest rumour is that Mrs P plans on banishing the mats to fill the dorm with benches and get more bang for her buck. I wouldn't put it past the greedy old bag.

The only good thing about Mrs P's is the hard and fast 'no kids' rule. No kids, no exceptions. I can't wait to wave Xiang goodbye in a few weeks. I wonder how bloody the fight for her mat's gonna be, and I reckon I'm going to make some credits on the outcome.

I sleep on a bench running down the west side of the room. I doubt anyone could call what I did for the past bunch of hours sleeping, but I decide I've had enough of it and unstrap myself for the morning. I switch on my tab and creep around the half-asleep and just waking bodies, back over to the window, yanking it open just a little. I nav to my email, see the confirmation receipt of my upload last night and can't help but smile to myself. As I'm about to close out, a little number one appears next to the inbox icon. I tap it. The mail is from Allnode.

Ms Mahoney, it begins. I scan across the words, guts ping-ponging up to my throat. *Thank you for the prompt return of your application. We are pleased to inform you have been accepted for the position of Trainee in Resource Location and Transport in the Logistics division. Please find attached an information pack detailing the specifics of your employment. Your contract begins at 9 am on the 11th of August. Congratulations on becoming a valued addition to Allnode!*

Sincerely, Zoya Safranek, HR, Allnode.

I did it. I fugging did it.

Well, me and the bribes.

But still: I found the right people to bribe!

'Close the fucking window, Mirii.' By her tone, I can tell that Una Pierce is repeating herself, and Una hates to say something twice.

'I'm busy, Una. I'll be done soon,' I say, not looking up. It's best not to make eye contact with the Pierce twins, it just makes them angrier. I really don't want Una and her sister Ildi to harsh this moment, a feat I've been working towards for the past six months. But what I want and what the Pierce twins want are rarely on the same wave.

'I said close the fucking window before I tear you a new hole.'

I look up to see Una's eyes glitter and her sister, Ildi, making her way across the room. Ildi can probably sense the fight about to start in her bones. The twins have a shared passion for brutality. I've seen it before, in the eyes of certain kids and guards, that weird, sick lust for violence. It's not worth the fight, so I shut down my tab, close the window and slip off the cupboard.

'Happy now, Una?'

'Give me the tablet, Mirii.'

'Fugg off, Una. Window's closed, I'm going to my bench and you can keep your undies on.'

I tuck the tab under my arm and walk off. The room is silent, all eyes on me and Una. No one dares breathe, the only noise a hushed bubbling of rice cookers. One switches over from 'cook' to 'warm' with a little click and everyone in the room jumps.

The blow comes from behind. I've never known a punch from a bully that didn't, and like all bullies, the Pierce twins don't distinguish between a clean or a dirty fight. Now that I think of it, though, I don't either.

All fights are dirty and everything is on the table. It's why I try to avoid them.

The tablet clatters to the floor as I go flying into a pile of dirty plastic dishes. Girls rush to the edges of the room, getting out of the way and clustering by the walls to lay quick bets on our impromptu melee.

I climb out of the dishpile, hands up.

'I don't wanna fight. You win, I'm out.'

Ildi grabs me by the arms, twisting them up behind my back. I lash out with my feet, kicking wildly as Ildi tries to hang on to my wrists. One kick catches Una in the ribs and she flinches a little. A blow like that might have dropped me or most of the other women at Mrs P's or just really any normal person, but the Pierces aren't normal by any stretch, yeah? They're, like, unable to feel pain. Or they do feel it, and they don't mind it, I can't tell which. It makes their fights pretty one-sided. The only way to win a fight with them is to let them get tired of punching you.

Ildi lets go of one of my wrists and slips an arm around my neck. She lifts me off my feet and Una starts in with the body shots. The punches make me see stars but I try to hang on, and I bring one knee up, slamming it into Una's nose. The sick crunch reverberates round the room. All the babes braced against the edges gasp as Una's nose shatters, pouring blood like I turned on a tap. I feel Ildi's grip go a little slack and I take the opportunity to twist free. Una stands, blinking, in the centre of the room and I wonder if I actually hurt her. Tears, blood and snot run down her face. I don't waste the effect, though. No way. I grab the closest rice cooker, yanking its cord from the socket. The hot plastic burns in my hands. I hold it aloft.

'Don't you dare,' says Ildi, but she's still moving towards me, so I'm not pausing for a second. Hot plastic, searing aluminium, boiling water and half-cooked rice fly as I chuck the whole thing in the general direction of Ildi's head. I don't wait around for the aftermath, I just scoop up the tablet from its landing spot and snatch up my bag then I run out the door. Ildi's screams follow down the stairwell and I'm sure I can still hear her even as I bolt up the street, breath coming hard and ragged.

—

I have enough credit for a few hours at the Caffinatrix on the corner until the sun comes up and I can start looking for a new dorm. I sit with my hands around a hot cup of synth coffee, silent, distractedly reading, but getting stuck on the same sentence again and again.

Mrs P's isn't a great place, but it was home, or at least home-ish. I've been there since I cleared out of Verity House. Even after the Pierce twins showed up, it wasn't that much worse than any other place I've lived, and in some ways it was better. Whatever nasty tricks Mrs P pulled, all the times the toilet overflowed raw sewage – leaking into the bedroom and across the mats – even the nights when Missy Burkus, off the planet with psychosis, had to be tied to the back of the door while she bellowed about nanobots burrowing into her skin, I always thought to myself: at least it's not the orphanage, at least I have control over my own life.

But do I? 'Cause even if I hadn't just had to flee Mrs P's, I'm about to plunge face-first into who-knows-what at Allnode, all on my own.

And even though the corp was mad-grim with the torture and the forced labour and all that awful shiz, I always had friends there. I was someone, with a function and a bunch of rad babes and brus, however transient the faces and the names, to make me all valid and stuff. We were in it together, a team with a common enemy, 'us against them'. At Mrs P's it's more like 'me against everyone'. It's every babe for herself. And when I take off to start my heavy mish into enemy territory, it's gonna be more of the same. Times ten, even. Me against the world.

That's no way to be.

—

'You, girl! Best refurbed tabs here! You want implants? Palm, aural, optical? We got clean choppers! Best in Sydney!'

The man buzzes at me, gesturing to a dirty shopfront, its window jammed with ancient electronics. He grins, his mouth spiked with blackened, broken teeth.

'Bugger off, mate,' I mutter as I push past. As if I'd let anyone with such a poor grasp of dental hygiene anywhere near me with an implanter, despite how much I wish I could afford an optic implant or even just a palm. It's not worth the hep, though – it costs big bucks to treat that shit. Hawkers assault me with promises of 'best this' and 'cheapest that' as I work my way deeper into the marketplace.

It's dark and warm in here, the spaces between the shops and stalls thatched and tarped to keep out the rain. Or most of it. Here and there, where the solar bottle-and-bleach bulbs thrust through the makeshift roof, drips and torrents pour through, making huge puddles underneath. Even here in the 'tronics district there are little carts everywhere frying up anything they can, so the smell of crispy crickets and breaded snags mixes in with the burned rubber and sparks stink from the workshops.

An old woman thrusts a handful of power cords into my hands, muttering in Cantonese, and as I try to pass them back they slip from her hands, coiling all over the pavement like snakes. The woman screeches after me, but I keep on, hurrying through the tight, crowded lanes 'til I reach Elton's door. His window is hung with a heavy black curtain, an electric blue sign the only thing on display, glowing cursive that reads 'The Blue Market'. I slam my hand on the buzzer, peering into the curved lens of the door camera.

'Mirii, is that you?'

'Let me in, Elton. People keep tryna sell me shiz electronics out here.'

'Don't let anyone penetrate you with an implanter without your express consent.'

'You're a sexist pig, Elton.'

The intercom goes silent.

I roll my eyes and sigh and after a few seconds – payback for the insult – the door buzzes. I heave it open. Metal plated and three inches thick, the door is serious.

The whole place is murky, lit with tiny lamps in different colours. The displays are spotted with soft yellows to highlight the exquisite quality of the antiques on show, but the corners and crannies glow with red, blue, purple and green lights. The colours pass across my skin in little waves.

Elton sits behind a huge, overflowing desk in a small room off the main show floor. Elton himself is huge and overflowing, bursting out of a giant office chair. He wears a headlamp strapped to his forehead and the implants in his piggy little eyes allow for 100x zoom. Something is in pieces on the desk in front of him.

'Whatcha working on?'

'This, my lovely, is a first-gen iPad. One of my pickers came across it in a 'tronic landfill out in Rooty Hill. Braved the Western Line just to bring it to me. That's loyalty, Mirii, you know? Speaking of loyalty . . .'

'I know, I've been really busy. I finished up my qualifications, then I got booted out of Mrs P's.'

'That's shit.'

'Right? How's this Elton – I got it.'

'Allnode?'

'Yep. You were right hooking me up with that recruiter Brandis, he's corrupt as hell, got me right in.'

'Pick and pack?'

'Yep, fulltime. *Housing.* I'll be in the Nodeplex, dude. Right there.'

Elton lifts an eyebrow and I can tell he's mad fuggin' impressed but he's playing cool 'cause he's such a badass. Or he pretends to be. He swings back around, picking up a wire. His fingers are surprisingly nimble even though they're like a buncha fat sausages at the end of his hands.

'You know what you're doing, Mirii?'

'Nah. No fugging idea.'

'I don't think you're gonna just waltz from the warehouse into the Psy division, just like that.'

'I sincerely doubt it, Elton. But it's closer than I am now.'

'Just don't get sprung, Mirii. You're okay, but you're just one little babe.'

'I know,' I tell him. *But I'm a determined little babe.*

'When do you start?'

'Tomorrow. That's why I'm here.' I pull my tablet out of my bag. 'Need a new power pad. Left my old one at Mrs P's and I'm not game to go back.'

Elton tsks me and opens a drawer, rummages for a bit and pulls newish-looking charging pad from a jumble of them. He throws it at me and I catch it gratefully.

'Thanks, Elton, I owe you.'

'Yeah, you really do. I'm swamped around here without your nimble little fingers.' He solders as he talks. 'Can you stay and help me with that?' He gestures to a pile of junk rising from the other workbench.

'Why, Elts? Imma big shot now, with a *fulltime job.* No need for all you small-time dudes,' I tell him, grinning, but I shed my jacket and sit down at the desk, sorting through the first few layers of the pile. Busted tabs, ancient hardware, a few gnarly antiques. Elton makes paltry creds repairing and reselling tabs to regular folk, but he always says that enough small transactions add up to big bucks over time. There is no amount of money that isn't worth his attention. The real funds come from collectors who pay ridic sums for his expertly restored antiques. I help him sometimes with the everyday stuff, and occasionally he lets me play with something old and fascinating, but Elton doesn't trust anyone with the good stuff. He'd sooner get up out of his chair than let me fiddle with a mint condish Galaxy or iPhone 5.

I reach into a drawer for a headlamp and magnifier. Slipping it over my head, I move the eyepiece into position and program it to 10x zoom. As I open the first tab on the pile, a Prion with a shattered screen, I smile to myself, even as my hands start to tremble.

—

I heft my bag to the other shoulder and sigh as the woman goes over the house rules. Standard fare: no this, do that, this way, that much. The landlord is a small woman of indeterminable age who introduces herself as Ms Wong and she charges me a mint for one night, but it's easier than fronting a deposit for a hotel or an Airbnb, 'cause my Worldcard balance is dire.

The room holds fifty women, fewer than at Mrs P's, but it's also much smaller: instead of mats there is a squadron of high-backed pew-like benches pushed to one side of the room for the day. Besides that, it's the usual dorm-fare, the same steamed windows, the familiar bank of rice-cookers bubbling furiously, and more mean-looking babes who peer at me with varying levels of interest. The room has a row of lockers on the wall closest to the door, and Ms Wong allocates one high on the left side. It's small, but looks big enough to cram my backpack inside. The number on my locker matches a number scrawled on a piece of tape stuck to a spot on one of the benches and I make a note of where it is. I went to a public Central Processing bank and printed out a new ration card on my way over, and I flash it to Ms Wong, who scans it before shuffling off.

'Hey, who are you?'

There seems to be no malice in the voice, but I'm heaps wary anyway. The girl is sitting by herself, cross-legged, her hands wrapped around the edges of a mini-tab. She looks around my age, with a long plaited mane of strawberry-blonde hair trailing out from the ratty beanie shoved on her head. Her nose is sprinkled with freckles and her lips are thick and chapped. From the dancing graphics on the tab, I can see she's deep into a game.

'Pirate's Bytes?'

'Nah, Colour Coins. I'm Jools.'

'Colour Coins is a bitch. I'm Mirii. I'm really bad at games.'

Jools gestures to the spot next to her, but I keep standing. Jools shrugs.

'Where you come from?' she asks.

'I was over at a dorm on Clarence Street.'

'Was it better than this one?'

'I dunno, not sure what this one's like yet.'

Jools powers down the tablet, tucks it into her coat pocket and stands up, stretching to her full height, which is just beneath my shoulder.

'Well, Ms Wong is pretty quiet unless you cause trouble, then she'll rail you out or bring in her sons.' She gestures over to the far right of the room. 'Your power point is over there, it's numbered like your locker and your seat.'

'Cool, thanks,' I say, even though I've figured that out already. 'How's the wifi?'

'Not bad, the signal's kinda low but you get it all over.'

'That's so rad.'

'You work?'

This Jools is pretty questiony, but I dig it. I get that vibe from her, the familiarity. Plus, there aren't a lot of babes my age in this dorm, just like at Mrs P's, so I'm kinda keen for the company.

'I tattoo, stick and poke, though there's not much biz coming my way with all the competition. I'm clean and that costs more, ya know?' I tell her and she nods, with a grin. I go on, 'I do some design stuff, too, but I'm mostly down with tech repair?'

'Sweet,' she says. 'I'm way into design. Games and stuff.' Jools sticks her hand in her pocket, and I can tell she's stroking the smooth corner of her tab. 'I wanna make games someday, the simple ones that everyone plays.'

'Like Colour Coins?'

'Yeah, or Wall Street Drop or Squirrel Street.' She grins, one blue incisor in a mouthful of otherwise neat teeth.

'This old bird at my last dorm loved Squirrel Street,' I tell her. 'She'd be up all night yelling at the screen. So, you do classes or anything?'

'I go on and off the FPP,' Jools says. The Free Public Education Program is available to anyone who can download it. 'And I use the W3 schools to teach myself HTML6 and Everscript, but it's hard, you know?'

I grin. I've been there, pulling down the school on my own, and trying to keep motivated all through Orphancorp and after with the courses I needed to qualify for entry-level into Allnode.

'I know,' I say. 'Keep at it, though, it's worth it.'

Jools grins again, mouth curving in such a way that suggests she doesn't smile often.

'You grow up in a corp?' I ask her, 'cause she stinks of it, like I probably do as well.

'Yeah, KidsCo. How 'bout you?'

'Verity House. How was Kidsco? I've heard they're brutal. Like, I heard they force-sterilised everyone, and the dorms and work weren't co-ed?'

Jools laughs. 'Well the dorms weren't co-ed, but we had a mixed crew in daily labour and no one got sterilised, babes was popping out little babes on the regular. Isn't it funny? I heard that Verity House was fraggin' diabolical. Is it true they have a room in the basement where they torture kids?'

They do. A white room, with a drain in the middle and dried blood in the grout between the tiles.

'Yeah, actually, that's true. You didn't have Consequences?'

'Kidsco calls 'em "Punitive Measures". But they weren't too brootal or nothing, just extra shifts and stuff. Shit dude, I'm sorry, didn't mean to trigger ya,' she says, awkward as and flushy in the cheeks.

'Yeah, nah, it's cool,' I tell her and we bump fists, her solemn and sorry, me trying to do the facials to let her know it's okay.

I take the opportunity to wander over to my new locker and jam my stuff inside. As I slam the door shut I catch Jools' eyes peering at me over her tab. She drops them again real quick and I close the door with a grin. There's something in that glance, and I can't be sure exactly what it is but I think I might know.

—

Town Hall is a grand old stack of sandstone hunkering down amidst the soaring towers. It's lit from below and the stone glows yellow as the early evening turns a darker blue. The place is surrounded on all sides by shanty-shacks and refugees huddled over little thermo-chip cookstoves, boiling rice rations. Rent-a-guards keep the steps pretty clear, though.

I'm here because I told her I would be. Vu. It's not even time yet.

Seven months, one week.

It's been six and a few days, but I come here most nights. I mean, what if she's made it out or something? What if she rocks up, all babeing and strong, maybe a little cut up from her daring and sexy escape and I'm not even here? I couldn't bear it.

I park my ass on the steps and an old bag lady wrapped in layers of mouldering cloth and ripped-up plastic shuffles over to make room for me, muttering. She's got a couple of pet rats living on her person and they poke their noses out of her hair and sniff at me. I stare out into the street, watching the bikes zig and zoom and weave, the railcabs, half-empty and silk-sliding across their line. I've got an old heavy-drone prog-rock album playing through my earbuds and there's this weird disconnect between the jittery scene outside and the sonic-soundwall music. Every so often, though, they sync up. I keep my eyes out amongst the bustle for her, her happy grin, round cheeks, that silly haircut. I watch until the night falls proper and the sky is midnight blue with the city lights. Full dark. No stars, though. Maybe that's why Vu isn't here. Maybe she can't nav without 'em. I know I can't.

I stand up and the old bag's rats, braved-up by my stillness, scatter back from where they were trying to sniff at my frayed jean edges. I pull a sharpie out of my coat pocket and start scrawling my message right there, on the step.

'You can't do that,' the old bag mutters and her ratties bob and wriggle their noses in agreement.

'I know it's wrong, I'm not usually a mad vandal, but I need to leave a message for my friend,' I tell her.

'The grafbusters'll just blast it off in a week.'

'I know,' I say, really working the ink in there, like trying to tattoo the stone. 'I'm not sure what else to do though.'

I finish my little note.

Vu! I'm looking 4 u. Like-like, Miz

'I live just over there,' bag-babe says, pointing to an alcove a little way over. 'What your friend look like? If I see her I can tell her you're lookin.'

I pause. 'About my height. Chunky. Vietnamese. Giant boobs. She had a part-shaved head and glasses. Her name is Adeline Vu.'

'And who are you?'

'Mirii. If you see her, tell her Mirii's looking for her. Tell her to mail me. Tell her I got an in at Allnode and I'm looking for her.'

The old bag's face crumples. 'You don't wanna work for them. They're bad folks.'

'I know. But I have to find her. I promised.'

'Most folks don't keep much by way of promises these days,' Baggy tells me.

'I'm not most folks.'

She looks me up and down. 'Nah, didn't think you were.'

'Oi!' The voice comes from behind us. There's a NewForce guard coming towards us.

'Go,' Baggers says. 'I'll deal with this one.'

'Thanks!' I say, and bolt, dodging sidewalking Hondas and leaping over sleeping-bagged refugees. Behind me I can hear the old bag screeching at the NewForce bru. At the road I flash my

Worldcard and a slick Kawasaki slips up beside me. The rider flips up his helmet shield.

'Ride?'

'You betcha.' I leap on the back and we peel out. 'Just ten creds worth, I'm on the lam,' I yell to him and he nods. I wrap my arms tight around his waist and close my eyes as the bike slip-skids through the throng with exquisite precision and skill.

I wonder if the bike bru has such precision and skill in any other areas?

—

I shift against the straps, trying to ease the ache in my ass bones. This bench needs breaking in, but there isn't time for that now. I ease my head against the high back and sigh, the noise lost in the low hum of female breath and snores and sleep-talk. I let my eyes sink closed but they fly open again when I feel a touch on my knee. Jools stands before me. She slowly eases my knees apart and steps between them. She bends low and I feel her warm breath on my neck.

'What are you doing?' I whisper, even though I know exactly what Jools is doing. I flashback to the deep nights in the orphanage – fumbling, grasping for comfort. Jools' lips brush my neck and despite myself, I feel a jolt go through me.

'I like you. I think you're nice. Is this okay?' Jools asks, running her fingers over my upturned palm, the skin there singing.

Is it okay? My thoughts race. No. Yes. No and yes.

'I'm going away tomorrow,' I whisper, grasping at the hand stroking the side of my face. 'I got a job with a dorm over in the Node district. I might not be around much.'

'That's okay. I can just keep you warm for a bit.'

She unbuckles the straps that tether me to the bench.

I think, bugger it. And then I try to stop thinking.

Jools leads me across the room to the bathroom, which is occupied, then out into the hallway. It glows green from the ancient exit sign that dangles from a few dangerous-looking wires by the stairs.

She unzips my hoodie and plunges her icy hands beneath my shirt, sliding up to hold my breasts with a firm grip. Her lips brush mine and our tongues meet. I can taste something sweet on Jools' tongue. Jelly beans? I run my hands through her hair. It feels strange to be pressed against the wall by someone so tiny.

Her hands make my body spark, hot threads flowing from the contact point of her fingertips right between my legs and I almost can't breathe. It feels like I've spent forever untouched but that isn't true. There was that Brazilian guy with the rakish grin and the rumpled jeans I met at the 'trix that one time, and those twins, the brother and sister who were into all that fun, weird stuff. And Benny, that friend of Elton's friend, and Gemma. . .Still, the touch fills something in me that feels long-empty. Maybe I just need more attention than most people. Maybe something in me is missing or dulled and I gotta be touched hard, and often, so I can feel it. I figure if I'm safe and I'm not hurting anyone, that's okay, right?

I don't know. I don't know any other way to be.

Above us, the EXIT sign buzzes and flickers, spilling a thick green light through the hallway, across our bare skin as it splits and merges.

DAY TWO

The bing of an IM on my tab shakes me awake in the dark.

—Hey Miz

—What's doing, Cam? It's four in the morning!

—Well. . .

—You got new info on the induction?

—Ah, Sticks has sent a few info packs. Standard intro stuff.

—I got all that already. Anything else?

—Nah, that's it.

—I mean, obvs they don't have any guides for what happens when you go in as a highlit hire. From peeping at some files I pinched from that recruiter Elton recced us, seems like about one-fifth of his hires are way subtle highlit and they just 'poof' from the sys after a week or so. I mean, the Node takes a look at your Centro file and depending on ya history and all that, they 'light ya if no one's gonna notice that you're gone.

—Sounds like you.

—Right?

—Right. So Miz—

—Hey, what about the recruiter's Worldbank deets? He gets a higher rate for the highlit recruits, yeah? Can you see what his comish is for me?

—Shiz, I didn't think of that. I'll get Sticks to look into it.

—Can you do it now?

—Not exactly. That's what I'm trying to tell you . . .

—Can it wait? I gotta get ready.

—Not really, see I been thinking—

—Shock :P

—Fugg up.

—What you been thinking?

—Just, like, how would you feel if I busted out?

—Bad idea.

—Why?

—'Cause escaping's one of the big five. You'll slam to Prisoncorp instead of ageing out if they catch you. WHEN they catch you.

—I know, but—

—Stay put.

—But IF I did. . .

. . .

. . .

. . .

—You've already done it, haven't you? . . . Cam? . . . CAM?

—Yeah.

—You little shit! Where are you?

—Town Hall station. Sticks is with me.

—Fuck, Cam! Shiz! It's my first day at Allnode! Stay there. No, don't stay there. Head up to George Street. I think I can meet you before I get the shuttle to the Node district. Bru, it's my first day! I can't be late, that's instant dismissal. Why now?

—I had to. They were coming for me. Yesterday. Told me to pack my stuff. It was a Sunday, Miz! They never transfer on Sundays!

—Just wait on the corner of George and Park. I'll meet you.

—

I'm wide awake now, shoving my sleep clothes into my backpack and dragging on my most decent outfit. I tie my hair back and give myself a momentary look in the mirror to make sure I look neat, which I don't. I tuck my shirt into my pants, concluding that it's about as good as it's gonna get, then swing my bag over my shoulder. I bash into the last row of benches as I pass, and exit to groans, yells and a poorly-aimed boot that sails over my shoulder, clatters into the door, and wakes up the rest of the dorm.

'Later, babes!'

I catch Jools' eye just before I race out, and give her a wave. I'm not sure if she sees it, she's half-asleep.

I race up Market Street and puff along George, past the old QVB, trying not to trip on folks sleeping on the footpath. Poor fuggers.

I see him before he sees me. He's taller, I can tell even though he's sitting down. I wonder if it hurts to grow so fast. I'm so mad, and so full of gut-punched feelings to see him. Him and Sticks are sitting right by my message to Vu, but they haven't seen it. Baggers, with the rats, is sitting just over and she's giving them a gnarly eye 'cause their whispering probably woke her up. They're trying to look tough but I can see that Cam is scared. His chest is puffed out just a bit, like he's tryna hide it, be a tough motherfugger.

'Come here, ya little bastards,' I say and they see me. Cam's eyes go all gleamy and I wouldn't admit it if he asked, but mine are too.

'Mirii!'

He hits me like a bodyblock, arms going round my neck and I almost fall on my bum with the force of him.

'Look at you. Look at how tall you are.' I bury my nose into his hair. It smells like the Corp, like a smell I never thought I'd nose again. I hold on tight to him for so long, for too long after he's tried to pull away. I can't rip the smile from my face.

'Gross, Miz, what are ya, happy to see me or something?'

Sticks stands there, looking sheepy, kicking his scuffed boots into the steps.

'Nah, no way. I could rip youse's head off, I'm so mad right now.'

'What was I supposed to do? Let 'em take me? You woulda been imming me like mad and you'd've never known what happened.'

He's right. But I'm not gonna tell him that. I pick up his bag and hand it to him, then motion that they both should follow me as I take off down George Street.

'We gotta figure out what to do with you.'

'What do ya mean? Can't we just stay with you?'

'No!'

'Why not? Where are we 'sposed to go?'

"Cause they've given me a space in the dorm at Allnode, shit-head. Plus, you've got no ID and no status. If they catch you with me, I'll go to Prisoncorp too, and you'll both just go back to Verity House. Hope you like Consequences, 'cause you'll be copping them for ages.'

'Oh yeah. Crap.'

'Crapsticks.'

I've only got one idea and no time. I hope it works out, 'cause otherwise, we're toast.

I flag a longie bike and flash my card, throw a leg over the back. Cam and Sticks slot in between me and the driver.

'Haymarket. Post haste.'

—

'No way, Mirii. No how.'

'Come on. They'll cook. And clean. Cam can even do simple repair stuff, he was a great runner back in my days in the buzzshop. I taught him everything I know. And don't get me started on all the ways Sticks could be useful. He's basically a prodigy.'

'I can't coo—' Cam says, but I throw him a look that's deadly as, and he shuts up quick.

'Elton, please. It's this or they join a ratpack. I can't have 'em running with the kidgangs, they'll put them on the game or give 'em a habit or get 'em killed or something. Look at them faces, you wouldn't want such a fate for two cuties like this, wouldja?' I squeeze Cam's cheeks, and he ducks out of my grip.

'I don't owe you anything, Mirii. In fact, you already owe me. Especially now you've woken me before the sun's even up.' Elton goes to shut the door on us, but I jam my foot in, which hurts like crazy.

'I'll pay their way. They can sleep down in the showroom, or under the workstations. They can just make up beds under the bench.'

I keep thinking of Cam like he was six months ago, not the

stretched-up gangle-kid next to me now, almost as tall as I am. I throw him a look that says 'be smaller', but he doesn't get it.

'I do not run a dosshouse, especially not for runaways. Some of my clients are from the Force, and Parliament. What if they see them?'

'They won't. They'll be invisible.'

Elton doesn't look convinced, but the pressure eases up on my foot. He's caving. Yes!

'I'd charge you dosshouse rates.'

'I thought you didn't run a dosshouse, Elts.' Shiz, my bloody mouth. Shut up, Mirii, oh god, shut up! 'Pretend I didn't say that.'

Elton gives me a withering look. 'And they'll have to work. And be quiet.' He looks Cam and Sticks up and down. 'I don't like children.'

'Nobody likes kids, Elts. But look, they're practically grown! You won't regret it, I promise.'

When Elton punches the price into the cardreader on his tab, I know I've won. I touch my Worldcard to it and I'm pretty sure my balance is in the negs now, but the charge goes through anyway and I almost swoon all over the doorstep with relief.

I grab Cam by the shoulders and give him my utterly-srs-look. 'Do not fugg this up, Cam. Do everything that Elton tells you. Stay close. In fact, don't leave the market at all. And avoid the NewForce like they've got the superclap, ya hear me?'

'I hear ya.'

'And you, Sticks. . .Argh, just don't destroy anything.'

'I won't,' Sticksy says, flashing me a gappy grin, but I don't buy it.

'I'll be back as soon as I can and we're gonna work something out.'

I can't help myself. I give Cam kiss on the head while he

swats me away, and then I tear off. I look back just once to see Elts eyeing each of the little bastards suspiciously before the door opens all the way and they all go inside.

Safe.

Now, to go and put myself in harm's way. I've got fifteen minutes to get the shuttle.

—

It's easy to spot the Allnode lightrail stop, 'cause of the large cluster of miserable fucks gathered around it, all in the same grey uniform in a zillion different sizes. Everyone here's headed off to some shitkicker detail, I can tell by the downdog expressions and dirty nails everyone's sporting. Besides, who of the higher-ups would be seen dead on the free shuttle? The tram comes rattling in and everyone crams on, wanting to get out of the cold morning wind that's whistling up George, flicking like a chilly whip between the glass scrapes.

'First day?' asks a portly old babe with grey hair in a tight bun at the base of her neck and a red nose surrounded by broken capillaries.

'Howdja know?'

'No uniform.' She gestures up and down at my probs-too-wrinkled shirt, coming out from its tight tuck into my pants here and there. I let go of the handhold, retuck, then almost topple into her as the tram driver brakes hard to miss some bagger dallying across the road. There's beeps and bells, but the bagger don't notice, or care.

'Hold on,' she says, and I nod, thinking, *no shit*.

'How long you been working for the Node?'

'Oh, ages. Four months.'

That doesn't seem like ages to me, but what do I know?

'You'll last,' she says, peering up at me. 'Turnover's high, but you look fit and strong.'

'Thanks. What do you do?'

'Maintenance, interior. Cleaner. How 'bout you?'

'Resource Location, Logistics,' I tell her, repeating the classification like she does, how it's written on the employee file they sent me. When in Node. . .

'Ah. Climber.'

I'm not sure what she means, but I say 'Yep,' anyway, to keep the conversation flowing.

'My advice, if ya want it, is to hold tight to that job. Don't let the workload beat you down. There's a line ten k's long for work at the Node, and every one of 'em'll work harder for less. If you don't keep up, you're out. I've watched a thousand kids like you show up on the shuttle, then boom, they're out in a week. Can't keep up. Burn out. But some of 'em, they stay. I don't see 'em again. In ten or fifteen years you might make it to management, get out of the dorms and into a subsidised single. Live the high life. If I was forty years younger, that's what I'd do.' She nods to herself, chins doubling and disappearing. 'And don't cry,' she says, 'they hate that. . .'

She stares off out the front window and I do too, thinking what it might be like to go the straight-life. If I was just a regular old babe without an agenda and a half-cocked plan. I could spend my twenties slogging through the bluecollar deets, maybe score a sweet supervisor gig when I hit my thirties, get my own room. Work my life away for a pass into norm-ville, if my body holds out that long.

Pretend to myself that it was enough of a life.

I dunno if I could do it, hey. Like I know I'm just one poor little chicky-face in a Pacific-sized ocean of poor jerks, but like, what if there was more? More than just trading my labour for some faceless bunch of rich jerks who'd work me until I died and just fill my spot with the next desperate babe. Maybe bust out Vu from whatever awful shit she's in, take Cam and Sticks and pay a mint for some forged docs to raise 'em up good, make sure they finish school. Maybe set up my own biz, like Elton did. Repair and tatt and live for me. Struggle, maybe, but strug on my own terms.

And I feel weird and ungrateful at the thought because there's ten billion other hopeless jerks out there who'd give an arm and a leg, a lung and a kidney for a chance like the one I've got.

The one I'm just gonna throw away.

Clunk.

The thought-train I'm on gets shook loose as we clunk across the rails crossing over and I focus on what's in front of me.

The Nodeplex.

—

'New recruits this way!' I hear from the other end of the shuttle station and I hold my bag tight to me and run-weave through the little groupy crowds until I reach the babe bellowing. She leads us onto another lightrail and we clatter across the 'plex.

There's about twenty-five new recruits and we peer at each other, eyelocking now and then and breaking, awkward. I look about. It's fugging weird to see streets not all cluttered up with dead or sleeping hobos and refugees. The Nodeplex is clean. Spotless grey concrete streets grid narrow between the towers, in perpetual shade and totally free of trash and splattered blood or vomit. Now and then, people zoom by on sleek bicycles, and the few scooters and one totally out-of-place truck are all sans oily clouds of biofuel behind. The thin streets are lined with garden beds, some raised, filled with brilliant green hedges, little wedges of grass, shrubs and trees. Trees! This place is dreamy, and a part of me wishes I could be in it for the long haul, just to spend a smoko or my lunch halfa sitting on that tiny slab of green, my back against the tree.

But that's not for me.

We pass all this plush junk, and things get more industrial. Past the pretty glass towers the green fades to washed-out concrete grey.

The wrangler babe stands up front and centre of the tram, her smile faux and toothy. Her eyes are too full, maniacal and kinda dead at the same time. She introduces herself as Vikke. Her voice is harsh and high and fake and I already feel like popping her one in the nose, just to make her stop talking.

'Welcome to Nodeville. With the towers, housing, warehouses and underground facilities combined, we maintain over a million square metres of floorspace, comprising the main functions of Allnode, besides manufacturing, which is, of course, completed offshore.'

All the recruits nod, wide in the eye and slack of mouth, like this is the most fascinating line of info they've ever received. If they'd bothered to read the induction packs, or done any homework at all, they'd already know alla this. She's babbling through the various divisions as we pass their towers, but there's only one that interests me and my ears prick when she says it.

Psynode. Just a tiny division, twelve floors of a sixty-story tower, but it flashes like a beacon. Drugs, training and recreational sims, bodyhacking. Neural networks. R&D. All that nasty shit. My life for the past six months has been stacking to this point. I mean, all I've got is a note to go on, just a scribble on a scrap of paper, but I can feel it.

Vu. She's there.

Brainfuckers, Inc.

The towers all sparkle like crazy, panelled in solar tiles and gleaming in the morning goldy beams. The solar panels reflect everything around, and get lost in each other's reflection. It's dizzying. My brain's circling like super crazy mad and I'm surprised the babe in the seat next to mine can't feel the max-volume thump of my heart. She's just sitting there, dumbstruck, while adrenaline surges around with every sledgehammer pump of my heart.

She's here, and I'm gonna find her.

—

The dorms are done up slab-style, brutalist. There are cranes on top, jamming on new levels. I guess business is good?

When we enter a smooth voice greets us. It seems to come from everywhere.

'Good morning, recruit batch four-oh-seven. Welcome to the Acacia Street Residential Dorms.'

'That's the Sys,' says Vikke-wrangle, herding us into a lift. 'Your chips will be 'planted tomorrow, but there's a temp ident in your packs, good for a few entries. There aren't any keys or cards, Sys'll just read your info and let you know where you can and can't go, and where you need to be and when.'

All the other recruits look totes impressed but I'd read this already, so I just feign poor urchin babe, all awestruck and wonder-ridden. I feel a little smug, like some stone-cold pro, hell-bent on espionage and radness. Way to face, Mirii.

The lift lets us off on the ninth floor, into a fresh-built dorm that still smells of paint and the formaldehyde-stink of new textiles, which jiggles my sensey-memory to the sweatshops of my youth. Ah, nostalgia.

'You lot are the second group in on this floor,' she says, and points off down to her right. 'The first group arrived last week. This hallway is yours, and the bays are org'd by employee number. Find your bay and get into your uniforms.'

No one moves or says anything for a few seconds. It's painful and awkward so I decide to break the silence, of course.

'Hey look, there's a list over here with our employee info on it,' I point to a plastic printout on the wall. Everyone follows me over like a bunch of dopey tots. I find my number, then skip-hop off down the hall to stow my stuff.

Dorms, man. My kingdom for my own room.

My bay is on level two, which is far more primo than level five near the roof. My bay is slightly bigger than my body, with shelves at the head end and a cupboard at the feet. There's a power point and a few different charger slots, with a little metre and a sign to say that we will be billed for all power usage. There's a membrane that slides out from the side and closes over the bay, though. Privacy! I pull it closed and take thirty whole seconds to revel in it, until Ms Wrangle bellows from the doorway that we have a minute-thirty to get dressed and out for our shift. My uniform is folded neatly on the pillow so I wriggle into it quickly, slip on the cheap socks and rubber-soled sneakers provided and use the last ten seconds to stretch out and enjoy my new digs.

For a little flash-second, I get that weird 'what-if' feel again. Like, if this wasn't a mish, if I could stay here in my comfy coffin-slot, work every day forever for a few bucks until I got a supervisor position or something. Meet a nice babe or bru, settle down in a double dorm off-campus, nurse each other's overworked bods. Maybe get a pet or something? A galah that would outlive us, or a sugar glider to shimmy up the struts of our loft bed. Yeah. Yeah, that would be peachy as.

But when I picture it, it's Vu I see folded up on the bed, knees crushed up against her boobs, looking out while our glider tangles up in her hair or teaching our galah rude words.

Without me, without us, she'll never get the chance to have that.

That's why I'm here. Not to build a cosy little life for myself, but to find Vu and make sure she gets the chance to try and build one for herself. 'Cause any life I could make would be hollow if I knew that my friend didn't get to have hers. I'd never be able to be happy, even with my job and my private two-by-one, thinking about where she might be, what she might be living through.

It's hard to do the right thing sometimes. But sometimes, it's the only thing you can do. Does that make me awesome, or a total sucker? I don't even know.

—

'This scanner,' Vikke says, holding up the offending piece of tech, 'is your everything.'

I flip the chunky unit over in my hand. It doesn't look like much to me, but apparently I'm wrong.

Vikke's voice echoes through the training space. There's little clusters of us trainees spaced out along a 'practice unit', a huge single row of shelving with bins and bays for stock and a flimsy scaffold wraparound that reaches to the ceiling. Vikke tells us the practice u is 'scaled down' from the real thing, and as my eyes follow the jut of bars and boards and boxes to the ceiling, my guts feel like they are gonna fall right outta my arse. Scaled down?

'Every piece of merchandise has a journey,' Vikke goes on. Did she say something before this? Did I miss it? 'And every step on that journey has a process, recorded by the Log.' She holds up a shrink-wrapped parcel. 'For instance, this box of Oat Bars has an entire history stored, movement-by-movement, on the Log.'

She zaps the QV code, and holds up the scanner. We all lean in and squint at it as she scrolls through line after line of codes and locations. These snacks have been through more ports and statuses since they were packed last month than I did in seventeen years of transfers through the Corp.

'This section,' she says, highlighting a few sections of code, 'is you. For a few lines of every process, your fates intermingle. . .'

We what?

To my left, a skinny dude with an underdeveloped chin snickers and Vikke throws him a deadly look, straightens and clears her throat.

'When an item arrives at the facility, it is unpacked by unit A, sorted into one of a hundred and sixty categories by unit B-1, is sent down the conveyor belt by B-2, where it arrives and is packed onto the shelves by Unit C. You are now part of unit D. Your responsibility is to source the merchandise when an order comes in and send it down the conveyor to shipping.'

A question jolts into my brain and before I even know what I'm doing, I've raised my hand like I'm some dumbshit brownnoser snotnose. Who raises their hand? Only total doofuses ask questions, it's like a one-way ticket to a beating. I know this. I snatch it down again, but it's too late. Our wrangler's seen it.

'Yes?' Vikke says, all bewildered like nobody's dared ask a question before.

'Just, ah, sorry. But what happens after that?'

She gives me a look so withering that I can feel myself drying and curling up right before her eyes. 'For you, your next order will come in and you'll repeat the process. For the merch, it's sent down the conveyor to E team, packed by F, processed by the logistics teams and sent out by rail, air, road or drone.'

Right. Outta the box, onto the shelves, back in a box, out to the masses. Easy.

'Allnode Logistics division employment works on a points-based system. Everyone begins at zero. Meet your targets by the end of the day, you're on plus one. Fail to, minus one. Failure to meet location estimates deducts from your rating by fractions of points relative to time percentages. At minus ten, you will be dismissed. Late arrival is instant dismissal. Coming back late from break is instant dismissal. But don't worry!' Her eyes gleam with something that's half joy, half fear. Something in the pitch of her voice scares me a little bit. I wonder how many times she's done this spiel. I wonder how many more times she'll do it today. 'Everything you need to know is in the manual!' She holds up a thick ream of paper and shakes it wildly. The pages flip back and forth, revealing text in print so small it just looks like black lines. 'All the OH&S guidelines are in here, so you'll need to make time to read it.'

'Now?' A teal-haired woman asks her.

'Not now. We only have fifty-five minutes of training left.' She brightens, her voice going high and whimsical again. 'You can use your breaks to look it over!'

Vikke hands out our scanners.

'I'm going to assign you a practice order. No pressure, now!

Take as long as you need. The scanners give you directions, a map and a timeline. The timeline is a guide, so you can try to beat it! Just don't go over. Okay everyone, have fun!' Everyone stands stupid-still for a moment before the first scanner 'bings' and then more and everyone's shuffling off, looking lost.

I'm about to accept the flashing order symbol on my scanner when Vikke steps in front of me.

'Maloney, is it?'

'Mahoney.'

'A word?'

'Um, okay.'

'It's best not to ask questions. You've only got this hour for training, then you're out on the floor. It's simple. All you need to know is your part of the process. Nothing else matters.'

'Gotcha,' I tell her, wrapping a stupid expression on my mug, tryna make up for having any kind of personality or enquiring mind.

She grins. She's bought it!

'Go!'

Out of the corner of my eye I see her grab the no-chin dude, the one who snickered at her.

'Jackson? You're out.'

I look up at the shelves and scaffold, trainees bumbling up and over the rungs and ladders, threading through the bars, and I take a big, shaky breath. I press 'accept' and launch myself at the shelf.

—

If the training bay was a single tree, then the warehouse is a jungle.

And every packer and picker is like a monkey, swinging through the boughs. Gnashing their teeth. Screeching.

It's like those old-timey nature docos with that ancient British dude, ya know, whatshisname? I can almost hear his smooth accent narrating over the grunting and screaming.

What have I gotten myself into?

The warehouse stretches on forever, rows and rows of metal shelving reaching to the ceiling, with grubby white conveyor belts threading their way through the rows, all lit harsh by giant spotlights in the ceiling, burning bright and faraway like suns. The rows of shelves are framed with the same scaffoldy frame of thin runners, ladders, and rails alongside.

And crawling over this like termites on a humungous mound are hundreds, maybe thousands, of babes and brus, threading through the bars and shimmying up and down the ladders at speeds that are simultaneously amazing and terrifying.

I don't know if I can do this.

I climbed a tree once. It was really hard, even before the Uncles from the Corp started chucking rocks at me, trying to get me down. I've done my share of fancypants scrambling on night mishes in the Corp, but nothing like this. Can my body even do that?

I guess I'm going to find out.

Vikke points to the clock on the wall above the entry, massive numbers flicking down to the second. It says six-fifty-eight-point-two, point three, point four. . .

'You need to be in position and accepting your first order at seven, when you clock on,' she tells us, all standing slack-mouthed in front of our bins. 'There's a bell at twelve for lunch, and another at four for smoko. You get ten minutes for each. Your shift ends at seven tonight. Have a great day!' she bellows over the din, and then she's off.

I eye the clock, then turn and peer up at the shelves.

A babe runs by me, in Allnode grey camo pants, a ripped singlet and bandanna around her buzzed head. She's glistening with sweat and her arms ripple with thin, corded muscle. She skids to a stop at the conveyor to my right.

'First day?' she says, puffing, reaching into a tight-net bag slung over one shoulder. She pulls out a huge canister of protein powder and slams it onto the belt, which whips it away.

'Yeah,' I tell her. She grabs her scanner with a practiced hand, and 'bings' her next order. Then she reaches into her bag, pulls out another bag and chucks it at me as she takes off.

'Take my spare. You're gunna need both hands up there,' she says. She takes a second to pause, crack her knuckles. Then she spins, winks and hurls herself onto the frame, zinging up four levels at a breakneck pace.

She's wearing gloves, grippy ones. With bands of metal across the top of each, just before the stubby finger holes. It takes me a sec to place them.

Brass knuckles.

'Ah, thanks!' I call, but I've already lost her. Maybe that's for the best?

The clock says six-fifty-nine-point-four-five, four-six, four-seven.

I thread the bag over my shoulder, lift my scanner and approach the shelves.

Five-six, five-seven, five-eight.

I hit the flashing order sym just as the clock clicks over to seven.

Cretaceous Friends Dino figurine: Triceratops. Colour: orange. 1 unit. Shelf 6, level 8, row 48, bin 3. Sourcing estimate: 1 min, 12 sec.

I run towards shelf six and hit the ladder. Just as I do, a man's scream rips out from above and something flailing streaks by on my left and hits the floor with a sound that's a mix of *crack* and *splat*. And a little *pop*.

He's like an egg, cracked open at the bottom of a tree. By the weird stuff that's coming out of his head, and the pool of blood growing around him, I can tell there's not much I can do. I look to his bent up body, the bag on his chest with the 'Soundseed' box inside, the way his eyes are already going cloudy. It takes everything I've got to tear my eyes away. But I do. I peep my time-frame, which has fifty-four seconds left, and I make my choice.

I haul myself up the ladder.

I gotta make the target, 'cause I gotta keep myself at the Nodeplex.

—

I'm on my fourth pick, back, neck and arms screaming already, and I've hauled myself up to *level ten, row twelve, bin 27* for a tube of *Puro-U Water purifying tablets, 60 pack*. I find the merch, pop it in my bag and turn, thinking 'bout how I read one time that accidents are more likely to happen on the way back down. I've got twenty-four seconds to get back to ground level and slam the water-cleaning tabs on the conveyor, and I'm trying real hard to integrate my dual desires to not go over-target and not wanting to, like, fall and die. The sound of that bru popping on the concrete plays in my ears like a catchy pop-tune, and I race across the worn plyboards that make the scaffold footing.

From behind me comes a thump-thump-thump.

I turn just in time.

The guy is lean and wiry, but ripples with wound muscle. He shoves another kid, who I recognise from training this morning, out of the way. The newbz goes tumbling into the bin to his right, crumpling the SUPER-BRO MUSCLE-GRO bar boxes as he falls on top of them. My mouth goes O-shaped and I duck as the wiry guy's elbow comes out for me. If he hits me with it, I go over the side and probs pop on the concrete floor. I grab a hold of the closest upright rail, swing out as the dude goes thundering past.

The split second that I'm out there, over the drop, feels like much longer.

I watch my legs fly up and over the space as I whip around the rail. It happens so fast that my hands barely register the weight of me, though their sweaty skin and the steel bar grip makes a screeching sound that echoes in my ears. Then I'm back on the kinda firma, panting and sparking with adrenaline.

He spins at the ladder, plants his feet and hands the right way so he can slide all the way down, and he throws me a grin.

'Nice move, newbie,' he says. 'You might just survive the rest of the day.'

Then he's gone.

I cling to the rail, crunched up and still heaving.

Then my scanner beeps. Target time is up and I'm over, again. I let out a cry that's curdled with frustration and anger and like, ten zillion other things, which scares a babe running by me so bad that she trips a bit and almost loses her footing.

'Ya gonna cry?' she says, jamming down the ladder. 'Go on, cry. See what happens.'

I don't cry even though my whole insides are all drippy and sobbing. I follow her down the ladder, slam the merch on the belt, bing my next order, and I use all the rage I got inside me to hit the shelves at a furious pace.

—

Vikke's eyes are all manic again, but not with joyful-Node-fervour, like before.

'The targets are not a joke!' she screams and even though every newbz on the floor hurts more than they've ever hurt, every one of us snaps to attention.

'Not one of you hit statistical new-recruit targets,' she says, holding up a tab with little graphs that we can't read, because she's waving it around. 'First day targets are intentionally lower, to account for your ineptitude.' She spits this and even though I know this isn't personal, I feel a deep bolt of guilt. What the? How is this unhinged biatch summoning a shame spiral in me?

'Bhatnagar, Cheema, Higgens, Joyce, Ngg, Tomkinson and Totah. You're out. Collect your belongings and report to exit processing within the hour.'

Some of them look utterly relieved at this news. Ngg starts to pipe up, with a ragey shake in her voice, but Vikke shuts her down with a flick of her wiry wrist.

'Take your complaints to exit processing.' She turns to a sorry-looking dark-haired bru nursing what looks to be a broken arm. 'Mifsud, you did well, but your rates dropped off after your. . .incident. Get first aid to take a look at it, then pack your things.' Mifsud shuffles off to the bays of med-staff along the back wall.

'Awad, Anderson, Haerewa, Mahoney and Price, you just scraped by. I want to see you lift your game.'

Even though part of me is all 'Eat shit, Wrangle,' another bit of me kinda. . .wants to lift my game?

'Everyone else, good job. You're all just under. Tomorrow, your targets realign with your experience level, and you're gonna need to work harder, be faster, be better! I'll see you here, in twelve hours, and I want you rested and raring to go!'

I want nothing more than to faceplant onto the floor right here, but somehow, I get my feet moving and exit the warehouse as the nightshift bell goes and the battle rages up on the shelves without me.

—

None of our group talks, we're all mute with the ache of the long day and the sting of scrapes and bruises. Shiz, twelve hours ago we were all fresh and brand new, nervous on the shuttle, and now we are here and battered to hell.

Back at the dorm, I stop by the food-chute and grab the hot silver pack with my name on a printout sticker on the side, then I go right to my bay. It takes everything I have to lift my arms to the ladder to climb to my bed – food under my arm – and once I'm in I lie there, almost comatose, while my shitty, pre-packed dinner cools in its bag by my head. From all around me are groans and some little sobs and the 'shick' sound of membranes pulling closed.

'Good evening, Mirii,' a voice says. It comes from all around me.

'Hi, ah. . .building.' I'm not really sure what else to say. I can't imagine me and the Sys have a lot in common. Its gentle but insistent tone, and the way it seems to come from everywhere and nowhere at once, is super annoying. Plus, I'm pretty sure the bitch is spying on me. I mean, why wouldn't it be?

'You have five new messages in your Allnode.all email. Message one. . .'

'Yo Sys, can we do this later?'

'Mail system set to 'postpone'.'

'Yeah, thanks.'

I've lived in dorms as long as I can remember. The crowded, chaotic bunkforests of the OC dorms, then the hardbacked pews and steamy madness of Mrs P's and Ms Wong's. Neither of those hellvoids have anything on the cushy, clean and comparatively luxe-as-shiz Psynode accom, but there's something missing here. At Mrs P's there were always babes around and down for an evening bitch session, even if I couldn't call them my friends. I wasn't at Ms Wong's for more than a night, but Jools was there with her ratty beanie and her expert tongue.

I make eye contact with the chicky across the way, a giant of a girl with folded ears who's from the batch of trainos who came in last week, but she breaks the eyelock as quick as she makes it, slamming shut her membrane with a crump. All the doors are pulled closed and everything's so quiet. It's not just an air of unfriendliness here, or just the fatigue. It's something else. In the hush grey-and-white there's this current of something cold and dark.

Is it fear? I think it's fear.

'Good evening, Mirii,' Sys says, and I open my eyes, groaning with the effort of it.

'Yeah, Sys?'

'You have six new messages in your Allnode.all email account. Message one: Balance and Performance Review.'

Balance?

'Ah, read?'

'Valued Allnode employee, number 2702575. Your performance is at minus 1.5 points. This places you in the top six of your intake and in the sixtieth percentile overall. Please ensure your targets are met on a continuing basis in order to retain employment. Your current employee balance is as follows. Eleven-point-three-three hours of Resource Location, Logistics at twelve dollars and seventy-five cents an hour, minus tax rate of four dollars and three cents per hour is ninety-eight dollars and seventy-nine cents.'

Rad, I'm freaking rich! All those hours gritting my gums and climbing the frame, and you know, only the complete and utter destruction of my body and limbs, but I'm almost a hundy richer.

'Cept it doesn't stop there.

'Minus uniform rate of sixty-seven dollars and thirty-four cents.'

Wha?

'Minus seven days housing rate in advance at seventeen dollars and twenty-four cents per night—'

'Hey!'

'Minus employee rations at six dollars and one cent—'

How much?

'Minus power consumption of point seven kilowatts at three dollars and sixty-six cents per kilowatt—'

Excuse me?

'Balance total for Employee 2702575, Mahoney, Miriiyanan: minus ninety-six dollars and thirty-four cents.'

DAY THREE

The wake-up bell goes off at five to grumbles and moans, and I roll onto my side, every muscle and tendon giving me hell. I think I feel worse than I did last night. What I wouldn't give for the good old days back at the Corp, where my labour was unpaid, but like, ten-zillion times less strenuous. I mean, if this is what it takes to make a buck, I'm not so sure I wanna be in it.

But I'm not really in it to make a buck, am I? I'm here for some shifty corporate espionage, if I can wrangle it. I dunno how I'm gonna find the energy to plot a way into Psynode if I'm pulling twelve-hour shifts in warehouse-hell, but hey, I'm in the Nodeplex, aren't I? That's closer than I was this time yesterday. I'm sure I'll figure something out.

'Maroney!'

Vikke Wrangle rips my closure open and sticks her straw-topped head in through the gap.

'It's Mahoney.'

She screws her face up and I remind myself that the aim of the game is not for her to know who I am or recognise me as any possible kind of human being, but more, 'yes ma'am, no ma'am, how high, ma'am'.

'Why aren't you up yet?'

'Well, I thought shift starts at seven. . .'

'You need to be on premises at six to have your chip installed. Didn't you read your mails?'

In between finding out I'm actually in the black after my first day, and becoming comatose with the most hard-earned fatigue I've ever brained, I just did not make the time. But I can't let her know, that's probably instant dismissal.

'Of course, I completely forgot,' I say, springing out of bed, and then instantly regretting it. I don't let her see my pain. I've got lots of experience in not showing my weakness to anyone higher in the foodchain than I am.

I enjoy my current status as 'undevoured'.

—

From the area at the front of the warehouse, I can just see the glimmer of the Psynode tower through the window. I focus hard on the division floors then close my eyes, wonder if I could feel her in there, somewhere. . .

What I actually feel is the sharp jab of the 'planter at my wrist.

'Argh!' I shout at the babe with the 'planter.

'Oh, I'm sorry,' she says. She pats my arm kindly, and crumples the single-use 'planter into a biowaste bag at her side. She's tall, much taller than me with her head scraped bald and big, dark red painted lips that pop out of her dark brown face. She's in the same Allnode grey that everyone wears, hers a boxy tunic hanging from shoulders like coathangers. She reminds me of a big insect I found in the playground one day when I was a kid – all twig-limbed and bulbous up top.

'I love your work.'

I've rolled my sleeve up for the jab and some of my tattoos are showing.

'Prison?' she asks.

'Orphancorp,' I say. 'I did most of them myself.'

'That's wonderful. They're lovely.'

'Hey, thanks.' I try to think of something nice to say back. 'I like your, um, head.'

Shiz. My fugging mouth. Good wording, Mirii. Way to talk.

But she runs a hand over the nanostubble on her head and smiles wide, red-painted lips stretching around a set of blinding white teeth. 'Oh, you're so sweet, thank you. I'm Rowena Hamilton-Singh. You can call me Rowe.'

I take her hand when she offers it, the long fingers and palm soft and cool in mine.

'Miriiyanan Mahoney. Mirii. It's good to meet you, Rowe.'

She keeps a hold of my hand and turns it over, runs a finger over the tattoo on the soft part of my forearm.

'Carina,' she mutters. 'The boat.'

I grin, wide. 'Yeah, how did you know?'

'I studied astronomy for a semester at the institute. You?'

'I've just always loved the night sky, ya know?'

'Oh, that's lovely. Self-taught, how delightful!'

'My name, it means "shooting star"—' I start to tell her.

'Maloney!' Vikke Wrangle is suddenly all up in my face.

'Mahoney,' I tell her, but she's not listening.

'What are you doing?'

I gesture to Rowe. 'We were just having a chat.'

'Get out of the way! There's seventeen other new recruits that need chips too.'

'It's no trouble, I started the conversation.' Rowe sets up for the next puncture and I hightail it out of the chair and work at sticking the crappy bandaid she gives me over my brand-new open wound as Vikke glowers over my shoulder.

—

As I'm limbering up and watching the clock count up to seven, Rowe taps me on the shoulder.

'I want to know more about your tattoos, and the stars! My friend and I are eating at Kuyu tonight and I want you to come with us. My treat.'

Food? Paid for? I'm in. I think. Am I allowed?

'I dunno, Rowe. I mean, I'm not sure if they lock us in at night or what.'

'Lock you in?' Her eyebrows crumple together like two fuzzy caterpillars sparring.

'Like, at the dorms. I'm not sure if they let us out at night.'

Rowe gives me a look like she doesn't quite catch the gist of the words I'm saying. 'You're an employee, not a prisoner. You can do what you like once you're outside of work hours.'

'Oh. Yeah. Yeah, of course. That makes sense.' I nod like this is totally obvs information. Shiz, Miz, of course they don't shutter the dorms once the sun goes down. Rowe probably thinks I'm some crazy institutionalised babe, fresh outta the Corp. I wonder where she'd get that idea?

'I'll send you a wave with directions later. Oh, and wear something nice!'

'I don't really have anything nice.'

'Even better! Wear something awful.'

—

I'm an hour in, on my thirtieth trip up the frame, when I finally do it.

I hit my first target. With three seconds to spare.

I slam the bulk bottle of Mouthsplosion-brand hot sauce on the conveyor with a triumphant scream, raise my hands in a wide V, and spin around. The lines of folk racing like ants carting crumbs across a summer kitchen floor, down from the racks to the belts, take a quick glance at me.

'Hit your first?' asks a tall glass of water, an Afro-albino bru coursing with sweat.

'Yeah,' I say and we fist bump real quick before I flick my scanner out of its holster and bing my nextie. We take off at the same time, him pulling ahead fast.

I only just hear him as he says, 'The more you reach, the tighter they'll get,' then he's on the scaffold and crawling up the side, sans ladder, as easy as he would crawl across the ground. I wonder how long it took him to be able to do that.

I've got forty-five seconds to get to *level 2, row 28, bin 3* and back though, so I don't wonder too long. I just get moving.

—

There's a bottleneck at one of the ladders, so I dry my sweaty hands, grit my teeth, and move across onto the bars like I see the pros do. It's faster, but so utterly scary and precarious. It's the inevitable evolution of the picking form, but. . . You can tell the new recruits by the way they cling to the ladders and cope with the bottlenecks, jiggling their feet with impatience.

I'm not sure what pushes me on. It's a weird mix. Like I know the targets are totes balls, but those steady counting down numbers *do* propel me. I wanna beat them to prove that I can. And I want to beat them so I don't get sent on my way. So I get to stay here, find some time to sus the cogs of the Node and reach my goal.

So in some weird, twisty way, in my brain anyway, it's like beating the targs is getting me closer to Vu.

Climbing the frame unsupported is slower in itself, but faster for the lack of dopey newbz getting all up in the way. I don't want to be one of them. If I'm gonna get better at this, I may as well start now.

The dull metal posts are too big to get my hands around all the way, so I've gotta hook my palms and fingers as far around as they will go, and hope that it's enough. It's lucky I'm tall, because the spaces between them are wide. There's one post under the floor runner, another like a handrail for each level. In a way they are kinda like a giant ladder. If I make a path beside the crossbeams running vertical, it seems more stable but that's probably only in my head. I try to copy the tight movements of the pros, elbows in, knees pistoning higher. Up, up, up, then a neat shuffle. Duck under the handrail, run to the right bin, find the merch, scan and swing out into air, reverse the motion back down to the floor. By my fiftieth trip, I feel like I've got it.

And I feel proud.

Sometimes accomplishing a thing is enough to fill you up, even when the thing is bullshit. Especially when you don't have much choice.

—

Stopping is worse than keeping on. When the break bell goes, I almost don't wanna stop, 'cause I'm really not sure I could start again. I'm grateful for the opp to wizz, though, and I slam to one of the portas they've got at the side of the facility, inside the warehouse so we don't have to go through security to the standard facilities just to slam a bladderful. That'd be time-wasteful.

Even so, there's still an eyecam in the corner of the john, like I'm really gonna sit in this foul little shitter and shove a box of stolen Superfood Muesli in my gob on the sly. I eye it for the sec that it takes to relax all the muscles I've been squeezing tight, but once I get a good flow going I'm too busy rolling my eyes back and sighing with the supreme-o pleasure of pissing and even just bloody sitting to care that I'm being scoped out on the toilet.

Lunch is a room-temp bag-and-straw deal of Node-brand squishy gloop. Carbs, protein, sugar, carcinogenic blueberry flavour. It's like what cat food would be if they made it for people.

I lay in a wide-arm, wide-legged plane on the concrete floor, bag propped on my chest and straw plugged in my mouth, sucking up lunch and trying to get a rest in. I didn't wanna lie down, but I couldn't help myself. All us newbz collapse to the floor. The pros, though, they don't stop moving. They jog on the spot, keeping warm and nimble for battle, and when the warning signal for the bell goes, they shoot their bags into the bins, 3-pointer style, and brace with their scanners while the rest of us piss and moan and stagger to our feet.

I set myself at the base of the shelves and poise my finger above the flashing 'accept' sign on my scanner with a few secs to spare, my whole body protesting at the forced movement, my ankles and knees and shoulders begging me for one more minute of repose.

I wonder how long my body can maintain?

But then I don't get much time to wonder before the bell rings and I'm back monkeying up the frame and wishing I was blissfully asleep or dead or something. When I'm halfway up to *Level 4, row 27, bin 2* and puffing and my joints are screaming, that's when I realise that I'm never gonna get a chance to infiltrate this bitch if I gotta spend my days busting ass this hard. My head is full of how much my body hurts, and fatigue and a weird, sick desire to meet my target even though I'm afraid it's gonna kill me. There's no room for anything else.

This is bad. I don't know what the hell I'm doing, or what I'm gonna do, and I want to sag against the rails and cry out, but that twisted target-fire inside me keeps me moving.

Even though all I want to do is let go.

—

I'm reaching into *bin 3* on *level 12, row 24* for a twenty-pack of Sharpish Markers, assorted *pastel shades* when there's a bellow from the bin two slots over. I peep out the corner of my eye to see two shelf-monkeys; an exhausted-looking newbie who I recognise from my intake and a grizzled older dude with the hardened body of a pro, every vascular, ripply limb visible under Node-grey skintight lycra.

They've both got a hand on a single unit LED lightglobe box.

'Give it up, arse-floss. Last one is mine.'

'I. . . I had it first,' the newbz says, her fingers clamped around the thin cardboard box so tight that it starts to crumple under her grip.

The pro doesn't hesitate. He flashes out an elbow so fast that it hits before any of us register that he's thrown it. The crunch is sick and the scream that comes a nanosec after is even sicker. Blood flies from the newbie's nose and her fingers fly off the box she'd held so tightly to. She drops to the runner floor, lap filling quickly with blood and the pro-bro takes the globe box and leaps over her as she sobs and tries to hold her broken face together. Her scanner beeps as her target window closes.

I wanna help her, I really do.

But my scanner is counting down, so I throw her a sympathy-glance for a moment, then ease off the side and down the rail. As I swing from level to level I feel a little sick with shame.

Why didn't I help her? Is this who I am now?

The most awful part is the overwhelming gratefulness that it was her and not me.

—

The wave Rowe sends says ten, so I'm standing outside the address by nine fifty-five, my body wracked with pain while I'm wrangling some borrowed creds from Cam to buy a pair of climbing gloves from the Allnode store, imagining the bing-and-battle raging to get 'em sent through on their Primo order program – they'll be drone-delivered and waiting at my dorm for me by the time I get back. Just the thought of them soothes my torn-up, calloused hands already.

I'm wearing my one nice outfit and trying to look like some normal babe who wasn't in a deathmatch six storeys high over canned ham a few hours ago when Rowe appears at three minutes past ten. She struts up in a pair of high-heeled shoes that elevate her at least six inches above her already enormous height, and peers down at me.

'You look very boring, Little Star. I expected you to be punk rock, not corporate casual.' Rowe is wearing a matte-black catsuit that hugs her from neck to ankles and wrists, with a huge, shapeless holographic shift over the top. The shift gleams out swirly galaxy and fields of stars.

'I didn't know how well ripped jeans and patched jackets would go at Kuyu. I've got a safety pin in my pocket, I could jam it through my eyebrow if you like?'

Rowe squeals and claps her hands. 'Ooooh, you're funny! I could tell you were funny the moment I looked at you. I can't say I've ever fraternised with any of the logistics staff before. But when you walked through the door, I could just tell you'd be different.'

She takes my hand and leads me in through the tinted glass door. I gotta work to keep my maw from dropping to the floor as Rowe teeters behind the host, who seems to know her well. It's a mega-swanky place right on the ground floor. Old money, ya know? The restaurant is arranged in a ring, tables either side, around a deep pit like a sinkhole in the centre of the room. The walls of the sunken hall are rough-hewn sandstone like it's been cut right into the bedrock. It thrums with dancers, strobing lights and an incessant bass.

The host seats us at a table right on the edge of the drop. A zing of fear goes through me when I peer over the rail. The people below look like bugs, mingling and buzzing. There seems to be a lot of flesh on show. Too much?

'Are they. . .naked?' I ask Rowe, who peers over the edge.

'Bah! I thought the Skinrave was tomorrow. I can't believe I missed it! Do you want to go down and dance later?'

'I don't really dance.'

'You don't dance?'

'Maybe I do. I've never had much of an opportunity to. Is it fun? It seems really. . .tiring,' I say, eyes flicking over the figures. From up here they look like they're convulsing. I dunno, it doesn't look very comfortable.

'It's wonderful fun. Everyone doses on psilocybin and the nudity is just kind of organic from there. It helps everyone to feel more connected. I've made so many wonderful friends.'

'Are they coming, your friends?' I say.

'Should be. Give me a sec.' Rowe moves her fingers across her palm, then looks down intently at the tabletop, at nothing. I've seen that engrossed stare before – Rowe must have an optical implant. She's not staring at nothing, but at a display projected across her corneas.

I'm totally impressed and jealous as shiz.

Rowe speaks quietly and I zigzag my eyes over the menu, not wanting to intrude.

'Well, Little Star, looks like it's just you and me tonight. Could you imagine if I'd come here and had to eat alone? I would have died.'

'That would have been. . .just awful.'

'So, Mirii. Tell me everything about you. Start with the tattoos and work backwards. Do you mind if I order for us? The wasabi emu taquitos are amazing. I know the chef and he was telling me about this emu problem he was having. . .'

She trails off as she flicks over the menu, selecting icons all over the place. Within minutes, waiters zoom up with little plates and cups. I start stuffing my face with food as I tell Rowe a highly edited tale of Orphancorp and the dorms, going into a bunch of detail about learning to tattoo and trying not to spit crumbs at her. She fills me in on growing up in Nodeville, her studies and travels, and their new place in Barangaroo. It's all about as odd to me as someone describing trips to outer space, but I go with it and nod politely, interjecting now and then around mouthfuls of food.

Then she mentions that her dad is head of research in the Neuro unit, and I almost choke on a stonefish rillette (which is like, wicked good and kinda makes my mouth tingle a little bit) and I cough behind my hand, because sweet holy shiz, that means Psynode.

What kinda luck is this? Looks like I just found my new best friend.

When Rowe dabs her red-lipped face with the napkin and asks me if I want to join her at the Skinrave, I mean, I can hardly say no. I do the maths on just how much sleep my body might need to ensure I don't plunge to a splatty death tomorrow, but the numbers don't add up and I decide that it's more important to try to make a good impresh and all that.

'Sure,' I tell her. 'Can you teach me how to dance?'

She waves her palm over a spot on the table which seems to settle our bill, then takes my hand.

'Of course,' she says, pulling a little tube from her wristbag. It looks like a lipstick or some kind of mad-expensive designer sex toy, but then she flips the top and a little sheet pops up. She presses it to her tongue and it dissolves right away. She flips it again and another appears.

'Psylocibin?'

'Um, well, I have work tomorrow. . .'

'Oh Mirii, it's basically essential.'

'Hey, I've heard about this. Is this peer pressure?' I ask, letting the sheet dissolve on my tongue. It tastes like hot sauce and lemons and a bit like tinfoil. I've had mushrooms before, a birthday present from a gardener back in OC, and I wonder how different the synth version will be.

Rowe pushes her seat back and pulls off her shift, throwing it on the floor of the restaurant. A waiter scoots over and gathers it up. She stands and pulls at a patch on her catsuit and the whole thing sorta separates into pieces that she shakes off one at a time. The waiter collects these too. Rowe is naked in the middle of the dining room and no one bats an eyelid. I'm not shy or anything, but I'm wary of making a scene in a place like this. Like, when I agreed to have dinner with Rowe, I didn't expect the meal to end with an impromptu stripshow in the middle of a restaurant where the lowliest of starters costs more than a month's rent at Mrs P's dorm. I look around, my cheeks getting all hot, and a sweet twisting sensation begins in my veins, rising up through my body and into my head. I remember mushrooms taking a whole lot longer to come on than this.

'Don't just stand there, Starface, let's go!' Rowe's mouth convolutes the words and I stare at her, memming how I thought she looked like an insect when I first met her and then wishing like all holy hell that I hadn't remembered it just now.

Shit. Oh shit.

I unbutton my jacket and hang it over the back of my chair with terror-induced slowness while Rowe taps an impatient foot that yes, is a foot, but now is a tarsus and then is a foot again.

Oh man. Oh no.

The room around me takes a skip to one side as I fumble to get my boots off, tripping over my feet. I hand my undies to the waiter who nods and grimaces slightly, and I wonder if his eyes are really flickering with flames or if it's just me? As I form the words to ask, Rowe takes my hand and pulls me across Kuyu. In the lift there's music growing louder and more intense as we descend.

'I'm so glad I met you, Mirii. We're going to have so much fun tonight.' She stares down at my body, eyes all over the place and I look too and all my tattoos animate just like that. Rowe's long spider-leg fingers trace the whirling, clockwork constellations and blooming flowers. Then the door opens and the music fills the lift, lights pulsing and she pulls me out after her, in amongst the bodies. All the faces are eyes-closed-smiling, the limbs twisting in time with the music and I'm panting already and I make my arms and legs do what I see everyone else's doing.

'Is this right?' I yell over to Rowe. 'Am I doing this right?'

'You're magnificent!' she tells me, and a group of people next to us, their smiles wide and growing wider, all turn and mimic her.

'You're magnificent, you're magnificent,' they chorus and I feel like maybe they're right and maybe I am magnificent, because just yesterday I was back shitkicking on the streets, living that life and suddenly I'm in the luxxest party in Syd, living this life. My head goes back so I can see all the way up to the soft-lit roundness of the room above us. It's like the walls grow and recede, the circle of light getting nearer, then further away. Around me, bare skin flashes with little clusters of light that the dancers hold in their hands, smear against each other, the glow spreading out across their skins in a way that could be my mind playing tricks, or just as easily real.

'Phosphorescence,' someone says close to my ear. 'It's from the sea.' They press something wet into my hands and when I move, it lights up. I move, it glows. I move again.

Then, in a switch-second, everything goes streamlined and clear. I stop dancing and stand, my heart pounding. The realisation of why I'm here strikes me like a zap from a faulty wire.

Vu is somewhere close, and she's probably not having as good a time as I am. Much, much worse.

'I've got to find her,' I tell Rowe.

She nods. 'You will! I'll help you!' she says, taking my hands, making me sway with her. 'Who?'

The music thumps into me and all the ways they might be trashing Vu come flickering in my brain in waves and pulses. I hafta get out of here. I don't wanna lose it now, not in front of all these people, not in front of my new best friend Rowe, I need her.

'I gotta use the bathroom,' I scream to Rowe, who points a long, long, long arm across the room. I push through the bodies, and sometimes it feels like my hands are going through them, or getting merged and sucked into their sweaty skins. I thump through the bathroom door, and it's quiet in here, the music fading to a dull beat.

But shit, the light in here is wrong, and the walls are so white.

There aren't grimy tiles, no bloodstains, so it's not exactly the same. It's some kind of fine stone, like marble or alabaster, but when I lean against it to catch my breath, it's cold, cold and it sucks the heat I've built up right out of me. One of the lights is on the fritz, and it strobes just a little, and that's enough.

I do not do well in white rooms.

In small white rooms with fritzy lights.

I've always wanted to be a perfect little hardass biatch, letting nothing touch me, but however hard I become, no walls I make around my head and my heart can hold against a flashback, and not one heightened and in full technicolour with the help of the 'shrooms. I'm bodymemming it hard – I can feel the pain in my feet and my arms, my kidneys aching, and the desolation of my whole self comes fast and full, flooding every inch of me.

I'm there again. Consequences.

There's a little bit of me that knows this isn't real, and I cling to that real tight and ride it. Like when you're tripping and you can cling to that little stable core inside that knows whatever is happening, however fast the ghosts of all the people you've ever cared for are flying in your face or whatever, that it's just the drugs. I'm not tripping so badly or flashing so hard that I really *think* I'm actually back copping Consequences, but I can't escape the tide pulling, the feelings that floodfloodflood.

Rowe comes through the door.

'Are you okay, Mirii? You're not having a bad trip, are you?'

She folds me in her sticky limbs and I let her pull me out of the horrible white bathroom, back into the crowd all grins and sweat, and the flasher stops strobing in my mind and in my heart. I can taste the simple joy and care these people have in this moment, like I'm sucking it up through a straw. They're all rich and clueless but they aren't evil. They just don't know.

I relax. I dance.

But there's a little core inside me, where I've got Vu encased.

I won't forget you. I'm coming. I just gotta dance a bit first.

DAY FOUR

I crack an eyelid gently, just testing.

Light blasts me through the tiny gap and I groan and roll over, trying to bury my face and thumpy head in the safey dark of the crook of my elbow. Instead, I get a momentary floating feeling before a sudden hard thump as I roll right off whatever I'm lying on and thud onto a slick floor.

I sit up, naked and wrapped in a blanket, my hip and shoulder throbbing. I'm in a room I don't recognise. The floor is made of shiny black stuff and there's no furniture except the couch I was lying on and am now leaning up against. The blanket is made of the softest, lightest fibres I've ever felt and I pull it tight around my nuddy body and blink against the light.

The light.

It pours in through the window, but it's not even a window, really, it's a whole wall made of glass. I rise up onto my wobbly feet and stagger over to it, hands up in front of my eyes to block the worst of the sun. Right up at the window I feel dizzy, like the whole world wants to flip at any second and tip me over the ledge. The glass is so clear that it looks like it's not even there. Like there's not a thing between me and the air, the water, and the city I'm looking down on.

From this high it doesn't even look real. It seems like it's close too, like I could reach out and quick-finger one of the shiny mirror buildings, pop it in my pocket. Like I could walk my fingers, one, two, three steps, to reach the dividing line between the city and the water.

And the harbour! A million glittersparkles on every ripple and wave. The yachts, ferries and dinghies plough in zags from north to south. And everywhere against the inun-wall, little house-pontoons made of rubbish, the ochre stain of rusted tin and blue of FEMA-emerg tarps topping them all. A view like this should make a babe feel small, yeah? But from up here, it makes me feel big. Powerful. I lift my palm and press it to the glass, covering a chunk of it with my hand right up to the horizon. I giggle, like it's a game.

I take it away, then cover it up again.

Look how much of the world fits underneath my hand.

Am I still tripping?

Behind me, someone clears their throat. I spin around and see an older dude, thick-creased in the face, but totally dapper, leaning against the door frame. He deftly knots a tie beneath his sharp shirt collar.

'You must be a friend of Rowena's.'

Rowe! This is her house. My brain jams out a bunch of images in flashes: the rave, dancing, lights strumming all over the joint, running through the empty night-time streets, laughing, knowing the cold on my naked skin but not feeling it.

'Fugg! I mean, shit! I mean, sorry. You must be. . .?'

'Doctor James Singh. I'm Rowe's father.' He comes over and

offers a hand. He doesn't even look up at the gnarly vista in front of us, to him it'd be old hat. He keeps his eyes locked firm on mine. They are so brown they're almost black. I shake with him, politely.

'And you are?'

'Oh! Mirii. Miriiyanan Mahoney. I met Rowe in the Warehouse, I'm training logistics.'

Something flashes over his eyes. I can't tell what it is. Maybe he's too wealth to mix with lowly warehouse types like me, but just as quick as it came, the look is gone.

'Nice to meet you, Mirii, it's always interesting to meet Rowe's friends. She has such eclectic tastes.'

I narrow my eyes. He thinks I probs don't even know what that word means, but I do. I do! He might as well have just said, 'Oh my wacky daughter, she's even friends with garbage people,' and been done with it.

Even though I'm in his spectacular house with his zillion-cred view, even though my nudey bod is wrapped in his delicious animal-fibre blanket, I can't help but feel a surge of hot, ampy rage. I take a deep breath and open my mouth and I'm about to let him know I don't dig his tone, thanks very much, but before I can pour out a word there's a clatter by the door.

'Mirii!' Rowe says, appearing in the frame, squinting against the light.

And it's probably for the best, because I should know better than to let my mouth get carried away like that, even almost especially considering who this bru is and what I'm here to do.

'Hey, Rowe, how you feeling?' I ask as she staggers over to her father.

'Terrible and amazing,' she says, collapsing against him. He kisses her bed-creased cheek.

'Sweetness, I've got to get into the lab,' he says and I almost jump out of my blanket. Work! Shiz!

'Rowe! What time is it?' I ask, totally interrupting their tender moment.

'Six-ten.'

'Argh, I gotta scramble!' I tell her. 'Do you know where my clothes are?'

She laughs, last night's smeared red lipstick stretching around her white teeth. 'Back at Kuyu? I'm not sure, Little Star! Don't worry, I'll have something you can borrow.'

She disappears and Dr Singh and I share the space awkwardly until she comes back, pale grey uniform in hand. 'It will be long, but you can roll the legs up! Just pretend it's a new thing and soon everyone will be doing it.'

Dr Singh shrugs into a jacket and goes to leave as I wriggle into Rowe's tunic, which is a weird combination of slightly too tight but much too long. As he kisses Rowe on the cheek and goes to leave, he gives me that look again, the same look he gave me when I said my name. And this time, I place it. A sharp bolt of fear zings through me and I drop the shoe I'm holding.

It's recognition.

He knows who I am.

—

—Dr James Singh. Who is he and why does he know my name?

—Hey Mirii, nice to chat you too. Me and Sticks, we're fine. Elton even let us go through his scrap heap this morning.

—Ah, Cam. I'm sorry. I'm just freaking out. And I got fifteen minutes before I gotta be at work. How ya doing?

—Good. Elts didn't speak to us all day yesterday, but this morning Sticks broke through some prob he was having with his new alarm sys, and now he's started grunting and pointing at things when he wants them.

—That's actually a really good sign. By the end of the week he might be up to whole sentences.

—Hope so. How's it going?

—Okay. The work is long and ridic, but the dorms are luxe, Cam, you'd be jealous as. I even made a friend, Rowena. Her dad is head of R&D in the Neuro unit at Psynode. He's sus as, I just know it. And he knows me, or my name at least.

—You're in with the head of Neuro? You been there a fugging day!

—Two days. And I'm friends with his daughter, not him. He don't really like me too much. But she befriended me. It's a totes coincidence.

—Right place, right time?

—You know it, bru. I'm stellar like that. Anyway, I looked his profile up so I got a handle on his general info, but I guess I need more? Like, if he has connex to anyone we already know, or if he's got anything to do with the highlit cases.

—Cool. We'll get on it. But hey, we still can't get to your file.

—Figured ya would've told me if you had cracked it.

—It's superheavy encrypto shiz. Sticks is having heaps of fun with it.

—I'm glad I can amuse you both. Okay, I gotta jam. James Singh, don't forget. I wanna know all about his sticky fingerprints, n how far up Psynode's skirt they go.

—No wuz, cuz.

—

My new climbing gloves grip the rails like a dream about maybe not dying in really high places. I'm busting targs and ducking elbows and fists left and right, like a tight and tricky song.

There's an art to this. It's a hard and painful art, but it's skillsy nonetheless.

Look, I can't help that I gots a thirst for skilling up. I dunno where it comes from or why, like maybe Dad or Mum was like this too and it passed down in the genes to me. Even in the Corp, I took a weird, pervo pleasure from getting good at things, stupid things that didn't matter. Maybe it's a control thing, ya know? Like, I can't choose what crappy detail I get assigned to, or what entry-level job I can wrangle, but sweet jeez, I've got a say in how I make the box they jam me into. Mopping floors or climbing shelves is balls in and of itself, but I can take those balls and squeeze 'em the best I can.

It's funny, though, because after lunch, it feels like my targets get tighter. I swear that jamming up to *Shelf nine, level three, row six, bin 4* had a two-minute, fifteen second window before. Now climbing up to *Shelf nine, level three, row ten, bin 1*, which is practically the same place, gives me a minute fifty-five. And I'm halfway there, scuttling across a gap to avoid a slippery, blood-splattered section of rail when I remember that bru telling me that the targets slim down the better you get.

I hang there for a sec, going a bit floppy with the realisation that no matter how good I get at this, it'll never be good enough. The exhaustion, the way things flicker in the edge of my vision from the drugs last night, the ache in my muscles that I'm starting to think may never go away, it all overwhelms me and I feel everything welling up inside.

Do not cry, do not cry.

I can't break down, so I pull something up from deep in my

gut, my stubbornness, my strength, all the things that have seen me get this far. They can take me a little further, right? Just a little bit further.

—

I don't know where I pull the energy from, but after my shift, as the wind whips up and the two or so stars you can see through the gleam of city lights come out, I make my way to the market.

It's not just because I gotta see Cam and Sticks and make sure they aren't doing Elton's head in, but also, because the dorms – they're pretty lonely. I watch the membranes close one after the other as I suck up my hot-packed meal-pack and remember the silky spin of the night before, the people press, and I can't bear to spend this night alone.

The market is a place of people as markets always are.

It feels real, crowded with vendors and people and spicy smells, loud and colourful with bright T-shirts and pastel headscarves and brown teeth in smiles. People smile here, laugh, shout, fight in a singsong cacophony of all the languages of the world, all in one little, filthy city block. It's a hive, but not like the warehouse. The people here smile and laugh, stop and stay. They work together, not against each other. I like that. I need that.

I get a locust skewer from a teen girl with curly black hair and grey eyes who stands behind a solar-stove, turning the insect sticks over and over, painting them with sauce in quick dabs with every turn. I stare down one of the bugs and then jam it in my gob. It's coated with jerk sauce and I can't taste much locust in there, just zingy spices, but the spices are really good. I get another one and press my Worldcard against the little square reader plugged into the vendor's cracked tab. She grins.

'Good, yeah?' she asks me and I nod. 'Yeah, I'm the boss of bugs. Best ones at the nightmarket. Bring a friend next time, I'll give you a freebie.'

She winks at me and gives me a funny look and I wink back and wonder if the bug girl is trying to crack onto me or if I'm just reading into it too much 'cause I'm stupid lonely.

There's stalls with the usual patched-up electronics jammed up tightclose to tables stacked with homemade sweet cakes; baklava and halva and kanafeh, next to vendors hawking ripoff synths. Tucked into a gap between a stand selling bananas and a stall crammed with shady-looking tech there's a little set-up that I recognise. The stink of rubbing alcohol and latex, the faint sweet smell of mixing ink that would be easy to miss unless you know it well, and I do. I hover around until the flap across the back raises. A bru in Allnode grey pants and a stained-up white shirt comes through, wiping his hands on a paper towel.

'You looking for a tattooer?'

I don't answer because I'm too busy gawking. The dude is one of the biggest guys I've ever seen. The paws he's drying are easily the size of my head and he's got shoulders that would have issues fitting inside my dorm bay, which is a comparison I make because I'm instantly keen to get him back there. Is that allowed? Could I get away with it if it wasn't? Would I be able to close the door with him inside?

'You okay?' he asks, tilting his giant head to one side. He's got long, wavy hair, dark eyes and huge arms. Arms. . ..

'Shiz, yeah. Yeah, I'm. . .I was just walking past. . .and. . ..'

Come on, Mirii. Use your words. Stop thinking about shimmying up him like he's a wide, well-muscled tree. Speak!

'Do you need to sit down or something?' he asks.

'Yeah, nah,' I say and collect. 'I was just looking at your. . .set-up. It's rad. I'm a tattooer too, or I used to be. Don't get much time for it these days.'

He gets a huge grin on his big, beautiful face and pulls a chair over.

'Nice one! Come in and take a seat. I always love talking shop.' I sidestep around the barrier across the front of his stall and take the seat he offers.

'Mirii.'

'Tane.' He takes my hand in his and gives it a firm shake.

'Much work 'round here?' I ask him.

'Some. It's hard to make a buck working clean when there's a hundred other scratchers out there who'll give anyone a shitty 'sign and some free hep for a fiver. I work security over at the Nodeplex,' he says, gesturing in the direction of Nodeville. 'But I can pull steady creds 'cause I've built a good rep.'

'Nice. I still have my kit but I don't really use it on anyone but me.'

'What kinda set-up you got?' he asks. I'm checking out the work on his arms, so it takes a sec for me to proper hear him, and when I do, I blush a little. His work is good, like mad intricate. Lines and shapes in tidy rows. I've never seen anything like it.

'Just a stick-and-poke.' I duck my head a bit.

'Nah, no shame, girl,' he says to my red cheeks. 'You grow up in the sys, teach yourself?'

'Yeah.'

'That's awesome, good on ya. I got taught by me mum. Her mum taught her, and her mum before that, like a family thing. Mumma taught me old-style and machine. You ever worked a machine?'

'No, I've always wanted to,' I tell him, watching as he pulls out a rig and passes it to me. It's big in my hands because he's got those giant bear paws and I just have regular, human-sized hands, but it feels good there.

'If you come by another time, I'll give you a go,' he says and I'd already planned to come by again, maybe just a sly drop-in as he's closing up, you know? But now I'll have to make a coupla trips. How awful.

'You Pacific Islander?' he asks. 'It's the tradition, you know. Tatau.'

'Nah. Indigenous, I think. Don't got no traditions, though. Unless you count what I learned in the Orphancorp.'

'Ah, gotcha. My tradition is important to me, ya know? Makes me feel tied to something.'

'I get that.'

I do. That's why I've spent so much time on the Wiki, checking out the stories of a people I might not even be a part of, with no link except the name and the hope that there's something there that I can hold on to, make me feel connected to the Earth, give me a past to feel a part of.

And too, I feel a spike of jealousy at his Mumma and his family biz that I instantly feel bad about. I just feel so. . .untethered. With no family, sometimes I feel like I could just float up and off the world and no one would notice.

But maybe that's what I'm trying to do. With Cam and Sticksy, why I didn't send them packing right away. And with Vu. Maybe I want her back so hard because I want to build myself a little family from the ground up. Try, at least.

All this thought-jumble comes in a quick second, but a look comes over my face that Tane must see, because he puts a heavy hand on my shoulder.

'That was a bit insensitive of me, I'm sorry. Must be hard to be alone.'

'It is. But I'm not alone. Well, I'm working on it.'

He smiles, his teeth shiny white. 'I gotta pack up now. But come back, girl. I'll teach you about the machine, tell you about the tradition. Show you old-school if ya want.'

'I'd like that,' I say.

Tane waves me off with a wink and I distract myself from my sorta-sad-spiral by thinking about being manhandled by those giant fists (just like, I don't know, kinda lifted up and put in places). I almost don't notice the kid following me. But I catch her in the corner of my eye, first ducking out from behind a frozen banana stand, then again slipping between a shock-shop and a Chinese massage station, each time catching my eye, then looking away real fast. I come up alongside the shock-shop's dusty tent flap and catch her as she's coming out the side, grabbing her by the neck of her T-shirt until the fabric pulls and the stitches crackle apart.

'So, why ya following me? Ya think I wouldn't notice?' I hold her tighter because I think she's gonna make a run for it, but she doesn't. She laughs. Then there are giggles all around me and hands pulling me back behind the tents. A man stumbles out of the shock-shop, his eyes glazed and mouth slack. I open my mouth to scream for him to get some help, but they've stuffed something inside it. The shocker's eyes bug a little and he reaches out a shaky hand as they slip something over my head and stuff goes dark and noisy for a bit.

—

Echoes. Echoes off close walls and the thump and scrabble of my feet as I get dragged. Two someones have their arms looped through mine. They aren't strong, but when I break away, there are more behind to catch a hold. They bump me from person to person and I career off them, all floppy and stupid with the bag on my head. When I trip and fall, they laugh, high-pitched giggles. Kids! Foiled and kidnapped by a bunch of bobbleheads! After a while their game of bounce with my body gets less fun, so they just march me regular-style, tiny hands gripping my shoulders and pushing me forward.

'Hey, shitkicker. Does ya mum know you're out this late?' I ask, trying to spice up this relatively tame kidnapping with some well-aimed antagonism. 'Isn't it your bedtime?'

'Shut up,' some little chick says to the left of me. 'Or it'll be your bedtime soon.'

'Oh no, you gonna send me to bed without dinner?' I'm not even sure where I'm going with this and she don't say anything, so I'm guessing she probably goes to bed without dinner a lot. Shiz, now I just feel like a nasty cow, I mean, in the OC they'd send us to bed without dinner all the time and it was the worst. I lean down close to her, or at least where I think she is and I tell her, 'Sorry about that dinner quip, that was a dog thing to say. I've got a Nutrobar in my pocket if you want it. . .'

There's a punch in my guts, just a little kid-sized one, but I'm not expecting it, so it floors me. Fugging kids! The bag slips off my face as I eat the floor and a bunch of hands riffle through my pockets, pinch out the packet and then there's a mean scrabble. The tots are waging a tiny war over the food. I seize the moment, reef the bag totally off my face and lift off from the ground. I'm in an underground storm drain, all dark, with pools of light every few metres. When I stacked it, I rolled around a bit so I've got no idea which way I was coming or going. I just pick a direction and take it, thinking that wherever I can take myself is gonna be better than where these grubs are trying to deliver me. I pelt down the way, sprinting from pool of light to pool of light and I hear the kids behind me yelling for me to stop. The tunnel curves and I round it wide and quick as, my legs twice as long as any of the littlies on my heels. I turn my head and jibe 'em as I go.

'Good luck catching up, shortlegs! Way to kidnap!'

Then there's a shout from above me. A big patch in the wall has been bricked up with cinderblocks, and there's a doorway up high, almost at the roof, big and steel with a windy handle. There's a girl up there, legs dangling down, clad in a pair of animal-print gumboots. She drops a rope ladder down the wall.

'Are you Miriiyanan Mahoney?' she says.

—

'Lacey, Lacey!' they bellow and she chucks down silver MRE packs to the kids, who fight like rats over the shiny bags.

'Now bugger off,' she says and they tear back down the tunnel, squabbles fading as they go.

'Come on up then. I'm Lacey,' she says, and sighs. 'Sorry I had to send the brats out for you. I'm having a flare-up, or I woulda come found you myself. I hope they didn't 'combobulate you too much. If it helps, I'm gonna be fucked just climbing down the ladder, ya know? I've got about half a spoon left today, I swear. Come on,' she says. I zip up the ladder, then wait at the top for her to go down the other side. She moves stiffly, like there are posts in all her joints, without a lot of give. It takes her a full minute to haul herself down. It gives me time to think. I mean, sure, let's follow this grumpy babe through this hole in the wall to who knows where, why not?

When I jump off the last rope rung, Lacey is easing herself into an old, duct-taped vinyl swivelley-chair in front of a bank of shiny screens arranged across a desk-top. The room is big, echoey and neat, a bed on the far side and the desk along the left wall. The rest of the room is taken up with humming server boxes, blinking lights and cables snaking all over. It's incredibly warm for such a big, damp place: the hot air from the servers like a bank of heaters driving out the cold from the concrete walls.

'Rad place!' I tell her.

'Yeah, thanks.'

'Does it flood? There's some pretty gnarly downpours and storms in the old Syds. You ever worried about an inun'?'

'Nah, the walls are all built-up and reinforced against the flashers. I get stuck inside sometimes, but never for long.' Even as she talks, her eyes are closed and she's puffing a little.

'You okay?'

'Yeah, yeah, gimme a minute.' She takes a deep breath. She's all freckles, with curly black hair jammed up in a messy tangle-bun on her head. 'Rheumatoid arthritis. I'm stiff as a rusty hinge today.'

'Shiz, dude, sorry. Can I get you something? I think I might have a spare Pernadol here somewhere,' I tell her, spilling out my pockets.

'Nah, wouldn't touch the sides. I'm guzzling Tarmeines these days, but me liver's shot to shit and as you can see, it's not having much of an effect. The drugs don't work and all that.'

'Balls.'

'Balls indeed.' She nods. 'So, aren't you gonna ask me why you're here?'

'Oh yeah,' I say, cramming my junk back in my pockets and taking a seat on the edge of her neatly made bed.

Hospital-corners, so I'm pretty sure she's a corp-kid because that shiz sticks, even when you've got the aches and pains. 'What is this? How do you know me? What is this place?'

'Finally some questions. I dig curious babes. And I know you're curious. This is, like, under. Gadi. We live here.'

'Who's we?'

'There's heaps of us. The Collective. Punks, crusties, activists, anarchists, ya know? Like, anti-caps?'

'Anti-caps?'

'Anti-capitalists. Pro-human.'

'Oh.'

'Delilah, open saved feed Mahoney, M.'

'Who's Delilah?'

Lacey goes a little flushy red. 'My sys. The computer. That's her name. What do you call yours?'

'I dunno. Mrs Tablet?'

'Real imaginative.' Her eyes go back to the screen. 'Look, I'm trying to show you something. You've ruined the big reveal. It was supposed to be more dramatic than this.'

I look. There, on the screen – the warehouse, all climby-shapes and floodlights. A lobby, looking familiar. A dorm-bay, empty, the crease of a body still on the sheets. I peer closer. There: a back-pack, up on the wall hook, a tab charging atop the sheets at the Allnode rate of a few cents per min.

All mine.

'I've been watching you.'

'Why?' I say, peeping at the feed of my life without me. I wonder what it looks like with a Mirii in there. Less empty? And there, in the corner – a feed of the marketstreet outside, half obscured by a flapping piece of tarp. I can just make out a tiny Tane. He's closing up for the night.

'I was just there. You're like, following me.'

'Only with my eyes. Non-corporeal. Is that less creepy?' Her face is half-lit by the screens, her freckles kinda blued by it.

'No, it's way creepier. Why?'

'Because they're coming for you. Soon. And I wanted to get to you first.'

'So I am highlit.'

She turns her head, quicker than I've seen her move yet. 'How'd you know that?'

'You said it yourself – I'm a curious babe,' I say. 'How did you know?'

'I've got a trace on the highlit files, took me forever to crack. You popped up and I started to watch ya. I can't do much more than watch these days, send messages. The Collective thinks I'm wasting me time, but what else am I gonna do? It's tough to get a word in to the 'plex – most of the time the highlits just blip out before I can get word to 'em. But you came out. You basically came to me.'

'I knew I was highlit, right? Quick hire, shady recruiter. Got no family, I'm fresh outta the Corp. That's the golden ticket? I'm expendable.'

'Do you know what that means, the proper definition?'

'Like, not worth much?'

'See, to them, though, you're worth a lot. They're not interested in anything they can't sell.'

'That's, like, a running theme of my life,' I say.

'Mine too. Expendable means to be used once and destroyed. But how they use you, that's worth something to them. I dunno, they could send you through to a med trial or something like that. Breeding, or dissections? I've got you pegged for storage, but. A lot of the youngies are off to storage these days, the ones I can't get to. Or the ones who don't believe me. Which is pretty much everyone.'

'Storage?'

She taps the side of her head. 'Neural networks. Human storage. A zillion kerjiggergigs in a human noggin. Cheaper than servers, far more powerful. More applications. They can harvest your experiences and use 'em for sims, sell 'em for a few bucks a pop. Turn you into a giant DNA data storage unit.'

'That's totally diabolical.'

'Do you believe me?'

'Of course. I actually thought it would be worse. I wouldn'ta been surprised if they were grinding them up into Soylent or whatevs.'

'Well. . .'

'Really? Oh, for fuggs sake, remind me not to eat anything here again.'

'I mean, I don't know what they do with the wastage, that's what they call it. I'm sure I can find out, but I really don't wanna. Whatever it is, it's something they can sell, no doubt. Fertiliser?'

I feel sick, sick at the thought of Vu in storage somewhere, or caged up in a lab with tubes all over and some scientician poking at her. Or fugg me, ground up and spread over a field somewhere to push up crops, or stuffed inside someone's dumplings. Shiz. Shiz.

'So you knew your file was highlit?' she asks me.

'Cheyeah, of course. I mean, not for total suresies, but why wouldn't it be? I'm their target audience.'

'Then why the bloody hell did you go there?'

''Cause I'm looking for someone. A friend. I think she was brought here from the Corp, just before I left.'

'They do take in lots of state wards. I think there's shady deals afoot with some of the higher ups.'

'*Vile*,' I say.

'Yeah, I know. Totally heinous. Delilah, search filecloud "Flow" for keywords "state ward".'

'Can you search names? The girl I'm looking for. . .'

Her head shakes before I even spit out the name. 'She might be on travel manifests or as a random name in a mail about a batch. But once they disappear, records get smoky. I can't find any link from a real person with a highlit file to the numbers that represent them. I actually think they're assigning them IDs at random so there's no traceable link. Names don't matter. All they want to know is what you're good for.'

I flop back onto her bed. It takes a good few seconds for it to really sink in. When it does, it comes sudden. Every scrap of air huffs outta my mouth and all my stomach muscles tense. I feel sick and winded. It's useless.

I'm not much of a crier. I mean, in the Corp, crying would get me a mark against my name, or a write up, as well as a fist in the guts if any of the nastier kids had seen me do it. I'm pretty good at holding in the tears, even when they're right there, even when they filmy-up my eyes and turn my voice low, I can still stop their spill.

But now they leak out. And it's like every single tear I've ever held back just pours outta my eyes. On this neatly made bed, in the glow of so many screens, none of which show anything that can help me, what's the point in keeping 'em in? Lacey watches me with her pinprick pupils, eyes flat.

'I'm sorry, Mirii.'

I hike up my tunic and dry my eyes on the hem of it. 'It's okay.'

'No, it's not. But honestly, what did you think you were gonna do, storm some lab? How would you even get in? And after that? There'll be a thousand sec brus with guns and zappers.' She gestures to her screens. 'Plus, everything's monitored.'

'I'm fugged.'

'Yep. Totally.'

'Thanks for the encouragement.'

'What do you want me to say?'

'I dunno.' I pull my knees in close to my chest. 'I guess I need a minute to be a sad lump.'

'Lump it up, babe. Have a cry, take as long as you need. Just don't wait too long. You gotta clear out. I can try and find a bolt-hole, if you like.'

'Nah. Nah, I went there to find her. I'm gonna do it.'

Lacey rolls her eyes. 'Good luck. Don't say I didn't warn you.'

'Yeah, thanks for that.' I get up and make to storm out of the place, but it's hard to do a stroppy stomp when I gotta climb a flimso rope ladder, and plus, the door is too heavy to slam for added dramaticals.

'Mirii?' Lacey calls after me. I slam into reverse and pop my head out. 'I'm sorry I was such a cow about it. I hurt, and it makes me fugging grumpo. You gotta listen when I say to get out. Do it soon. Come find me when you do, I can help with that at least. There's a place for you here, under.'

'I dunno. I got stuff I need to do.'

'Well, you may as well gimme her name. Your friend. I can almost guarantee I won't find anything, but I'll give it a try.'

'It's Vu. Adeline Vu.'

'Nice name.'

'Yeah, she's a nice chicky too. She deserves more than whatever they've done with her.'

—

The Node-streets are pretty empty in the late hours. I try to look nonchalant but the night gardeners and street cleaners give me eyes as I pass. Plus, I gotta smoothstep off into an alley when a truckload of rentacoppers rumble past. It don't matter anyway, 'cause I've seen those divided screens at Lacey's and I know that every move is recorded by a zillion eyecams on every nook and corner of this fugging place. I just gotta hope that no-one's paying too much attention to the screens right now.

Sys tries to batter me with emails, but I'm not in the mood. I set her to wake me up ten minutes early so I can check them then and I crawl into bed, tireder than I have ever been, but I've got thought-circles spinning in my brains. Sleep's just not coming even though it's stupid o'clock and everyone not tortured by, like, woefully underplanned industrial espionage and dirtbags in drains, is in a dreamy state of pure black sleep. I'm so jealous.

Then I hear the whisper of a footstep. Just a tiny brush. I wonder if someone else is up and if they might want some company or a friendly ear, or even just a nod to know that they aren't the only one battling a case of the no-sleeps. I dunno, maybe they wanna make out – I'd be up for that. I've heard good things about Psynode's range of new-gen sleep aids, but there's nothing like a good, old-fashioned getting-off to send a babe to triple-z-town.

I roll to my side and crack the membrane just a smidge. I can't see anything at first, just a strip of black, which is weird because there's always light in here: the serene green of the exit sign, cool blue from powerbank LEDs and soft purple of the walkway nightlights. Then the black shifts, letting in a sliver.

Someone's standing right in front of my bunk.

I almost leap outta my stiff new soft-grey Psynode flannelette winter-issue jarmies and hit the roof of my bay.

They shift again and there's the quiet click of someone opening the membrane across from me, the one that belongs to the girl from an earlier intake, the one with the pair of folded ears. I can't see much, but it's enough and I can hear too. A low 'shick' noise that's so familiar, then some shuffling, and shadowy shapes move away from the dormbay. They're carrying something.

I stay still, like so still, and I'm scared every beat of my heart or pump of my guts might shake my skin enough to let these shadow SWAT dudes know I'm here. I don't breathe or blink or twitch. Even after they're gone, the squad of silent bru's in gunmetal grey with their loot, I still don't move. Not for a while. Because that 'shick' noise is the same noise that a drug-shooter in an action flick makes when it slams against someone's skin, and that bundle they're carrying? Person-sized.

I reckon that poor babe was highlit.

DAY FIVE

I wake before the alarm sounds and lie under the blanket, back
sore from work and my roughhouse kid-napping last night. I make
a little world under the blankets for a bit, a world where I'm just a
reg kinda gal, havin' a lie-in before work detail, and not like I just
saw a scary night-time secreting-away, or at all messed up or too
deep into like, anything. Just reg. I pull my pillow out from under
my head and push it along my back, trying to pretend it's warm,
like a person lying alongside me. Maybe it's Vu, and maybe she's
back there, nuzzling into my neck and murmuring in her sleep. I
run my hand over my own side, slip the warm fingers up under my
shirt and then down, playing in the waistband of my pants for a
bit. They stray a little lower and in my head Vu is waking up next
to me, blowing morning breath into my ear and slipping her hand
inside my undies just like this and then I'm in a different kind of
world, with images flashing through my head. Scanty mems of
rough calloused hands on me, a look in someone's eyes like my
body is their whole world, whispered phrases here and there that
sent bolts through me then and do again now.

I'm so close, I'm almost there when my tab beeps three times, then again three times fast.

'Shiz, shiz!' I whisper-shout and fumble for it by my bed before it wakes up half the dorm. That's Cam's call sig and I plug in my sat line and make sure I'm sec before I open his chat bubble.

—Where have you been?! he asks, the text appearing in a big clump like he's typing mad furiosa.

—Nice interrobang, dude. I'm right here.

—?

—Bah, nvm.

—I've been trying to IM you. Sticks cracked your file, finally. You gotta get out of there, Mirii! You're highlit!

—Ah shiz, Cam, I knew already.

—You knew? Thanks for telling me. What else did you find out? Have you found Vu?

—Soz, dude. I found out last night. Some little brats tyke-napped me and took me to this grouchy punk babe who lives in a drain. She's got eyes all over Nodeville and she warned me.

—?

—Yeah you know as much as I do on it. This place, Cam. And no, I haven't found Vu. Lacey, the drain babe, she told me that it's pretty pointless trying to find her. The records go anon after they nab ya.

—Fugg.

—Fugg is right. I don't know what to do.

—How 'bout your other friend. Head-neuro-dude's kid? Can she help?

—Rowe? I'm still trying to figure out that angle. I dunno, it could take a while.

—Maybe you gotta call it, Miz. Get out while the getting is good.

—I know. But it's such a waste. All this work. And what if she's here and I just give up, when I'm this close. It's just not like the Corp, hey. I don't know how it works here. You can't play the sys if you don't know it. There, I was a big shot, ya know? Now I'm a small flea on a big dog, and I think I'm about to get bit off.

–Fugg.

–Yep.

—

'Where's chunko?' some dude from my intake asks me and I snap back to the assembly point from wherever the hell I've paranoided off to in my head.

'What?' I ask him, and get back to stretching out my quads.

'Chunko. You know, whatshername, with the huge jugs. And the ears,' the dude folds his ears in half and my heart zings.

I just shrug and hope to holy shiz that he don't see it writ all over my mug. I try to fold my features into a caj look that says something along the lines of 'not sure, but I totally didn't see her juiced up and secreted off into the night by a band of shady brus, definitely not that.'

He buys it and goes back to rolling out his neck. My thoughts are twirling and I didn't sleep, not one blink.

Too much is happening, you know? Like I could deal with just a fruitless search for Vu, or just the whole general shadiness of Dr Singh, Lacey in her little pain-drain, worrying about Cam and Sticks, or just the night-time trainee-napping. . .For any one of those things I'm totes sure I could drag together a band of scrappy kids and have rad, sexy adventures solving the mystery and the whole thing would close with us pulling a mask off some old codger, gee whiz, just like in the old webrips, you know? But I feel like every string I yank on pulls out ten more strings and I'm getting all tangled up like a stray kitten in a textile sweatshop.

Out of the corner of my eye I see Rowe passing by the entrance to the warehouse. Her proportions are unmistakable. I eye the clock and see that there's a few minutes left before I gotta get climbing so I jog over.

'Hey Rowe, how ya doing? I had a great time with you. Didja get my wave?' I keep bouncing around trying to stay warm.

Rowe looks to the side, then is like, 'Oh no, I must have missed it.'

'Oh,' I say, pulling my arm up and over my head, pulling out whatever muscle that it stretches.

'What are you doing?'

'Limbering up.'

'How come?'

I point at the shelves, the last shift apeing across the rails. ''Cause I need to be able to move tomorrow, so I can do all this again.'

'Is it hard?'

'It's the hardest thing I've ever done, and I been working in sweatshops since I was six, so. . .'

She nods. With her long limbs she'd make a great climber, but I can't see her ever needing the cash that bad.

'So,' I say, 'you busy tonight? I was thinking we could do a thing. I can't treat you to Kuyu or anything, but we could head to the market and get a locust skewer. I could show you how the other half parties.' I honestly can't imagine doing anything else after my shift but collapsing in a pile to sleep, but cosying up to Rowe is kinda important.

She looks away, but. 'I can't. I'm busy. And, my fa—'

Ah, the old mid-word trail off.

'Your. . .?'

'Nothing.'

'I'm pretty sure that was something there.' I cock an eyebrow, 'cause I reckon I might know. 'Did your dad tell you not to hang out with me?'

Rowe's face flushes as red as her lips are. Bingo. Does old Singhy know who I am? Or what I'm up to?

Is it simpler than that?

'It's just that. . .'

'That I'm an orphan? I'm a climber? Am I too grubby to hang out with his presh kid?'

That I'm engaged in wholly unplanned and currently unfruitful corporate espionage? I don't mention that.

'It's not like that!'

'It kinda seems like that.'

Rowe looks all hopeless and she mumbles something I don't catch before she walks away. I don't follow because the clock's at six-fifty-eight and I don't feel like getting fired today. I get into position and run gently on the spot, scanner in hand and ready to go. I'm mad too, for some reason. Maybe I kinda cared if Rowe liked me or not? I mean, technically I am using her, even though it's in a pretty indirect way and I actually really dig her so maybe it's more like just a bonus to us potentially being best friends forever that maybe she can help me find Vu.

Using someone isn't so bad if you also like them as a friend, right?

And hey, if I keep telling myself that, maybe it will be true.

It doesn't matter anyway. Her pops don't want her talking to me, so I'll need to change tack.

And I'll have to think of how after this twelve-hour bloody shift.

—

I'm getting good at this.

I'm swinging up and down levels like I never went bipedal. I take the hotshots of adrenaline from last night, the fear and uncertainty of what's gonna become of me if I can't brain this whole thing before I get disappeared, and I funnel it into the climb.

I smash all my morning targets and Vikke gives me a half-hearted grunt before she launches into her manic-freak-out at the rest of the team. I suck on my midmorning break meal-pack allocation, bouncing on the spot to keep warm while the rest of my cru, slowly dwindling down to the superfit, true-believers and bloody stubborn, gets a railing about what a useless pack of lazy sods they are.

I might not get a verbal thrashing, but I do get my targs shaved down for the middle seg, so I don't kid myself that I'm spesh or nothing. If I don't lift my game, it'll be me copping insults by lunch-time.

It's a game no one can win. Do better and beat the targets, and instead of a pat on the head or a shiny prize, you win smaller targs and the opp to bugger it all up again. I look up at the pros, the corded wires snaking up the sides and wonder if their targs just dwindle down to nothing? How low can it go? Where does it end, or does it just keep thinning and thinning until they break?

There's no time to find out though.

Not when there's targs to meet.

Over-confidence is a killer, but.

I'm up on *Shelf 2, level 13, row 1, bin 1,* trying to cram *2 units* of *So-soft Toilet Tissue, sixty-pack* in my stock sack, and wondering how I'm gonna get down thirteen levels with a hundred and twenty bloody rolls of loo paper. Who buys their bog paper online, for fuggs sake?

I cram one into my bag, the net straining around the giant plastic pack, and I tie one to the bottom with a set of straps I ordered instant delivery on my lunch break the other day. I feel like a laden ass, like the donkey kind in one of them pictures I seen on the wiki of burdenbeasts piled up with stock on the side of a mountain somewhere. I'm so bulked out by the TP that I don't fit on the slim passageways running by the bins, so I couldn't use them even if I wanted to. I've gotta turn at a crazy angle to fit through the rails to get onto the outer frame. I contort, easing as slow as I can while hyper-aware of my targ-time flicking down. There's nothing like a slow-go out over a huge drop to make a babe's heart all thumpy-thump and maybe it's the fear of heights, maybe it's the fear of that slim minute-five counting down, or the lack of sleep from last night's witness. Maybe it's a combination of it all. But I'm not quite with it and I make that last little inch out, prepping to turn mega-careful to start down, when there's a soft squeal of plastic-wrapper on aluminum rail and yep, I'm jammed.

My load jammed soft-but-tight between the rails, my body twisted up and out and thirteen levels below, hard concrete.

'Outta the way, twerp,' comes a voice from above and I look to see a hardened older babe, her Allnode grey shirt with the sleeves sliced off all soggy with sweat and her face a ripple of burn-scar tissue. I'm blocking the way and a little line starts building behind her, everyone grunting and some screeching before they slip over the side. A big dude with a nose that looks like it's been broken ten times for sure climbs right over me, his elbows battering my face for a sec as he passes. He bellows at me, just a long, deep wail, no words. I'm looking as he passes, so I don't notice her until I feel the bump, and it comes so hard it almost knocks me off the rail. The sweaty cow pulls her leg back again and goes for another kick so I quick-smart start to wriggle my arms out of the straps of my stock bag.

BOOM.

'I just fucking missed my targ because of you!' she screams, and goes for the goal, dealing a huge blow to the squishy packs. I pop my arm out as it comes free, and the TP sails out over the void and falls to the floor, bouncing once, then twice, while I fumble to swing around and keep my footing.

'Stupid goddamn newbie bitch!' she says, but flies off, with a look that says, *later.*

Hey, even though I nearly died, it's a helluva lot easier climbing down without the stock. And when I reach the bottom, it's undamaged so I slap it on the conveyor and send it off, only five seconds over my target.

Coulda been worse.

Then, at lunch, it gets worse. I'm peeing hard and fast in a tight, odorous porta-loo when the whole thing rocks. The contents slosh up over the edge and patter on my shoe.

Uh oh.

'I got ripped a new one by me unit manager because'a you. I haven't had a missed targ in seven weeks, novice.' The last word gets spat out, like it's the worst thing I could possibly be.

It's Sweaty. And she's not happy. She wrenches the door open, because of course they don't lock, that would make spring-attack searches impossible, and who knows what we might be doing with misappropriated stock in here? I try to pull my pants up but don't get time, and when I look up, it's just at the perfect moment to see her fist flying towards my face.

Thwap.

It's been a while since I felt the force of fist on face. She gets me right on the cheek, with the old scar on it, and I start laughing 'cause I'm in shock, but also because I got this scar on the toilet as well, and now it's opened up again and oozing a bloodsy stream down the side of my face like a sweet little harmonious reminder that you can't ever, ever escape the past. It'll catch you up as you go faster.

She gets a bit put off by the way I'm cackling, sitting on the john with my pants around my ankles, covered in blood, so she slams the door. I stand, buckle up and try to pull it open, 'cause I'm gonna cork her one right in the tit for that, but she's holding it closed. The Porta-loo rocks. Back. Forward. Back. . .

And it's teetering there, on the bottom edge and I'm all, *no no no*, but it can't recover and the whole thing tips over.

I tumble out on a gusher of human waste, and Sweaty has the audacity to still be standing there, a smirk pulling the ripply scar tissue tight over her face. I get up, and she holds her hands in front of her, flicking her fingers towards her, like *bring it.*

I do.

But I've rethunk my prior notion to pop her one in the boob, so I just approach her real slow, then at the last second, pounce on her. I catch her in a tight hug, and she gets covered in all the muck I'm covered in.

'You little cu—'

'Break it up!' The warehouse fuzz is here, and they're stopping the fight as much as they can without touching either of us. One scans my wrist for my chip.

'The cost of cleanup's gunna be deducted from your accounts, botha you! And you can't get back to work like that. I'm adding a new uniform to your tally. Go and wash up, now!' She looks at my face. 'Have medical take a look at that wound for you. You wanna hope they get here before ya lunch break is up, or you're out on your arse.'

There's only one place to clean up, so I take a reasonably comprehensive bath in the emergency eyewash station. Half the warehouse eyes me as I rub-a-dub, and Sweaty snarls at me, waiting her turn.

'It's not over,' she says as I rip open my new uniform bag and wonder how far in the negs this has got me.

—

Rowe's waiting with a first-aid pack when I reach her in the warehouse entryway.

'What happened, Mirii?'

'Can I explain while you fix me up? I've got seven minutes to be back out there or I lose my job.'

She's got me in a seat and is applying some kind of sick-smelling medglue to my face before I know it.

'It was just a fight,' I tell her. 'They happen when it's all stressy up there.'

'I see it a lot,' she says. 'People get explosive in high-stress situations like this. Don't move, that needs a minute to set.'

I check my watch. Three to go.

'I can swing that.'

'Mirii, I'm sorry about this morning. I didn't mean to offend you.'

'I know.'

'I went to see my father at his office in my break today.'

'Yeah? He have a change of heart? Gonna let me sleep over?'

Rowe grins, the smile splitting her dark red lips.

'Not exactly. He wasn't there, anyway. So I had a look around. . .'

'Snooping? In Pop's office? Find any sweet meds? Wanna share?'

'This is serious! I thought I'd just take a look at your file, see if there was something he wasn't telling me about you.'

'Rowe—' I start, wondering if she's cottoned on to my little disaster-infiltration, but she stops me.

'Your file, it was strange.'

My highlit file. Of course she doesn't know. Why would her daddy tell her that he trades in human stock? How could she look at him again?

My scanner goes with a two-minute warning.

'I have to go.'

'Please Mirii, it's important.'

'I can't. Can you meet me? Tonight? Away from here?'

'The nightmarket,' she says. 'Take me out for a bug skewer.'

I nod, pat the side of my face where the medglue has hardened over the twisty mess of scar tissue there. Then I race back to the stacks, to start working off my brand-new debt.

—

I think Rowe's trying to look inconspicuous, but she's drawing a lot of attention to herself. Her black glasses cover most of her face and she's got-up in ripped jeans that look sprayed-on to every millimetre of her data-cable-thin legs. Her top is a hessian sack sewn together at the sides, with a hole cut out for her head. She's leaning against the wall next to the locust stand, head-and-shoulders above everyone around her. Even in her rough clothes, she's like a beacon. Everything about her – her height, her insect-limbs, her designer-applied dirt and precise-cut tears – screams 'totes sus'.

'This your friend?' the girl at the stand asks me, brushing the skewers with one hand and gesturing towards Rowe with the other. 'She's scaring away my customers.'

Rowe gapes and I tell the locust seller that we'll take everything she's got. Rowe waves the Worldcard chip in her wrist as the bug-babe fills my hands with a marinated swarm. We wander over and take a seat on the gutter, cramming the bugs in our mouths.

'So whydja wanna see me? What's with the incogneets?' I ask her around a mouthful of crunchy insect.

'You're not here just to work, are you?' she says, locust legs moving around her mouth, smudging her almost-black lipstick. 'You're up to something.'

'I might be.'

'So, since the night you spent at my place, my father's been asking about you. Just in a roundabout way, but he's suspicious. Then when I searched his sys for your name and found your file, it looked funny. Different from a normal employee file. And it wasn't pulled from the employee cloud.'

'Where did it come from?'

'I don't know. Somewhere else. I don't know enough about the employee files to say. It just didn't look right. I think you're in trouble.'

I start poking the empty skewers into a half-eaten bánh mì cast off into the gutter by my foot. I don't think I can wiggle my way outta this.

I gotta tell her.

Maybe she'll freak, but maybe she'll help.

'Just before I left the OC, my friend got 'napped,' I say, driving a wooden spike deep into the stale roll and still not looking at Rowe. 'She went completely off the sys, like she never was at all. A friend in the Corp got wind of some connex with Psynode. So when I got out, I started working on getting into the Nodeplex, though it's not quite jamming to plan. And my file looks funny because they're gonna disappear me just like they did to her.'

Rowe's all agape at that, and she flips her shades up and looks right at me.

'People don't just disappear, Mirii.'

'Maybe where you're from, babe, but where I'm from, they do all the time.'

'You think I don't know how the world works because of how I was raised, don't you?'

'Not even! I think you know exactly how your world works, just like I know how mine does. But I don't know what your life has been like, and you don't know mine.'

Rowe puts the shades back down and kind of stiffens a bit. 'I spent a whole gap year volunteering with Planet Vision, doing vax shots for refugees in the Gulf,' she offers up. 'My father was against it, but I have tried to learn to check my privilege, you know.'

'I know. You aren't heartless, Rowe. And I'm not trying to say that you don't know anything 'cause you got born cashed up. I'm just saying that this is real. Psynode has its fingers up some shady skirts. They take people who no-one's gonna miss, and they're fugging with them. I don't know how or where, but my friend Vu is one of them, and I'm gonna be too.'

Rowe processes a bit and then she jumps right up.

'You think my father's involved in this!'

'I never said that,' I tell her, looking way up to meet her eyes.

'No, you didn't, but that's what you think, isn't it?'

I stand up and look her right in the face. 'Okay, yeah. I do.'

'My father is a good man.' She actually crosses her arms at that, and I'm just waiting for her to stomp a foot, too, but she doesn't. Everything about her closes right up. I've lost her.

'I'm sure he's a good father, Rowe.'

'He's an excellent father!' she screeches, and then she's storming off, so I run after her. I get it because it's easier to run away that to think someone you love could be capable of awful shiz.

'I just don't think that being a swell dad stops you from doing shady shiz in the workplace, yeah? If he's got my highlit file up, then he must have something to do with it all, dontchathink? Maybe he doesn't know where the folks are coming from, maybe he just works with 'em. Maybe he just tinkers on the neural networks for storage or whatever.' I don't believe it though. I reckon the sly old rat knows exactly whose heads he's playing with. He knows and he doesn't care.

Rowe stops. 'Storage?' she asks, looking at me with big old eyes, sparkly with recognition. She's frozen there for a second, like she's trying to parse something. Then she shakes herself off, just like a dog, and her twinkle-eyes harden. 'Were you using me to get to my father?'

'It's not like that, Rowe. I didn't set out to—'

'What exactly *did* you set out to do?'

I slump a bit at that. 'Ugh, I don't even know. I thought maybe if I got into the Nodeplex I'd be able to find a way in to Psynode, and maybe find my friend. But so far all I've done is work stupid crazy hours in the warehouse. I've got no plan and in three days, if I'm not gone, what happened to her is gonna happen to me.'

'How did you arrange for us to meet?'

'Arrange? If I could arrange something like that, Rowe, I wouldn't need you in the first place. It was an accident. It was great fucking luck! But I didn't want to use you and I haven't, have I?'

'No.'

'See? I knew the only way I'd have a chance is if I told you why I was here, but I couldn't, I don't want to get you involved.'

'But I am involved now. I can't just hear something like that and not do anything. If what you're saying is real, it's an utter violation of human rights.'

'No such thing for me and mine.'

I jam out my tab, ping off a few IMs while Rowe miseries up in the gutter.

Two bings back.

'Come on,' I say, pulling her up by a soft, long-fingered hand. 'There's someone you should meet.'

—

It must've started raining since we ducked underground, 'cause the middle of the drain is filling up with dirty water and rubbish. Rowe watches a healthy-looking rat run by like she's trying to cope with some real, serious horror, but I just pull her along faster and hope like hell everyone gets here before it starts to flood.

There's a stranger at Lacey's door, throwing the rope ladder over. They're a hard-looking babe with a ratty mohawk and a few wobbly facetats, and they gesture for us to come up.

Good thing Lacey was watching. I think she's probably always watching.

When we're in they go to pull the ladder back over, but I tell them to wait.

'Two more. Coming soon, I hope.'

Rowe's already all gapey at Lacey's sneaky-peek screens.

'This is highly illegal,' she says, running her fingers over her head-stubble, all nervous.

'Rowena Hamilton-Singh,' the mystery babe says from their high-point up by the door. 'First and only daughter of Dr James Singh. First-year med student at USyd. Part-time Advanced first-aid officer at Allnode warehouse division. Apartment 2712, Packser Building, Barangaroo. One hundred and eighty-eight centimetres of pure daddy's-little-bougie-sweetheart, following in his footsteps.'

Rowe's mouth opens and closes, but there's a clatter at the door before she can say anything, and Cam and Sticks leap off the rope ladder and both tackle me to the concrete floor.

'Miz! We've missed you! This place is rad! Elton says he's had jack of us. He's let us sleep in the workroom the last two nights! I think it's gonna flood out there, how cool is that?' I can't tell who's yelling what, just that I've got about ninety or so kilos of pre-teen boy squirming round on my person.

'Argh, gerroff me!' I say, squirming to the top of the pile. Lacey, Rowe and the mohawk babe are all bugging at the sight of us on the floor, so I push the kids off and struggle to my feet.

'Cam, Sticks, this is Lacey, and Rowe, and. . . I'm not sure of your name, Mohawk.'

'Tat,' they say, latching the thick door against what I assume is a rising tide outside, and climbing back down to thump on the floor in a stompy pair of combat boots.

I turn back to my little brus, who are fawning over all of Lacey's rad 'tronics.

'Did anyone follow you? Were you careful? Sticks, please don't touch anything.'

'Why would anyone follow us, Mirii?' Cam asks, grabbing Sticks and pulling him away from Lacey's keyboard.

'Because you're all fugitivey and—'

'How the hell do you know who I am?' Rowe says, looking at Tat with knivesy eyes. Rowe's voice rings loud and clear over the din of teenage giggs and rising water in the drain outside. She's overcome her case of gapey fishmouth and her face is righteous anger and fury instead. Her bald head pulses with a stress vein just above her eyebrow.

'You're pretty hard to miss, hey,' Sticksy says, standing beside her, neck craned way back to look up at her. It breaks the tension, a little.

'Your daddyo is number three on our shit-list. We know everything about him.' Tat scowls from the corner where they're sitting, wide-legged on a tape-patched office chair.

'Why? What has he done?'

Lacey scoots over on her wheely-chair and shoos Cam away from her set-up. 'Delilah, open filecloud James Singh.'

The screens fill with text, pics and vids.

'Where do I start? I mean, the speriments and med trails on human subjects are just the tip, but that's his forte. And while he's by no means responsible for the human traffic legwork, he's a big market for it. The experimental drug trials on unwilling participants, harvesting of mems for experience sims, creation of neural storage networks—'

'Storage. . .' Rowe and I say at the same time.

'I've tapped that feed and it's about as grim as you can imagine.'

'So, whadaya got to say for yourself?' Tat asks from the corner, crossing tattooed arms.

'I've got nothing to do with this,' Rowe replies, glowing blue in the dim light of the screens.

'Well, you sure do reap the rewards.'

'Hey,' I say, holding up my hands like I can stop the waves of hatey indignation flowing back and forth across the room with the thin skin of my palms. 'Rowe's right. Go easy. She didn't know. I reckon if we give her a chance to brain this new info, she might be able to help us.'

'What can *I* do?'

I approach her with a tender voice. 'Well, Rowe. . .you do have access to your dad's office.'

'Last time was just luck and timing! He was at a lunch meeting!'

'Maybe you'll have it again?'

'I know how she can help us,' Tat says. 'And we won't have to wait.'

We all turn and look at Tat. They stand and crack their knuckles, pop-pop-pop, while we wait for them to go on. But I know it's not gonna be good. Tat's got the scowl of someone who knows how to get the job done. Lacey has this soft, practical vibe to her, keen but floaty. Tat feels vicious, more determined. I can feel them crackling with potential from the other side of the room. I wish I'd sensed it earlier. What the bloody hell was I thinking? I always assume people are just gonna want what's best for everyone. I don't know why I think it, because it's almost never true.

Fuck me, I can be an idiot sometimes.

'Rowe,' I say. 'I think we should go.'

Cam and Sticks read the tension after a lag, and they both look at me. I wave them over and we all bundle together, the four of us.

'She's not going anywhere. How's our luck? You brought us something we can actually use.'

Lacey actually gets up out of her chair, real slow, and she puts a shaky hand out towards Tat. 'We haven't discussed this with the others.' She turns to us. 'You can't go out there yet.' She gestures to a screen with a tiny feed I can't properly make out until she tells me what it is. 'The drain is still flooded. You can't risk it, you'll end up in the harbour if you lose your footing.'

'They're gonna side with me and you know it, Lacey. The majority has wanted more action for a long time. Your soft-angle watch-and-learn tactics can only take us so far.'

'Our statement says we don't revert to the tactics they use. We don't bloody kidnap.'

'It's a trade. Her for the members of our crew who've been captured and imprisoned fighting for the cause.' Tat's puffed up, all full of righteousness now.

'And what about the rest of them?' Lacey says, her voice husky and tired. 'The thousands passing through their black market trade? Every poor fucker drained and rinsed and hung out in storage? What about the sorry mobs working for them every day in inhuman working conditions? The offshore manufacturing deaths? A trade implies consent to all that. We'd be working *with* them! Copying their tactics, negotiating a trade-off. That's against everything we stand for, collectively. All because you want Trala outta prison. It's not gonna happen.'

Tat fires Lacey a venomous look. 'I've heard the rhetoric. We wrote it together! Back when you were useful.'

Lacey winces at this blow.

'But if I put this to the others,' Tat goes on, 'you know they'll come out in favour. Everyone's missing someone. She could help us re-establish our numbers.'

The four of us are watching all this discourse quiet in the corner, and Rowe's got a bony hand wrapped around my shoulder, brown fingers going white with the pressure. I can hear the rush of water real faint behind us, the hum of electronics in front, the sharp jolt as Sticksy sniffles now and again in the damp air.

'Rowe, I'll get you out of here,' I say, real soft.

'No,' she says, just as soft, but then she gets louder. 'I'll stay. I will. But I'm not your bargaining chip. I want to see evidence of everything you've told me, because if it's true, then I'll work with you to help those people,' she says, nodding to Lacey. 'And free your friends,' she adds, throwing a dagger-look at Tat. 'In that order.'

I'm about as shocked as Lacey and Tat are, but, like, not totally shocked because I always got the feel that Rowe wasn't a bad person. She's totally privileged out, but her heart is right and I could sense that from the start.

'Deal,' Lacey says, as Tat and I both open our mouths to speak.

'How can we be sure she's not gonna get bound up and bundled off as a hostage for the cause?' I ask Lacey.

'You can't agree to a deal like that without putting it to the Collective!' Tat says.

'You have my word,' Lacey says to us, then to Tat, 'and if you're so concerned about making decisions on behalf of the group, let's get them on the blower. I reckon they'll all be more amenable to a friendly coalition than a switcharoo in cahoots with the enemy.'

Tat makes a 'pah' sound, and slinks off to sit on the bed in the corner, scowling all the while.

My tab pings with a reminder. I've got a halfa 'til the last shuttle back to the 'plex. Bloody hell, right in the middle of, like, vitally important political negotiations, and I gotta toddle home to bed!

'Lacey, how long do ya reckon before it's safe for me to leave?'

'Ten minutes or so? The rain stopped a while ago, and the water level's already going down out there.'

'Rad.' I turn to Cam and Sticks. 'I can't believe I'm saying this. You gotta stay here and keep an eye on Rowe for me. Make sure no one does anything bad to her. If anything even a little bit untoward happens, I wanna know right away.'

The little dipshits nod, big beamy faces like they've just been asked to mind a lolly shop for the night. I think they're just super proud that I'm trusting them with something important, so I can't bring myself to tell them that I'm only doing it 'cause I've got no choice.

'Just don't, like, break anything. Or touch anything. Or say anything!' I say, but they're already crowding up on Rowe and puffing their chests like they're her bodyguards or something.

I take Rowe by the hand. 'Rowe, shit, I didn't plan for this to happen, I'm so sorry.'

'No, it's fine. I need to know. If my father's involved. . .I want to know the truth.'

'Whatever you find, I hope you're okay. And I want to help. But I didn't come here to fight some anti-cap battle. I'm trying to find my friend. Please, if you can, help me find her.'

Cam and Sticks nod. They knew Vu, knew how good she was.

'Tell her,' I say, starting up the ladder, nodding goodbye to Lacey, and giving Tat a farewell scowl. 'Tell Rowe all about about Vu. How much it hurts to know what might be happening to her.' I heft the heavy door open and peer out to see the water is slowing to a calf-deep trickle, just low enough to splash through and not fast enough to knock me off my feet. 'Make Rowe see she's a real person, and that we need her back.'

—

Sys opens the door back at the dorm and hushes a few words about my mails before I shut her up. I lean against the mirrored walls of the lift, watching myself played back again into infinity – muddy legs, eyes all dark-circley with fatigue.

Seems like every time I try to catch a thread to follow, it just tangles me in something new. My brain is all like, 'abort, abort', 'cause this mish is more than I ever bargained for. Every step I take forward is actually like a huge tumble backwards. Into a patch of stinging nettles. And brown snakes. Nettles and snakes backed by a multi-nat corp with its own police force and a whole host of shady places to put me if I get caught.

Ugh.

I've made this mish my purpose, my whole life. Since I left the Corp, I've held my plan and Vu up in my head like a finish line I can push toward. Without it, I'd be lost. I'd have nothing but myself and what then? I'm clinging so hard to all these threads, and the harder I hold on, the more they come lose.

I'm slipping.

I smoosh my head against the closest mirror and look into my own eyes. The light in here turns the green to black.

The doors split apart on level nine to the empty, pastel-glow hallway and I think I've managed to slip in all sneaky-sneak. Nice work, Miz. At least you've done one thing bloody right today.

My membrane comes apart with a crunchy click that bounces off all the walls and I wince and slip into my bay, hoping that I'm all undetected, but no luck. Vikke Wrangle is there all of a sudden, hair scrunched at the back with sleep. She shines a torch in my eyes even though it's never bloody dark in here.

'Mahoney, this is the second night you've come in late.'

Fugg.

'Yeah, er, sorry Vik. Was out seeing a friend.' I pull the covers over my grubby clothes quick-smart and make to close the cover, but she pops a hand in the way. Though I'm tempted to slam it in there, I probably shouldn't.

'Who?' she asks.

'Ah, I don't think you know them. I was just at the nightmarkets, you know, enjoying some of the local locusts.'

She crosses her hands over her crumply Node-jamas, eyebrow raised.

'If it happens again, I'm going to report it to HR.'

'So we aren't allowed out at night? Like in our own time, after work? 'Cause I haven't read anything about a curfew in the employee guide.' I cock an eyebrow. It's probably not the time to get cocky, but I feel pissy and miserable and so, so tired and if I can take it out on VW, then why not?

'Of course you are. This isn't a prison!'

They do keep telling me that, don't they? I pull back the covers, sit up on my bed, ease off my dusty shoes with the opposite foot and pull my hair into a scrunchy bun on my head. 'Then what's the problem?'

Vikke scowls at me. 'The manual recommends an eight-hour rest period, Mahoney. You've got six until the bell. Get to sleep.'

I'm already pulling up the covers, so I just look at her with both eyebrows trying to lift up off my forehead and into my hairline. Her face goes all pointy. She blows her hair out of her eyes and shuts the membrane with a crump.

—

I've only been scrunched up in bed for a little while when the soft pad, pad, pad of rubber-soled boots rises just above the usual night-noise hum. I wonder who the shadow-team is coming for this time and it's not 'til I hear the footfalls stop right outside my bunk that I even consider the obvious – they're coming for me. Zingy fear-juice sits me up, and I reach for anything to defend myself, but all there are just bedsheets and a pillow.

'You're early!' I scream as they ease open the membrane.

I guess they aren't used to 'napping someone who's not zonked out already from the long day of work, because the drug-shooter is slow to come. I take the opp to bellow enough to wake the entire floor. As they fumble my twisty bod out through the membrane I catch a glimpse of two beady eyes peering out from the bay opposite, and when I thrash my head towards the other side, two more eyes, all big and fear-shot. They disappear as the latches slam home.

'It's gonna be you next,' I whine and my voice kinda flattens out at the end because a shooter gets jammed up against my neck and fired, the punch coming quick and the 'shick' noise echoing through everything. It feels like lukewarm soup flowing into my veins, and my brain goes soupy too.

'It'll be youse guys next,' I say again, my voice blurry through my lips and I give a few half-hearted thrashes as the pull of a zip grows up and over my body, like the sound of the world ripping in two.

DAY SIX

'It wasn't personal, Miss Mahoney,' Dr Singh says, clinking away with something off to my right.

I'm strapped on a hard metal table with soft vinyl straps, small ones around my wrists and ankles, big, wide ones looping over my legs and pelvis and torso and chest and shoulders. I've got about two centimetres of give when I wriggle, so there's not much point trying to move and I stop after a few half-hearted strugs. Plus I'm too tired. I've never been this bloody bone-weary in my whole life, not even after a day climbing racks.

'It was business,' he continues.

Something yellow flows through a tube snaking down past my left eye, and then there's a sting and a sliding sensation below my ear. I feel the cold spread out from my neck, down to my heart where it thump-thump-thumps all over my body.

'This kind of questioning isn't even my business, really. I'm a researcher, not an interrogator.'

The yellow junk really perks me up. I wonder what it is? I feel really great, maybe better than I've ever felt, and there's this burning feeling inside me, coming from my guts and through my chest, like I want to tell Dr Singh something, something super vital. I want to tell him my life story and the life stories of every single person I know, and all my hopes and dreams and every single one of my secrets. The words try to puff their way out all at the same time but they jam all up in my throat and come out all at once.

All those things, all mixed together, sound a little bit like, 'Trrrrghaaaaaaaaa,' which I scream repeatedly, jolting up against the bonds.

Someone I can't see mutters something about dosages, and another person, an older babe with yellow hair under a hat like a nurse you might see in an old-timey flix, comes over and pats me on the arm and tells me to relax.

'This kind of thing is not usually my business,' Dr Singh says, 'but you made it my business when you ingratiated yourself with my daughter. Who sent you here?'

'Me!' I scream, so excited that he's asked me a specific question and that I get to tell him something, like, finally! Like all my birthdays have come at the same time! 'I sent me, me!'

'Who do you work for?'

'Allnode!' I pant at him and to everyone who might want to listen, because wow, shiz, they just have to know! 'I have a job in Logistics! My employee number is 2702575. I'm assigned to warehouse crew D7-328, resource location. . .'

'How did you come into contact with Rowena Singh?'

'Luck, hey!' I gush at him, 'Isn't that rad? Rowe's so great, huh? But I think she hates me because I'm using her. Not even intentionally, it just happened, right? I never meant to, but when I realised I could I was gunna. That's bad isn't it? Rowe doesn't deserve that. She looks like a cluster of data-cables, don't you think? But, shiz, don't tell her I said that because it sounds, like, kind of offensive, yeah? But it's not in a bad way, like a really beautiful cluster of cables.' I bellow and thrum against the straps because it's so hard to get out what I really mean and I feel like if I just keep talking and talking and talking, I'll be able to say it. 'Nice cables!'

Singh looks puzzled, and he takes a step back. 'Is she having a reaction to the Certiburinex?'

'Her levels seem normal, Dr Singh.'

'Have you ever been in the employ of Euphrates?'

'No!'

'Pharmaglot?'

'No!'

'Are you here on behalf of the Central Bureau?'

'Nuh!'

'Are you sending dispatches to anyone with information about Allnode, or Psynode?'

'My friend, Cam, when we can get a sec line in,' I pant.

'Is Cam in the employ of any of the previously mentioned companies?'

'Nah, shiz, he's like, twelve!'

'Anyone else?'

'Some punks in a drain. I don't know how they can help me, but. They got their own shiz going on.'

He peers down at me. 'Why are you here, Ms Mahoney?'

'I'm here to find Vu, my friend Adeline Vu, I'm pretty sure they brought her here, and it's not that I love her, okay, maybe I like-like her, but she doesn't deserve to end up some speriment or Soylent or anything, and I just wanna take her home, and it's not like we have a home, right, but we could try and make one, ya know?' I feel every muscle in my body strain and all the veins in my face close to popping as I grind against the straps. 'Ya know?'

I scream to Dr Singh, because he's gotta know.

Singh looks at me, disgusted, and I peal with tappy jolts of shame 'cause I just wanna give him what he wants, but I can't.

'This is personal?' he says, snapping off his gloves and chucking them in the bin.

'They took my main babe away, Singh-y!' I shout in a dull roar. 'It don't get more personal than that, right? They sold her like she was a chunk of bloodsy horsemeat, and you bought her! Her whole life, jerks like you in big bloody corps have just been buying and selling her! And me too! Me!'

'This is a waste of my time,' Dr Singh says, his voice fading out as he walks away. I can just hear him as he opens the door. 'Put her into storage. Erase her file.'

'Howdja feel if they did that to Rowe?' I scream after him, my voice shredding at the end.

There's not even a pause in his step as he keeps on walking away.

Yellow-hair nurse leans over me again.

'You came here to find your friend?'

'Yes!' I scream. 'And it was all for fuck-nothing but it was worth it!'

She plugs something into the tube to my neck, looking right into me. Her eyes are different from Dr Singh's, different even from when she first jammed me.

'Would you do it again if you knew it would end like this?'

The secret-bursting feeling fades away, replaced by a sharp, sober clarity. I wonder what they're filling me with this time?

'I dunno. Probably,' I tell her, the words rasping up against my throat. 'I think she woulda done the same for me. I hope so, anyway.'

I remember Lacey telling me that they crop out all your

memories for their experience sims before the one-way to storage. Is that what they're prepping me for now? The nurse fiddles with my straps, and the pressure on my limbs eases just a little. Mems fire in my mind's-eye, rapid, just in case this is it. I wanna feel 'em one more time.

The fuzzy mum and the dad, kind eyes and soft hair, and the hum of love in the places around a tiny blobber me.

The hard lines and hard eyes and seepy wet-pants feel when I pulled up to my first corp house.

The hair-mouth and sweaty tangle of my first cuddle party in a late-night corp dorm.

The first time I took a took a broken plug apart and put it back together and it worked; the sweet, warm pride bubbling all over me and the way the Uncle on duty told me to wipe the smile off my face, and I did, but he couldn't get to the smile inside.

Lonely nights in Time Out cells, regret and defiance brimming over.

Crowded early mornings in the bathrooms in the twisted limbs of friends: showing kindness with tongues and lips and bits.

How big the night sky was when I got released from Verity House, the way the stars went up and out and deep-away and how I coulda jumped the train and been in the city in a flash, but I just kept walking, just kept looking up and feeling everything inside me expanding out into freedom, feeling so small and so big all at the same time.

The way that big, free feeling sucked back into me as the shuttle came through the Nodeplex gate and it slammed closed behind me like another prison.

Nurse-features leans down real close and whispers in my ear. 'Storage is on sub-level fifteen.' She slides a single sterile wrapped scalpel into my hand. 'Your chip'll have to come out. It will track you and the sig it gives out will block access if they code it to.'

I nod, just slightly.

'They took Steveo away and I just let them,' Nursey says. 'I always wish I'd done something.'

She leaves without a single look back.

The strap round my right wrist – it's loose enough to slip through.

—

I've thought about slicing myself before. You know, when stuff hurt. It's the same kind of thing as making a tattoo isn't it? Pain to match up the pain inside, a mark left to nurse and care for, to remind me. But I never could. I'd see my arm there, all soft and brown and innocent and I'd be unable to open it.

This time, though, I dive right in.

The chip isn't far underneath, but it's hard to find and slippery when I try to take a hold of it with my clumsy fingers. So instead, I slip the tip of the blade underneath it and jimmy it slowly, until it gives and flies out of the hole I've made, spattering red drops as it arcs across the room and pings on the floor somewhere in the corner. I'm bleeding a little crazy, but there's gauze in a rack by the door, so I stuff a pile of that on and tape it down as best I can. The white gauze turns red-red. There's a painful throb there, but it feels far away. I ignore it. There's more important shiz to think about.

Now: I gotta make my way underground. Sub-level fifteen. But how? Can I shifty it through the aircon tunnels to the lift shaft?

The only ventilation grate in this room is in the ceiling and while there's a bunch of shiz I could pile up to reach it, I can't see myself twisting the screws open and getting inside without copping a big, clattery tumble and bringing a crowd running, half with snoozy-time drugs, the other half with AKs or whatever.

I pad-pad-pad across the tiles, and open the door heaps careful, just enough to pop an eye out. The hallway's clear so I skippity-jump out and fly along it, feet tangling in my long PJs. There are lots of doors along the white hallway, all unmarked, and I reckon they're all in use for some shady purp, so I ignore them. Finally, by the elevator, there's a door with a sign on it: maintenance.

That's my jam! It's not locked. Inside there's the usual armoury of cleaning junk, but there's a couple of smoky-grey coverall uniforms hanging from the back of the doors too, and after I strip and slip into one, I also find a toolbelt that I sling around my waist. I tuck my hair under an Allnode-branded cap and my disguise is complete. Cunning as!

I'm not sure what the nurse slipped me, but whatever it is, it makes me feel sharp as a diamond-tipped drill, and fearless too, every muscle seething with potential. She musta knew I'd need more than just my wit and natural charm to make it through this. After all, I'm not just posing some radtacular escape, I'm going deeper inside.

There's no link from the cleaning closet to the vent system, so I casually amble out the door to the elevator. It's the usual Psynode kind, with no buttons, just a slim reader for chips by the door. When I hear footsteps coming along the hall, I yank out a screwdriver and wave it in the general direction of the lift. The steps pass behind me and on down the hall and I'm midway into my giant sigh of relief when a husky voice pipes up.

'Ah, where are your shoes?'

Shiz.

I look down and yeah, my bare feet poke from the folded-over hems of the coverall. This is just like some lame flix where the whole plan comes undone from some stupid little thing that the protag totally should have noticed before. Fugg me, I'm so basic. I look up and there's this babe in a labcoat, eyeing me.

'Can I read your ident?' she asks, coming over.

'Nah,' I say and everything that happens next just flows like choreography.

She goes to cry out when I come towards her, but I'm too quick. I slap a hand over her mouth at the same time as I sweep around and get her in a tight headlock. She's small and slender so it's easy to just haul her up off the ground. It's only a few steps to the maintenance cupboard and once we're in I yank up a roll of ducto-tape and wind it around her mouth a few times as she strugs hard, giving her all because I could be anyone, right? She doesn't know that I don't want to do this. She gave a high yelp when I first took my hand off her mouth, but she's quieter when the tape goes round, little mouth-noises muffled. I fix her hands behind her back, then I push her, face-first, into the ground, sit on her and tape up her feet.

'I'm so, so sorry about this, babe. I don't normally kick it with the impromptu non-consensual bondage, but it's important. I promise I won't hurt you.'

She thrums under me, muffled screams grinding up through the tape. I pull her legs up to her hands and hogtie her, looping the tape round and round and ripping off the end with my teeth.

Her eyes, looking up at me, are all mad fear, rimming with tears.

Then, I get an idea. It's not a good idea. It's an awful idea, but it might work.

'Do you have access to sub-level fifteen? Please tell me the truth.'

She is still for a second, like she's frantically running through her options. Then, slowly, she nods.

So I come at her with the scalpel.

—

Getting my own chip out was tough, and I was a cooperative patient.

This babe isn't.

And I get it, I really do. If some mysterious jerk trussed me up then dug in my wrist with an already bloody scalpel, you wanna bet I'd be fighting her as hard as I could. I tell her this all before I make the first cut but it don't make any difference.

'. . .and I had a full path panel before I came here, so I'm clean, don't worry about the scalpel. And just think, as soon as you wriggle outta this, you can jam it right to the medbay for a nice hot-shot of anti-bios and the best painkillers that Psynode has to offer!' I say as I try and lever the chip out of her wrist, being as gentle and careful as I can be on someone who's fighting me as hard as they can. Finally, it pops out and flicks across the room and I leap off her and chase after it so I don't lose it.

She looks at me, all agony and fear and I feel a deep pang of shame because I know she's probs gonna be living this trauma for the next bunch of years, maybe forever, and I'm responsible for that. I get down to her level and look her in the eyes.

'I'm sorry I did this to you.'

She won't look at me. I don't deserve her forgiveness anyway. Doing something awful to someone just because you think it's justified doesn't make it better, because every person probably feels like all the terrible stuff they do is justified, don't they? Like when an Auntie or Uncle in a corp takes a bat to a kid's foot in the naughty chair, they go home and think 'I was just doing my job, hey?', and all the scienticians hard at work fugging with Vu's brain, they're probably saying, 'I'm just an employee here, following orders.' When I try to explain this away to myself later, *I'll* be all like, 'I was just trying to save Vu, yeah?' and that's the same thing, so basically I'm a total fucking monster. Ugh.

I reach around the back of her and put the scalpel in her hand. 'You don't owe me or anything, but can you just give me ten minutes before you cut yourself out, please?'

The look on her face tells me that she's not thinking, 'Yeah, no problem.'

I'm about to head out the door when I notice my hands covered in her tacky blood, so I go to the sink and give myself a quick rinse. I can hear her struggling behind me even over the sound of the running water, but as I dry my hands off on my coveralls, she goes quiet. I turn around and she's right there, tapes deftly sliced through and she she's got this fierce look on her face.

'Shiz, I thought you'd take longer than that. You done this before?' I say to her.

And then I feel a sharp little zing against my belly.

Ever see a thing that your brain can't make sense of? I once saw a kid get his arm jammed in a broken washer that sprung to life while he was fixing it. My mind just couldn't fathom the new bends in his wrist. This is kinda like that. Like, I know that there's a blue plastic-handled scalpel sticking out of my guts because I can see it just fine, see the instant spill of blood go down the front of the coverall, but it takes a few good seconds for me to brain it properly, and think about what it means for my immediate future and what-not. A few seconds doesn't sound like much, but when you're punctured in the belly, and gushing a bloody slick down your pants, it's probably too long. I look up at her and she's all wide-eyed and shocked like she can't quite believe that she's done it, but also a little bit triumphant, because, after all, she's just incapacitated the monster who trussed her up for a little impromptu surgery.

'Good for you, babe,' I say, as I puddle onto the floor.

She's on her way to the door and I'm a pile on the floor in a slowly-spreading pool of red, and I know I'm toast if she gets out, but I don't have the strength to stop her, not physically, anyway. All I have is my winning personality, so I guess I'm totally buggered.

'Please don't!' I say, and she pauses. 'I'm sorry I hurt you. I'm just trying to get to storage. I'm just trying to save my friend.'

She's got her hand on the door handle, smearing blood all over it, but she hangs there. 'If your friend's in storage you won't be able to save her.'

'Why not?'

'No one comes back from storage. They're wired in.'

'What does that mean?'

'You're really here just to save your friend?'

'Yes. Her name is Vu. Adeline Vu. Have you seen her?'

She snorts. 'Trying to find one person in storage is like trying to find a speck of sand on a beach.'

I groan and roll a bit, feeling another hot gush of blood glug out from my gut.

'Can you help me?'

'Ha! Why would I help you?'

'I dunno. 'Cause it's the right thing to do?'

'Was it right to slice the chip out of my arm?'

'Probably not.'

'Well, there's your answer.'

'Yeah, that's fair.'

She bolts out the door and I can't blame her 'cause if it was me, I'd be doing the same. If it was the other way round I woulda given her a good boot in the ribs before I went, too.

There's one thing though – I take my hand off the hole in me and press my other hand into it. Curled in my slick hand is her chip.

I can still do this.

—

There's only one way to do this now, and it's slash-and-burn style. There's no other way for it. I'm fucked, glugging blood like crazy, splattering a trail from the maintenance cupboard to the lift, but now I've got the chip, so the door slides open for me, a happy welcome. I slap the button for sub-level fifteen, leaving a red smear on the plate, then slip over in my own blood and clunk on to the floor. I mean, I was gonna sit down anyway, so it's cool, but the jolt stings like a biatch and knocks free the bundle of oily rags I've pressed to my gut wound, a dual measure that soaks up the blood and might even give me a nice infection that I probably won't even survive to enjoy because I might just bleed out right here on this elevator floor.

The lift falls fast and then clunks to a stop halfway between levels fourteen and fifteen. The little box goes black for a sec, which jolts my heart and sets it racing, the blood speeding up its pour out of my gut. Then the light lifts to a low red and an alarm begins to blare.

That's for me.

It's no big surprise.

First, the gut-hole. I'm glad I slung the toolbelt around my now blood-soaked pelvis, 'cause it's full of handy shiz, like the tube of medglue in a little pouch on my hip. I open the coverall down to my belly-button and do my best to mop up the area. How does so much blood come outta one little opening? I peer into it for a second, the brown skin split deep, before the whole thing wells with blood again. In a different place and predicament, I mighta sat here, doing a little study of my innards, but this is neither the time or place. I sop up the blood around the wound once more, glop most of the tiny tube in and around the split, then do my best to hold it together. After a few tense minutes, success! Look at me, no longer pouring my lifeblood out on the floor. I feel practically med-trained right now.

Now I've got that pesky bleeding problem sorted, I yank a flat-head screwdriver out of the toolbelt and work the door. Bit by bit it opens. I get my hands in between the doors and pull them apart to reveal a slit of sub-level fifteen. Is it Mirii-sized? Only one way to find out. I wriggle forward and pop my head through, but the floor of the lift is only a little bit below the roof, so I change tack and spin around, sliding my feet through and shuffling back until my legs dangle down towards the floor. It's a tight fit, but once I pop my bum out, the rest of me slithers over the ledge and I even land on my feet.

There's just one door off the lift lobby, which is a boxy-type stark white space that I mar with sticky, bloody footprints as I cross it. My heart thuds in my chest, a deep, slammy thump like the time Evan Alvarez climbed into a dryer in the Blacktown corp and Sian Middlestein shut the door on him and turned it on. The pain in my wrist and my gut falls away and all the fear too. The door looms big as I get closer. I barely notice my hand lift the blood-sticky chip to the reader plate. The little beep is far away, then the slick sliding sound as the door opens. Cool air rushes out to fill up the space around me.

I make a little 'guh' sound and it moves into the space, getting lost. It's the biggest enclosed space I've seen, or the second biggest, after the warehouse. It goes on forever or close enough.

It's the world's sickest warehouse and it is stuffed with grim stock.

It's storage.

—

I keep making the 'guh' sound while my numb feet carry me to the first row, the first of many from floor to high ceiling. The bodies hang from racks like suits in a dry-cleaners, like fruit on a tree. Their oval plastic sacks are clear enough to just see through, see their faces. I grab at the one closest, feel the plastic give a little under my hand. I think it's a she, but it's hard to tell. She's hairless and a thick cluster of cords thrusts down from a connector at the top of her bag and into her head, *right into her fucking head*, through some kind of metal connector or seal.

She looks peaceful. I don't think she's there any more, you know?

So it makes even less sense when I fumble at my toolbelt and pull out the first sharpish thing I find, then thrust it in through the side of the bag. Just seeing her in there, it's so wrong that my first instinct is to just get her out. The need fills me up, bursts out my sides, spills over.

The plastic repels me, but I push harder and scream like that's gonna give me the strength to break it. For some reason it does. The Phillips-head pops through. There's a hideous ripping sound and then the stuff inside, this warm, thick gel, bursts forth and flows out over my feet.

I didn't think this through.

She pulls out of her curled up fetal-pos in her warm tummy-sack as the gel empties out. The plastic sucks tight to her skin and she's hanging, hanging limp from those wires that connect her to the top of the bag, that snake out through the opening at the top and away to the next and the next and the next.

'No, no, no,' I say and try to hold her up, the floppy weight of her, but she's slick with the fluid and keeps slipping. The whole row groans and creaks with the weight of her and just as I think she's gonna bring it all down, there's a loud tearing as the cords break away from her skull and she slumps to the floor, taking me with her.

I hold my hand over the hole in her head, trying to staunch the flow of hot blood and fluid.

'No, no, no,' I moan at her. 'I'm sorry, I'm sorry.'

I didn't think it through.

Her eyes open for a sec before she goes. They blink up and out, but past me. Her mouth moves gently around the tubes thrust between. She doesn't know I'm here. She's not there. And then she's really not there because those empty eyes close and all the wishing and regret on my part doesn't stop her from dying right there in my arms.

And the only safe thing I can think to bind up these hot, flarey feelings, is that maybe she wasn't really alive before I killed her anyway.

—

I've always felt like a bit of a product, as much as I've tried to fight it.

Like a thing and not a person, maybe a cog or wheel that keeps something turning inside something else. A part, easily replaced when I'm worn out.

Everyone is just a little superfluous bit of a bigger machine, and whatever it is we're churning out isn't for us, doesn't benefit any of the parts.

I mean, I don't feel this way in myself. Not to my friends, all the other cogs and wheels.

But to the ones in charge, their faces always changing but who always stay the same, I know that's all I am to them.

And this room.

This room is what happens when that notion, that a person is just a product or the sum of their labour or whatever, reaches its supermax conclusion.

This is the pinnacle of that process.

This room.

This is what happens when people aren't people no more, when they're just cogs.

But these poor babes aren't even cogs. They're less still.

They're things. They're expendable.

They're stock.

—

Time gets stretchy.

Things come to me in bursts like some kind of flashback, but it's happening in real-time. Black, black, then I'm sifting madly through the bags like I'm cruising the racks at a recyc store looking for a pair of jeans that fit both my limited price-range and my round bum, but not, 'cause I guess I'm looking for Vu's deep-set eyes and smooth, round face but all the faces look the same through the thickness of the goo and they're not like hers, not like hers.

I want her to be here, but I really, really don't.

Now, black.

Now: panting against the warm plastic for a sec, the face inside floating next to mine, and the gauze has come off my wrist, the wound opening again, so there's blood dripping onto the floor and smearing against the sack. Black. Black.

And, staring up at the racks and racks that back-and-forth up to the ceiling and think how Vu could be up there, could be any-where, and this is pointless.

Black with flashing lights.

Black, black.

More clarity, and this time, my fuggy brain clears and I'm like, *shit, I gotta get out of here.* Gotta wade through this panic and horror and up the other side. I'm like, even if she's here, there's no point. Even though this isn't a life at all, it's better than if I killed her trying to get her out. It's something. I'd know her heart's still beating, even if her brain's not in it.

Then I hear the soft, faraway sound of the lift opening and the clatter of boots in the hall, and I know I'm boned, utterly boned, so I do the only thing I can. I'm really good at it, now. The racks holding the pods are perfect for it.

I climb.

DAY SEVEN

A faraway bang twirls through the giant space as they open fire. The first bag by my reaching hand bursts and empties out, the poor fugger inside dangling for a sick second, then falling all the way to the floor in a gush of gel and blood, and two more land below with wet thumps just after.

'No!' I bellow, looking down. 'Don't shoot them!'

They smart-up to what they're doing, damaging the stock and all that, do the sums of what a whole bagged body might equate to in docked pay, so they all sling their guns and the head dude gestures that the biggest bru should start up after me.

He slips off his night-vis rig and looks up, then back at head dude, who screams at him to follow.

'Fuck,' I say and haul myself up higher.

I don't know what I'm climbing to. Just away? To my own death? He's after me, there's nowhere else to go, and my brain is just pushing my body up to the furthest point away from their shiny barrels.

He's below, puffing. I'm lighter and can climb fast, but it's not easy pulling myself up. I've got the skillz from monkeying around on the warehouse frame, but I'm gut-stabbed and woozing, still a bit flashy from all this new bullshit trauma I'm trying to brain. He's got muscle-arms toned from brainless hours and reps in the company gyms, no doubt, and he's gaining. Every time I look down, I lose precious height and seconds, and the span 'tween me and the ground makes my heart skip-trip.

He gains.

My breath comes out in raggy chunks and I watch my blue-lit hands grip the next rung, the next. I can feel the frame rocking with his weight, hear his grunting getting louder. My arms are screaming as I pull myself up to the eighth level, dead-slow and my lungs fry between my ribs. I can feel the slow trickle of my gut-blood moving down in the gap between the coverall and my legs, a drippy tickle off my toes. My head hangs limp against my raised-up arms for a second, just a tiny little rest, and then I look up. I'm almost to the top. Two more levels, two more cool rungs to grip between my shaky hands, and above that, the smooth surface of the roof.

And nowhere left to go.

The grip on my ankle comes quick. It's strong, it's so much stronger than I am, but from somewhere I draw up the last of what I have, hook my elbow around the steel frame, hang on tight and use my free leg to kick, blind and screaming. I use all the rage I have to power me 'cause I've spent everything else. My bare heel hits and splits flesh, there's a surprised grunt and a gargle of a blood-filled mouth. The grip on my foot is still tight, then an immense weight pulls at it.

He's fallen.

The hold around my leg the only thing between him and air.

And the floor.

It all happens in half a second, but seconds can stretch sometimes.

I wail with the pain of his weight and mine, the cut into my tender elbow flesh as the joint and the pulled skin take all my weight, and his too. I look down my bloody coverall, down to the hand on my leg, the fingers blood-covered and tattooed underneath. His eyes boring into me, pleady.

I know those eyes. From where?

It's only after his grip starts to slip on the fresh blood dripping down my leg, after he realises that it's happening and tries to hang on, and after it's pointless and I feel his hand glide the last few centimetres past the point of holy fugg, and the weight and pressure eases as he drops, slow and fast at the same time. . .

And after I hear the sick thud as he crashes to the ground and I wince but still feel the relief course through me because I'm still alive, still!

After that, I remember where I know him from.

Tane.

Tane, who worked in sec and tattooed for extra change of an evening. Whose mum taught him the trade, who was gonna teach me if I wanted. With his kind eyes and his huge body and his strong arms, strong enough to hold on to me after losing his grip on the frame.

Just a dude, doing his job. A nice dude, following orders, and now he's smooshed flat on the ground, probs dead or if not, wishing he was.

And I feel even sicker as the debt of my collateral builds.

I pull myself to the top of the racks and roll over for a second on the grating, lying between two big bundles of cables and tubes. The rough metal cuts into my back, and a big yelpy cry pulls up out of my throat. What's the point of trying to save someone if in the process, you just destroy all these others? I'm a monster, a fucking monster.

I roll back over and pull myself up to the lip of the grating, look down through the soft-lit baggies and their grim yolk and for a second a thought flashes in my brain-eye.

Just a tiny little movement. A quick roll, a long drop.

I could pretend to myself that I'd never thought a thought like this before, but that'd be a big falsey. Even those times where I was totally brimming with hot defiance, and the urge to live exploding in my heart and guts, to live for me, or for anyone else, or even just for spite, a quiet voice sometimes piped up. As much as I'd try to stuff it down and cover it with hopey bullshit, it was there, is there.

No more cold sweat and trembles in the mornings. No more getting set to 'stun' every time I walk into a white room, or flash-backs of red blood filling up grimy tile-grout. No more being bought and sold. No more watching my friends bought and sold away from me. No more crowded dorms or dosshouses. I wouldn't have to sell my youth, or my labour, or my pixelated webcammed-ass to the lowest bidder, just to keep my guts full and my head under a roof. It could all just be over so easy.

Roll.

Splat.

So easy.

—

I even scared myself there for a second.

The drop goes all elastic in my view and I roll over onto my back.

Like, it would be even worse to top meself now, 'cause then I'd never have a chance to make up for all the terrible things I've done here. So it's settled.

No rolly-splat.

But every time I blink I see Tane's face in the spot behind my eyes, that look of doom and shock all juxtaposed, so I concentrate really hard on keeping my eyes wide open and they water as I scan the ceiling for a vent, an aircon tube, a power supply access point, any kind of opening. . .I can hate myself later. There'll be time for that, if I can make it out.

There. Six or so rows over, two or three across, a little rectangular seam in the ceiling. I peer down at the crew of sec dudes clustered around the horrible jumbled shape on the ground and then I careful-pick my way across to it, fumbling in my toolbelt for whatever's survived my mad scramble. I've got a flat-head screwdriver and I almost lose my guts when I see that the screws are for a Phillips-head. Mine is still somewhere on the floor, floating in a pool of egg-whitey gel. My brain goes a bit whomp-whomp for a sec. I try to shake away the mem and the feel of that babe dying in my hands, and I almost drop the driver. When I get past the horror again, I look closer and the screws have that long bit in the head that means my flattie will fit, but I can barely get the driver into the screw, I'm shaking so bad.

'Don't you dare, you little shit,' comes a gruff voice from below and it spurs me into action. I've got three of the four screws out before they decide to send another bru up after me, despite his protests. When I twist out the last screw the cover clatters down to the ground, and I look up into the space as the racks start to shake with the weight of sec bru number two, who I really bloody hope I don't kill as well, hey.

The void is stuffed full of wires and cables, but I pull them aside to make room, and I reckon there's just enough space to fit in through the opening, though it's gonna be a squeeze. It's too dark to see if it even leads anywhere, but it's my only option aside from capture or the old 'splat', so I take it.

I tell you what, sometimes I get so tired of all my options being bullshit.

—

As I wriggle through the cramped, cabled space, I know I'm safe for the moment. There's no way anyone bigger than me is gonna get in here. I barely fit in here. I'm ripping cords out left and right, and it feels like this data tube is endless. The torch I grabbed from my belt is clamped between my teeth and strings of drool pour down my chin around it.

I try to brain how long the storage room is, how far I might need to thresh through this, but it's too hard to do the distance maths. I'm getting woozy. I reckon I've lost a buncha blood by now, and I feel like I can't breathe in here. For a sec it feels like the metal case is closing in on me, and I start to flip out a bit.

Breathe, Miz, breathe, I tell myself. The torch in my mouth feels like it's expanding, choking me, hitting my gag reflex even though it's only just past my teeth. I spit it out and things go dark. The black edges of the tube go white and I'm thinking, *shiz, not now, not now.*

I sift back through the images in my brain-eye, tryna think of something calm, and right.

There, that's it.

I'm at Elton's on a cold, rainy night, my hair's still drying from the walk over from Mrs P's. He's let me play with a PC he's building from ancient parts. I watch my hands fiddle with the bits, join the clips to each other, knowing that I've got it, hoping that I won't let him down. And I don't. I'm good at this. There's a Nutrobar in my pocket that I take little nibs from now and then, and a super-large takeaway cup of synth-swill coffee from the 'Trix, still hot, on the bench in front. I've got a date later on with a babe I met out the front of the dumpling stall on my way in. It's so simple, and good, and I'm grinning ear-to-ear.

It's two days before I put my app in for Allnode.

It's the last time I really felt free.

My breathing is normal again. I know I can do this. I put the torch back in my mouth and the way ahead is lit with yellow light again. I make a promise to myself to just go as far as the light shows me, to the furthest cable-tie along that I can see. I count them, one, two, three. When I get there, I make the same promise again.

I don't know how long I play this game. It feels like ages and ages and it probably is. But when I lift my head the last time, and see the tube end ahead of me, I almost hurl with relief. Maybe it's just the end of the tunnel, maybe the cords just snake away through an opening I won't be able to get through, but it's something.

It's not a dead end, but. There's an access door with an opener and everything. I need to use all the strength I got left to lift it open, and it groans like a teener getting dragged out of bed for an early morning shift, but pop, there it goes. I tumble out and into a small, LED-lit room.

I'm not expecting to see anything, but what I do see makes my eyes bug and my mouth flap open and closed.

About twenty babes and brus, balaclava-ed and dressed like it's the end of the world, because maybe it is, and every one of 'em has a weapon lifted or pointed in my direction.

'What's up?' I ask them, putting my hands up high, but then I'm melting through the ground as the world warps and white-whitewhite spills from the corners of my eyes and over everything.

—

'Miz?'

'What?' I say, but my mouth is thick and pasty and I'm not sure it comes out sounding like anything at all.

'Mirii, can you hear me?'

'Well, this buggers up everything, doesn't it?'

'Shut up, Tat! Give us a hand here, willya?'

'Don't move her!'

'Is she gunna die?' That voice. Jug-ears. Freckles.

The stars.

Am I going to die?

'Where's the blood coming from?'

'We don't have time for this! Comms say the security forces are massing on the ground floor.'

'I don't know if I can help her!'

'You're a med student! Do something!'

'I'm a first year!'

'This is a disaster. I'm calling it. Time to get the truck outta here.'

'You're not in charge!'

'Someone needs to make a decision! In about five minutes there'll be fifty Allnode rentacoppers up our bums. We've gotta haul.'

'I dunno if we can move Mirii.'

'Then we leave her.'

'No fucking way!'

'No!'

Freckles.

I find my voice again. The world comes back a bit, and I can just make them all out. Rowe and Lacey, bent over me. Cam, cradling my head, his little doofus face all crumpled up and pleading. Sticks hovering, jangling. Then Tat, and the others I don't know, clustered above me, looking vicious and, underneath it all, scared.

Everyone's so scared. Not just now, but all the time.

Except me.

In this floaty, coming-back-from-passing-out place I'm really peaceful. It's nice not to feel the fear, for once. Too bad it took getting gut-stabbed to get me here, but while I'm here I might as well enjoy it.

'Stop talking about me like I'm not here,' I say, and sit up, groaning.

'Oh Mirii, we're in the shiz,' Cam says, helping me to my feet which feel weird and fuzzy and faraway.

'Cam, why are you here?'

'We couldn't leave Rowe.'

'You told us not to leave her,' Sticksy says, and Cam nods in serious agreement, like we'd signed a contract in triplicate or something.

'And Lacey, how'dja get here? Are you okay?'

'I'll need to take a few days in bed after this, but I had to come. I know the security cam sys layout by heart, and I usually just relay it to 'em, but I wanted to make sure Rowe would be okay.'

'Mirii, you've lost a lot of blood. I should try to contact my father, he might help us,' Rowe says, steadying me with a red, sticky hand.

'Ya dad's already on his way,' Tat says. 'He's meeting us in the lab on the other side of that wall. It's being repurposed so the camera system isn't up.'

'What?' Rowe says. 'Why?'

'For the trade. You and her for our people.'

'I did not agree to that!' Rowe says, her voice all shrill. 'You promised you'd work with me to find a resolution.'

Lacey looks at Rowe, then me and Cam and Sticks. 'I didn't know about this, I swear. They didn't discuss this with me!'

A snort. Tat.

'Too late. It's done. Why do ya think we're in this building? Bloody hell, Lacey, you can be so naive sometimes. Must be all the drugs.'

I sense Lacey stiffen, and even from dreamy-land, I can tell this is a low blow.

'I thought we came here for Mirii?' she says, all uncertain, like now that she thinks about it, why would they?

'Why would they?' I say.

Tat snorts again. That sound! It pulls me all the way up and out of my lull. It grates against everything, and I want to grab them and shake them. I grip Lacey's hand real gentle in mine.

There's nothing for it. Where are we gonna go anyway? We're hemmed in, with rentacops on one side and Dr Singh on the other. Between a doc and a rifle-butt to the face.

'It's okay,' I say to Rowe and Lacey. 'There's nowhere else to go. We'll go with them. Just take Cam and Sticks with you, Lace. Get 'em out of here.'

'No,' Rowe says to me. 'No,' she says again to the rest of the room. She raises up to her full height, like a butterfly unfurling out of a chrysalis, but the cycle is in reverse, from a soft butterfly into a spiky caterpillar. She looks so mighty, her face lit in all the wrong places by the LED light, hands and that awful sack-shirt streaked with my blood. She's so different from when I first met her, but the same too. Her face looks older, like all the things she's realised and seen have sucked some of the kid out of her.

'If you do this, you're as bad as they are. As he is!' Her voice goes trembly on the last bit. She knows. Maybe they even showed her the feed of storage. That'd be enough to quake the base of anyone. I wonder if she's reeling?

She takes my hand, and Lacey's too and I grab hold of Cam and he grabs Sticksy's and my blood is sticky on Rowe's fingers, then she's moving across the little room, and she pulls us with her. The babes and brus part like she's a big rock dropped into a little stream. They don't say nothing, 'cause they've got the look on their faces like they know this has already gone too far.

We're almost at the door when Tat lifts the gun, and aims it right at Rowe's head.

—

Everything freezes.

The gun is one of them three-dee printed numbers, done up in blue plastic, the kind everyone has. It looks silly pointed up at Rowe's head, and I'm this close to letting a big snicker out, because jeez, I'm always laughing at the wrong time, but I hold it, 'cause I don't want my snorting to be the thing that makes Tat's finger slip. It looks dumb and shoddy but it'll get the job done.

Rowe's grip on my hand gets tighter, and on her other side, I see Lacey wince as the grip on hers does too.

'If you do this, you'll have nothing. My father will find you and send you to prison, I can guarantee that. He's got reach you can't even imagine.'

'Eat shit, rich bitch.'

'Tat, give it up,' a dude with ultra-gross blond dreadies says, scratching the back of his neck. 'This isn't right. I think if we put it to vote right now, consensus will be that we abort.'

In the low light, everyone nods, murmurs.

'I can't! Trala! I need her back! I fucking love her!' Tat doesn't budge. A vein pulses above their right eye.

'If everything you've said about my father is true, you know you won't get your friend back.'

A chick with a red buzzcut puts a hand on Tat's arm.

'We miss Trala too,' she says, gentle. 'But this isn't going to work. We gotta scramble. We'll find another way.'

'We're so close,' Tat says, but with a shade over their voice like they know it's true.

The gun inches down.

I can just make out the sound of radio through a set of head-phones. The dreadie dude listens, looking vacant-eyed, then he comes to quick-smart.

'Looks like there's been a breakout from the containment areas in one of the labs, they must'a used the commotion and the alarms as an instigator. The rentacoppers are diverting forces. I say we skedaddle, right now.'

The look in Tat's eyes is pure rancid hatred, but the gun comes down.

'Right-o,' Dreadies says, giving his ear a scratch. 'Out the west door, up the fire stairs, across the way to the hole in the fence. Keep low, move fast.'

'Us as well?' Cam asks, and Lacey scrunches up her brow.

'I guess. Where else are ya gunna go?'

'I'm coming too.' Rowe's got the blaze in her eyes still, but it's spilling out little by little, in eyeliner-black tears and in the way she's bowing down and in from the shoulders. There's something so sad about a very tall person slouching like that, trying to disappear into themselves when there's just so much of them and no place to hide.

'Rowe, are you sure?' I ask her. 'What if something happens? We could get caught. Ya dad is just there, you could go distract him or something. Send him in the other direction or something sneako like that. Then you could go home.'

'And what then? Just go back to school and work and parties like nothing's changed? Act like I don't know what he's done?'

'But you'll be safe.'

'No one's safe from him. There's so much you don't know. My mum. . .'

She doesn't finish and we don't press her.

Lacey takes Rowe's arm and wraps in under her shoulders. 'I'm gonna need help to get out, Rowe. Cam and Sticks have to help Mirii. You can come to my place. It's no Barangaroo, but it's not so bad for a hole in the ground, hey? You can keep an eye on your Pops from there and figure out what to do.'

Rowe hiccups and nods and Cam and Sticks take a pos at each of my shoulders.

We watch the dude on point open the door a nanometre at a time. When he sees it's clear, he gives us a wave and everyone flows forward and out all smooth and quiet, like they've got a bunch of experience sneaking through places they don't belong.

The only sounds in the stairwell are the trippy thump of rubber-soled shoes on the cement, the huff of people trying to breathe real quiet in an echoey space and soft whispers from Lacey about where the blindspots in the cam sys are.

'To the left, the left!' she whispers, and we all slide quickly from this side to the next, working along the edges of the blindspots. I try to ignore the way my bare feet leave perfect bloody footprints on the tread of every step, prints that look black and oily in the low light.

Don't look at them, Mirii. It's fine. It's a perfectly normal amount of blood, yeah? Just one more flight, then across the way to the fence, then through the fence, then a nice trip home in the back of the bumpy van, then you can get some stitches and maybe a sweet blood transfusion and have a gnarly scar to impress all the babes. Easy peasy.

Dreadies and Ginger Buzzcut stand either side of the door as everyone waits with gleamy-wide eyes in the sick green light of the exit sign.

'We've got no cover from here to the fence,' Lacey tells me. 'But our pos is in the way back of the view so if we go fast, maybe they'll miss us.'

Ginger opens the door real slow. Her eyes bug and she lifts her silly plastic gun up fast, like an instinct or a reflex.

And then her head comes apart in front of us, before we even register the shot.

'Sticks, Cam, run, NOW!'

—

When they saw the blood and what was left of Ginger's head, everyone dropped their weapons real fast, which is why we're lined up against the outside wall instead of dead and littering the stairwell.

I dunno where Cam and Sticks ran to, but the sec brus do a sweep of the stairwell and surrounds, and don't come back dragging them. I bloody hope I haven't sent them into something worse. Then again though, what could be worse than this?

They did my flexcuffs up too tight. It's weird how familiar it feels to be restrained like this. Is that institutionalisation? That the dig of cuffs is kinda like an old friend? Like I always knew I'd end up here, hands behind my back and nothing left to run to. And I feel too, like I deserved this. All the things I've done and people I've hurt trying to get my way, trying to get her back. This is the debt of that, and I deserve to pay it.

Fuck.

Lace is crying and Rowe's got her chin jutted out but her eyes still look scared, and when the head sec dude walks the line of us and looks her up and down, he gets a slammy facial of recognition.

'Ms Hamilton-Singh?'

'Cromley,' she says in her best private-college accent, but with a mad-subtle tremble that she's working double-time to mask. 'I think there's been some mistake. I was just showing my friends from college through daddy's lab. This is just all a terrible mix up. Maybe you should call him?'

Cromley looks us over: me, going green at the edges, barefoot in a blood-drenched maintenance coverall, the collective kids all got up in stealth blacks with their tattooed faces and hands, their taped-up old jungle boots. Rowe, herself, in that now-filthy sack shirt, hands gloved in blood and face smeared with mascara tear-tracks. It's the middle of the night, alarms are wailing, drones are silent-sweeping over the entire Nodeplex, slicing cold white beams of light across the dark bitumen. Nice try, Rowe.

'Wouldn'ta picked you for turnabout. Just wait 'til ya pops hears about this.' He gestures at Rowe with his gun barrel, and she jumps as he booms, 'Lookit, blokes. It's Singh's kid. She's playing for the other side.'

Rowe makes a weird sound in the back of her throat, 'cause it's one thing for her to say she can't abide someone for the terrible things he's done when she's safe and warm and free, but with a gun barrel jammed in her face, I'm pretty sure all she wants is for her dad to come and save her. Shit, don't we all? If old Singhy showed up now, maybe I'd leap into his arms myself.

It starts to rain.

Far off, a siren starts, loud enough to be heard over the drumming rain and the alarm sys. The circular whooping gets closer. That'd be for us. I look over at the fence. It's only five metres away, a little ripple in the links showing the bit where the Collective kids cut a passage through. We were so close. I look back down at my feet going white with the cold, and as I do, there's a flash in the corner of my eye.

A white flash.

There, past the fence. Another.

People. Running, one at a time. Dressed in white hospital-type gowns, flapping heavy and soaked with rain.

The breakout? From the labs?

Go, go, go, I think, 'cause if I gotta be cuffed up against this wall with a rentacopper van bearing down on me, then it makes my heart wither just a little bit less to know that someone else might be free.

Another shape takes off, from right of my vision to left. It looks over to make sure the sec guys aren't watching, and I look at the same time and our eyes meet.

My heart thrums, then stops, then explodes into ten billion starry pieces, swirling like a galaxy inside my chest. Even from this far away, and even through the drumming rain, I'd know that face. I've spent the past six months scanning crowds with that face in my mind's eye.

Vu.

—

Vu.

I shape her name with my mouth at the same time as she shapes 'Mirii' with hers.

She stops.

Her hair is plastered to her face and down her back in soggy black strings. The rain has made her gown all see-through and I notice how the curves of her body that I knew in my brain and hands so well have withered. She's like a ghost but harder, like a vision I've waited too long to see, almost pulsing and glowing and blurred at the edges. I get a flash, a sick and horrible doubt that maybe she's not real, maybe it's just all the blood I've lost. . .

Nah, she's real. If she was just a spectre from my brain and sick body and longing, she'd still look the same. Still chunky with glasses and that silly haircut. Not this sharpened, worked-over shape.

Her face. The look on her face is the same, though.

The sec crew hasn't seen her. Not yet. But all the kids against the wall can make her white-clad form out against the black of the night and the rain, and I know it's just seconds before someone says something or flashes an eye in a way that will alert the guards.

Go, go, go.

Her face is a round mask against the shining black asphalt and it crumples. Her hand comes up a bit, then drops again. She can't reach me. It's like she can hear my thoughts and she knows there's nothing she can do.

She mouths something before she sprints off into the dark. I feel a relief so hard in my guts and bones and muscles as I watch her fade away.

I'm sorry, she said. *I'll find you.*

—

We all get our trial in the van. There's a sick pause while the Judgesys electronically reviews our case and then issues the verdict (guilty, what else?) in a robot voice over the comms. The sentence is ten years apiece, pending affidavit and evidence lodgement, and further review. Everyone sinks, as if we weren't expecting it. I reckon we'll all have an industrial espionage charge tacked on to the criminal trespass, as well as various weapons charges, and maybe some grievous bodily harm and murder for me once the statements are in from the babe in the storeroom and the sec dudes from storage.

The coppers have a duty of care now that I'm in their custody, but they're not happy about it. They begrudgingly stick a bio-patch across my wound and hook me up to a fresh bag of O-neg from their kit. I rise and perk up a bit with the transfer, like it's filling up some huge void inside. But one little bag isn't gonna cut it. I've lost a whole bunch of blood – but even more of something else, something that they can't replace.

No one looks at each other. Lacey's going white with pain, Tat gnashes their teeth and body and soul against everything and everyone. Rowe sits straight-backed, head bowed over to fit beneath the roof, but with a dignity still, and defiance in her eyes, but her bottom lip is trembling. I wonder if she ever saw herself here, and I can't help thinking that she mighta been better off ignorant to it all, happy and oblivious, scarfing down emu taquitos and tripping on synths between classes.

Clipped to the side of the van, everyone's in their own personal hole, and sinking like everything that's happening is digging the floor out from beneath them a bucketload at a time. For every rock-bottom, there's a new strata of stone that can get scraped away. There is no real rock-bottom, just layer upon layer until the top is so high up that you forget it's there.

The one thing that keeps my head from cracking open is the mem of Vu, the way the words shaped on her mouth in that moment when our fates swapped over, my freedom and hers.

I'll find you.

I have to believe that she will.

EPILOGUE

It doesn't stop raining all through processing. Through the slick, grey-painted cinderblock walls I can still hear it thrumming against everything. I can hear it over the metallic clank of doors closing, and the guards bellowing, the wails of prisoners and the hiccup-sniffles of my peers. They separate us, men from the women and the genderless, the slightly-underage from the old-enough-to-know-better. Some navy-clad guard lady rips out my cannula too hard, chucking the empty blood-bag into the bin with a wet sound. She's saying something to me, something probably mean and unnecessary, but I focus on the sound of the rain against the barred windows and I don't hear her.

I hear it hammering against the roof of the van that hustles us from the Pyrmont Street processing centre out into the streets. Through the metal grille I get glimpses of the roadways, but I don't know where they're taking us. It's too hard to make out street signs in the grey haze from the rain. I can't make out anything except the blur of lights passing and the grey-black of night.

I can't see the stars from in here. I'll never be able to get back home.

Lacey huddles as best she can against Rowe, who dips a head down down down to rest in among her hair. We'd all be holding each other, but you can't hug when you're handcuffed to a security rail. We each try to hold ourselves.

There are two voices inside me, polar.

One chants *no, no, no* like a little snotnose dipshit who can't accept this, can't go back inside.

The other just says calmly, *you deserve this.*

No.

You hurt people.

No.

You buggered this for everyone.

No.

YOUR FAULT!

I CAN'T I CAN'T I CAN'T!

YOU!

I try to shake 'em off or shut them up, but they just sink and fade into the background noise like rain. It's hard to tell how long we've been driving because it feels like no time and all of the time. Then there's a pause, and a jolt as we bump over something, and through the grill and the downpour I can just make out the sight of a heavy, barred gate drawing closed.

Prisoncorp.

The crunch it makes as it locks breaks through the hammer of the downpour and echoes through us all.

There's no drowning out that sound.

PRISONCORP

DAY ONE

She's expecting a right, so I telegraph it, then clock her dead centre with a head butt. You know, just to liven things up a bit. A good old Campbelltown kiss. The skin of Freya's forehead cracks like broken glass. She goes down. I stand over her, heaving, bleeding, then I raise my hands up in a V and the crowd goes wild.

By crowd, I mean the two babes in the cell opposite peering through their check window into ours, who scream like feral foxes in the night, and bash on the door so loud it brings the screws.

'What's happened here, prisoner?' the stubbier of the two screws says, looking in through the glass. Freya groans from the floor and sits up.

'Nothing,' we both say, at the same time.

'That's right,' says the other one. 'Hey Maloney, you're out today. Collect your shit and we'll be back for you in ten.'

'Mahoney,' I correct her, but she's already walking away.

I look around the Protective Isolation and Secure Rehabilitation cell. The PISR. There's nothing in it but me, Freya, two foam mattresses, a toilet built into the floor and about a square metre of empty space, just enough for me to kick her arse all over. We don't even get real clothes, just paper drapes with ties in the back. Maybe the screw means to collect my shit metaphorically? I can't see her being that deep. She's probably just being a bastard.

I step over the mattress and glare at Freya, who glares back at me. We've been doing a lot of this. There's not much else to do when you're stuck in a two-by-three metre cell, twenty-three and a half hours a day with your worst enemy. One of them, anyway.

I thought Freya and I might have sorted out our shit in our final showdown just before I left the Orphancorp. I mean, *I* worked through my beef with her in the act of beating her to a pulp, came to a conclusion about the futility of my hatred for her, and like, how it just played into what the system wanted of me. You know, like how we clashed because the whole corp jam was just wiring us to hate each other, a distraction.

Freya, on the other hand, had just been waiting for me to walk through the door of this prison. Like she knew I'd be here some-day, just like I always knew, deep down.

We glare. Sweat moves down my body, turning the paper gown all spongy. We're smack-bang in the middle of a heatwave and these rooms are like tiny ovens, with us stewing inside. I go over to the toilet, the only fresh water in the room besides the ration they give us, already drunk, and I dip my hands in to rinse the blood from my face. Freya's eyes never leave mine, and I don't look away either.

'Oi, screws!' she bellows, still glaring at me. 'What about me?'

'Not you, Ferguson. Now pipe down!'

Freya's eyes are knivesy sharp.

'Perfect Mirii, sliding right out of the PISR after a month.

What special favours did you give the screws for such an easy ride?'

'Didn't you hear 'em, Freya? Pipe down. Who knows why they do what they do?'

We go back to glaring. Freya doesn't wash the blood off her face, and I watch it mix with sweat and run down her face in the heat of the tiny cell. They said ten, but the screws take what I think is a few hours to come get me.

It's hard to tell. There's no clock in here, no proper light, no window to the day. Nothing but Freya and me and the way we hate each other filling up what little space we have left. Not much else but the heat and the sound of our paper gowns crinkling, the toilet dripping and the squeak of our pointless movements across the mattresses. Has it really been a whole month? Has it really only been a month?

Time gets stretchy in here.

—

Seeing as Freya corked me one about ten minutes after I walked in the door, starting a big fight and getting us both thrown in the PISR, I didn't get a chance to acclimatise to my delightful new home. Home is a medium security Corrections Co facility somewhere in the desert, and they let me out just as the sun is rising. I breathe in the warm desert breeze and marvel at the air, and how much I didn't realise I'd missed it in the stuffy box of the isolation cell.

I'm out in general pop, still in my paper gown which rustles around my knees in the hot wind. Maybe a stint in the PISR first up did something good—after that anything is bearable. At least out here there's fresh air. I'm on the edge of a dusty yard, below an enormous brick monstrosity that rises five storeys above me. The PISR must be in there. It acts as a watchtower too, guards patrolling with guns and binoculars on a balcony three storeys up.

I look towards the rows of tents that are our housing. Here in Female General Population, the tents stretch endless, packed dirt paths winding between them. Every spare spot has shanties and box-houses whacked up, leaving only the barest minimum of walking space. What the shit is this? How'm I gonna find Rowe and Lacey in all this? I get panicky and my heart starts to palpitate, glugging hard and wrong in my chest.

No freaking out, Miz. Be methodical. You can do this. I walk across the yard to the first row of tents, seeking calm and breathing slow until my heart stops clunking. Phew. Everything's gonna be okay. I can do this.

Then the bucketful of piss hits me dead in the middle.

'Watch out!' comes a voice from the closest tent and I shake myself off as a chicky waltzes out from behind the flap.

'Shouldn't you say that *before* you dump the bucket, not after?'

'Shut your fucking mouth,' she screams at me.

'Duly noted.'

I shake the wizz off my fingertips and squeeze it out of my gown, which starts to disintegrate in my hands.

Great, just great.

There's a bank of showers at the base of the Block, so I backtrack to them, step inside the closest one and turn the tap. Nothing comes out.

A wrinkly old babe sitting on a flattened box in the shade of the shower block points to the side of the recess. There's a coin slot there.

'You need a token.'

'A token?'

'You need a token,' Wrinkles says again, real slow, pointing at the coin slot.

'Can I scab one off you, then? I'm good for it, I promise.' I am not good for it. I've got nothing, not even a shirt on my back. The screws just dumped me out in the yard. I don't even know where my tent is.

'Go fuck yourself,' she says, and turns away.

Great. Just great.

I've got no idea what to do. I'm covered in wee, my gown is falling off me in clumps so I'm basically naked, and some nasty-looking inmates are eyeing me from a row of tents up front and muttering to each other, even though I've got nothing they can roll me for. I try to blink away the harsh glare of the sun off everything, and the world starts to warg warg, feeling really big, and full, and just so . . . populated, while I'm here, and small, with nothing. For one sick second, I wish I was back in the PISR where it didn't matter, with only Freya's eyes on me and the guards through the visual check window, where the concrete walls kept me relatively safe, and small and contained. I even miss Freya, just for a tiny sec, because I knew we were an even match. The devil you know, ya know?

Shiz.

'Mirii?'

I look around, but I can't see her. 'Rowe?' I call.

'Here!'

There, in the third line. Rowena!

'Mirii!' Rowe is there, tall and skinny as ever, with dark circles around her eyes, deep-set into her angular brown face. She looks different without her red lips, and her hair is longer, just buzzed and not scraped bald. She's got a towel and a pair of clean knickers for me, plus some of the same mint-green scrubs that everyone's wearing, boots slung over her shoulder by the laces, and a little disk in her claw, but she doesn't hand them to me before she takes me in her long spider-arms.

'Don't hug me, Rowe, I'm covered in muck!'

She hands me the token, I slam it into the shower slot and scrub myself as best I can with no bloody soap, which probably costs two bloody tokens. My paper gown comes to pieces in my hands. I haven't showered in a week and it feels like I'm showering off the mess and the PISR the longer I stand under the water. There's nothing quite like being clean after a long stint in the dirt.

'We didn't know how long you'd be in there! Are you okay? You look terrible, did they even feed you?' She hands me the towel. 'Oh Mirii, did the screws beat you?'

It sounds funny, Rowe saying 'screws'.

'Nah, there wasn't much else to do in the PISR besides get into it with Freya.'

'I thought you were in solitary!'

'I was. There's overcrowding though, so it's two or three to a cell.'

'They threw you in for fighting with that girl, then put you in a cell with her? Who is she? Why did she start a fight with you?'

'Riiight?' I say and grab the uniform from her because I'm so down with this happy reunion, but less so because I'm naked. I tell her all about Freya while I dress. '. . . but it was okay, we worked through a lot of our issues in there, you know, hugged it out.'

'Really?'

'No.' I pull the top over my head and my hair soaks the back of it, but I'm dressed, like a real human! No more paper gown or bare skin for me. I can see what they mean about solitary breaking you down. I didn't realise how unlike a person I felt with everything stripped away; not until I got some back.

But the traces are still there. I don't know, a month alone with my thoughts and Freya's hatey eyes, and I'm struck too hard by the openness of everything. It feels weird talking, and my voice sounds too loud in my ears. There's a bang and a shout off to the left and I jump, then feel like a complete 'tutionised idiot.

'You got out fast,' Rowe says, helping me towel off my hair. 'We heard that people can do three, four months in solitary for fighting.'

'It didn't feel fast.' It didn't, it felt like one endless day. Always light, always hot.

'So, where's my tent?' I say, following Rowe as other prisoners pass us, throwing me deadlies.

'You'll sleep in with us, we've made some room.'

'I'm in with you? How lucky is that?'

'It doesn't work like that, Mirii. You have to buy your housing here. Well, they call it a security deposit,' she says, then comes in a little closer. 'But between you and me, I don't think we will get it back.'

'Buy it? What if you don't have any money? I don't have any money!' My voice goes all jumpy on the tail end, like I'm freaking out, because I kind of am.

'There are loan sharks, or your family can wire some into your account, if you have one. Otherwise you sleep in the yard until you can afford one.'

'Did your dad . . .'

Rowe goes all rigid. 'No. Daddy is not speaking to me. My aunt, my mother's sister, she sent enough for a single unit deposit and a few things to set me up.' She brightens a bit, but I can tell it's just a put on. 'There's enough room for all of us!'

—

There is not enough room for all of us.

There's barely enough room for one of us, because this is, as Rowena said, a single. It's slightly bigger than the isolation cell. There's one bed along the left side, where Lacey is lying down, groaning. She and Rowe sleep there, though I've got no idea how—Rowe must curl around Lacey's tiny body like a cat, some kind of long jungle cat, around its kitten.

'Look,' Lacey says. 'We bought you a mattress. Ages ago. We knew you'd be back.'

They did. It is a typical Prison-slash-Orphancorp issue foam mattress covered in a sweaty, slick vinyl coating in a stain-resistant forest green pushed up against the other mouldy canvas wall. There's a small passage left between the beds for us to move about, just like in the PISR, but I foresee a lot less brawling going on in it, or at least, I've got hope. Rowe flicks a muddy white sheet over it, tucks it in around the edges. I flatten myself against the wall to give her room to do it. She's adapted to the size of the room, made it work with the size of her, but I'm not there yet. I'm still too used to hugging the walls of the PISR cell trying to avoid Freya.

Rowe flops onto the bed next to Lacey and wraps an arm around her. Lace is in pain, I can tell. If they're charging for accom, I can't imagine that they'd be chucking out meds for free, and especially not the kind of painkillers Lacey needs for her arthritis.

'How you coping, Lace?'

'Oh, you know. Detoxing was hell, the pain plus the withdrawals . . .'

'I thought she was going to die,' Rowe says, giving Lacey a squeeze.

'I'm better now. But during withdrawal I kept thinking that the pain from my joints would be so easy to take without the jonesing. I was wrong, though. Tarmeine is easy to come by here, but it costs big bucks. We're talking black market bucks, and work detail only pays a few cents an hour.'

'Work? What kinda work is it?'

'Like sweatshop stuff. Manufacture, sewing piecework. There's tech shit, online help and content mod.' She gets a little shiver at that. 'Then there's the farms. Plus, you can make money doing other stuff too, like tradey, under-the-bars kinda stuff.'

'Like tattooing?'

'Sure, but you'd have competition. Plus, supplies. You'd have to cosy up with a guard or make your own stuff and I know how you feel about cleanliness and all that.'

'Shiz, right.'

'I've got work in the sewing shop,' Rowe says, and I try to imagine her bent over a machine, long fingers picking apart threads. 'But I make more taking patients.'

'You're a doc? That's perfect.' Rowe studied medicine. She could have joined her father messing with heads in the neuro department at Psynode, but instead she's here, probs pulling teeth and stitching fight wounds. I get a pang of guilt, because I know that if she hadn't met me she wouldn't be here. I look to the floor, like I want to sink right into it, into the hard-packed dirt where I belong. The toll I've taken all comes flooding back and even though I thought I'd tortured myself as much as I deserved in the PISR, there's always more regret waiting. It's an endless self-hating free-for-all! As much regret as I can handle!

'There's so much to do, too little time and not enough supplies. It's so hard, Mirii.' Rowe doesn't see my little pity party, and I'm glad in a way and not in others. I want her to know how sorry I am, and I don't know how to make the words to her.

'They do nothing for the prisoners, there are people here really suffering. I do what I can, but it's not enough.'

I nod. Bloody hell, she's so good. I don't deserve her, or her making room for me in this impossibly tiny tent, or even the token she gave me to wash my putrid body.

'So, what about food? We don't have to buy that, do we?'

'Well . . .' Lacey says.

'You're kidding me.'

'We get the standard rice ration, plus the minimum protein and a piece of fruit or vegetable, whatever has been damaged on the farms that they can't sell,' says Rowe, and I think back on the solitary gourmet meal we shared when we first met, the way the expensive meat fell apart in my mouth.

'Per meal?'

'Per day,' Rowe says, looking grim. 'Half the women I see in here are malnourished. It's horrible.'

'We can get other things on buy-up but the prices are a joke. Nothing else, except the veg that the girls smug back from the farms. And once again, big bucks,' Lacey says.

'Okay, so I guess I knew it would be like this. We need a plan, yeah?'

'What kind of plan?' Lacey asks.

'Like, I don't know, a plan. We gotta find some way to contact your friends. And Cam. And Vu!'

I think about Lacey's collective friends: Cam, who's like my kid brother, and I get the quickest flash of my babe Vu, the last time I saw her, drenched in rain and mouthing to me that she was sorry. I shake her out of my head. 'Babes have got sneaky comms in here, right? Handhelds, tabs?'

Lacey and Rowe nod, and then both intake air, about to say something, but I beat them to the smack. 'Big bucks, right?' They nod.

I start making the list in my head, all dot points. I wish I had my tab, so I could make a spreadsheet or something. I wonder what happened to it, and imagine it sitting solitary and battery-flat in an evidence locker somewhere. 'I'll get to work, start bringing in some money. Get us fed, get you some meds,' I say and give Lace a rub on the knee, which makes her wince. 'Shit, sorry.'

I don't tell them the secondary plan. That's just in my head. In my mental document, I make a second page. I call it 'BUSTING OUT'. All caps.

'We can do this,' I tell them.

Lace and Rowe look at me, heaps dubious.

'We can! It's kind of like how we grew up. Hey, Lace?'

Lacey's face is stony. 'I don't think you understand, Mirii. It might feel like that because some of the bits are the same, but the system's different. In an Orphancorp you're just marking time 'til you age out. You know you're gonna get out, and you just hold hope until then. Here, well . . . This is nothing like an Orphancorp. It's way worse. We'll die here, Mirii.'

Lacey's words slam around my head as Rowe leads me down into the yard. She can't mean it. We can't die here.

I won't fucking allow it! Not Rowe, not Lacey.

I guess not me, either.

There's a roiling crowd of women by a barred roller door set into the north wall of the Block. Hundreds of them, agitated and pushing, building up to some frenzy that's obviously on its way.

'What is this?' I ask Rowe.

'Distro. You'll see. Come on, we're late.'

Dainty, spindly Rowena Hamilton-Singh, of the Barangaroo Singhs, fashionatrix and first in her class at medical school, charges into the throng of prisoners with her hands stretched out, weaving and pushing her way in. I follow in her wake, ducking as the babes she's barrelled out of the way wash back in, weaving around and squeezing between the clustered, fighting bodies.

'Rowe! Rowe, what's going on?'

We're close to the front now. With a great screech, the roller door starts to rise. Slow and noisy, it opens to reveal a truck surrounded by screws. They point tasers and guns at us as one of them unlocks the bars and pulls them apart. No one bats an eye at the guns, though I flinch a little as one swings towards me. The sight of the screws sends my blood cold, and suddenly I'm super aware of the crowd I'm in, like I've just been magic-plonked right in it, instead of fighting my way through. My heart double-times.

'Get back, you filthy cunts,' one growls.

It's like a punch in the guts. Us women, sorry, us bunch of filthy c-bombs, ease up the clamour a bit. The truck begins to beep as the tray tilts. It's almost at forty-five degrees before I realise what's in it.

Food. Our food.

Our food which slides down the rusty tray and into the dust at our feet and the prisoners go wild, snatching up the bags of rice, the dirt-encrusted meat, the floppy, wilted veg.

'Oh god,' I say, but Rowe grabs me as the crowd in front turns, arms laden.

'Get in there, Mirii!'

I coil back and slam forward into the throng. I pick up a plastic sack of rice, a gov-issued single daily ration pack, and then I scramble forward to grab a hunk of fatty, gristly, dusty meat and some bug-eaten bok choy from the ground. Rowe's gathered up her share, and Lace's too. I'm shell-shocked with the crowd and the screws and the guns, and the outright indignity of this, like they gotta really put us in our place by dumping our food out on the goddamned ground like we're pigs scrabbling at a trough.

I turn to Rowe, my mouth all gapey, when someone grabs me by the hair, yanks me back and I drop everything as I thunder to the ground. It's some tough-looking babe with a mouth full of brown teeth who bares them down at me, grabs all my stuff, and peels off, cackling.

'Too slow, bitch!' she says, just audible over the shrieks and groans of everyone fighting for their meals.

'Rowe! She took it . . . That chick just took my stuff!'

'Don't lie there, Mirii, go back in, or we won't have enough!'

I get up off the ground, wobbly as a bub, and I clamber through the crowd until I see the feeble pile of stuff left. I leap on a bag of rice, curling my body around it, reach out for a chunk of meat, half-ground into the dirt. My fingers close around it, someone steps on my hand, but I keep a hold even as I bellow, and then I roll over and crawl out of the brawl. Rowe's waiting for me and I look up at her, feeling pathetic. She peers down at me, weird pride blooming in her eyes.

'Good job, Mirii, you did it!'

My hand throbs, my scalp too. The crowd is clearing, and I can hear the screws laughing as they lock up the bars and tilt the truck tray back down.

'Buncha animals,' one says, and oh, don't they have a good chortle at that. I bet he says it every day.

I come up, clutching my bag of rice in one hand and my disgusting lump of meat in the other. There's fear in me, a remnant of the PISR cell, but rage too. Fucking fury.

'We're the animals?' I say, and everything goes a bit quieter. '*We're* the animals?' I yell this time, and Rowe grabs me just as a taser prong flies out and catches me bullseye in the chest. She lets go real quick.

Good shot, I think, and then everything is pain.

The screw keeps the shock going long past the standard limit. I lose myself in the pain, there's nothing else to be done until he relents.

'Yeah. You're the animals,' he says. Rowe rushes forward and picks the prong outta my shirt. She grabs my food up off the ground and tries and fails to help me up with laden hands. The tough babe from before, the one who took my stuff, she's above me, helping Rowe to help me up.

'Fucking screws,' she says to me. 'You okay?'

If I had it in me, I'd punch her.

'Why are you helping now, you bloody thief?' Rowe says to her. It's the first time I've heard her come even close to swearing.

'Because fuck screws, that's why,' she says. Then she storms off.

'Unbelievable,' Rowe mutters. 'Some of these women . . .'

I get it. It's all of us against each other, and all of us against the screws.

'It's okay Rowe. I'm okay.'

'Come on, can you walk?'

'I think so,' I say. 'Wow, I haven't been tased in ages. Feels like coming home, hey?'

Rowe takes my handful of rations and I shuffle behind her towards our tent. Inside, Lacey's got a banged-up tin pot of water boiling on a little thermo-chip stove already. Rowe sits and takes a bucket between her wide-spread knees, pouring fresh water from another bucket over our meat and veg to wash off the dirt. I don't know what else to do, so I just flop on the bed and take a minute to work through the trembles from my tasing. I don't know where I fit into this little picture of domesticity, like Rowe and Lace have fallen into a routine with each other and I'm just an interloper—worse, the interloper who caused all this.

Then Rowe chucks me the bunches of bok choy and a few gnarled carrots and tells me to get prepping and I feel a bit better. They don't have knives or anything like that, so Lacey shows me how to break everything up into little pieces, bending the stems and twisting. Once the rice is done, she pours the water off and sets it aside, filling the pot with the meat and veg. Rowe digs through the sack containing her earthly belongings and brings out a few little packets: salt, pepper and a mixed spice bag.

'This cost a mint, but it's worth it,' she says, grinning. Her teeth are dirty and yellowing already, but her smile seems to take up half her face and it zings my heart to see it. She adds it to the pot and a dreamy smell fills the tent. My mouth floods with saliva. I haven't had much more than rice with some stringy, unidentifiable protein mixed in for the past month. My stomach gurgles out loud and we all get giggling, even though it's not really funny 'cause I'm actually proper starving.

It's nice. I feel normal for a sec, cooking a meal with my friends.

Then the tent flap flies open, and a blood-gushing babe falls in, splattering the dirt floor with dark spots. Rowe rushes over and collects the girl in her arms.

'What happened, Arrow?' She brushes Arrow's hair out of her face, trying to find the source of the blood.

'Got jumped,' Arrow says, 'in distro.'

'Every morning someone's in here,' Rowe says, pressing some clean-looking rags to the cut she's finally found on Arrow's head. 'You think they'd find a better way to do it.'

'Not so fast.' Lacey turns the stove off and drops the spoon into the pot with a dull clunk. 'You still owe us for last time.'

'I'm good for it, I promise.'

'That's what you said when we yanked that wisdom tooth.'

'If you made it to rations on time, Arrow, you'd stop getting caught up in the fray.' Rowe's got her hand pressed hard over the wound, trying to stop the flow of blood. 'I think this might need stitches,' she says, lifting the bandages off for a sec.

'You can't afford stitches,' Lacey says, 'and we can't afford to keep doing treatments on tick, Rowe.'

'I've got rice, I've got meat,' Arrow says.

'No, I'm not taking your rations. Lace, we can't send her out of here with a giant hole in her head.'

'You're too soft, Rowe. You can't afford to keep being kind.' But Lacey goes back to stirring the pot, so I know she's given in as well.

'Mirii, can you take that bucket and boil some water?' Rowe asks, so I slosh a bit into the other pot and Lacey grunts as I steal the stove to heat the water. Once it's got a good boil going, Rowe drops in a sewing needle, and leaves it to heat while she washes her hands in the bucket.

'That's the last of the water. The least you can do is spot us for some more,' Lacey says, and Arrow hands over a token.

After fifteen or so, Rowe drains off the water to save and waits 'til the needle is cool enough to touch. Then she pulls a roll of string out of her sack, threads the needle and goes to work.

The sight of the blood makes me feel kinda woozy, the dip of the needle in and out stinging me almost as much as it stings Arrow. Nah, with the string of profanity she unleashes every time Rowe pushes the spike in, I'm guessing it hurts her more.

Rowe's in her element. The stitches are as neat as any I've seen, and a bunch more profesh than any I got by kid-docs back in the Corp. She ties off each one with a practised hand, even if the hand is sticky with blood and probably not totally on the aseptic up-and-up. Once she's done, she douses the whole thing with splashes from a bottle of iodine, lord knows how she came across that.

'There. Arrow, get to ration distribution early from now on, okay? It's not worth the fight, understood?'

Arrow nods her bloodied head. 'Thanks Rowe. I owe you.'

'Yeah you do,' Lacey pipes from the corner. 'Double now.'

Once Arrow is woozing off to her own tent, and Rowe cleans up, we get to eating.

'What do they pay you in?' I ask her.

'Whatever they can,' Rowe says around a gristly lump of meat. 'Food, medication, water tokens, things they steal from work detail. I get a lot of supplies from service trades, so it's a self-perpetuating cycle. Daiyu from three tents to the right got me needles from the textile shop after I pulled her tooth on our second day here. And,' she says, gathering herself up all proudy and grinning, 'I stole the thread myself! I'm a common thief!'

Rowe takes my arm. 'Come on, it's time for work,' she says, pulling me out of the tent. Lacey follows, slower.

'What do you do, Lace?' I ask her as we wind our way through the tent city, tripping over guy ropes and babes in boxes and under blankets. I can't imagine that she's able to labour on the farms or bend over a sewing machine all day.

'I'm on DIC—"Disabled Internee Consideration"—'cause of me arthritis. Get an inside job, with a seat and all, but it's content moderation.'

'Oh babe, no. They outsource that here?' Content moderation is the hideous armpit of tech work. Even in my most desperate moments, when I went to bed hungry or sent my Worldcard balance into the negs, I'd never taken a CM gig.

'Yep. I gotta look at every piece of porno, torture and troll bullshit in the Twaddle feed and flag it.'

I can't imagine how awful it must be. No wonder Lacey seems harder now. There's a steeliness to her she's cultivated to cope with having to lay eyes on the murkiest scum of the net all day. And it's only been a month. I can't imagine what she'll be like after a year. Or ten. Jeez.

Rowe leads us through the tent-maze again, back to the admin block where there's the same mass of women as before at food distro, but much more subdued this time. There's a lull that speaks of a long day of labour for a few measly cents ahead.

'I don't know where they're going to have room for you,' Rowe says. 'You might end up out on the farms. I know you wanted manufacture but it's probably full. We'll just have to wait and see.'

The babes are all making wobbly lines by various doors along the admin-watchtower-PISR-whatever-else block. There's a small line forming at one of the doors and Rowe points towards it.

'That's sign-up,' she says. 'Go and stand in line and they'll send you somewhere. I might not see you again before they take us to the sweatshop, so have a good day! You can do this, Mirii. I've figured out that work is just a state of being you have to exist in until it's over, but it will be over.'

'I came to that conclusion when I was about six,' I tell her, wondering how she's managed to stay on the PMA in here. Of anyone I've known, Rowe would have been in my top three least-likely to succeed in a prison-based environment, but she's going gangbusters. Maybe she's the kind of person who can bloom anywhere. Maybe she always has been.

'Well, then it will be so much easier for you! Good luck,' she says as her line starts to move. She gives me a quick, pointy hug and she and Lacey shuffle off to join their lines.

I glom onto the grim little posse of babes snaking to the sign-up window, and it's not long before the woman at the desk dead-pans, 'Next,' at me. She tells me that someone just died and I'm lucky enough to get assigned to the yard. I dunno what she means, but I am a little grateful I won't have to back-break labour in the sun all day on the farms.

I fall in line behind one of the roughest, toughest looking chickies I've seen in here. She's about forty or so, maybe younger, but hard-lived in the face area. She's got scratchy prison tats all over every visible bit of skin. When I step in behind her, she looks back, then up and down my body before huffing out a breath.

'Hey,' I say to her, making friendly because we're on the same deet and all that.

'Mmm,' she says. 'I'm Clayton. You heard of me?'

'Ah, no. I've been in the PISR for the past month. I'm Mirii, nice to meet you.'

She grunts. 'The PISR, hey? What you do?'

'Fighting.'

'That's my girl. Well, Missy—'

'Mirii,' I correct her before I even realise what I'm doing, then wince and wait for the inevitable smackdown because this one looks totally srs.

'Whatever,' she says, and I unclench. 'Mirii, I run this bitch, so just remember that.'

I'm not sure what she means. 'Like this deet, or what?'

She scowls at me, and puffs up, then turns to face the screw at the head of the line. 'I run this whole fucken place!' she says, and the women in front of us cringe away from her.

The screw caresses the taser at his hip. 'That's enough, prisoner.'

Clayton flips him the bird, but he just waves her away and I wonder who this babe is that she can pull a move like that on a screw and not cop a tasing. I'm scared to find out. When the line starts shuffling along, an oldie with full silver up top gives me a pat on the arm.

'Don't worry about Clayton. You just stay out of her way.'

'Does she really run this place?'

'Oh, she wishes. Delusions of grandeur, that one.'

'So, what's yard deet like?'

'Not as bad as the farms, but still pretty bad.'

'Great.'

At the door they're handing out pairs of long, stained rubber gloves. I take the pair handed to me and peer at the streaks along the side.

'What're these for?'

'First job of the day is to clean out the latrines and send the waste for compost processing,' Oldie says, and my guts sink so far that they almost drop out of my arse—but not quite. I mean, I'd be on the deet that'd have to clean that up.

I knew my sentence to a Prisoncorp would see me elbow-deep in shit, but I didn't think that it would be so literal. I've never been so grateful for a pair of gloves in my life.

The crappers are composting units—urine to the front to be recycled as part of the water that we get in little drips and buckets with the tokens that come weekly as a ration. The hard waste goes to the back and is processed into compost on the farms. I wonder how the recipients of this vegetable matter would feel knowing it was grown in actual human shit. I mean, it's safe after processing, but the idea isn't exactly pleasant, and the process itself is pretty much totally gross.

'So,' I say to the silver lady, 'I'm Mirii.'

'San. You a snitch?' she asks, cocking the place where her eyebrow might be if they weren't thinned into oblivion.

'Me? Never. I went right to the PISR as soon as I got in. Only been out a day. I wouldn't even know who to spill to.'

'Well, yard detail isn't all shovelling crap. Being in the yard allows for certain other pursuits, if you know what I mean.'

'Like shady stuff?'

She doesn't say yes, but then, she doesn't say no. 'You might have noticed that screws aren't really thick on the ground.'

'Why is that?' I ask her, because I've been wondering why the guards don't have much of a presence in the yard.

'Why would they? It's a clusterfuck in here. They've got the spotters on the Block and the cams on every corner. And when spilling gets extra rations and better conditions, why would they need to get down here with the muck?'

'Makes sense.'

'They only come out when it's time for a beating, seems. Or a surprise turnover.'

'Turnover?'

'Search. They come in here and wreck everything.'

This fact doesn't surprise me. What kind of person signs up for a job way out here, in this barren hellscape? Seems like only the desperate and the cruel would make it out all this way.

When we're done unloading the stinking bags of human waste, we haul them to a row of trolleys and take them to the drop-off area. Apparently, they go from here to the processing plant, and I'm just glad I'm not on that deet because I've dealt with enough crap for one day. I strip off the gloves and wish I could spend the next hour under a stream of hot water, rubbing myself down with disinfectant, but there's more work to be done. We scrub out the latrines, and I get my disinfectant wish when I spill half a bottle on my hands. I'm secretly very pleased. It only burns a little, but it's worth it.

The screw approaches me, hand-on-taser, as I heft the last crapper-bag into the trailer to get sent off for processing.

'You Mahoney, M?' she says, spitting the words at me like she's five parts venom and two parts sour.

'Um, yeah?' Shiz, what now? My body starts to shake instantaneous, and I feel my mouth flood with saliva like I'm about to hurl. What have I done?

'Come with me.'

She walks me into the Block and passes me off to another screw. The hallway is cool after the heat of the day outside. My eyes take a minute to adjust to the low light. The screw leads me down past what I remember is the entryway to the PISR and I get another mad shiver through my torso. Are they sending me back? What did I do? But the screw waddles right past it and I huff out a breath like I've just won the most primo happy prize ever. One month in this place and the best feeling in the world is only being confined to the regular oppressive prison instead of the super hideous version. Bloody hell, this place is gonna do a number on me, right?

For a quick-step sec I wonder how Freya's doing down there in isolation, if she's fighting against herself now she has no one else to fight with. Who knows, maybe they filled my spot up with some other poor chicky who's copping all of Freya's misplaced rage? One small slice of me wishes they'd let her out. The rest of me wants her in there forever.

'Keep up, Mahoney,' the screw grunts, and I skitter across the painted concrete floor to catch up with her.

She leads me on to a door, which opens to reveal a tiny room with a chair, table and screen on the wall. Nothing else.

'What is this?' I ask her.

'Meeting with your legal rep.'

'I've got a legal rep?'

'You do now. Court appointed. Looks like you got yourself into enough trouble to warrant a real, live lawyer instead of Legalsys.'

'Where are they, then?'

She points to the screen and waves at the chair, so I go over and sit down. She leaves, the door clanking as she bolts it closed, like I might just tear off through the Block and into dry, hot, desert freedom without the proper locks involved.

The screen lights up. A harried-looking babe appears, black hair coiling down past the view in thick braids.

'Inmate Qiū?'

'Um, no. Mahoney? Miriiyanan?' I say, like it's a question. That's me, isn't it?

'Mahoney, that's right,' she says, and I'm convinced she's got no idea who I am. She taps and scrolls a bit on her tab. 'Oh, Mahoney. Yes. Wow. Industrial espionage, breaking and entering a private facility, criminal trespass, grievous bodily harm, weapons charges, manslaughter. What kind of rampage did you go on?'

'Manslaughter?' My jaw locks and an image of Tane flashes up in my brain-eye and I go cold from my toes to the crown of my head. 'That . . . that wasn't in my list of charges.'

'Your case was pending evidence and affidavits when the initial verdict and sentence was delivered. Now all documentation has been filed, you've had extra time added to your sentence.'

My head fills with a dull droning sound, and the screen seems far away, like I'm looking at it from another room, another place, another life.

'How much time?' I hear myself asking.

'Twenty-five years.'

'Years . . .' I say, and I try to remember my initial sentence, but I can't, and it doesn't matter anyway, because it's like adding one seemingly infinite amount to another and coming up with a different answer every time.

I almost don't register when the screw comes in and lifts me up out of the seat.

'Come on, Mahoney,' she says, almost gentle.

I didn't notice that screen-lawyer is gone, the monitor back to black.

'Twenty-five years,' I tell her, and she turns me around, then does something totally unexpected.

She hugs me.

I stiffen. But then I realise that there are no cameras in here, it mustn't be legal to snoop while a babe and her lawyer chitty-chat about law junk and the total annihilation of most of a person's life. Who knew this place had any laws? So, I hug her back, and she pats me a few times on the head.

Lacey was right—I will die here.

—

I drone through work, deep in a shocky fug.

'You, girl. We're done.' San gestures at me and a screw comes to collect our gloves and tells us to fuck off back to the yard.

'Mmm,' I reply. There's not much in my head but the law-babe saying 'twenty-five years' in a reverby loop. When I get to the post-work headcount, Lacey's there looking grim and hollowed out, and Rowe pops up right behind me.

'What's wrong?' Lacey says after the quick-count, as we wind our way back to the tent.

'Saw my lawyer today,' I tell her. I can't stop staring past her. I feel like there's nothing inside me, my body and head voidy and light, like I could just float up and off the planet. That'd be one way to get out.

'Lawyer?' they both say at the same time. Rowe flips up the front door flap of our tent and holds it up as I go in.

'You've got a real, human lawyer?' Rowe says. I try to look at her but I can't, I can't.

'Yeah. New charges. More time on my sentence.' The colour in their faces drains.

Rowe takes my face in her hands. 'Look at me, Mirii. How much time?'

I close my eyes so she can't see into me. 'Twenty-five years.'

Lacey sucks in a deep rush of air. Rowe squeezes my face. 'Oh Mirii.'

'Concurrent?' Lacey asks.

'Don't know. Don't think so, they would have said, huh?'

'Twenty-five years?!' Rowe says, storming through the tent and picking up bags of rice, waving them around as she speaks. 'On top of the ten we already got? For what?'

Ten years. My initial sentence. The concept of thirty-five years here slams around my head louder than the notion of twenty-five, but it can't find anything to cling to.

Rowe slams a pot on the stove and sloshes water into it, spilling it all over the floor and turning the dust into mud. 'This is ridiculous,' she says. 'We have to do something!'

Lacey limps to me, takes me in her arms. 'I'm sorry, Mirii,' she says.

'Me too,' I tell her.

'Look,' she says, turning me around. Outside, past the Block, in the setting-sun sky, clouds gather in a tight cluster.

'What is it?'

'Seeded clouds. For the farms. To bring the rain,' Lacey tells me.

It's like nothing I've seen. They're deep purple against the red of the rest of the sky, and when I look out further I see more gathering in little masses above the horizon. Grey streaks of rain, real enough, stretch from the clouds to the ground, and the last rays of light push through them. I feel Lacey slip an arm around me, then Rowe too, and we stand there, watching the make-believe clouds empty over the farms until the sky goes dark.

DAY TWO

The bleat of a siren wakes me from my poor sleep on the floor of the tent. Above me, Lacey and Rowe groan in unison.

'Wha?' I say through thick, sleepy lips.

'Assem,' Rowe says. 'Come on, we only have a few minutes to line up.' She throws off her sheet and helps Lacey to her feet.

'What's assem?'

'Assembly. Headcount.' She slips on her boots and I shove my feet into mine, struggling to stand. It's hot, too hot for this early in the morning.

We file out of the tent and join the rows of women trudging down the paths between the tents. We trip on babes emerging from lean-tos and humpies in the road, and finally come out into the yard in front of the block. Guards are suited up in stab jackets with the standard tase-belt and a few even have guns in their hands, deadly black barrels pointed down at the dirt. It's weird seeing screws out in the yard. From what I had seen so far, they tend to stick to the Block, hunting around the edges where they couldn't get muck on them.

Babes form lines in front and guards thread through them, scanning the thick plastic bands around our wrists, with our prisoner number and Q code stamped on top. I can't believe how many of us there are. Hundreds of women, in all manner of disarray. There are ten guards on this many babes and I wonder how easy it would be for us all to turn . . .

But everyone stands stock-still and silent while the screws zap-zap-zap to record our presence. I crane my head and watch them meet in the middle, confer, and then a thick-as dude guard stands up on the steps coming down from the Block and starts to bellow.

'We're six down this morning! You better be dead or close to, or I'll have your hides. Hastings, Htet, Jogi, Ornlamai, Smith, and Varley, if I don't see your sorry arses up front in the next sixty seconds, every putrid bitch in this place can forget rations for the day.'

Within a minute, five girls trickle in late, and it's right to the PISR for them, with a clip over the ear and a hell of a serving from the thick bastard up front. We're still one down, but they seem to think this is acceptable and give the nod for us to unassem. The lines go loose, and the chatter starts up, but a bark, this time electronically delivered, gets us all springing back into line in instant quiet. A woman appears at the rail from the watch level two floors up, loud-speaker in hand. She's done up in a white pantsuit, and she shines from the balcony, clean and sparkling. Her blonde hair is scraped back into a severe bun and her face has the puffed up linelessness of someone who hasn't just had some work done, but is entirely work.

'Who's this bird?' I murmur to Rowe. 'The warden?' Me and wardens don't end up having the best rapport.

'No, she's the COO.'

'What's that mean?'

'Chief Operations Officer. She's in charge, represents the Board.'

Lacey jabs me with an elbow. 'Be quiet, you'll get us sent to the PISR.'

Whoever she is, I wonder if I'll get on this babe's bad side too. Though, to look at her, she doesn't get down here much. There's not even a trace of dust on the hems of her pant-legs.

'Inmates! I have a report from the Board.'

There's a little ripple in the lines of prisoners. It's like a soft groan and the screws pick up on it, but there's too many to start tasing so they throw us deadlies instead and things go quiet.

'The first quarter report has been delivered and certain projections were not met. We are hereby increasing daily working hours by sixty minutes and implementing new efficiency measures within all work programs.'

Now there's a roar, real noise from the crowd as women cry out in protest. The screws spring forward, flicking out batons, and they start beating chickies at random until everyone shuts up. Soon there's silence but for the little whimpers of the women who copped a beating, which seems to be acceptable because the COO babe starts up again.

'Also, as of this week we are receiving two hundred female inmates from the Rutherford Immigration Detention Centre.'

Another surge of anger rises from the crowd and there's not much the guards can do because it seems like everyone's got a thing to say about this. I brainflash to the crowded rows of tents and makeshift housing in the yard and wonder where the hell they're gonna put these babes. Seems like everyone's wondering the same thing.

Pantsuit lowers the megaphone and smiles an immovable smile before smoothly gliding back inside the block, leaving the screws to deal with hundreds of outraged babes.

They do it with sticks and zaps, in the usual way.

—

I slam in, elbows out and neck tucked in tight, shoving away some babe who's creeping up on my left side, and I zone in on a little pile of rash packs and soiled meat. *Mine.* I make short work of a bodyblock by dropping low and to the side, then skid, throwing up dust, and scoop up my bounty.

There, the greens. Ducking a big chicky growling past, I scoot around two women going at it over some bug-eaten kale leaves, and I swoop then bring up a handful of veg without even stopping. I'm in and out in under a minute.

'Mirii, that was amazing,' Lacey says from her pos off to the side. 'It's like you've been doing ration distro your whole life.'

I'm puffing, but proud. 'It's a lot like the warehouse back at the Nodeplex. You gotta think smooth and flowy, let the adrenaline slow everything down.'

'Good work, Miz!' Rowe says, coming back out with the beginnings of a nice shiner on her left eye.

'Rowena, no!' Lacey says, gesturing for Rowe to bend down to her. She takes Rowe's face in her hands and looks her over, clucking.

'Makes you look tough, Hamilton-Singh,' I tell her.

'Really?' Rowe asks, all sincere and excited.

'Really,' I say.

'It just hurts, mostly. I wish we had some ice.'

'Animals,' the same guard from yesterday calls, and I don't even think before I shout, 'We're the animals?' like a callback. A few other girls yell it out with me, then we look at each other and get to giggling. The guard gnashes his teeth, but he can't tase all of us, can he? Well, ya know, he probs can, but he *doesn't* and that's the thing. It kinda gives me a little boost, like me and those three other babes are in this together, which is a good thing seeing as this is the next thirty-five years of my life.

If I can't get out.

Or unless I die first.

Ah, what a great buncha options.

We get back to the tent, cook breakfast and Rowe sets the arm of an old bird who got it snapped by a screw at assem. It goes in with a loud crack that gets girls peering in the tent, as Oldie howls like a banshee. This already feels like a routine.

On our way to work deet, Rowe takes my hand. Holding hands with her makes me feel like a kid, she's so tall and I've got to bend my arm at the elbow to send it up to her.

'How are you coping? You know, with the whole . . . *sentence thing.*' She drops to a whisper for the last bit like it might soften the blow, or soften my blow 'cause she's brought it up again.

'I dunno, Rowe. It don't feel real, hey? I can't imagine that amount of time.'

'Neither can I. I thought ten years was incomprehensible.'

'It is. I'm just trying not to think about it.'

'Oh dear,' she says, and I want to honk with laughter 'cause only Rowe would say 'oh dear' with a nice, ripe shiner in the middle of a prison yard. 'I'm sorry I mentioned it.'

'Yeah nah, it's okay. I can deal.' I can deal because my mind is whirring with other thoughts. I can cope with anything if I'm busy enough, and I can keep my mind busy in one real way: thinking up how I can get us out of here.

—

We line up, get our gloves and then we're right off to the latrines. I stick with San, the golden oldie from yesterday because she seems like the kind of babe I might want to glom to. I'm not sure why, she just exudes this air of patience and strength. I wonder how long she's been here.

'You two,' booms a guard from a door in the Block after we're done with the dunnies and showers. 'Dead run.'

San nods and chucks off her gloves for decontamination. 'Come on, young'un,' she says, and I follow her to the window.

'What's a dead run?' I ask, at her heels. She's got a mad stride for such a yearsy babe.

'What does it sound like? There's a dead body somewhere in the yard. We gotta go and remove her.'

'What?' I'm all incredulous. 'Us?'

'Yep,' she says, no nonsense.

'Row seven, in a humpy somewhere,' the guard says, a real hardarse bitch with a flattop haircut and tattooed knuckles.

'Right-o,' San says. As we walk off down the rows, she gives me a little frown. 'I was hoping for a tent, we coulda scored on her stuff. Oh well.'

'Like steal her things? That's not very . . .'

'Not very what?' she says.

'You know. She's dead.'

'Lotsa ladies die here. In this heatwave, we'll start dropping like flies soon. You'll get used to it. Stay here long enough and you'll get a lot less sensitive. It's every woman for herself.'

I hate the thought that one day I'll think nothing of rifling through a dead babe's things and pocketing the choice bits.

'What's your sentence, anyway?' San asks me, as we start up row seven and peek into the little lean-tos set up here and there.

Again with the sentence. 'Thirty-five years,' I tell her, saying the numbers like a robot. They still don't mean anything to me, it's like I'm parroting back a language I don't understand.

She whistles between her few remaining teeth. 'What'd you do?'

'Industrial espionage, break and enter, GBH, weapons charges, manslaughter.'

'Didn't think you were worth much, but what do you know? You're a proper criminal.'

I don't feel like a proper criminal at all. Just some babe in over her head, but I try to puff up, because I can sense that I've gained a little bit of respect, and the respect of this babe feels important.

'How long have you been here?' I ask her as I gingerly throw back a piece of ragged canvas to find nothing underneath.

'Eleven years,' she gruffs at me. 'I organised a sit-in at the Zap Factory for fair pay.'

'You got eleven years for peaceful protest?'

'I got fifteen years for *organising* a peaceful protest. It didn't even happen.'

I whistle between my teeth and lift a piece of old cardboard off a lean-to. The smell hits me right away, and the vision of her, the dead babe, blue in the lips and 'round her open eyes. Those eyes.

'Shit!' I say, dropping the cardboard back onto her.

'Guess you found her, huh?'

I've seen dead people before, but not like this. She looks like she suffered, the grimace on her face and the curled-up posture of her body telling. I hate to think of her, of anyone, dying alone like this, in a box, in the dust of the yard.

'Come on Mirii, let's see what we've got here.' She throws the rest of the cardboard off the dead babe and starts looking over her things. There's a little chip stove, which San puts to the side, and a blanket and sheet. Apart from that, the woman has nothing but the clothes on her skinny, dead frame and the boots on her feet. San slides one off. 'So, what size are you?'

'Um, eight I think.'

'I'm a nine, these are a six. Take 'em and make a trade.'

I really don't want to take the shoes off a corpse, but needs must and I wonder what I might get for them.

'Wanna second uniform? A good wash and this'll be brand new. She looks like she might be close to your size.'

I nod, dumbstruck. Two days in this bitch and I'm already stripping the newly dead for spoils. Shit. If I die here (and a little voice chimes up in my head with a 'when you die here', 'til I squash it back down) will some yard deet babe takes the choicest bits for herself? Will they plunder the clothes I die in and wonder what they might get for my boots?

We undress her. She's a little stiff, and the smell starts to fade away the longer we handle her. Soon she's naked and San and I wrap her in the sheet, one of her five worldly possessions now a shroud.

'What now?' I ask as we prepare to heft her up.

'Now we take her to the block. Then, well, then they'll compost her.'

'What?' The word glugs outta me like vomit. 'They won't even bury her?'

'No waste. Even in death we'll be working for the Board,' San says, then spits off to the side.

———

Our second job of the day is to move the fences—broaden the boundaries of the jail to accommodate the new prisoners who simply would not be able to cram in any other way. It's heavy work, as we dig out the concrete feet of the fence, drag them over, then sink them into the new holes. A couple of guards lead us through a gap in the fence, into the red dust outside. They finger their weapons and tell us not to bother trying anything, or it's a bullet in the back. Yes ma'am, yes sir, I'd like to avoid one of those today.

The fence feels flimsy as we climb through, and I wonder how the air seems fresher out here, the sky a more vibrant blue. I'm struck by how simple it is to not be in the prison, just a few measly steps between 'in' and 'out'. The fence is a boundary between the world and the inside, and it's so negligible, so easily moved.

We help the other crew drag the chain-link panels over, avoiding the heavy razor-wire edge, and wrangle them into pre-dug holes. Just like that, the outside becomes in, red-dust nowhere becomes correctional facility. For a second, the whole place feels made up, arbitrary, but then it feels worse than that—it feels like anywhere can become prison with the right attitude and the right number of fences.

'Oi, you. Snap out of it,' a screw says to me, and I shake my head out of its mini- philosophical debate and crushing realisation.

San struggles with the job in the heat and when they give us a five-minute break as the sun reaches its blistering pinnacle, I share what water I have with her. The heat rises from the ground, making a wavy haze in the distance, while the dirt at my feet is in deep cracks that catch on the soles of my boots.

'Thanks, Mirii,' she says, and I get that feeling again, like there's gravity to her words, like her thanks really means something.

As the sun strides across the sky, we keep up our cracking pace, crackling in the heat. Manufacture brings over the new fence panels and we sink those too. As the last one drops into place, I get that feeling again—we're back *in* now. A little part of me withers, and I wonder if I'll feel that feeling again, the wide-openness and quick flash of freedom that I had for just a second as I stepped through the fence and into the outside. Like, if I'll ever feel it again before I die.

The last panel screws into place with a sick finality, and then that's it, it's over. Onto our next daily drudge with the knowledge that it's all just arbitrary, this place, but that I'm stuck inside it anyhow.

—

I'm bent over in the late afternoon sun, aching in the lower back and scooping up garbage from where it's blown up against the fence, when I hear a male voice. For a second I think it's a screw and I snap up fast. I'm half-expecting a blow to the head or a tase or something and I get a hot flash like I'm doing something wrong, even though I've been told to come and do this. But when I'm up I can see it's a standard bru, on the other side of the chain-link. The men's side. There are two rows of fence between us, topped with the razor wire you'd expect and an empty space between the two. He's dressed in scrubs too, the same mint green, and he gives me a smile that turns his dark face to radiance and dimples. He's a babe, and I feel a stab between my legs like a zingy treat on an otherwise bleaky kind of day.

'Hey there, how's tricks on the women's side?'

There's a shout from up on the tower.

'No fraternising!'

We both step back from the fence. I go back to picking up empty rice ration bags and bits of weathered cardboard, and so does the bru, but I keep an eye on him and him on me.

'Tricks are pretty standard, I guess,' I mutter over to him, trying not to move my mouth too much. 'How 'bout on your side?'

'Yeah, brutal and dreary, same as always.'

'I'm Mirii,' I say, shuffling over to a plastic bottle and jamming it in the recyc bag.

'Mohammad,' he says.

I don't know what else to say to him. What do you say to the first bro babe you've seen in forever, let alone got a bit flirty-flirt with? Normally I'd make some sly and witty comment that'd insinuate some kind of making out later on, just to make my intentions clear, but this is not the time or the place. Our tongues wouldn't be able to reach across the no-man's land between the fences, and I reckon that'd be considered 'fraternising' of the highest order.

He breaks the pause in banter between us. 'So Mirii, can you pass a message for me?'

'A message? I'm in.' I make out like I'm stepping down inside my garbage bag to make room for the rest of the trash up alongside the fence, and it gives me a reason to pause a few seconds. Smooth as, Miz.

'Tell San that we've seen the transfer list, and Saif is on it.'

'San? The old bird?'

'Yeah.'

'Why?'

'Why not?' he says and goes all dimples again.

'And she'll know what this means?'

'Of course.'

'Um, okay. I can do that.'

He smiles again, and I blush a little, I actually blush like a lovey teen, sheez, and then I remember I *am* a teen so maybe this is okay. I forget sometimes. I wonder how long it'll be before I feel boy hands on me again, big and rough, and then I realise it'll probs be never and my blush drains away, leaving me withered and empty. Older again.

'Prisoners!' The voice pipes up again from the tower. 'Away from the fence!'

I step back, automatic, and Mohammad does too. I look past the glare to the block, where the voice is coming from and then my heart stops. It actually, like, skips a beat and I thought that just happened in the flix or in books or something, but no, here it is happening in real life, and I don't know if it's legit or not, what I'm seeing.

She looks different. Thinner, that round face sharper and the curve of her chest slighter beneath the standard issue guard uniform. She's got her head shaved all around the bottom, long on top, piled up on her head, and a blunt fringe. Thick, black-framed glasses.

I turn back to the last few dregs up against the fence, shove them in my bag, and stagger away, forgetting Mohammad, and the message he gave me, forgetting what I'm doing, where I am, how long I'm here for, what my name is.

It's Vu.

Vu is a screw.

—

'What's with you?' San asks me, 'cause I'm totes reeling and my eyes must be the size of bloody planets.

'I just, I saw . . .'

I shove the garbage bags into her arms and trip over my own feet, thumping down onto the ground.

'What did you see?' she says, emptying the bags into their right receptacles, then holding out a hand to lift me up.

'That guard. I know her.'

'Which screw? You know one of the screws?'

'Asian. Glasses.'

'Tran? She's new. Been here about a week. She's okay, a bit young though.'

A week? How did she get here so fast? We spent eight hell-weeks in the holding cells before placement, two days for trans-fer, and four weeks here. That's just over three months to apply, to train, and she must have had to get a new ident somehow. Tran.

'Where do you know her from?'

I come back a bit, and realise I'm making a bit of a spectacle of myself in front of San. 'I think we spent some time in the same Orphancorp, that's all. It was just weird to see her.'

San furrows her already wrinkled forehead, like she knows there's more to it. She's a cluesy babe. 'Okay,' she says.

Not long after, we get called for another dead run, and I barely see the fresh corpse as I heft her towards processing. There's a train of thought going 'round my mind, like: how did she do it, how did she get here?

There's a quieter one too, a bright voice in there, trilling golden just below everything.

She came. She found me.

—

The sun's gone way down by the time we knock off, then there's the headcount, and finally we drag our sorry arses back to our tents. Rowe slumps—minus the verve she usually has. If the Board wants to break us down, it's working.

Lacey's eyes are dark. I bet she's got to turn herself off inside to look at the endless stream of nasty shiz all day. I get a stab in my guts again that it's my fault she's suffering here. I look at Rowe, her fatigue and the way even she is fading, and I get another jab. Then boom, it's that sick-rising guilt coming back, and I feel the spiral sucking me down, shit, not again . . .

'Look what I've got,' Lace says, and I snap back from my misery-fest. She glances around, furtive, like there might just so happen to be some screw lurking right outside, even though yeah right, as if they could be bothered coming down here. She scrambles through her prison-issue Personal Effects sack, then pulls out a mini-tab. It's busted as hell but it almost hums with potential to me, like strings rising at an important moment in a flix.

'I can fix that!' I squeal, maybe pre-emptive because I don't even know what's wrong with it, but damn it, I got magic hands. 'I can like, probably fix that!' I get my grabby mitts on it and let my fingers pry at the joins, the broken bits.

'I knew you could. A babe with a rolled ankle on temp DIC brought it to me. She knew I'd been wanting to use it, but she's been holding out for a tastier trade. She bartered a week of use if we can fix it for her. I knew you could, Mirii, I thought of you right away.'

'It'll be rough,' I say. 'I don't got no tools, but I can give it a burl.'

I'm so excited with my dirty fingers all up in the tab that I almost forget. Then, right as Lace's got the rice boiling by lamplight, I remember, almost dropping the tab into the dust but I catch it again at the last moment.

'Vu!' I say.

'Yeah, if we get it working we can try to find her,' Rowe tells me from her collapsed pos on the bed.

'No, no, she's here!'

Rowe sits up and Lace ignores the rice.

'She's here? She's a prisoner?' Rowe says.

'No, she's a frigging screw.'

The rice boils over but Lace doesn't even see it. 'A screw! What?'

'I dunno how she did it,' I say, going over and turning the stove down. 'But she's here. She must've got a new ident, they call her Tran, but it's def her.'

'She came all this way . . . Did all that . . .' Rowe says.

'For me. I know. I guess I did it for her.'

Everyone sits back for a second, thinking on it.

'She must be trying to bust you out,' Lace says finally, straining the rice. 'Why else would she be here?'

'Yes, but how? We're in the middle of nowhere, where would you go? How would you get past the block?' Rowe asks.

'We. I'm not leaving without you. This is something. We've got the tab for comms, we've got Vu on our side. I dunno how this is gonna work, but this is more than we could hope for. Something's gonna happen. We don't have to die here.'

—

I've been in bed a good tenner when I'm shaken out of the Vu-reverie going 'round in my head.

The message for San! Bloody hell, I forgot.

'Lacey, Rowe, you awake?'

'Mmmmm,' Lace says.

'You know an old babe called San?'

'San? Of course we know her.'

I wonder for a sec why that is but put it aside. 'I got a message for her today, just before I saw Vu. I completely forgot to tell her. Where does she stay?'

'She's in row twelve, tent twenty.'

Wow, they really do know where she's at. I clamber up out of bed and slip my feet into my boots.

'Won't you see her tomorrow? You can tell her then,' Rowe says in a thick, sleepy voice. I mean, yeah sure, I could, but I'm not sleeping anyway, so why not just go tell her now? I feel bad for forgetting.

The night-time yard is filled with the hum of babes chuckling, fighting, crying. I count the rows and then the tents in the low light until I find San's. It's still lit from within, so I don't feel bad about interloping. But, crap, how do I knock on a tent flap?

'Um, San? Hello?'

'What is it?' comes a hoarsey voice from within.

'It's Mirii, from yard deet? Can I come in?'

The flap flies open, and San greets me, 'What is it, Mirii?'

'I completely forgot earlier, I have a message for you, from Mohammed?'

She looks around a bit, then yanks me into her tent. It's spacey as, a triple I think. Bed, desk, books. San has it *set*.

'Sweet digs,' I tell her, and she looks me up and down with her grey-eyed stare.

'What did Mohammed say? How did you talk to him?'

'We were at the fence at the same time today. He said to tell you that . . . he's seen the . . .' ugh, what was it? 'The transfer sheets? And Said is on it.'

'Said? Do you mean Saif?'

'Yeah, that's it. Who's Saif? How do you know Mohammed? He's a total babe.'

'None of your business, girlie. He should never have said anything to you.'

'Well, he kinda made it my business,' I reply, feeling a bit dismayish that she's turned so hard and cold all of a sudden. I thought maybe we'd be friends or something, that she'd be a good influence on me with her wisey ways and we'd have nice times. Like she'd teach me to knit or something? But here she is, all hard-eyes and focus.

'He had no right to say anything to you. This is none of your concern. Go back to your tent.'

Whoa. Instant dismissal, hey? Fine then. I bluster out the flap and fling it back down. That's the last time I get out of bed for San.

DAY THREE

I'm in Time Out again.

The cold-creeping concrete at my back, the roof stretches up and away from me, going long and giving me a tilting sense of vertigo to go with the racking despair that I'm back here again. I'm bruised, the blood oozing from my face the only warmth in the place. The walls close in, slowly getting tight around my body until I'm crawling through the vents above storage at Psynode, all squozen and stifled, the air turning foul. My torch has gone out and I keep feeling for the end of the tunnel, but it's never there.

I wake up still feeling trapped, still feeling stale hot air in my lungs. In the dim half-light from the spotlights outside, I can see Lace looking at me, big liquid night-time eyes shiny in the dark.

'Bad dreams?' she says, soft.

'Always,' I say. I wouldn't know a good dream if it bit me on the arse.

—

Assem is the usual clusterfuck. The COO lady is probably off thinking about how best to next bugger us in the name of profit, and is absent. But in the tiny space between distro and work deet, when we are supposed to eat, the screws flood out into the yard. I didn't know there were this many.

'What is this?' I ask Rowe and Lacey, who rolls her eyes.

'A turnover. Contraband search. Don't worry, we've got everything well hidden, they won't find nothin' in here.'

Rowe isn't as confident, and she worries her smooth hands against each other.

'You don't know that, Lacey. They very well could, and it will be straight to the PISR for all of us.'

I get a pang at the thought of going back into isolation, but it dissipates into surgey zings all through me when I see the screw approach our row.

'Prisoners, stand at the front of your tent,' she says and I'm too busy with my eyes bugging out of their sockets to move, so Rowe drags me over. She looks at me like I've gone over nutso. She doesn't know. How could she know?

It's Vu.

Or Tran. Or whatever.

'You,' Vu says, pointing at me. She holds up Rowe's sack of belongings. 'Come here and empty the contents of this.'

I step into the tent without feeling the dusty ground beneath my feet. Like I'm hovering a foot above it. Vu looks out into the yard at the screws busy foraging through everyone's junk, then takes my hand. Her fingers thread through mine and even though it's just a touch there's something sparky in there, something powerful.

'I've got a plan, Mirii,' she says. 'I'll get word to you somehow.' Then she lets go of my hand, stiffens up, flips the bed on its side and kicks over our stove, spilling boiling rice all over the hard-packed earth floor. Shit, I know she's gotta keep in character, but the rice? Low blow, Vu.

'Clear!' she bellows to no one in particular, and she's off to the next tent.

I'm still inside, frozen like I'm caught in headlights.

'What was that?' Rowe says, coming in, eyes bugging. Lacey limps in behind her, just as bemused.

'That . . . That was Vu.'

—

'Oi, you two,' Vu says, coming up to San and me as we wait in line for work deet. She spits on the ground by our feet. She's really getting into this character, and I can see a bit of gleamy snark in her eye.

'Dead run?' I say, pre-empting her, because why else would a screw interrupt our work? Vu or no Vu, there's not a lot that brings 'em in off the Block.

'You got it.'

'Where?' San asks.

'South side. Row ten.'

San and I get going and as we walk away, I sneaky a glimpse at Vu. *I'm sorry,* she mouths.

When we make our way through the tents in row ten, peeking in them one by one, and finally find her, I see that neither of us is gonna win this bet. I can see why Vu was sorry to send me on this run.

I've known people to end it. Life in an Orphancorp wasn't all shiny, happy friend-gangs and sneako mishes and cuddle parties.

I've had my share of babes choose to die rather than suffer any more, live with their shizzed up memories, or the promise of a life spent going from one institution to another. We'd have whispers in the morning of those who couldn't make it through another night, little memorials for them that the staff turned a blind eye to.

But I've never been this close to it.

When I see her, I make a noise that I can't believe is coming out of my mouth. It's the noise of someone else, seeing something that they know they won't ever unsee; that person is me, though it doesn't feel like it. I feel this sweeping disconnect from my body, like I'm pulled loose and placed just to the left of myself. I can only just feel San come up beside me, push me away.

'Get back, Mirii,' she says seemingly far away. 'You don't need to see this.'

But it's too late. And running through my head is the wonder of all the things this poor babe suffered, and how hope sometimes isn't enough for some people. I wonder what was so bad that she felt like she had to resort to this—I kinda know, and I don't at the same time. Then, feeling selfish, I think of myself, and how lucky I am that I've got a thread of hope through me that can't get beaten down. That at my core, I believe life is good and meant to be lived, even though I don't know why 'cause it's not as if I've seen much evidence of it. I wish I could have given a little bit of that to this stranger-woman, like I could have done something to help her back up from where she'd fallen.

I don't know, man. I just wish I could save everyone.

San deals with her while I stand by the tent flap, waiting to slam back into my body again. It doesn't happen. She stands up from the shrouded body and starts shuffling through her things.

I'm agape at her feet. 'No. San, no. We can't.'

'We can, and we will. Her things will help people. She'd want that.'

'You don't know what she'd want. Maybe what she wanted was to make it through the night, but she couldn't. I can't take her stuff, San, it's wrong.'

'Someone will. It might as well be us.' She throws me a bag of rice, and then, like a monster, I tuck it into my pants. She's right. Feeling light in the head, I rifle through her things. A stove here, a pair of boots there. A couple of beat-up old pots. I bag it all up and sling it across my shoulder. In her blankets I find a folded slip of paper. I open it, and it's a photo. A baby. Gender indeterminate, they're sitting in a chair and waving at the tab or phone taking the pic. I wonder where that baby is, how old they might be now. If they're filed away in an Orphancorp somewhere, dragging through the days 'til they age out. I let the photo flutter to the floor.

As we carry her out of the tent and towards the Block for composting, I'm still just a little off centre, like maybe there's a part of me that won't ever feel like it's tethered again.

—

It's mid-afternoon before I'm given my set of bags for general clean-up. I take them into the centre courtyard to begin. I've barely scooped up the first ratty scrap of kale when there's a clamour at the Block. The roller door shudders open and I'm wondering 'What now?' when there's a flood of babes backed up by a squadron of screws. Hundreds of women pour out into the courtyard, all of them looking confused and horrified at the motley sea of shelters in the yard.

'Prisoners!' shouts a skinny weasel-screw on a megaphone from inside the Block. 'Welcome to your new accommodation. We trust you will enjoy our five-star facility!'

Groups of newbz huddle around each other, some wailing and clutching their chests, others in a dumbstruck stupor. I'm stuck on the spot, stunned, even though I knew this was coming— the influx of new prisoners from the immigration camp that we were expecting. I just didn't think they'd arrive so soon. A woman close by me collapses into the dirt, sobbing hard, and I drop my bags and offer her a hand.

'It's alright, hey. It's gonna be okay,' I tell her, but is it? How will we go with all these new babes? Like how will the facilities, already stretched so much, cope with two hundred more drains on the system?

I feel about as hopeless as they do. I wonder where they're all from, how they thought their new life in Australia might go. Did they expect to be rounded up and put into this dusty camp, to waste away on starvation rations? Weren't they seeking something better, and is this better, or is it more of the same? All this way for same shit, different country. Or is it worse? I feel a hot, sinking sorrow for them, and a deep shame, that this is the best we can give. A spot in the yard, and labour in the camp. It shouldn't be this way.

A brave few move into the rows to seek out the new cleared spaces up the back. I decide to follow, stopping now and then to pick up an empty ration pack or used menstrual product, like, look, I'm totally working. I peek out from between the tents and watch.

On the empty dirt, they lay out blankets, chattering in different tongues I can't understand. I watch them, wondering at their resilience to just get on with it, and I'm amazed and humbled. Look at them, making a go of it.

I'm here as well. I haven't come from war or famine. While my life been its own kind of war, a different kind of famine, it's got nothing on what these babes have been through. All we can do is keep our heads up, spread our blankets on the ground, and get on the best we can.

—

Rowe's bartered a few hours with some tools, and she and Lace sit outside in the warm night air, keeping watch while I start to fiddle with the tab. I crack the case, gentle-like, and realise it's a pretty simple fix. I'm actually disappointed. I'm gunna have to spin a yarn about how hard it was to repair or the other babes will be totally unimpressed. I piece together a story that includes wonky power connectors and I switch it on. It takes forever, this tab's a hunk of junk. When it finally gets up and running I see that someone's already hacked the Block's wifi, thankfully, because I'm shit at that kind of thing. Two bars and everything. I download an open-source encrypted message sys and log in with my old username. Immediately hundreds of messages pop up, and I scroll through 'til I find Cam's chat window.

He's been messaging every day.

He knows I'm not gunna respond, but has kept at it, telling me stories of what he and Sticks have been up to. I gobble up every word, speed-reading the little bubbles of text. They're safe! They're with Elton, like I thought. I wonder if he still makes 'em sleep under the tables in the workroom but it doesn't even matter, as long as they're safe.

It's so sweet to see him tell me about his days. And sad.

I've got tears streaming down my face as I read his hopeful

entries, thoughts and dreams. It's like a diary: an endless letter to someone who might never get to read it.

Cam, I miss you.

I get to the end and start to type, fingers flying over the cracked screen.

—Cam! It's Miz! I'm okay, in a priz in the middle of nowhere. I've got access to this tab and comms for a few more days. I'm so glad you are okay. I'm doing my best to get back to you soon.

—Mirii!

I can almost hear the longing in the letters.

—I thought

—I dunno

—I just hoped you weren't dead.

—I'm not dead, little dude. Just filed away in here. I'm working on it, but.

—Tell Sticks I said hi!

—Do you know where Rowena n Lacey are?

—In here with me. Freya too. She says hi.

—Really?

—No.

—Did Vu get to you?

—How do you know about Vu? She's here, she's a guard!

—I know. We met up with her on the night you got arrested, she escaped from Psynode! Elton's the one who helped her with the new ident. Gave her a bargain. He said it was coz he was feeling generous, but it was really coz he misses you. He won't say it but I know. Are u gonna get out soon?

—I dunno. We're trying.

—I miss you Miz.

—I really miss you too Cam. U keeping out of trouble?

—Trying.

Tears keep coming outta my eyes the whole time I'm typing. I'm so grateful to Elton for keeping Cam and Sticks safe. He didn't have to. No one was paying their way. I don't kid myself that he's doing it out of the kindness of his own heart—the boys are handy kids to have around, they're hard workers after a life in the OC. He coulda chucked them out when my fund transfers for their accom ceased, but he didn't.

—I'm gunna get out. Somehow. I'll come and get you.

—I know Miz. Keep trying.

I type the words, 'I love you, little dude', then hover over the little 'send' icon.

Before I can tap it, a msg comes through.

—Love you, Miz.

I make a noise, a strangly little sob-cry thing.

I hit send.

—

We're not long in bed when there's a cry and the shuffle-shuffle-thump of bare feet outside. A shape throws open the tent flap. It's keening in the moonlight and grossly swollen and I give a yelp as it comes towards me, falls forward onto my bed and me.

'It's coming, it's coming!'

There's a rustle of sheets and a flare of light as Rowe flicks on the lantern.

I see her now. She's on all fours, writhing next to me. She's hugely pregnant, heavy belly hanging, and she throws her head back and lets out a surge of sound that almost doesn't sound real. From the sounds of it, she won't be pregnant for much longer.

'Zoe! Deep breaths!' Rowe says, leaping out of bed and rubbing

Zoe's back as the woman tries to breathe slowly, air catching in her throat.

I've seen a few babes in labour in my time, but they've always got to this stage and been hushed out of the dorm to the Orphancorp's med rooms, so I've not seen what comes next. I climb out of bed, leaving Zoe to bury her face in the sheets and cry, muffled in the rumply fabric.

I sidle up close to Rowe. 'Have you, like, made a baby happen before?'

'No,' she says, 'but I think I've got an understanding of how it will go.'

Oh good.

'I've been around for a few deliveries,' Lacey says. 'Rowe won't have to do much, Zoe will do all the work.'

'How is she pregnant?'

'She probably came in already up the duff,' Lacey says. 'Or one of the guards.'

Zoe had quietened for our little hushy convo, but she lets out another cry and starts wriggling.

'The contractions are very close together now. I told her not to come until they were about a minute apart, there was nothing I could do for her before this.' Rowe leans down to her. 'Zoe, how long have you been in labour?'

'Since this morning!' Zoe cries, rocking back and forth on her knees. 'Work deet was a bitch, let me tell ya. Oh!'

'I'm going to have to examine you. You'll need to lie down on your back and drop your knees open.' Rowe takes the small amount of water we have left over from the day, a tiny chunk of soap, and she washes her hands. Lacey helps Zoe turn over.

'Is she gonna, like . . . have the baby in my bed?' I ask Rowe. I don't want to sound ungrateful, I'm just worried about the sheets.

'Oh, Mirii,' she says, annoyed. I drop the subject.

'From what I know, she'll need to be ten centimetres dilated before she can push.' Rowe holds her thumb and finger about that far apart and I wince.

'Really? Shit, that's insane. How?'

Rowe ignores me. 'I'm going to take your pants and underpants off, is that okay?' she says to Zoe, who agrees. She does and then Zoe drops her knees apart. 'Zoe, can I check your cervix?'

Zoe grunts and nods. Rowe examines her, brow creased. 'I think you're fully dilated,' she says.

Lacey crouches down beside her. 'Do you have water tokens?' Zoe shakes her head, so Lace heads off to find some spares from the little crowd that's gathered at the door, peering in like it's the best show in town. 'Oi, youse! Stickybeaks! You wanna watch the show, ya gonna hafta cough up. We need water and blankets.'

I just stand awkward at the top of the bed, arms folded because I'm not sure what else to do with them. Rowe looks up at me.

'There's a little more water left. Wash your hands, I'll need your help.'

'Me?' I croak, frozen to the spot. I'm not good with kids, and who knows what I'll bugger up in the arrival of one? What if she wants me to hold the baby once it's here, and I drop it? I can imagine trying to pick it up and dust off the dirt while everyone looks on in horror. 'I'm not sure—'

'Just do it, Mirii!'

Shit. I lather up my hands. How do I know I've gotten all the germs off? What if I get my filthy hands on the baby and bugger it up? But then, babes been having babies since forever, if it was that easy to screw up as all that, there sure wouldn't be that many of us left. I make the decision then, that I can do this. After all, look at Rowe, taking charge when she hasn't even done this before. Look at Lacey, coming back in with a bucket, a second stove, and a clean sheet scrounged from the watching crowd, which can't have been an easy task. Look at Zoe, the poor babe riding her pain in this horrible place.

Lacey puts the water in our biggest pot and sets it to boil. 'Whenever a baby's bein' born, they always want clean water. I don't even know what for,' she says, giving me a grin.

'Do you feel the urge to push?' Rowe asks.

'I don't know!' Zoe cries. 'What does it feel like?'

'Um, I'm not exactly sure.'

Zoe lets out a peal of profanities.

'I think it feels like that,' I tell her, 'maybe you should give it a go.'

Lacey drops down by us and shows us a beat-up old pair of scissors. 'Will these do for the cord? I about had to promise *my* firstborn just to borrow 'em.'

'They'll do. Can you boil them for me?'

Lace sets up the second stove. Rowe peers down between Zoe's legs and lets out a little yelp.

'Look, Mirii. It's crowning.'

I do look. There, in between the folds of skin and hair, is a split filled with what I can only assume is a baby's head. I can't decide if it's beautiful or hideous. It's both. I zing with fear and something a little like joy. I'm not at all ready for this, but it's happening. I wonder if that's how Zoe feels, times ten. Times a million.

Zoe starts to writhe again, and Rowe helps her into a squat position. Lace and I each take a side, helping her stay up.

'So, Zoe. When you feel the next contraction coming I want you to bear down and push as hard as you can.'

'Okay!' Zoe says, and a few seconds pass. Then she lets out an almighty cry and screws up her face, forcing all her muscles and will to have this baby out. She pauses, then pushes again, the cry coming from her sounding both inhuman and *all too* human, base and primal. The head emerges, and I'm frozen as I see its tiny ears, the soft down of its hair slicked to its head.

'Very good, Zoe, that's the head! Now, you'll need to push out the shoulders, and then the hard part is over.'

I feel like Rowe is right, and not right. I suspect the harder part will come later.

Zoe gathers herself, winding all her muscles up, and she bears down hard, strangely silent for a moment. Then she breaks out in a scream as she pushes, a scream that seems like it's less about the pain and more about mustering everything that she has inside herself to make this happen. I watch, totally struck, as Zoe pushes the shoulders out. Then it comes quick. The baby slithers out and into Rowe's hands and it's floppy and purple, streaked with blood and goo. The baby doesn't move for a moment, and my heart dips and drops to my belly, but then the baby seems to realise they're out and reaches their arms as Rowe sweeps her fingers through the baby's mouth, clearing the way for the first breath.

Rowe holds the baby up, and Zoe, panting, falls back, pulls up her shirt and reaches out. Rowe places the little wriggly form gently onto Zoe's chest and then we all just stare as the baby nuzzles into her chest, cord stretching long and ropy back into Zoe, still connecting the two of them after all this. Everyone is quiet, us and the little crowd gathered at the door, and the baby starts to cry, a pealy little sound that splits the night air.

DAY FOUR

I come back from chucking the placenta into the compost as the sun is rising, and I flick open the tent flap quietly. Inside, Zoe and the baby snuggle in my bed, dozing comfortably on our last pair of clean sheets. The heat is rising quickly, making the earthy blood-milk smell in the tent just a little sickening. I'm not one for babies, but the sight of them thaws something in me just a little, the baby's hand wrapped tight around Zoe's finger. I stand and watch them breathe for a while, until someone pushes past me. I was so wrapped up in the domesticity of the scene I didn't notice them coming.

'Was there was a baby born here last night?'

It's the surly guard with the flattop, and Vu. *Tran*. Who fucking told them? I mean, it was bound to happen, but the crack of dawn? Snitches work fast, I suppose.

Really, what did I think was going to happen? They'd just let Zoe keep the baby in here, let her strap it on her back for work detail, let it learn to crawl in the dust and the dirt of the yard? Of course not. I knew they'd come from the moment Zoe plonked her pregnant ass down onto my bed, keening. So did she. We all just conveniently forgot for a second, trying to take a smidgen of peace and pleasure in the way the two of them curled into each other as the night faded and the sun rose. It's how we protected ourselves.

'No, no, no, no, no!' Zoe screams as Flattop pulls the sheet off them. 'Not yet! Please not yet!'

I gotta give it to her, Flattop is all business as she gathers up the baby, pulling it away from Zoe's grabbing hands. I wonder what it takes to turn a heart so hard? How many babies you gotta rip from the arms of their mothers before it's just another day on the job? Vu tries to keep her face hard, but it wilts as Flattop hands her the baby, saying, 'Take this,' and she pulls out her taser.

'Not another word outta you, ya little trollop,' she says, and Zoe shrinks back a little.

Rowe goes to stand up, saying, 'Hey . . .' but Lacey pulls her back down. No need for Rowe to cop a tasing for something that we can't stop.

'It got a name?' Flattop asks.

Zoe can barely speak for crying, but she manages to hiccup the name out. It's this or the Orphancorp it goes to will just assign it something stupid. It's the one thing Zoe can give to the baby now, the last thing. 'Mani.'

Vu jiggles Mani gently as they start to cry, and I remember how she used to work the nurseries back when I first met her, how good she was with the little blobbers and how much they loved her, followed her around in their own little wobbly ways, toddling or crawling or just dragging along on their bums to be close to her. How when I first met her she smelled sour like milk, a little like this room smells now, and I want to reach out and take her hand because I can see her eyes get filmy.

'Toughen up, Tran,' Flattop says, but before she can say anything else, Zoe is up and on her, screaming words that get lost in the volume. Flattop pushes Zoe off like she weighs nothing. She arms her taser and shoots, prongs burying into Zoe's naked, swollen chest. When she's done delivering the zap, she strongarms Zoe up and off the bed.

'Why fight it, girlie? You think you'd get to just keep a baby in this trashheap? Now you gonna spend ya post-partum in the PISR instead of out here with your friends.' She drags Zoe out by the arm.

Vu looks down at Mani, then up at me. She gulps down a sob, turns, and follows Flattop out, cradling the baby. I follow to the door, but there's nothing I can do and Vu gives me the most sorrowful look I've ever seen, and she mouths the words, like an echo, like a de ja vu, leaving us alone in the tent with its milky, bloody smell the only evidence that any of it happened at all.

I'm sorry.

—

Food distro doesn't spike the usual hunger in me today, and I let myself get trodden on twice before I drag myself out with a sorry ration of meat, a split-open bag of rice leaking grains onto the dirt, and a broken carrot.

The guard calls us animals, and I don't have the spirit to ask him who the animals really are, but I don't have to because a buncha women call it back to him like it's a singsong little game we all play now.

I feel a dim zing of glee at this tiny display of defiance. The screw looks pissed, but he just fingers his taser, hitches his belt up around his gut and leaves it at that. The glee fades as the sun rises higher into the sky, blistering the ground and bouncing off the Block to blind us as we scrub the dunnies. On a downward spiral, I wonder what it might be like to do this every day for the next thirty-five years. I can't picture it, can't insert a *me* into my mind's eye. I try to draw up a picture of myself, old and cracked by this place, by work and horror and stolen babies, hair greyed and mouth sunken with lost teeth. It doesn't come. Is this because I won't last that long? Or can I not picture it because it's not my destiny, to age and wither in prison? I dunno. I shouldn't be making symbols outta nothing—it's just that I've got too much time to think. All the time in the world. Thoughts tumble, and for a second I wish I could have a quiet brain, wonder what that might be like. Like if there was a pill I could take to keep it all soft and silent in here, would I?

It's tempting, but nah. I like the clamour. I'd miss it if it was gone.

My thoughts are all I have now, aren't they? This place will take everything else: my life, my youth, my everything, but they can't take away my thoughts. They can't get into my head, that's mine.

It's the only place I've got left.

—

The heat barrels down like never-ending punches in the face from the sun. The latrines were hotboxes of baking waste and as I scrubbed 'em out I'd cursed yard duty. Though I can't imagine the farms would be any better, and the factories and warehouses are probably amping the heat; big, airless tin sheds that they are.

At least here in the yard there's the promise of little pools of shade here and there, like oases.

On clean-up I stalk through the yard with my waste bags, hunting shade patch to shade patch, sweat beading on my lip and coursing in tickly little drips down from my armpits. My whole body is a swamp. Water is such a scarce resource, but I wonder if Rowe and Lace might not wanna set aside some tokens for a shower tonight. We could all jam in, make it worth the while. It's been days since I felt clean. I can't imagine how I smell, but if it's anything like everyone else, then it's bad. We could rinse out our uniforms, even. What a bloody treat! A month in this place and I'm thinking of a shower jammed in with two other babes and a quick spot of laundry as the ultimate in luxury.

I'm 'tutionalising fast. It happens. After a childhood in the OC I slip back into it easily, a familiar rut, a hole I fit into because it's already in the shape of me.

I shake the negs out of my head. No rushy misery-thoughts. No use in spiralling further.

The refugees have a day off before work deet starts for them, to set up and acclimatise, get provisions from a special buy-up organised just for them, though I wonder if they've even got the means. I'm sure most of them gave every cent they had to people smugglers, sharks who took a fortune off 'em to jam them on some leaky boat to cross the Arafura Sea and live or die at the ocean's whim.

Calling them sharks does a disservice to real sharks, 'cause at least sharks are just following their nature. People smugglers are colder than that. There's nothing worse than making a mint off desperate people.

They can't all have been cleaned out, though, because as I mosey around, trying to look nonchalant and jamming little scraps of refuse in my bags, I see a few tents flapping in the hot wind. Babes are gathered around a couple of thermo-chip stoves, sorting out ration bags of rice. One gestures to me, her prison-issue minty-green headscarf fluttering in the breeze.

'You!' she says. I look around, but she is staring right at me, so there's no one else she could be talking to.

'Me?' I ask.

'Yes, you. Who else would I be talking to?'

Oh, she's feisty. I like her already.

'How do we start this?' She waves her hand towards the stove. They are a weird, cheapo knockoff brand and pesky little bastards to get going, you need to get the hang of it.

'Um, well, you put the fuel pellets in here, then you have to work this button a bit, see . . .' I show her, and a little crowd gathers around us.

'Yes, good. You have pots? We need more. So many of us, not enough to cook all the food.'

'I do,' I tell her, thinking of the booty I'd razed from all the poor dead babes I'd carted off to compost.

'We have nothing to trade right now,' she says.

'That's okay.'

'From what I know, help never comes for free,' she tells me, her eyes narrowed.

'You can owe me.'

'I do not like to owe people.'

'Me either. But if you want some pots, you're just gunna have to trust me.'

She gives me a look like she doesn't trust anyone, and maybe never has. But when I gesture at her to follow me, she does. I lead her through the tents until we get to mine, rummage through my Personal Effects sack, and hand her two battered pots.

'What you want for them?' she asks.

'I really don't want anything for them, hey. I got 'em off babes who died here, it feels kinda gross just having them in my bag.'

She sighs, like me gifting her the pots is some huge imposition, but she takes them and then takes my hand.

'Thank you.'

'No wuz. I'm Mirii, by the way.'

'Nabeeha.'

'Where you from?'

'Everywhere. Nowhere. Born on the move. You?'

'Born here.'

'Lucky you. How long have you been in this place?'

'A month. How long have you been in detention?'

'Four years. Came by sea. We got captured up by the Force when we made it to the Peninsula. They move us from place to place. Seems like each is worse than the last. This is the ultimate shithole.'

'That's a perfect description,' I tell her.

'My grandmother, she was a very educated woman. University,' she says, with reverence. 'She gave me lessons my whole life, until she drowned in the sea. I'm smart, I can make something of myself here. Make all this worth it. There's a review of my case in seven months, my residency application. Maybe I get out of here.'

I want to tell her how hard it is, how much everyone thinks that they could have a chance here, and how most fall along the wayside, but I don't have the heart.

—

I'm cruising the Block with my garbage bags, picking up all the flotsam that's blown up against the walls, when a door in the facade bursts open. I jump like I've taken a scare in a horror flix and my bag upends, sending trash flying all over the joint.

'Out of the way, prisoner!' says the screw, a burly dude with a gut that protrudes over his hard-working belt. He pushes a babe out through the door and she stumbles, then fall onto the baked ground.

'Pick that shit up!' the screw says, and I make busy with the tidying, jamming scraps back into the sack. As soon as he closes the door, I stop, reach down and help the babe up.

'You okay?' I ask.

'I think so,' she says, and dusts herself off. 'I'm Cady.' She picks up the pack she dropped, dusts it off too.

'Hi.'

'What the fuck is this place?'

'What do you mean?'

'What kind of rehab is this?'

I look her up and down, confused. I see that she's shaking, sweaty and glowy-pale. Poor thing. 'I hate to be the one to break it to you, but this isn't rehab, babe. This is prison.'

'I . . . I signed up for rehab . . .' She trails off, looking around the yard, her bottom lip setting to tremble.

'Was it free?'

'I couldn't afford to pay . . . The Mercies Ministry arranged it all for me . . .'

Oh, this is rough. It clicks together in my head real quick. I bet it's some church-group that has a bit of a handshake dealio with Corrections Co, sends their addled babes along under the guise of treatment. She'll detox all right, just not under any kind of medical supervision. She'll detox while working the farms and I bet the measly few cents she'll earn per hour will go to the Ministry as well.

She's crying now, wailing even, and it hurts to hear her, so I give her a bit of a pat, pat, pat on the shoulder 'cause I'm not sure what else to do. Bloody hell, why did I have to be the one to break it to her?

'Come on, Cady. It'll be okay.' I pick up the pack she dropped on the ground and open it up. 'Looks like the Ministry gave you a tent! If you'da come in as a regular old inmate you'd probs be sleeping in a box tonight. Ooh, a stove too! That's some kinda something, isn't it?'

Cady just looks at me like I'm responsible for the mess she's in, and she cries harder. Bloody hell, I'm so bad at this.

'Come on, it's almost knockoff time. We might have some spare food for ya, and my bunkmate Rowe can look you over, she's a doc.'

'Does she have any Fentalyn?' Cady asks, hiccuping.

'No,' I say.

'Oxynim? Tarmeine, even? Can you get smack in here?'

'You'll probs be better off just forgetting about all that, hey. Unless you're rolling in spare bucks, you're just gonna hafta brave it out. My friend Lacey detoxed when she came in, she can give you some advice.'

Cady starts to cry harder, then she doubles over and spews a bit in the dust. I wait for her to finish heaving, then steer her by the trembly shoulders towards our tent. I feel some hint of empathy towards her, but it's faint.

I feel like I'm switching off inside. Like, I gotta, to protect myself. After Mani and Zoe and the dead bodies and my sentence and just bloody everything, if I really let myself feel anything I wouldn't be able to drag my sorry arse off my mattress in the morning. Like, if I let myself feel even a bit bad for Cady, then all the horrible things and sad stories going on in this joint will loom, and my feelings will spiral outwards, picking up on every one until my heart just stops or something. I can feel myself icing over a little already.

Not even the heatwave afternoon can touch that kinda cold.

———

It's late and there's quiet—almost. I can hear Cady sobbing constantly, pausing only to retch in the little single tent she's put up close to ours so that Rowe can keep an eye on her.

I feel like I won't ever know real silence here, but then again, I haven't had much of it in my life. With whispers, tears and other night rumbles in every dorm I've ever lived in, silence has only ever happened in solitary: the PISR, Time Out. Maybe real silence here would set me to shiver, bring the flashbacks cascading. I can imagine it, though—the night silence of the desert out there, beyond the black.

I wiggle down under my blanket and worm around until I'm as comfortable as I'm ever going to get on this hideous mattress. Sleep is almost on me when I hear footsteps. They're soft, rubber on dry, sandy dirt, but I can just make them out. The tent flap lifts a little and I hear a whisper.

'Mirii?'

I'd know that voice anywhere.

'Vu?'

She slips in, blinking at the darkness inside after being out in the spotlit yard. She's slight in her uniform, utility belt heavy at her waist and she's got her taser in her hand. She clips it to her hip as she comes inside.

'Down here,' I say, and she sidles carefully around the bed where Rowe and Lacey are sleeping. She sits down on my mattress, her knees cracking with the bend, and she takes my hand in hers.

'I have to be quick. I think I can get you out. I've seen blueprints, been watching the cameras, exploring the block. There's a corridor, it was supposed to join this place to a second part of the facility, but it was never built. If I can get you into the Block, I dunno how, steal a guard's uniform or something. We can take the tunnel and come up through an access panel.'

'No fucking vents. No way. Not again . . .'

'I've got a car waiting, it's just outside of the township.'

'Even if we could make it, I won't go alone. I can't leave Rowe and Lacey here.' I gesture up to the bed, where Rowe adjusts herself then resumes her soft snoring.

In the low light I see Vu's brow crumple. 'I don't think I can get the three of you out, but.'

'It's my fault they're here. I won't leave them. We'll have to think of something else. I got the time.'

'I get what you mean Mirii, but I dunno how long I can keep the mask on. This work . . . You don't know what it's like to have to treat these women this way. It hurts. We gotta do it soon. What if you get sent to the PISR again? What if they find out I've got a fake ident?'

I can see I'm breaking her a little bit with my insistence that I won't leave Lace and Rowe behind and I feel like a regular jerk right now. She's trying to calculate, to do the new escape maths, and she can't work out the answer. I don't know what to tell her, or what to do, so I do the only thing I can think of and I kiss her.

Kissing is easy. It makes my brain shut up and I think it makes hers quieten too, because I feel the tension in her body drop just a little.

'Don't even think about it,' comes a voice from the bed, and we both look up at Lacey, whose open eyes glimmer in the dark. 'Find somewhere else for your little reunion.'

'Gotcha,' I say, and we fumble up and off my mattress, trying not to wake Rowe up too. I take my blanket and we slip around the back, laying it out in the small space between our tent and the one behind us.

Vu runs her hands through my filthy hair, across my neck, back up to my cheeks. I fumble at her waist, get her bulky belt off, and hold her tight to me. Then it's just our bodies pressed, gradually more skin to skin. Everything slips away while her mouth is at mine, this place, the time that's passed between us, all the distance we've come to get to each other.

She lays me flat on my back and I clamp a hand over my mouth to keep myself quiet. Her mouth is at my neck and her hand on me feels so good that I can't bear it. It comes quick, and everything rushes away. The weight of my sentence, the fences and the Block and the dust.

I could be nowhere, I could be anywhere.

It takes a while for me to come back to myself. I can't remember feeling this good. When I'm back, she kisses me again, grins white in the dim light.

I'm kissing down her belly when she says it.

'I think I love you, Mirii.'

I stop right around her bellybutton. Fear bubbles up from my guts, but I try to swallow it. That word, why is it so scary? But why else did I go so far to find her, why would she come all this way to save me? We've had so little real time together, just a few days, and been apart so long, but that feeling of what we *could* be has carried us both over so much time and distance.

I still can't look at her while I say it, though, so I stare intently at the curve of her stomach and murmur, 'I think I love you too, Adeline.'

'Ugh,' she sighs, her fingers slipping through my hair, catching in the tangles. 'Don't call me that.'

But it gets so much more intense after we say it. It's like the words spark off something huge in us and we careen into each other, the world receding more and more with every kiss and bite and sharp breath. There's not much else besides the hot feel of her thighs on my ears, and I reach up to cup her cheek but then there's the clamp of her teeth on my fingers as she catches them in her mouth. Every time I get her there I want to make it like a gift for all the way she's come for me, and me for her.

—

Vu said she was just going to tuck me back in to bed, but tucks turned to cuddles, then sleep.

We aren't even awake when she comes. I crack an eye to a bitter laugh and then blink against the spotlights coming in through the tent door. She's backlit but I still see her just enough to know we're in deep shit.

'You fucken two,' she says.

She's pale from all that time underground, and too thin in her paper gown. Face a shadowy mess of bruises and cuts, remnants of our scrapes and clashes in the PISR. White-blonde hair, that missing canine tooth a black hole in her twisty smile.

'Oh, this is rich,' Freya says.

DAY FIVE

'So, whatcha gunna give me to not wake up the entire camp right now?' she says.

Rowe's getting out of bed, bewildered, and Lace sits up, wincing and looking confused.

'Whatever you want, Freya,' I tell her, getting up off the bed with my sheet wrapped around me all awkward, tripping over. 'What do you want?'

She lets the tent flap go, sending us into a hushy darkness.

'Hmm, what do I want? I'd love to see you go back to the PISR, mostly. But I'm guessing you've got some kinda plan going on with Wu here.'

'Vu,' Vu says.

'Whatever. I reckon you've got a plan to get out of here with *Vu*, and I want in.'

I crumple just a little inside. I've got to do it.

'You're right. We're getting out of here, and if you keep your big mouth shut, maybe we'll take you too.'

I mentally kick myself for saying it, but what else could I do?

'How can I trust you?' Freya asks, curling a lip and I ache to whack her right in it, but keep my fists bunched at my sides 'til the knuckles ache and go white.

'I dunno. You're just gonna have to. I've got nothing else but my word.'

She looks doubtful, but what are her choices? She can get me thrown in the PISR right now or take a chance on escape with nothing to go on but my say-so. If the roles were reversed, I don't even know which one I'd take. This is her shot, right now, because once Vu is back on the Block it will be Freya's word against hers.

What it comes down to is what she wants most.

Does she wanna hurt me, punish me for all the things I've done to her and the things she thinks I've done to her? Or does she want to have a life outside of this place, a chance at a future, something more than this yard and labour and starving until she's too old and too institutionalised for freedom to make a difference?

Everyone's holding their breath, the room a big, silent, sucking vacuum. There's a sudden fox-cry in the distance and we all jump, everyone except Freya who's all iron-focus.

'Fine,' she says, finally. 'But I want all your extra rations and any other little sweeties you might have hidden away in here.'

I breathe out, close my eyes and start digging round for the extra rice.

Vu leaves first, so Freya can't go back on her word and start clanging pots and pans after making off with all our juicy treats. As she leaves, Vu gives me a dark look and a quick kiss.

'I'll try to come again when I can,' she says. 'We need to talk.'

Freya watches her go then narrows her eyes on me. 'Shake on it, Mirii. I want outta here.'

'What's your sentence?' I ask her.

'Five years,' she says, and I wonder at how little time she really has in the grand scheme of things. If she had forethought or hope or anything, even the tiniest glimmer, she'd keep out of trouble, serve her time right and get out legit. Not escape and spend her life on the lam, always wondering when the big hand's gonna swoop down to scoop her up. That's the kind of life I'll have—but I'll trade paranoia for the prospect of thirty-five years in this joint. It's just that Freya don't see a future for herself. She lives in the right now, the heartbeat thud of one second at a time, all reaction and no time to consider.

I reckon she'd be back here within a month even if she did serve out her time.

I reckon she'll be back here in a month even if she does escape.

I shake on it anyway. What else am I gonna do?

Freya skips off, leaving me, Rowe and Lacey gaping in her aftermath.

'What the hell just happened?' Lacey asks, sinking back down on the bed.

'We're in the shit,' I tell her, because there's no other words that are gonna cut it.

—

When the sun comes up it gets so much hotter.

Like, actually hotter, not all metaphorical, though that argument could be made.

Assem is at six and already there's sweat beading on my forehead and little runners dripping down my back to soak into the waistband of my pants. We stand at attention before the block, getting scanned as the sun rises, pushing out what little coolness the night brought. It's gonna be a scorcher, way worse than any of the days previous, and I give a thought to the poor babes going out to the farms today, to back-break bend-over in the midday sun. There's four of us missing this morning, and after a few good bellows and a threat of the PISR, no one appears, so I know that I've got some corpse-collecting to do today. Wonderful. Are all these babes keeling over from the heat?

The crackle of the loudspeaker announces the presence of the COO. She's got up in pale blue this morning, the same colour as the sun-blasted sky, and she holds a brilliant white parasol to shade her taut skin from the early morning sun. It catches the light and sends it back down, blinding us as she comes forward.

'Inmates!' she begins. 'Productivity is already up 40 percent! The Board is satisfied with the progress being made, and as a tribute to the hard work you've put into this initiative, we are increasing your water rations by 200 millilitres, beginning today.'

There's a half-hearted murmur of thanks from the crowd, but we're all too warm and pre-empting a long day in the stinking heat to cause much of a ruckus this morning. I guess we're all just glad we get a little more fluid to sweat out today.

Isn't it funny how if they take away everything, giving us what constitutes 'still not enough' makes us thankful? Even so, I click the extra water token against the others in my hand and then wipe the sweat outta my eyes, linking arms with Lace and Rowe as assem breaks up and we head towards distro.

—

As we're cooking breakfast Rowe sits up suddenly, spilling out half of her little plastic bag of spices out onto the floor.

'Watch it!' Lacey says.

Rowe doesn't even notice. 'Did you hear that?'

'Hear what?' I ask her, and then I hear it too. The crackle of gunfire. Underneath it, bellows and howls.

'Is that coming from in here?' I say, and rush to the doorway to see a bunch of babes with their heads poked out too, noseying towards the Block. I can see guards running across the balconies, guns poised.

'I think it's coming from the men's side,' Rowe says.

The steady gunfire pops keep up. Rowe and Lace and I look at each other with wide fear-eyes and then a siren starts to howl, blocking out the gunfire sound, blocking out everything. It drowns the whole world, it's so loud. Lacey and Rowe drop to the ground, face-down in the dust. My brain feels like it's gonna start dribbling out of my ears at any moment. Just when I think I can't take another second of it, the wail stops and there's a great void of silence that feels massive after the blaring sound.

'It's a lockdown!' Lacey says. 'Get on the floor, the guards'll be here soon and if they find you up, they'll bash you to the ground!'

I drop down to my knees and then my belly, turning my head towards Rowe and Lacey and we all flick our eyes back and forth to each other.

'What now?' I ask.

'We wait until the guards come by,' Lacey says. 'Then . . . I don't know.'

We wait. The dirt gets inside my nose and my sudden sneezes echo in the quiet. Finally, there's the sound of rubber-soled boots on packed dirt and a guard sticks her head in the flap. It's the nice screw, the only one other than Vu who's not a complete bastard. She's got her tase unit out and primed, and all of us reflexively cringe away from it, but when she sees it's me, she drops it down a bit.

'You can get up, prisoners.'

We struggle to our feet.

'What's happening?' I ask her. I'm reaching, but I feel like she might tell us.

She looks back out through the entryway, then comes just a little closer.

'It's the men's camp. They've taken over their yard. They've got ten guards as hostages and they're trying to take the Block. The whole women's camp is on lockdown, no work detail, no leaving the yard. They're trying not to let this spread.'

'Now what happens?' Lacey says.

'We dunno. Corrections Co is sending in their riot squad. We're hoping this doesn't take long, but that don't seem likely.'

'Has this happened before?' I ask her.

'Yeh, once, in a facility down on the South Coast.'

'And what happened there?' Rowe says, her voice going all high pitched at the end, like maybe she doesn't really want to know the answer. The screw takes another look out of the tent, double making sure she's not being watched, then she goes on.

'They had the yard four days. Big breakout. Then it was a bloodbath, what else d'ya expect?'

I close my eyes. Of course it was a bloodbath. Sure, our labour pays their shareholders, but us prisoners don't mean that much to them. Not enough to stop 'em from gunning us down like plinking cans on a fence, one by one. Prisoners? In this world, they are pretty easy to come by.

I sneaky-peek out into the yard after the screw is gone, watching the other guards go by, two by two, guns and tasers poised, fingers braced on triggers. The sitch is knifey-sharp, tension rising like heat off the ground. I only feel safe when I've closed the tent flap again though I don't know why. Like these canvas walls wouldn't just fly to tatters under a rain of bullets. It's just an illusion of safety, the soft domesticity of Rowe and Lacey boiling rice when outside is like leaf-litter drying, a forest not burnt for years, just waiting for a stray spark to ignite. I feel like burrowing underneath my mattress, down into the cool dirt where I can hide from expectation and responsibility and fear. From screws with guns and girls with shivs. From this whole mess, my life, my memories, and the entire world.

All I'm feeling right now is like I don't want to die, and if I hide long enough I might survive this. Until a situation hots up like this, it's easy to forget that guns are real, and that people are really just fragile buckets of guts and blood.

'Do we use this?' Rowe says.

'Like how?' I ask.

'Do we take advantage of this situation? Escape? That's what you're planning with Vu, isn't it?'

I was afraid she'd say that.

'I need to talk to her,' I say, lifting the tent flap just a bit and peering out, like speaking her name might summon Vu. It doesn't. Outside, the yard is eerie silent. A plastic wrapper floats by on the hot breeze. I watch the wind pick it up and send it over the fence, easy as that.

Why can't it be that easy for us?

—

The sound of my boots is just a soft thunk, thunk, thunk over the dirt, but it echoes deafeningly over the silence of the camp, the quiet of this place feeling so wrong in my ears. I'm slipping through the gaps in the tents, nav-ing carefully over guylines and pegs sticking up from the crackly ground. I'd spotted Vu on patrol with some beefcake screw, this square-jawed bru with an M16 and a filthy look on his face, and now I'm following them ultra-careful and quiet. I'm not the only inmate out, now and again there's the soft shuffle of some prisoner zipping between the tents and the harsh staccato of a guard ordering them back inside.

I can see panic in their eyes when I peer out from behind a canvas wall and I watch Vu and the Jaw twitch as gunfire pops from across the fence.

I don't know how to get to her. I can't let her partner know that I'm trying to talk to her, but I can't just follow them forever. I summon up every bravey scrap I got inside, and carefully ease out onto the pathway in front of them, eyes on that gun barrel.

'Inmate, back to your tent!' he barks, swinging the gun my way. I try not to wince as he aims it. Visibly shaking. I throw my hands up.

'Aye aye, captain,' I say, and give Vu a Look.

I can't, she mouths at me, subtle.

I throw her a facial that says, I know, but . . .

'Go on, fuck off back to your tent!' the dude-bru screw says and I scuttle off, wondering how I'm gonna get her away from him. All I can do is hope that Vu can throw him off somehow and come to me. I'll be waiting.

I'm halfway home when the boom of gunfire sounds, close. That's not on the men's side, that is coming from here, and my insides turn liquid hot and cold at the same time. I'm right by San's tent so I rush at it, throwing myself through the flap as if the bullets are coming for me. I land hard on the packed-earth floor, eyes squeezed tight and arms up like they could protect me from the deadly lead.

'Mirii?' San says. I open my eyes and look around. She's not alone. The tent is not shot to ribbons or nothing and I feel kinda stupid as these babes all peer down at me with shiny fear-eyes.

I've interrupted something. I can tell by the absence in the air, like this party was full of important whispers just before I crashed it. I stand up and dust myself off, feeling foolish, then I wait with this weird mix of chicas and we all listen for more shots. They don't come. Were they just a warning?

'Out, girlie,' says one of the women.

'No, she's okay,' San says. 'She works on the yard with me.'

'What's happening?' I ask. I don't know if I mean in here, or out there.

'We're taking the yard,' says a young woman from the back. She's tall, with short, dark hair and a hard, brown face. 'That, or we're all going to die.'

'Shush, Tarni,' San says, throwing her a loaded look.

'You Indigenous?' she asks me, ignoring San.

'Um, I dunno. I think so.'

'Who your people?'

'I'm not sure. I'm from an Orphancorp. But my name is Gamilaraay. I looked it up. Means shooting star.'

She nods, gives it a little consideration. 'There are a lot of us in here, from all nations. 'Cause it's a crime to be Koori in our own bloody country!' She laughs a bitter 'Ha!' that twists her features hard and cold.

'Now isn't the time, Tarni,' San says, but Tarni scoffs at her.

'Don't talk over her, San,' comes from the back. 'Let her speak!'

'I've got sisters primed and ready,' Tarni says. 'We could have this yard in ten minutes. We've got numbers, weapons, and the will. The men are acting, why can't we? You've been talking about it for years now, San. It's what you do.'

'I organise people. I don't have the power to organise a riot.

That's a contradiction in terms, isn't it?'

'You could focus it, though, couldn't you? The energy? Towards the screws. Towards the fences!'

'You've been planning this, San?' I ask. 'Is that why you're getting messages from the men's side?' Stuff starts to make sense, like why San has such gravity in the camp.

'I haven't been planning this! I don't want a bloodstorm. Which this is going to be.'

'Only if we don't have leadership!' Tarni says.

'You want to step up?' San says. 'Try and unite all these women into something cohesive enough to take down the Block? The screws? Good luck.'

'Or we just sit by and let it happen? Let the guards take us out one by one? Not on my watch, San. We can take action now, before they get the upper hand.'

'They've always got the upper hand,' San says.

'Not if you have hostages,' Tarni says.

'Ha! The Corp cares as much about the screws as it cares about us.'

'There's one person who the Corp will care about, though,' I say, my mouth just kind of moving on its own, before my brain has time to catch up to it and tell it to bloody stay out of this. 'If we can get her, then they'll have to hold their fire.'

San and Tarni and all the other women look at me like they all get it at exactly the same time. Then they look at each other like they don't know why they didn't think of it earlier.

'I mean, we'd have to storm the Block . . .' Tarni says, and now I'm flooded with that realisation as well.

If they're storming the Block, then me and Rowe, Lacey and Vu can get in there too. We can use the riot as cover.

We can get out of here.

'. . . sixteen shivs, two maces, a slingshot, and some babe made a bloody pipe bomb, who knows how she hid that from the screws,' Tarni says, listing out the weapons she's got prepped.

'If we have a pipe bomb, then we could blast open the dock door on the Block, where they do morning food distro,' San says.

'Is the mad bomber down to party with us?' I ask.

'Oh yeh,' Tarni says. 'She's been wanting to riot for ages, we've had to hold her off.'

'Good.'

'We're really doing this, aren't we?' I say.

'Looks like it,' San says, her eyes bleak. 'Have you thought about what you're gonna do if you get out of here?'

'Nah,' I tell her. 'I can't think that far ahead.'

Like, if I start thinking about that, then I start thinking of all the little things that will crop up along the way, and then my brain just starts to spiral. I can only take this one day at a time.

One hour, maybe.

—

I've never felt quite as tense as I am now, with the fuse lit and a bunch of women hunkered down around me in a tent we've crammed into in the first row. The anxiety is a real, living thing weighing down heavy on my chest and head and limbs. The moment the fuse sputters to life, every babe in this tent clenches their teeth, their fists, their everything. I've got the glass shiv tucked into the waistband of my pants and I'm just waiting to shift the wrong way and stab myself, the first casualty in this probs totally doomed plan.

Plan? I don't even know if you could call it that. We're just a bunch of babes with a bomb and a few knives against at least forty screws with guns and tasers and mace and stab vests. The only thing we've got on our side is the diversion of the male population, and the fact that there are a whole lotta us and not so many of them.

Screws are still filing two by two up and down the rows. But the women are coming out now, collecting in furious little mobs, and the guards are having a harder time keeping them at bay. Now and then one will shout something angry to the screws, and they'll point their guns and puff up, but I think they know by now that any shot is gonna spark something off, something they wanna keep down. The roller door to the Block is thankfully clear. Like I need the fear that I'm gonna explode some poor babe or screw along with the door weighing on me. I've got enough worries already.

I mean, once we're in, there's still screws with guns to contend with. They'll fire then, oh yes. People will die today. Everyone says they've made peace with that, but I don't got serenity thinking that I might lose any one of these chicas, let alone any of my friends.

Rowe crouches to my left, whispering, 'Oh dear, oh dear, oh dear,' softly. Lacey is breathing hard with the pain she's trying to ignore so she can be in on this and not just listening and hoping from our tent. San's towards the back, and I can feel her eyes on me from here, her gaze heavy, like it's loading me up with something huge.

The fuse's at halfway now. I don't know how any of the screws haven't noticed the little burning flame puttering along towards the Block, but they haven't.

I try to go to my happy place, but I'm having trouble finding it. Used to be that I could call it up at will, a sweet mix of memories of my free days, the tiny point of time just after I got out of my Orphancorp and before I got myself into this mess. A few months where I worked for me, breathed free, tripped and zipped and fucked my way around Sydney. It's so close that I can almost feel it, but I can't let it centre me like it always did before.

Instead I feel the salty wash of fear inch through me. It creeps like the sweat creeps down my spine in this hot tent, stifled by the breath of so many women tucked in tight, stinking of dread and unwashed bodies.

Two-thirds burnt now, and there's a commotion off to our right as a little group of women explodes with foul language directed towards the screws. There's the soft metal clatter of guns being drawn and cocked, and I'm thinking, *Not now, not now!*, as the shouting match between them continues and intensifies. Into my vision in the little sliver of view between canvas sheets come Vu and her guard partner, hurrying towards the Block.

No!

I don't even think, just bust out of my hidey hole. Rowe grabs for me and misses, and I feel the soft brush of her fingertips along my arm as I go. I glance at the fuse, now more than three-quarters of the way to the detonator. I race towards Vu, mouth open, but nothing coming out and I see the other screw swing up his gun as I approach her. He aims it, and then I've connected with her body and we go down just as he fires, and misses. The shot stuns every-thing into silence. One quiet second, long and fat with shock and awe, and I feel Vu's body under mine, and then . . .

Then . . .

Ka-bam!

Dust flies.

Dust obscures everything, the door, the Block, turns every-thing a hazy orange like the end of the world. Vu breathes hard beneath me, warm and alive, and me too, I can't feel anything missing. No sticky blood between us. Shots ring out, and into the short, dusty view falls a babe, bleeding. I hear the thump of boots, and I can see a bit more now, shapes moving forward, hear the guttural cries of women long-suffering, as they see the opportunity and take it. There's the thud of fists on flesh, the crack of a gun butt smashing a face, and a sick gurgle that comes from a shivved screw who falls alongside us.

I can't think of what to do besides hold on to Vu. She holds me back and we lie in the dirt like that until things clear a little, the sky peeking blue again through swirls of soil. Around us are fallen babes, bleeding screws. I can see the door to distro now, the aluminium a peeled-open flower, and there's women rushing through, armed now with the guns they've liberated from dead guards.

This is not your fault, I tell myself. You just set the spark, you can't control the fire when it goes wild.

But I've got my eyes locked onto the forever-open eyes of the woman who fell by us, and try telling her not to blame me, right?

'Mirii,' Vu says. 'Get up! We can use this. Let's get out of here.'

'I know. But Lace, Rowe!'

'We'll find them.'

When I finally roll off Vu, and scramble to my feet, I find them back in the tent where we set the fuse. Rowe's got her hands clamped tight over Lacey's ears, and they're curled up on the ground, low against the flying bullets.

'Come on,' I say, dragging them up. 'We've got to go!'

We run towards the Block, low. Inmates flow in through the jagged hole, and we join them, leaping over the ripped-up door.

'This way!' Vu says, reaching for my hand, and she leads us past the babes with their newly-liberated guns pressed tight up under the chins of screws, hurrying so they don't notice her. As we hightail past the distro point for the men's side, we hear the heavy boom of the roller door as it takes hit after hit. Not everyone has a pipe bomb lying around, ya know? We just got lucky.

We could help them. We should help them. But I don't want to think about the men's side. I don't want to think about the secondary chaos that it will cause when the men breach and flood through, though it sounds like they're close. Look, it's not that I don't like bros or whatever, it's just that they'd be a new level of tumult on top of an already stacked strata. And then, sometimes dudes are the worst.

Vu presses her pass against a door and it beeps and opens to let us through. Then, silence. A hallway, perfectly normal, grey-painted walls clean and lino floor squeaking under our feet.

'The corridor, it's this way.'

We take the hallway slowly, knowing that there are probably screws holed up somewhere, scared and armed and just ready to be startled in a deadly kinda way. My jaw aches from the stressy clench as we round a corner, but everything is clear and startlingly silent except for the squeak of our boots on the painted concrete. When Vu points at a door, we open it slow, knowing that we've got nothing if there's a screw on the other side. I peek around, and there's something there that takes my mind and my eyes a second to comprehend.

Black, round. Real close, lined up with my eye.

I do the first thing that comes into my head, which is to flail out a hand and push the gun barrel up as it booms. My ears ring. The gun flies out of her hand, and our door crashes open. I barely think, just lash out with fists and feet, feeling the thud of flesh against mine, but it's far away, my brain still echoing with the sound of the shot.

I'm tired of fighting.

But I can't stop. It's my life. It's our lives.

I come back to myself when my head meets hers with a sharp crack, and I've got her by the shoulders, her face bloodied and she's not really there any more, her eyes just whites. Someone grabs me, and I spin and lash out an elbow, clocking them on the chin, but when I look closer, it's not a guard, it's Vu.

'Mirii! It's me. It's over, she's out.'

I can barely hear her for the high-pitched din in my ears.

'I'm sorry, Vu, I'm sorry, I didn't see . . .'

'It's okay. I'm okay.' Vu rubs her jaw and looks at me, her eyes flashing with hurt for a second.

Rowe and Lacey stare at me as they shuffle past, probably wondering what kind of monster I've become that I can bash my own babe in the face during a fight. I wonder too. Where does the line fall between fighting to live and living to fight? I don't even fucking know any more. I've been fighting my entire life, one way or another.

We leave the guard slumped on the floor by the stairwell door and creep through the hallway, Vu on point and armed with the rifle she took from the screw, handling it with a sureness that I hadn't expected. We come to a heavy gate. I remember this. It's the way down to the PISR.

'I'm not going back down there,' I say, knowing very well that I am.

Lacey glares at me, white-faced and sweating. 'For fuck's sake, Mirii.'

She holds open the door to the PISR, a grey stairwell lit with hideous fluorescents, and I tremble, gulping at the huge amounts of spit my mouth suddenly decides to flood with. Flashes of all the hideous underground places I've had to endure come at me, making it hard to breathe.

'I'm having flashbacks,' I whine as Rowe slips past me and through the door.

'Deal with it,' Lace says, and I try to be strong for her, as strong as she is being. I'm not. I'm not that strong. For a flash second, I hate her for her sharpness, all the spiny, pointy bits of her that she juts out to protect herself in here, the twisted carapace she's cultivated just to get through. But the hate is twisted up with jealousy because I'm struggling now, real hard, and I wish I could put on my game face and get this done.

I pause at the top of the stairs as everyone clatters down. I try to gather up some strength, but it's like a bucket on a rope scraping the almost-empty bottom of a well.

Then Lacey comes up behind me and pushes me off the top step, spurring me to catch myself then trip my way down the first flight before I even know it.

'Look at that,' she says, clutching at the rail as she grunts down the stairs behind me. 'Easy.' She actually flashes me a grin that's half grimace, but still. I try to grin back at her, but my face doesn't want to cooperate, and I think I really just bare my teeth. I slip an arm under hers and help her the rest of the way down.

The solitary cells are alive with screams and rattles.

We forgot about these women.

Oh my god, how long would we have forgotten them for?

'We've got to let them out,' I say.

'Do you know how?' Rowe asks me. I don't. I stumble into the screws' booth and hit the biggest, reddest button I can find. A siren wails and there's a big grinding as all the doors slide open. Babes flail out, screeching.

'We've got the yard!' I say, and point vaguely upwards.

They tear up the stairs, leaving us with only echoes barrelling up and down the row. All except one. I can see her shadow looming long up and out of her door. She doesn't move. I already know who it is.

'So, you've come for me. Didn't think you would,' Freya says.

'Um, well, I always keep my promises,' I say to her, but she can tell I'm lying. Anyone can. I'm so fugged with shock and echoing shots and booms that I can't fake anything right now. I didn't even know she was here, though I did wonder where she was when all the action went down. Freya loves rough and tumble. A riot woulda been her element. She would've been front and centre, anything for a bit of violence. It's just her nature—the Corps and this place can't tame it out of her. Freya's been fighting her whole life, and she's not tired of it. It sparks her. It's how she thrives. It's how she must have got put back in the PISR a day after she got out.

'We really have the yard?' she asks us.

'Kinda. Like, how else would we be here?' Lacey says.

'Whatever,' she says, and stomps out of her cell, paper gown flapping. She eyes up Vu, gives her a sneer, and puts her hands on her hips. 'So, Wu, what now? What's your amazing escape plan, then?'

Vu looks set to deck her, but holds it in. 'Down here,' she says, and pushes past Freya. She strides down the hall, getting smaller, fading in and out of the pools of brightness made by the intermittent lights along the way. We follow, Freya glaring at every one of us as we pass her, then bringing up the rear.

The hallway stretches on, cells lining the way until they abruptly stop. There's a blockade made of yellow-striped tape that Vu pulls down. Beyond is nothing but a bored-out hole, the lights reaching out their glow.

'We need a torch.'

Rowe dashes back to the screws' booth and comes back with a

tiny pen torch. Totally insufficient, but it'll have to do. Vu takes point, and we step over the piles of torn-down tape, careful not to trip.

The bored-out tunnel takes a slow curve, and we round it, Vu shining the lights on all sides, looking for an access panel, a man-hole, anything. Then . . .

It ends in an abrupt wall of rough, crumbly rock that glows red in the small circle of light from the torch.

The tunnel—it doesn't go anywhere.

Vu scrabbles at the stone. 'No, no, no . . .' she wails. She's sob-bing, low and soft, body shaking with each shuddery breath. Her fingernails bend and break on the rock wall and I pull her away from the stone as her hands bead with blood. I don't know what she's gone through to get here, and what she went through before that. What she did to get the money for the new ident, who she might have bribed and how she bribed them to get the job here. I don't know what they did to her at Psynode. I don't know her life, her convoluted path here, all the stuff she's seen and done and had done to her that led her to this point, to grating up her hands trying to get out. She's just as trapped as I am, as we all are.

I gather her up in my arms. Rowe and Lace look respectfully at the floor, faces glowing ghoulish in the torchlight, but Freya watches us like she's trying to work it all out, like she's studying the way humans exhibit emotions.

'There'll be another way, babe. We'll get each other out of here.'

'It's over,' she says. 'We'll go back to the yard and we'll die out there.'

'No way,' I whisper into her hair. 'I wouldn't let it end like that.'

—

I knew we were walking back into a riot, but I forgot what it might look like, sound like.

In the late afternoon light there are babes aiming guns up at the third storey, trying to take out the screws who duck and hide below the rail. Others vicious-taunt the growing crowd of guards they've got bailed up, hostage-style, in the yard. Other prisoners, more level-headed than the rest, try to hold them back from the screws, but they're fighting a pointless battle against a roiling tide of fired-up women.

Treat a babe like an animal, and who can say how she'll turn on you when it all comes tumbling down?

We duck our way out of the block, bending to avoid stray bullets—moving low and fast across the yard. In the distance comes the thwack-thwack-thwack of a chopper. We watch it swoop over the fence and everyone freaks and drops for cover, but no shots follow. It bends in the air, angling up, and disappears over the rise of the Block.

'The COO,' Rowe says. 'I think they're evacuating her from the roof.'

'Good luck with that,' Freya says. 'I bet she's in pieces already.'

'No way,' I tell her. 'She's the perfect hostage. She's the only thing that might save us from whatever they've got planned to squash this.'

Everyone in the yard stares at the roof of the Block. We can't see anything, but we hear it. The chop of the rotors, then the small pop of gunfire beneath. Who's up there? What's going on?

The chopper lifts up, coming into view. It hovers just a bit, hanging in mid-air, then something flies into the rotor, and clips it, just so slightly. Then it goes all wrong, the angles off. It seems to come out of the sky slow. We respond slow, too, a heavy pause before the running starts. Everyone scatters as the chopper sails down like a feather on the breeze, tilting wildly. I don't see any more, just my own blind panic as I throw myself to the ground and cover my head with my hands like that's gonna save me. The sound of the crash is everything, all around me, and something whizzes by my head, close enough that I feel the air split around it.

The silence after is crushing.

I stand on quivery legs and there's carnage every place I look. The downed chopper, flattened like a crushed can and looking incongruous in the middle of the yard. Here and there, babes and screws split apart. I try not to look, but can't break my eyes away.

It's funny how we all look the same on the inside.

And then there's the far-off, growing sound of jeers and celebration. Through the remnants of the roller door for distro comes Tarni, M16 raised up above her head, and behind her, dragged scrabbling and crying, is a familiar shape. Pale blue suit, high-lit hair. Tight features, the face a mask, even as she is dragged, struggling and screaming, across the yard.

The COO.

We've got her.

—

For a while the COO doesn't seem like a person, just a token, but then I catch a glimpse of her eyes, bright blue and set into her taut face. There's terror there, such boundless, wide-open fear. Who knows, maybe she's afraid that we'll treat her the way she's treated us.

I watch her as she's pulled across the yard, stumbling on the baked-dirt ground in her spike heels. The legs of her pantsuit get streaked with dust, and it pleases me to see her get dirty.

Yep, I'm that petty.

Prisoners surround her, whooping and cheering and calling for her head. Tarni hustles her into San's tent and when I find Rowe, Lace, Vu and Freya, I beckon them along and we fight our way past the crowd. Tarni's friends bail us up at the tent flap, but she tells them to let us in.

The women surround the tent, shaking the canvas, and we try to talk over the din.

'This is gunna get out of control soon,' Lacey says.

'We need to say something to them,' I say.

'Go on then,' Tarni says.

'Me? No way. Where's San?' I look around the babes crowded into the tent, but don't see her among the dirty faces.

'Someone's got to!' Rowe says, and she's right.

'Fine, shiz, I'll do it.'

I go to the tent entrance, flip the flap with a dramatic gesture, and hold my hands up. 'Shut up, everyone!' I bellow, but no one hears me.

Rowe puts two fingers in her mouth and rips out a massive whistle. Things go quiet.

'Nice work, Rowe. I didn't know you could do that!' I look back to the crowd gathered, twisted down the rows, some climbing up the poles that hold the spotlights to get a better look. Someone drags over a chair and I climb up on it, so that everyone can see me. I clear my throat and say in my loudest, most grown-up voice, 'Um, okay everyone. As you might have noticed we've taken the yard and have a hell of a good hostage. Ah, just so you know, we won't be roasting her over a fire today.'

The crowd boos.

'Nah, nah, we need her for leverage. With her in here, the riot squad won't dare storm the yard. She's too important.'

'How do you know that?' someone calls.

'Well, I don't, I just have to believe it. And now we're gonna need help. There's babes injured, others who died taking over this place. We need to set up a triage. Then we gotta talk about what to do next.'

'Bring the fences down!'

'That's an excellent suggestion, but what then? We wander the desert? We've got to agree on a course of action and we hafta organise to keep this place running smooth. I want everyone to chill, go back to your tents or whatever, and think about what you might want to do next. We need your input!'

'Who died and made you boss?'

'Look, I'm just trying my best here. Um, in the meantime, no one harms the COO, you got me? We're gonna have her guarded, so don't even try.'

There's a grumble from the crowd, but to my utter surprise they start to disperse a bit and things quieten down.

I climb down off my chair and swing back around to face my little crew. Someone knocks into me, almost toppling me over. 'Shiz, watch it,' I say, but then I see what they are carrying.

It's San. She's limp, her grey hair is mussed and there's dirt on her face. A shittonne of blood covers her uniform, spreading from a hole in her gut.

She's dead.

DAY SIX

San looks peaceful, but so old and small. Tarni sits at her head, spitting on a cloth and wiping the blood from her face. Everyone's stark-silent.

We've been sitting here for hours.

Even the COO, who doesn't know San from a bar of soap, can sense something big is happening and has quit her whimpering.

'What now?' Tarni says, like she's asking San what to do, San who can never answer. Everybody's still looking at her, and I bet they're thinking what I'm thinking.

That she can't really be dead. That she can't not live to see the end. I wonder if her plan looked anything like this? Like women and screws bled out in the yard, turning the ground to blood-mud?

It's Tarni who starts the shroud. She slides off each of San's boots and places them gently onto the floor. Then she folds San into the sheet all soft and careful. 'I don't know what we should do with her body,' she says.

Surely we can't let her get composted, spread across the ground to push up crops for the Corp. We can't leave her here either. I kick my feet into the hard-packed earth and realise we can't even bury her. Not that I'd want anyone buried here. What a final resting place, this isolated tent-city of misery.

'We burn her,' I say. 'Viking funeral.'

'We don't have a boat,' Rowe says. 'Or a lake.'

'So just a regular cremation, then,' I say, huffing a bit. 'Maybe we can find some fuel in the Block somewhere.'

'I'm on it,' Tarni says and skitters off out the tent door, relieved to have something to do besides sitting here, staring at the shape of San's face beneath the sheet. She comes back with a jerry can of fuel. 'This was by one of the backup gennies.'

'Perfect,' I say, but flat and dry, because it's not perfect at all. It's messed up beyond all measure.

We carry San into the clear space at the front of the yard, by the Block where we usually assem. Women come out to watch us pass and whisper that it's San we're carrying. We lay her out on the dirt. Tarni pours on the fuel and I'm thinking, no, San can't be dead, let's check her again, but it's no use because no matter how many times I rest my head against her chest, there'll be nothing but hollow emptiness.

'Get back everyone,' Tarni says, and all the women take a few steps out, expanding the circle. She comes to me with a box of matches that she's pilfered from somewhere. 'You do it, I'm covered with petrol.'

My hands shake so much that when I strike the first match it just breaks in half. I try to remember the last time I ate or drank. My body feels empty, strung out with jangly, post-adrenaline shakes. The second match takes, though, sputtering to life and I walk a few steps in, not too close, as the match burns down towards my fingers. I feel the hot bite of the flame touch my thumb and forefinger, like a jab, like a punishment, and then I throw the match. There's a sound like 'Whump!' I get myself back as the shroud flames, and Vu takes my hand. She's out of her guard's get-up now, dressed in one of my spare uniforms, so she blends in with the crowd. She stands behind me, body pressed into mine and she threads her hands around my waist. I link my fingers in with hers, but I don't take my eyes off the fire. I breathe deep the stink of the burning body, the fuel, because there's this deep feel inside me like I must, like this is a penance that I've got to cop.

I keep watch long past when most of the crowd disperses, 'til it's just a few holdouts feeding the fire with more petrol and busted up bits of desk and chair from the Block. Until the body turns to bones and embers. Until the sun rises behind the fences, low and hot on the horizon.

'Proud of yourself?'

I snap awake, only just realising that I've dozed off, and drooled all over Vu's shoulder. In the cool blue light of the early morning I can see it's Nabeeha. Her mouth is twisted in anger.

'What do you mean?' I ask, as Vu helps me up.

'We came here to escape death. Now there's more.' She comes closer. 'You don't know what you've done. We'll never get out here alive.'

'Mirii didn't start this,' Vu says.

'You don't have to defend me, Vu,' I tell her, and turn back to Nabeeha. 'This woulda happened with or without me.'

'I came here in search of peace.'

'Did you really think they'd just approve your claim?' I ask her, feeling vicious. This is not my fault. Not entirely, right?

'Now I'll never know,' she spits. She points at one of the bodies on the ground. 'She'll never know, either. Did you know her story? Do you even know her name?'

I don't. I feel the guilt rising. Fuck. Don't own this, Miz, don't own it. But how do I not? How do I parse all these poor babes caught in the crossfire? Nabeeha walks off, keeping eyes locked and pointy-sharp on me until she is swallowed by the crowd.

'She don't speak for all of us,' a passing woman says in a low, musical lilt. She's priming a liberated taser as she comes by. 'I've got a feeling that this is our only chance.'

—

I'm so tired. I've never felt so bone-ragged weary in my life. I'm on guard for the COO with Vu at my side, but I'm struggling hard. Tarni comes up and chucks me her pillow.

'I'll take over, you two get some rest.'

I try, I really do. I curl onto the mattress feeling like sleep will come quick, like a punch to the face, but it doesn't. Every time I close my eyes I see a parade of hideousness and blood and death and I can't sleep, I can't, I can't.

Beside me Vu snores lightly, mouth open. I look at her face, trying not to blink, because when I do I just see bleeding bodies, the screw made meat by the helicopter rotor, the inside of the PISR, the tight squeeze and absolute black of the vent above storage at Psynode, a white room splashed with blood and a drain in the middle of the floor . . .

No, think about something else. This is not the time for any kind of PTSD spiral, not now, not now. Look at her, look at Vu. She's here, right now, she's real.

I breathe in through my nose and push the fear through my mouth, making a tight O as I breathe out.

Does Vu always fall asleep so quickly? Does she dream about

the things she's seen too? Does she feel them when she's awake?

There's so much I don't know about her.

This is only the third time we've shared a bed and it feels right to have her wrapped around me, but I have to fight the urge to wake her up and ask her questions. I mean, this whole thing with us is insta-love, I know that. We've had so much time apart and so little time to get to know each other. It's like our loyalty to each other, the way we've come so far is an obligation—not the grudging kind, but a loyalty that comes from us both wanting to not see the other suffer. But who is she, really? What kind of music does she listen to, what kind of books does she read? Does she even read books? What does she like to eat, you know, when she can choose? What would she wanna do with her life, if she got to choose? I start to ache a bit inside to have the time to really talk and tell each other all our secrets. But then I'm scared, like if we ever got to have a super long D&M, maybe we'd find out we aren't a good match.

Shit, now I'm really not going to fall asleep.

I unweave myself from her arms and legs and leave her to soft-snore nap. Slip on my shoes, tiptoe around the sleeping bodies on the floor of San's tent. I go on the hunt for water tokens, to wash the smell of blood and death off my skin and out of my hair, to rinse myself of the fear and the memories and the images I bargain with myself to keep outta my head.

At the distro door, a bunch of babes are sorting through yesterday's ration delivery. They lay it out in little bundles, one rice, one veg, one meat; all on a big blue tarp they've nicked from somewhere. To eat food that hasn't touched the ground! It's the simplest things that we've missed out on. I'm worried though—I didn't think of the whole ration thing. How long have we got food for? How far will we be able to stretch it?

Not now, Miz. One thing at a time.

'Oi, can I get my rash of water tokens?' I ask the babe closest to me. She points me over to another woman who counts me out a few. I go over to the showers and strip off, slam in a token and feel the water zap my senses. I scrub myself pure again, rubbing the soap I'd snatched from San's tent through my hair, and over my body once, twice. This is a waste, I know. This water should be for drinking—after all, I'm not down with how the water here works . . .

The thought slams into me. Does it get trucked in? Is there a mains switch somewhere that they can shut off? That's one way to stop the takeover in its tracks—cut the water supply. I leap out of the stall, don't bother to dry myself, just slip my uniform right back on and run through the tents to headquarters.

'The water!' I say to Tarni. 'Can they turn it off?'

'Fuck, I hadn't thought of that. We need to store as much as we can, right now!'

The next few hours are dominated by buckets and bins and whatever we can find to fill with precious water. Seems like half the camp is at it, the babes who are down for this whole shebang, anyway. There's a real divide line—women who want to be a part of the takeover, and those who really, really don't. They are hiding out in their tents, or sticking to the edges of the camp. I feel them. A part of me, a huge chunk really, wishes that I'd stayed out of this too. When the sun comes up a bunch of prisoners line up for assem like it's just a reg kinda day. We shoo them back to their tents with promises of a ration distro soon.

I tell ya, even the ones who aren't up for a bit of riot mayhem look relieved they won't have to skirmish for their food this morning. What a treat!

'Hey Mirii, I think we're ready now,' Tarni says, looking tired even though it's early. 'Wanna get on the bullhorn and announce distro? I can't find the public-address program on this thing.'

I don't really, but I take the handheld from her and fiddle with it until I find the PA program.

'Um, hello. Hi.' My voice echoes around the yard, tinny and far too loud. 'Food and water distribution starts now. We need you all to form, like, an orderly line or something because we're handing it out today. We won't be scrambling in the dirt for it. Everyone gets the same.' A whoop goes up from the yard and that brings a bit of a smile to my face even though I'm still mortified to hear my voice projected from every single speaker in the place.

A line starts forming at the door right away. It's pretty neat in the front, women slotting in behind each other. At the midline babes are tapping their feet and crossing their arms, a bit impatient, looking up the row wondering what the holdup is. San's little inner cadre are on distro, handing out rash packs as quick as they can, but as the line gets longer and feeds up and through the rows of tents, little fights start to break out as people jostle for position.

'Fuck off, I was here first!'

'Ah, don't push,' I tell them, the sudden sound of my voice projected making everyone jump a bit. 'There's enough for everyone.'

Now I reckon I know why the guards just let us fight it out for rations. It takes so long any other way. But we're not like them. We're not gonna dehumanise these babes just because it's easier.

A familiar face reaches the front of the line. 'Why is this rash so small? Where's the fuckin' beef? Shouldn't we get it better now the screws are kaput?' Clayton says, face wrinkling around her scratchy tatts.

'We've got to make this last,' Tarni tells her. 'We don't know when the next delivery is gonna come.'

'What, so you're gonna starve us more than the bloody screws would?' Clayton's voice gets louder with every word, and a murmur goes up through the line, brows furrowing one after the other.

I can feel it in the atmosphere, just a tiny shift in the air that brushes past my fingertips and raises the hairs on my arms. The electricity of brain circuits switching from positive to negative. Like the feeling when you're doing something maybs a little shady and feeling great about it, then suddenly the doubt creeps in and it's too late to go back.

I look around the yard, hundreds of women milling around, the wreckage of the block, the blackish pools in the dirt where babes fell and died, their bodies hushed away to the compost chute.

It is definitely too late to go back.

I can hear a soft rumble of noise from among the tents as we dispense the final ration pack.

What is that?

My guts drop about a foot. 'Uh, who's watching the COO?' I ask.

'I left some of our girls back there with her,' Tarni says.

'They trustworthy?' I ask her, and she throws me some narrow eyes.

'Yeh, what of it?'

Suddenly a cheer goes up, and there's a wail, a series of dull thumps and laughter. Tarni and I exchange a quick glance and then we both break into a run. As we round the corner closest to the big tent, a crowd blocks our view. We fight our way through the throng of babes 'til we can see the scene laid out before us, like it's frozen, tableau-style.

A group of prisoners have the COO out of the tent, one

holding each of her arms. Clayton is cutting her long yellow hair off in huge hunks with a knife. She is stripped down to her underwear, the angular lines of her thin form glowing pale in the noon sun. Her clothes lie in a tattery pile at her feet. They cut them off her.

One of Tarni's friends rushes us.

'I'm sorry, Tarn, we tried to stop them . . .'

Tarni storms over to Clayton, and plucks the knife right outta her hand, mid-hack into that fine, highlit hair. The strands get caught on the hot wind and sail away over the crowd as they go quiet.

'No fucking way,' Tarni says. She crouches down, stabs the knife hard into the baked earth at her feet. 'This is not how we act.'

'Who even are ya? What makes you think you can talk for us?' Clayton fires back.

'We won't be talking nothing if anything happens to her,' Tarni says, jerking her head at the COO, who is sobbing and clutching at her face, running her hands through her shorn-off hair.

'Says you,' Baldy replies.

'We need her! She's our only bargaining chip. You think the Board will negotiate with us over the bloody guards? They care as much about them as they do about us.'

'Yeah, about them . . .' says one of the women holding the COO's arms. There's a chorus of laughter from the crowd.

'What did you do?' I say, my voice real quiet, but everyone hears.

'They tried to stop us getting to . . . what's your name, honey?'

'Ava,' the COO says in a quivery little voice.

'Tried to stop us getting to Ava here, so we had a little bit of fun with them first.'

I storm through the crowd, rip open San's tent flap and immediately wish I hadn't. It takes me a sick few seconds before I recognise Flattop, or what's left of her. And the snarky one, Vu's partner from yesterday, he's in there, too. All through it. I can't identify any of the others, not by what's left. Vu's caught up to me, creeps in behind me now, and she peers over my shoulder, then drops to the ground and starts to heave.

'This is not what we do,' I say, letting the canvas drop, covering up the horrific mess.

'Not what you do, but this is how we do. Where do ya think you are? This is a prison, babe. You think we all got here stealing loaves of fucking bread to feed our families?'

The crowd goes wild for that one.

Things are getting out of hand.

'They weren't bad people!' Vu says. 'They were just doing their jobs!' I wrap an arm around her, scared that she's spoken up. I kinda hoped they'd all conveniently forget about this whole Vu/Tran thing, but now she's reminded them.

'What, your job was to torture us every day? Feed us nothin' and work us from morning 'til night? Leave us to bake in this fucken hellhole?'

'There's more to it than that! When you're desperate, when you have nothing, you'll take any job you can get. You know what it's like!'

'I don't give a rat's arse who's desperate. There's doing ya job and then there's being an inhuman prick. They made their choices. That screw had it coming, don't try'n tell me she didn't. I been putting up with her shit for six bloody years. She didn't just do her job; she loved her job.'

'No one had that coming!' Vu says, throwing her arm towards the vicious scene in the tent. I move stealthily between Clayton and Vu, trying to get some distance between them.

'Who even are ya, huh? One minute you're a screw, now you're a prisoner? What's the fucken go with that?'

I pluck up every little gram of bravery I've got in me, which isn't much. Everything inside me is depleted, I'm feeding on scraps. I just hope it's enough.

'She's with me,' I say, holding my arms out to block Vu. I never thought I'd human shield for anyone, but here we are. I'd say I'd never thought I'd be in the middle of a prison riot, but hey, I always secretly thought I'd end up in here eventually.

'And who the fuck are ya, abbo?'

'Oh, you did not just call her that,' Tarni says, coming up alongside me and helping me block Vu.

'What are you gunna do about it?' Clayton hisses. Tarni is coiled, a mass of seething rage, jaw working hard, and hands balled at her sides. Clayton rolls up her sleeves, making a big show of it, a scratchy but stark swastika tattoo on her upper shoulder revealed like a flashing beacon.

We're in enough trouble, now we gotta deal with this shit? Bugger it.

'You see this Nazi crap? You all on her side?' Tarni bellows out to the crowd. The prison is a sea of faces, every shade of the gradient from peachy-cream to darkest brown. We're a multi-cultural bunch, and by the looks of the set lips and furrowed brows, they aren't gonna take this lying down. There's a chaos-roar as the crowd goes nuts and I take my chance, push Vu back, and race over to Ava as the grand smackdown begins. I grab her as the babes holding her drop her arms and rush to defend Clayton from the mob. I drag Ava alongside me, Vu and Freya tailing behind. We need a safe zone, something more solid than a flimsy tent. We stamp through the rows of tents, the noise of the crowd getting further away. As we approach the blown-up roller door I spy Rowe and Lacey folding up the tarp we used at distro. They look to me, Vu, and the ragged scrap of the COO and their eyes go as wide as they can go without completely bugging out of their heads.

'Come on!' I say, leaping over the split remnants of the door. They drop the tarp, Rowe grabs Lace's hand, and they limp-sprint alongside us, eyes all questions, but this is not the time.

The Block. Concrete walls, steel doors. Locks.

The hulking, throbbing heart of this place.

And the only place we can be safe now.

We make a run for the watch level, to get a bit of an idea of what we're up against. Rowe suggests it, and I can't think of anything else to do but get away from the thrashing mobs of babes in the yard.

Up we go. The staircase is all tiny echoes as we carefully round each corner, but there's no one there, just the grey walls and the sound of our boots bouncing off the concrete. Vu opens the balcony door to a shock of natural light that sets me blinking.

The sky is sandblast blue and endless. Small clouds gather over the farms: seeding, building. I don't want to look down. I just want to stare at the sky until my ears stop ringing.

'Fuck,' Rowe says. Hearing her say that word shakes me up. It sounds incongruous, that harsh word coming out in that private-school voice. Something must be wrong, something must be very, very bad.

The yard is filled with babes, some fighting, some crying, some sticking to the corners. The tents pack in around tiny paths like some terrifying maze, stretching back and back and back. Then, the fence. No-man's land. Another fence. Red dirt, dry scrub follow.

Then there's the riot squad.

A rigid line of men in body armour. Each of them holds a gun, pointed at the ground. Same angle, every one. They are just standing there, looking hot and pissed off, and every now and again one lifts his hand to scratch his nose or adjust his armour, but apart from that, they don't move. They are waiting, but for what?

I look at Ava, stripped and skinny, sheet-white and shorn.

Oh yeah.

'Get her inside,' I say in thick words like golden syrup pouring from my mouth. 'Before they see her.'

It's too late. A shot I didn't even hear explodes the concrete wall right beside Rowe's head. It clips her ear, and I see the blood spill down her shoulder as she screams, all fuggy with shock, turns and bolts for the door.

'Get down!' Lace screams and I duck behind the rail, dragging Ava down beside me.

A hail of bullets now, peppering the concrete wall, and I lunge forward to grab Rowe and pull her down.

I'm too late.

It happens like a slo-mo scene in a flix, 'cept this is real.

The bullet goes right through her, carving a neat little chunk out of the wall behind that pings off and almost hits me. Her blood splatters warm across my face. Time gets stretchy as she slumps to the ground and Lacey wails and scrabbles her way to Rowe. Lace screams, 'Help me!' and I feel my arms numb as I try to drag her back through the door. It's like I pull back from the world and my vision goes tunnel, as the blood pools, and spreads real slow in an imperfect circle on the pale blue lino. Vu pulls off her shirt and presses it to Rowe's side, and the blood soaks it through in a quick second. I'm chanting, 'No, no, no,' and Rowe's eyes are big and deep-brown endless, eerie calm as she whispers,

'Apply pressure,' and I press the fabric against her, like the force of my will, my rage and my regret, my guilt could seal her, make her whole again.

It can't though. She takes a long, shuddery breath, breathes out with a sigh, and dies there on the floor.

For a second I wonder how to go back, do things differently, and it takes a moment before I realise that I can't, that the freight-train careening of time only goes forward.

Lacey wails, a hideous sound that is all sorrow. I try to hold her but she fights me, lashing out blind. I let her. I can barely feel it, the blows dim and distant. Vu pulls her off me and she collapses next to Rowe, her long hair dragging in the blood, painting it across the floor. I look from Rowe, to Lacey curling around her, Vu with blood gloved up her hands, Ava bedraggled and gaping at the scene, to Freya, stepped back and staring at the ground, trying not to engage with all this misery and mess. I don't know what to do. I don't know what to say. I can't feel anything besides guilt, and grief and fear. Rowe was too good, too kind and weird and beautiful for it to end for her like this, a ripped-open shell on the floor of a hell hole in the middle of nowhere. I want someone to say something, anything, that can make sense of all of this.

Then Lacey looks up at me, face a mix of blood and tears, her eyes all poison and she says, 'Not her. It should have been you.'

And I don't say anything, because she's said it all, hasn't she?

'We can't leave her here,' Lacey pleads.

We can't take her with us. We don't even know where we are going.

'Stay with her then,' Freya says. 'When the riot squad gets here, you can join her.'

'Shut up, Freya,' Vu says. She kneels down next to Lacey, who's threading her fingers through Rowe's. Outside, the guns throb and the mob roars. 'We need to go, Lacey.'

'We can't leave her here,' Lace repeats, but her voice is quiet now, resigned.

'We can't take her with us,' I tell her, but she won't look at me and I can't look at her without it ripping shreds off my conscience, setting it to scatter. I wish I hadn't spoken and I wish I could fix this all, and I wish more than anything that I'd never met them, never dragged anyone into this, into cages and death and sorrow.

'I've got nothing of her,' Lacey murmurs.

She's right, there's nothing to remember her by, no token we can take except the blood drying and cracking on our hands. Every tiny realisation is a stab to my heart and my guts, all the sober realities spinning off new threads of guilt to tangle with the rest. My brain is chanting, *It should have been you,* and I can't tear my eyes away from the blood pooling, the body on the floor, the shell that was once my friend. A shell that should be mine.

'Where will we even go?' Vu says.

'They could have hit me,' Ava whispers from the wall, her back pressed up against the concrete like she wishes she could just sink right into it and back out into her old life. Her voice is so soft we almost miss it. 'They could have shot me, just now.'

'Shut up, Ava,' I say, dripping vicious, 'cause I've got no time for her shit right now.

'They could have hit me. They aren't coming for me, are they?'

'What did I just say?' I roar at her, the sound of my voice making everyone jump, and Ava starts to cry.

'There's a truck,' she says, sniffling. 'For the food delivery. It should be in the bay.'

'There's no point, Lacey says, not taking her eyes off Rowe. 'It's over.'

'No, it's not,' Vu tells her.

'They'll shoot at anything that comes out,' Lacey says.

'Fuck it,' I say. 'We'll go kamikaze. What do we have to lose?'

She looks up at me for a second, her face a scramble of misery and hatred. She glances at the body on the floor, then reaches out and closes Rowe's eyes.

'We have nothing. We have nothing left to lose,' she says, finally.

She's right.

It's this or the inevitable bloodbath, and even though I'm racked with guilt and sorrow, there's something in me that wants to live, or try.

Or at least die trying.

'Well, I'm definitely in,' says a voice behind us. 'I'm always down for a doomed plan,' Freya says, then flashes us a bit of a mad grin, the missing tooth in her smile like an omen.

—

The truck is a battered, ancient hulk of a thing that stinks of oily biodiesel. Ava was good for it—it's parked right where she said it would be, in a tight, shadowy bay behind an aluminium roller door that can't lead anywhere else but outside. Through the door I can hear muffled voices and shuffles. The riot squad is right there, probably leaning up against the corrugated tin, shuffling their combat-booted feet and just aching hard for some action. I'm zingy with their presence, the fear sending jolts of adrenaline through my heart, waking me right up.

'Who's driving?' I say in a hushy whisper.

Silence.

'Someone's got to,' I say, easing open the truck door as soft and gentle as I can. It lets out a mid-level squeak that sets everyone to freeze, eyes goggling and fear-shiny. But how's our luck? The keys are in the ignition.

'Come on, who's gunna pilot this thing?' I ask. 'I mean, I can't drive . . .' I glance at the gearstick. 'I could probs fake it 'til I made it in an auto, but this is manual. What is this thing, a hundred years old?'

Lacey breaks her distant stare to say, 'I can't drive,' then looks off to the side again, unable to engage.

'Vu?' I plead. 'You can drive, right? You've got a car waiting.'

'Yeah, but it's automatic, babe. Who can drive a manual? I didn't know these things still existed. I could try, but I'm not sure I can even start it.'

'Ava?' I ask, really clutching at straws here.

'My Lotus is self-driving,' she says.

Reality grabs me around the heart and squeezes vice-tight. Shit. Shit! I peer at Ava, who's looking at the ground, small and almost naked, her jaggedy hair standing up in chunks and tight face almost regretful. Almost.

'Did you know this?' I say, grabbing her by the shoulders. 'Did you know we wouldn't be able to drive it?' Out of nowhere, I start to cry. Like actually, really, uncontrollably cry, not sobs or any-thing, but tears just start streaming out of my face. I wipe at them with my dirty hands, but they keep on coming. Everything that's stacked up on me: Rowe, San, the spit of gunfire and boom of the pipe bomb, the dead runs, my sentence, this place, this place, this place, it all crumbles, trapping me in rubble.

This is it. It's over. This is the end of the line.

'Me dad taught me to drive in a hack-slashed Mazda 808.' It's so quiet we almost miss it. 'Took me forever to get the hang of the clutch.'

Everyone turns slow to see Freya, her white-blonde hair glowy and eyes gleaming in the low garage light. Not with scorn, like usual. With tears.

'Why didn't you say that earlier?' I hiss.

'I dunno,' she says, and then the unthinkable happens. Her eyes spill over. Freya's crying. 'Don't like thinking 'bout me dad,' she says.

I want to shake her, hard, and hug her at the same time. I restrain myself and instead sniff up the tear-snot that's pouring out of my nose. It's weird, I didn't ever think of Freya having feelings. Or a family. I thought she musta hatched from a soft egg in some snake den or sprung full-formed and maniacal from a swamp somewhere. I try to think of her as a bub, cradled in her mum's arms, and then I get the flash of the Mum and the Dad that I get sometimes, just soft eyes and fire-lit hair, holding me and keeping me safe. I look at Freya and she looks at me and we're both tearstained and mortified, but then something passes between us, an unspoken thing. Like we both feel the ache of all the things we've lost and that hurt careens between us for a quick second.

'Bloody come on then,' Lacey says, looking disgusted at us, and the moment slips away. Just as well.

There's not a lot of room in the cab, but the four of us cram in. I've got to push Ava in by the bony bum. She don't wanna come with us, but I convince her by offering to take her back to the Nazi babes in the yard instead. She wriggles across the bench seat quick-smart after that. I help Vu in, then climb up after her, sitting practically in her lap. I open my mouth to tell Freya to take it easy, but before I can she turns the key and the truck rumbles to life. She revs the engine hard, once, twice, then throws it into reverse and backs up in a jerky motion, swinging around so fast that all of us groan and slam up against each other.

'Ready?' she says, filmy eyes gone and replaced by that gnarly sparkle that I always thought was kinda evil, but now I realise it is just defiance, pure and simple.

'We can't drive through the door,' I say. 'It's too heavy!'

'We aren't going through that door,' Freya tells her, then jams it into gear and takes off across the concrete. The truck flies through the dim space, and after a quick, confusedy second, I know where we're going.

Through the yard.

The sides of the truck spark against the blown-open edges of the distro door as we bust through into the light. Freya swings the truck to the left to miss a small crowd of babes hovering nearby. She lays on the horn and inmates scatter before us, trying to get out of the way. She takes a hard right around into the space between the tent-rows and the fence, clipping edges and sending mouldy canvas flying. Horn blaring, we race across the dry earth, dust in a red-tinged wake behind us.

The boundary fence comes up on us quickly, we're going so fast. Freya cackles, shifts the gears and speeds up. The riot squad takes a knee, rifles poised and ready to spew out deadly flecks.

They hold.

We keep coming.

Ava's screaming, 'Stop, stop,' but Freya is steel and focus. I don't think she hears or feels anything over the sound of the engine and the fire of her will. She screams, slamming the accelerator to the floor, as the fence gets close, closer.

They don't start firing until we hit the first fence, peeling open the wire, poles flying. The windscreen shatters in a shower of bullets and everyone ducks, everyone except Freya, and the sound of the bullets mixing with the roar of the engine and our screams makes deafening chaos. It only takes a second to cross no-man's land, and the soldiers scatter from our path as we slam into the outside fence and rip it open in a momentary burst. The bullets shatter windows, covering the cab in a rain of safety-glass chunks. We race right past the riot squad and I spy them in the dangling side-mirror, turning to fire at our rear, the bullets pinging off the sides of the tray.

In, then out. It only takes a second. It's almost too easy. That sweet, free, wide-open feeling that I got when we moved the fence, those scant moments when I moved between the inside and the out, it comes back in a slow drip that turns into a gusher as we get further away.

We move at an incredible pace, barrelling over shrubs. A roo bounds out of our path. Things are quieter now, just the rev of the truck and Ava sobbing audibly above. There's no more ringing of bullets against the tray or the cab, and I come up, wary, looking first in the mirror, and then leaning out the window. The goons aren't shooting us because there's a flow of women pouring out through the gaping hole in the fence we've made. I cry out as I watch rows of them mowed down, figures falling as they grow smaller in my view. Guilt rises from my guts like bile.

We left them.

I left them.

Tarni and all the babes from the meeting. Nabeeha, and the refugees, aching to be free. Cady and her dope-shakes. Zoe, who's suffered so much.

San, burnt to bone and ash.

Rowe, her body cooling all alone in a hallway.

I'd always known that I'd turn tail and run if I could. *Selfish, selfish,* my brain chants. And even as I berate myself, I'm feeling the wind on my face and it feels like free air. It feels good and I hate myself all the more.

Bloody hell, I can't even enjoy escaping from prison, I'm such a killjoy.

I keep watching so I don't forget what I've done.

But it's not long before the tide turns. There's so many more prisoners than rentacoppers, and they get swarmed by babes in short order, guns turned on 'em.

I should be there. I should be helping, or fighting, or bleeding out slow from a chunk of lead in my guts. I should be standing vigil over Rowe's body as the riot squad storms the Block, and I should go down in a spray of gunfire.

I'm not though. I'm free, speeding away with the wind catching my hair and red dust coating the inside of my nose.

The facility grows small, smaller. Gone.

It won't ever be gone though, will it?

There'll always be a PISR cell in my head. A Time Out cell. A tight-squeezing air vent crushing me from all sides and dark and endless in my heart. I'm gonna be escaping one prison or another in my mind as long as I live.

But at least it's just in my head, ya know? For now, anyway.

I keep looking behind like maybe if I blink hard enough I'll still be able to see, but then it strikes me as stupid. I come back to myself, feeling the softness of Vu beneath me, her hands on my waist, holding me. Lacey looks out the shattered windshield, face full of righteous rage but eyes gleamy with tears. Ava sinks onto the floor of the cab and cries softly, and Freya just chuckles to herself, small cuts oozing little runners of blood down her face, from all that shattered glass. She doesn't know where she's going any more than I do, but she's just happy to be at the wheel.

We drive until the sun gets low, turning the desert brilliant reds and pinks and purples.

We drive long after the sun goes down, outback sky a riot of stars. I whisper their names to Vu as she holds me tight in the warm desert air.

We drive until we run out of diesel.

And when we can't drive no more, we walk—into the night and the future and to who knows what.

All we can hope is that it's better than what we're walking away from.

EPILOGUE DAY 365

The gun vibrates in my hand, a high whine from the motor filling the space. My client groans a little, and shifts almost imperceptibly, but I feel it, and murmur, 'Stay still,' my voice just sounding over the rotor whirring. 'We're almost done.'

Cam's over my shoulder, eyes gobbling up every tiny move I make. I dip into the ink, pressing down the foot pedal just so, to coat the needle, wipe off the excess with a paper towel, and lean back over Cheikh. He takes a breath and holds it as I begin.

'Breathe normally,' I tell him, and he relaxes a little.

'It looks friggen rad,' Cam says. He mimics my movements with his gloved hands. I've not let him touch a human yet, but he's been practising on pigskin and he's got a good eye, a great sense of style. His sketches are fantastic. He could even end up better than me, but I'm not gonna tell *him* that.

Out of the corner of my eye I see Sticks look up from his tab, assess and nod. 'Really awesome,' he says, then slams right back to his code.

I release the pressure on my foot and the buzz stops. 'All done for today. You sat really well, Cheikh.'

'Yeah, thanks,' he says, sitting up and huffing a few times. 'That was rough.' He stands slowly and goes to the mirror, angles himself to look at his back, which is angry-skinned and raw, but beautiful. The tattoo is coming along nicely. I don't often get the chance to do big work, I mean, who has the creds for it? But sometimes there's a babe or bru who's cashed up from some score or another, and I relish the chance. Big art, complex and intricate, it's becoming my favourite.

My studio is really just a section of our place that I scrub with bleach to keep it clean. I can't believe we scammed this sweet pad. It's an old shopfront on Smith Street that we rent on the cheap from a shady dude called Kevin. I've actually no idea if it's his or he's just taken it over with squatter's rights, neither would surprise me. He lives upstairs. Me, Vu, Cam and Sticks built two little bedrooms at the back with old office partitions when we first got here. It's ramshackle, but it's ours.

A home.

I've made a home. I never thought I'd get to.

I message Lacey once a week or so. She never answers, but I can see that she reads them. Maybe one day she'll forgive me. I've read the story they put on the news pages about Ava, who they found wandering in the desert. We offered to take her with us, but she just shook her head and wandered off towards the township, skinny body fading into the landscape as we took off down the road.

Rowe. Rowe. I keep my guilt locked in a box inside. I'm afraid of what's gonna happen when I let it out. I don't know if I can ever forgive myself. I dream of her all the time. The dreams, they are never good.

I wouldn't know a good dream if it bit me on the arse.

I often dream that I've woken up in prison, or in an Orphancorp, or even once, that I woke up in a clear plastic bag full of goo in storage at Psynode, and that *this* was all a dream. But as much as I pinch myself, it's not. This is real.

Sometimes I hear a sound like gunfire, or a distant boom and I'm right back in it. Sometimes I see a red the same colour as Rowe's blood as it pooled on the floor and I'm overwhelmed with grief and guilt and I cry and cry. Sometimes the sky goes a certain colour at dusk, and the clouds don't look real and I'm sucked into the feeling like I'm there again, trapped, my sentence looming endless over me and that's when Vu or Cam or Sticks will pinch me and say, *Hey, you are here. This is real.*

Our names aren't real. *Mary-Anne Maloney*, but everyone still calls me Miz. Cam and Sticks took my name. Fake name. We're siblings now, and it feels real, even though our faces are so dissimilar. No one questions it. *Different mums*, we say. I'm their legal guardian. Sticks fixed it that way in the Central Bureaucracy, so no one can try and take them away from me. We're so far from where we came from, a year and a twelve-hour drive down the highway away. I've come so far for them, I don't know what I'd do to anyone who tried to take them away from me.

I love them, fiercely.

I can say it now, though it took me a long time to be able to form the words, not just in my mouth, but in my head. To admit it to myself. I feel free enough to love a lot of people fiercely now. I never knew that tying myself to people would make me feel *more* free.

I love them all, fiercely.

Cheikh leaves and I follow him to the door and blink out over the night street; the trams rattling up and down the rails, motorbikes zipping around them, bicyclists' wheels turning lazy circles up and down the road. It's hard to see anything much in the sky with all the light pollution, but Jupiter is there, shining bright, a little gem between the soft clouds.

I've got all the stars in my memory, though.

Like how, at night looking out of my tent in the desert, or in an Orphancorp in the outback, no moon, or on the wane, they'd glimmer incandescent, backed by the hazy spray of the Milky Way. I can recall it so well, it's almost like I'm there.

Like I'm there.

When I let the image flood me, the sick, tight feel of institutionalisation grips heaps hard. I fight it.

I'm so tired of fighting.

I can't stop though; I won't let that trapped feeling run my whole life. I'll fight it whenever the feeling creeps into my guts, and I'll keep fighting. I'll fight anything that wants to keep me trapped, be it in my own head, or something, someone, some Corp . . .

I fight it daily by living my life the way I want to, loving freely.

I feel a hand slip around my waist, and then Vu is snuggling into my neck and her mouth there is right, and it's true. *This is real, she is here with me.* I take a deep breath and try to push out the feeling like I'm stuck.

'Looking for the constellations?' she murmurs.

'Yeah,' I say.

'No luck?'

'Maybe later on, when it's darker.'

She turns me around, kisses me. I will come out later, after we spend a sweaty hour or two in our bedroom. I might be able to see them then. After love, I'll seek 'em out.

They haven't ruined the stars for me.

ACKNOWLEDGEMENTS

Thank you to Kij Johnson and the Clarion West Class of 2014 as well as the instructors and students from the 2017 novel-writing workshop at The Gunn Centre for the Study of Science Fiction at the University of Kansas in Lawrence for all their help in making the Orphancorp world.

Thanks to my first readers: Tim McDivitt, Arcadia Lyons, Anna Spargo-Ryan, Jae Steinbacher, Marisa Wikramanayake, Emma Wortley , Tahlia Norwood, Jessica Walton, and Michelle Goldsmith.

To David, Alice, Rod, and everyone at Seizure, and to Zoya Patel, thank you for helping me to get Mirii out into the world. I am so grateful for their support and encouragement, letting me work at my own pace and applying just the right amount of gentle pressure to help me along. I appreciate everything they've done immensely.

Thank you to Sally Evans, Alex Adsett, Nick Joyce, Cat Sparks, James Bradley, Margo Lanagan, Charlie Jane Anders, Shady Cosgrove, Gab Snowdon, Rosie Lourde and heaps of people I'm probably forgetting.

My sincere thanks to every supporter from the Australian literary and sci-fi communities. Let's keep writing and championing each other.

Thank you to Corey J White for everything.

Finally, thank you to everyone who loves Mirii. I love her too, and I'm going to miss her. I'm glad she got to have her happy ending.

Marlee Jane Ward is a writer living on Wurundjeri Land in Melbourne, Australia. She grew up on the Central Coast of New South Wales, studied creative writing at the University of Wollongong and is an alum of the Clarion West Writers Workshop.

She is the author of the award-winning Orphancorp Series. Her short fiction is published in Aurealis, Apex, Interfictions, Terraform and others. You can find her non-fiction in Overland, Meanjin, KYD, Scum Mag and more.

She spends most of her time managing the inside of her own head but is also living her dream of being someone's fabulous goth aunt.

Website: marleejaneward.com